CALL TO DUTY

Without warning the man turned around and looked straight at me. I felt trapped in the stare of his black, Indian eyes.

"You are Jesus O'Hara Martinez," he said in a voice as soft as sliding sand. "He said you would come."

A quiet panic held me in place. No one had known where I was going. "Where'd you get my name?"

"Tohil told me your name and where to come for you. He said, 'Jesus O'Hara Martinez is a son of Great True Jaguar. And, you, son of Great True Jaguar must halt the ice in the sky—or our sun will disappear from the sky behind the dust of death and all men will die.' "

"An enjoyable, contemporary excursion into Mayan mythology. Fast, often funny and always serious under the whimsical surface."

—*Carole Nelson Douglas*

ALAS, BABYLON by Pat Frank
ALWAYS COMING HOME by Ursula K. Le Guin
A CANTICLE FOR LEIBOWITZ by Walter Miller, Jr.
THE BREEDS OF MAN by F. M. Busby
CHERNOBYL by Frederik Pohl
CHILD OF FORTUNE by Norman Spinrad
DESOLATION ROAD by Ian McDonald
DHALGREN by Samuel R. Delany
DRAGONWORLD by Byron Preiss, Michael Reaves and
   Joseph Zucker
EMERGENCE by David Palmer
FANTASTIC VOYAGE by Isaac Asimov
THE GARDEN OF THE SHAPED by Sheila Finch
GREAT SKY RIVER by Gregory Benford
The Harper Hall Trilogy (DRAGONSONG, DRAGONSINGER
   and DRAGONDRUMS) by Anne McCaffrey
LINCOLN'S DREAMS by Connie Willis
The Majipoor Trilogy (LORD VALENTINE'S CASTLE,
   MAJIPOOR CHRONICLES and VALENTINE PONTIFEX)
   by Robert Silverberg
THE MARTIAN CHRONICLES by Ray Bradbury
MEMORIES by Mike McQuay
THE PROTEUS OPERATION by James P. Hogan
The Riftwar Saga (MAGICIAN: APPRENTICE, MAGICIAN:
   MASTER, SILVERTHORN and A DARKNESS AT
   SETHANON) by Raymond E. Feist
RUMORS OF SPRING by Richard Grant
TEA WITH THE BLACK DRAGON by R. A. MacAvoy
TRUE JAGUAR by Warren C. Norwood
THE UPLIFT WAR by David Brin
WEST OF EDEN by Harry Harrison
WHEN GRAVITY FAILS by George Alec Effinger

TRUE JAGUAR

Warren C. Norwood

BANTAM BOOKS
TORONTO · NEW YORK · LONDON · SYDNEY · AUCKLAND

All the characters and events in this story are entirely fictitious and any resemblance to actual persons living or dead, and actual incidents or events is purely coincidental.

TRUE JAGUAR

A Bantam Spectra Book / February 1988

ISBN 0-553-27127-X

Published simultaneously in the United States and Canada

Bantam Books are published by Bantam Books, a division of Bantam Doubleday Dell Publishing Group, Inc. Its trademark, consisting of the words "Bantam Books" and the portrayal of a rooster, is Registered in U.S. Patent and Trademark Office and in other countries. Marca Registrada. Bantam Books, 666 Fifth Avenue, New York, New York 10103.

PRINTED IN THE UNITED STATES OF AMERICA

KR   0 9 8 7 6 5 4 3 2 1

To Richard, Sandy, and David.
I could not have hand-picked better siblings.

Special Acknowledgment

The Crain Predator Machete used in this story is an original Jack W. Crain design, and the trademarks Predator Machete and Crain Predator Machete are his and are used here with his permission. My special thanks to Jack for his enthusiastic assistance, his willingness to give freely of his time and expertise, his generosity, and his superbly inspirational craftsmanship. Anyone interested in more information about Crain Knives should write directly to Jack W. Crain, Rt. 2, Box 221-F, Weatherford, TX 76086.

A note on pronunciation: The Quechean *x* is pronounced like the English *sh*. Thus, Xibalba is pronounced *shǐ·bähl·bǔ*.

Chapter One

I was following the self-guided tour through the ruins of Pueblo Bonito in the Chaco Canyon National Monument when I noticed a man wearing a faded blue seersucker suit. He stood off the marked path with his back to me and seemed to be studying one of the unmortared stone walls. Probably a professor or some visiting official, I thought. Who else would wear a suit in the ruins of Chaco Canyon?

Without warning the man turned around and looked straight at me. I felt trapped in the stare of his black Indian eyes. There was something too familiar about him.

"You are O'Hara," he said in a voice as soft as sliding sand. "He said you would come."

A quiet panic held me in place. No one had known where I was going when I left Weatherford two days before. In fact, except for the neighbors whose son had agreed to clear my mailbox every day, no one even knew that I wasn't home.

Who was this Indian in his dusty, ill-fitting suit and blue and white polka-dot tie? He certainly didn't have the look of a security agent.

"You are Jesus O'Hara Martinez." He pronounced my name *heysoos*, not *geezus*, which—even given his appearance—surprised me just a little.

"Sure, I'm Martin O'Hara," I said, giving him the American version of my name. "So what? Where'd you get my name? From the park registration office?"

"Tohil told me your name and where to come for you. He said, 'Jesus O'Hara Martinez is a son of Great True Jaguar.' That is what his spirit said to my spirit. 'And this son of Great

True Jaguar will halt the ice in the sky.' Tohil said that, too, Jesus O'Hara Martinez."

I had signed the park register my normal way, J. Martin O'Hara, just like on my driver's license, not the Spanish way with mother's maiden name last. Besides, mother and my aunts were the only people who ever called me Jesus, anymore. I pulled my shoulders back and took a deep breath, drawing myself up to tower over this misplaced stranger. "Look, mister, I don't know how you got my name, I don't know what you're talking about, and I'm not the guy you're looking for. *Con permiso. Adios.*" I turned to walk away, the sand grating under my boot soles on the stone path.

"Your mama wore the name Maria de los Angelos Martinez de Concepcion." His voice was almost feminine in its softness.

Twisting around to face him, I nearly lost my balance. How could this stranger know—

"Her father carried the name Jesus Martinez Garcia y Garcia. His father, your great-grandfather, carried the name Antonio Martinez de la Queche. His father carried the name Mercado Nacxit de la Quitze. His father carried—"

"Stop it," I said, frightened by his knowledge. Looking quickly around I saw that the plaza of the Pueblo Bonito ruins was empty except for the two of us. "If you know all that, then you know more than I remember." Again I pulled my shoulders back and squared my body in front of him. No more than ten feet separated us and I stood five or six inches taller than he did. "Now just who the hell are you?"

"I carry the name Cacabe Reyes Campos. Cacabe means red road, but it makes no importance to me what—"

"That's not what I mean." A solitary cloud blocked the sun, filling the plaza with shadow as I pushed aside my usual shyness. "Who are you that you know so much about me?"

"It is written in words that Great True Jaguar and his wife, Macaw House, produced no children. But no matter how powerful the written word *esta*, all is not written. Tohil said there was born of True Jaguar and Macaw House a son named Uucubalam, Seven Jaguar, who went through the underworld Xibalba and came out in the far north past Tulan to—"

"Dammit! What is all this gibberish? Who the hell are you and what the hell do you want from me?" The faint breeze across my bare arms and neck felt unnaturally cool and I wished that damn cloud would move on.

A crooked smile split Reyes's face. "I forget that we must start at the beginning. You have knowledge of the big *cometa*?"

"Lana's comet? Of course. The whole world knows about Lana's comet. It's coming sometime next year, bigger and better than Halley's, they say."

"Good. *Aqui*, I must tell you a terrible thing. The *cometa* has come through *ube Xibalba*, beyond the Milky Way. Unless a male *descendiente* of Great True Jaguar stops it, our sun will disappear from the sky behind the dust of death, never to return, and all men will die."

The cloud shadow slid away. I felt a sudden relief of tension along with a return of warmth, and it was all I could do to keep from laughing. "Are you drunk, or what? That's the biggest crock of bull I've ever heard."

Reyes stared at me, the crooked smile still on his face, and when he spoke, there was no anger or excitement in his voice. "Did I not know your family names? Would you have me name your family all the way back to Seven Jaguar and True Jaguar? Tohil has shown me the names and I can speak them for you *de punta a punta*."

"So you can recite it from beginning to end?" I said, pleased that I remembered the phrase. "That doesn't prove a damn thing."

"Then perhaps this will convince you."

He held out his hand. In it was a photograph of me standing in front of some kind of—I took it and looked at it closely. It showed me standing in front of a Mayan temple.

"But, but, this is impossible. I've never been . . ." An image of stones and jungle flashed through my brain, then another and another. With a shake of my head I held the photograph out to him by its edges. "I don't know what you're trying to pull, Mister Reyes, but this doctored photograph doesn't prove anything to me."

"I have the negative," Reyes said, taking the photograph and handing me a glassine envelope. "Look at it with your own eyes. The photograph is real."

"It can't be. I've never been there before."

"I know you haven't, senor."

"Then how . . ."

"This picture was Tohil's way of showing me your *cara*—your face, how you look."

"I don't know any Tohil," I said, examining the negative against the bright sky. It certainly didn't look retouched, and it matched the images in my brain. But what in the name of—"

"Tohil is our god, yours and mine."

"Tohil" echoed through my thoughts, repeated by a voice more fluid than Mr. Reyes's. Again I felt a chill of fright, but there were no clouds blocking the sun. *"No explico,"* I said. My grandmother's phrase slipped out from behind my consciousness and made me all the more aware of how strange—

"That is why you have me," Reyes said. "It is my job to read the signs for you so that you may understand and stop the *cometa.*"

"There you go again with that comet. Even if I did—"

"It must be stopped, Senor O'Hara, and you are the only one who can do it. You are the only living son of True Jaguar."

Without another word, and without trying to decide if this Reyes was drunk or crazy, I turned my back on him and walked away. Only when I got to the road did I look back. I couldn't see him, but at least I could see that he wasn't following me.

Slowing my walk to a normal pace and forcing myself to take long, deep breaths did little to quell the uneasiness I felt. Whoever Reyes was, he knew more about me than anyone had a right to know.

Maybe he worked at GenDARF and had gotten a look at my personnel files. But that didn't compute. GenDARF probably had one of the toughest security programs in the industry. Besides, there was no information in my personnel files about my great-grandfather—at least I didn't think there was. But if not there, where? Where else could he have learned about me? And where could he have gotten that picture?

I thought about the few real friends I had managed to make at GenDARF and about Miss Spiegel, the engineer who had agreed to go to the Fourth of July picnic with me, and I had an unusual feeling that I wasn't going to see any of them for a while.

A little chill rippled up my spine, and a dark shadow moved across me and the road. My eyes followed it to another set of ruins, and a sign that read HUNGO PAVIE. Suddenly

I saw myself in a jungle clearing, standing in front of a wall that was carved with rows of hieroglyphs.

The cloud passed by, the picture dissolved, and there in front of the Hungo Pavie ruins stood Senor Reyes in his faded blue seersucker suit. Without understanding why, I left the road and went up the path to meet him.

Chapter Two

"You believe me, then, Senor O'Hara?"

"No, I don't. And I don't know why I'm talking to you. I should turn you in."

"What do you mean?"

"I mean a call from me to the Defense Security Agency and they'd have agents out here in no time to haul you away for questioning." I could tell from Reyes's expression that he didn't comprehend what I was saying.

"You're a security threat," I said. "You know things about me you have no right knowing."

"But what is this security?"

"National security."

Reyes shook his head. "Senor O'Hara, this security you talk about is something I do not understand."

"Where do I work?" I asked.

"Senor O'Hara, Tohil did not tell me that. Is it important?"

"You don't know that I work at General Dynamics Aerospace?"

"No, I do not know this information. I do not know what this *Guneral-Die Namicsair-O Space* is. Where you work and where you live are not important. Tohil directed me to come here to find you. Because he directed me, that is what I did. I flew in a great aeroplane from Guatemala City to Mexico City to your city called Albuquerque. Then I rode a terrible bus filled with cold air that brought me here where I have waited for you to come."

"From Guatemala? How long have you been here?"

"Almost a month."

"Impossible," I said. "I didn't decide to come here until two days ago."

"All things are possible if the gods wish them to be. Why did you come if Tohil did not send you to meet me?"

I sat down in the shade of a collapsed wall and Reyes sat opposite me in the bright sunlight. "I don't believe this god of yours did that, Reyes. Actually, I think you're some kind of spy or something. Either that, or you're crazy. Or maybe you're a crazy spy. Doesn't matter. So, if you don't tell me straight exactly who you are, I'm going to fill this canyon with our government security agents and they're going—"

"Cacabe Reyes Campos. I am Cacabe Reyes, a daykeeper of the Queche. I am Chuchcahau, mother-father, attendant to the gods. If these security people of yours must hear my words before you will believe me, let those people come. Cacabe Reyes has nothing to hide."

Suddenly he looked smaller, less threatening, and his words rang true. "All right, Senor Reyes, let's pretend for the moment that you are who you say you are. Tell me again what all that has to do with Lana's comet."

"This Lana's comet, as you call it, comes to us from *ube Xibalba*, and if you do not stop it, the comet will strike the earth and kill us all."

I shook my head in amazement as much as in disbelief. "Lana's comet is not going to hit us. But even if it was on a collision course, just how in the name of this god of yours would I stop a comet?"

Reyes glanced down at his calloused hands before bringing his eyes up to meet mine. "Senor O'Hara Martinez, I do not know the answer to that question. My visions and my readings have not brought me all the answers. But if you do not know the answer, either, do not worry. Tohil will tell us when it is time."

"Dammit, man, you must think *I'm* crazy if you think I can believe something that bizarre." I could see by the expression on his face that I had hurt his feelings, but there was an even deeper pain in his eyes, so I tried to push my frustration aside.

"Listen to me, Mr. Reyes. I don't mean to belittle you or your beliefs, but I have no way of relating to the things you've told me. You have to understand that I'm a fourth-generation American. My great-grandparents came here from Mexico over a hundred years ago. Nobody in the family speaks much

Spanish anymore, and they're all Catholic except me. I'm agnostic."

He looked completely placid and accepting, like nothing I said made any difference.

"*Por favor*, Senor Reyes, try to understand. I don't believe in religion. I doubt there ever were any gods—at least none that cared about humankind. I'm a technical writer, for crying out loud, a technical writer for an aerospace company, and even if I wanted to help you stop this comet, there's nothing I could do. I can't help you." He just looked at me.

"Do you understand that? *Comprende?*" I asked as I pushed myself to my feet. "You're looking at the wrong man, so please, leave me alone."

Reyes nodded, and I left him sitting there in the ruins. I walked back toward the monument headquarters and the campgrounds, not at all convinced that he understood. A warning signal in my head told me to call the DSA. But if I did call them, what would I say? 'Excuse me, but there's this Guatemalan nut case here in Chaco Canyon who knows an awful lot about me and thinks I can help save the world from Lana's comet. Do you want to come talk to him?' They'd come for Reyes, all right, but they'd probably lock both of us up.

No, better not call the DSA yet. Reyes seemed harmless enough. If he refused to leave me alone, then a phone call might be appropriate. Besides, technically I should have told the DSA that I was going to Chaco Canyon. They liked to keep tabs on all of us with top security clearances, but after thirty-three months of working on the Stealth-Six rocket program, I thought I deserved a little time alone without tabs.

Failure to notify the DSA of my whereabouts, however, could get me in a lot of trouble—could even cost me my clearance and my job for talking to a foreign national.

Dammit! Where was my brain? Had I forgotten what happened to Gleason? As soon as Reyes told me he was from Guatemala, I should have run to the phone and screamed for help. I'd just had a very unusual conversation with a foreign national. Gleason had lost his clearance and his job for not reporting his conversation with that Yugoslav at Disneyland. Now, I didn't have any choice. They'd drilled the security rules into our heads, and if I wanted to keep my job, I had to call the DSA.

The small public phone booth outside the monument headquarters building was hot and stuffy, and for a second I thought about waiting until after sundown—but only for a second. They were already going to read me the Security Act forward and backward, so there was no sense in aggravating them further.

One ring preceded a soft female voice saying, "Please enter your identity number after the tone." Two, two, four, two, one, seven, five.

After a long pause an abrupt voice said, "Agent Butler. What do you want—O'Hara, is it?"

"I have to report contact with a foreign national."

"Where?" Butler asked.

"Chaco Canyon, New Mexico."

Another long pause.

"What the hot blazes are you doing there? Did you report your travel plans?"

"No," I admitted. There was no sense in lying to him.

"Contact male or female?"

"Male."

"Nationality?"

"Guatemalan."

"Guatemalan? You sure about that, O'Hara?"

"That's what he told me, Mr. Butler. He didn't exactly show me his passport."

"Did he mention the *Raza Unida* to you?"

"What's that?"

"Never mind. How intimate was this contact?" Butler's tone insinuated more vulgarity than a mouthful of obscenities.

"Conversation only," I said.

"We'll test you on that, you know."

"Yes. I know."

"Name?"

"His?"

"Of course, his. I know yours, O'Hara."

"He said his name was Cacabe Reyes Campos."

"And what did Mr. Composte say to you?"

"Mr. Reyes," I said. "He said he knew—"

"You said his name was Composte."

"He told me his name was Cacabe Reyes Campos." I

pronounced each syllable as clearly as I could. "In Latin America the last name given is usually the mother's—"

"I don't give a shit what they do in Latin America. Is his name Reyes or Composte?"

"Reyes," I said.

"Spell it."

I gave him my best guess at the spelling.

"All right, what did Mr. Reyes ask you?"

"To help him stop a comet."

"What's a comet, some kind of secret missile you GenDARF boys are working on?"

"No, he means a real comet, Lana's comet."

"Where are you, O'Hara?"

"At Chaco Canyon National Monument."

There were some strange clicks and a long pause before Butler spoke again. "Okay, and where is this Reyes person?"

"Here. Same place."

"Well, you stick around the headquarters building now, and we'll have someone out there to help you as soon as we can. You got that?"

"Yes."

"And O'Hara, listen to me."

"Sir?" I said without thinking.

"You're in deep shit, O'Hara. You've already broken five or six regs, and God only knows what that's going to cost you. But don't you panic on me, O'Hara. Don't you rabbit out of there, you understand? If you do, your ass will be in a vise forever. You got that?"

"Yes, sir."

"Good. You just hang tight. Shouldn't have to wait more than an hour or so."

"Yes, sir." I felt like I was in the army again.

He hung up and so did I, feeling like someone had kicked me in the chest. Just as I stepped out of the phone booth, I saw Reyes crossing the road and walking down toward the campgrounds. After a quick glance at my watch, I decided to follow him. Maybe I could find out something about Reyes that would slacken a little of the pressure the DSA was going to put on me.

Chapter Three

Reyes never hesitated and never looked back. He walked straight to the campsite where my truck was parked and sat himself down at the picnic table. His face revealed no surprise when he saw me coming to join him, as though he thought it was the most natural thing in the world. That disarmed me. How could I be suspicious of a man who acted so openly?

"You have talked to these security people of yours?" he asked when I sat down across from him.

"What makes you think that?"

"A bird told me."

I would have laughed if his expression hadn't been so serious. He probably *had* heard it from a bird. Suddenly I felt guilty about what was going to happen to him. "Look, Reyes, when the Defense Security agents come, they're going to arrest you. Maybe you ought to try sneaking out of here."

"But I wish to speak to them so that you will be convinced of my words."

"You don't understand. They're going to lock you up and interrogate you and probably throw away the key. Because of your crazy ideas, you and I are both in a lot of trouble."

"I do not think so, Senor O'Hara."

The odd glitter in his dark eyes didn't tell me a damn thing. "Where did you learn to speak English, anyway?" I asked, looking for something about him I could use to get him to leave.

"Tohil taught me the words and the form for speaking them. The meanings I already knew."

"Now wait a minute. You're telling me this god of yours taught you how to speak English?"

"Why do you not believe? Why do you have such *escepticismo*?"

"I'm a skeptic because there's damn little evidence to support your claim or any other religious claim, that's why." This wasn't at all what I had in mind. How could I reason with a man who claimed to learn his English from a god?

The slightest of pouts shaped his lips. "But before Tohil

came, I spoke only Queche, the language of our ancestors, and Spanish, the language of the Invaders of Cristos. Now I speak English." His face brightened. "There is the proof."

Maybe I could have argued with him, but where would it have gotten us? With a sigh I said, "Señor Reyes, I'm already in trouble with the DSA just for being here without telling them. Talking to you only makes my case that much worse."

"This I do not understand."

"Just listen to me. As far as I'm concerned, you haven't done anything wrong—strange, certainly, but not wrong. So I'm trying to help you. Would you please take the chance to get out of here and get yourself back to Guatemala?"

He shook his head vehemently. "Tohil sent me to find you. The *cometa* cannot be stopped from Guatemala. It comes from *ube Xibalba* and must be stopped from Xibalba."

"Where the hell is Xibalba?" It amazed me how fast he could irritate me.

"Xibalba is here"—he pointed toward the ground—"under your land and under ours. The traditional—"

"You believe the comet comes from under the earth?"

"No, no. Xibalba is the underworld. It controls the *cometa* and calls it from *ube Xibalba*, the road to Xibalba, through what you call the Milky Way."

"So the comet's coming home to the underworld Xibalba?" At least I was getting the idea of what he was talking about, even if it didn't make any rational sense.

"*Si*, Senor O'Hara. *Bueno*. The entrance to Xibalba lies under Tulan, what the Yaquis now call Mexico City. The most secret exit from Xibalba lies north from here in the seven canyons of Weatherhill. Do you know these seven canyons of Weatherhill?"

"North from here?" I tried to remember. "No. I mean, I think I've heard the name, Weatherhill, but I don't . . . Mesa Verde." The name jumped onto my tongue. "Weatherhill was the rancher who first discovered and excavated the cliff dwellings in Mesa Verde."

Reyes nodded and smiled. "Already Tohil gives you the information you need."

"Tohil didn't give me that. I learned it from some book about the Anasazi, the old ones who built—"

"*Si*. I know these Old Ones you call Anasazi. The whis-

11

pered words say they are the tribe of Seven Jaguar. The Old Ones were directed by the Sovereign Plumed Serpent to guard the secret exits from Xibalba. That is the reason why there is no picture writing here"—he swept his arm in a gesture that encompassed all of Chaco Canyon—"so the lords of Xibalba cannot steal the words that give men and gods great power."

He looked to his right and pointed to a small ruin in an alcove under the canyon wall north of the campground, and I realized in a moment that I hadn't been paying close enough attention to all of his babble.

"The Old Ones built here and lived here after Seven Jaguar went home to Tulan," he said in a tone that suggested he was revealing a great secret. "They lived here until the Spanish Invaders of Cristos touched the soil of our continent. Then the gods closed the entrances and exits of Xibalba to ordinary men." He looked at me as though waiting for a reply.

A glance at my watch told me we had wasted ten minutes, and that DSA was probably cranking up their fastest helicopters in Albuquerque by now.

"Great," I said. "I'm glad to know all of that. Now, will you please pay attention—*atención, por favor*? The American *federales* are coming for us. You've got to get out of here because you've got less than an hour to get lost."

"Please, Senor O'Hara, there is no need to talk down to me. I understand your English quite well. You believe I am in danger from your National Security Agency?"

"Absolutely."

"You want me to leave?"

"Yes," I said, the frustration reaching explosion levels in my head. "I think you should leave immediately."

"But you will come with me, of course?"

"I can't. They'd hunt me down."

"Would they not hunt me down?"

"Yes, but you've got a better chance to get away. They don't know much of anything about you. By the time they figure out who to look for, you could be back across the border into Mexico."

Reyes shook his head. "I cannot go to Mexico. I cannot go to Guatemala. I cannot run from your Security. I can only stay with you and interpret Tohil's messages so that you can stop the comet. That is my task, Senor O'Hara. That is the duty I must perform, *mi obligación.*"

There was something in Reyes that I was quickly becoming attached to, something earnest and honest, simple and trusting, something that almost made me risk my life. Fortunately, or unfortunately, I was too attached to my life and my career to do something that stupid.

"All right, Reyes. I give up. We will sit here and wait until the Security boys come to bag us up and ship us off to one of their interrogation centers."

I paused, thinking that maybe Reyes would tell me something he wouldn't tell Security, and I could still buy myself a little relief with that information. Maybe I should have felt guilty about asking him to incriminate himself, but I didn't.

"Senor Reyes, since Security is going to grill me about all this anyway, you might as well tell me everything you can about this comet mission of yours."

"It is more than a *misión*, Senor O'Hara. It is the fate of the world we are concerned with."

"So, is there anything you forgot to tell me about stopping Lana's comet? Like maybe you want me to use a missile or something? Did you forget to tell me that?"

He pursed his lips and shook his head very slowly. "If Tohil says you should use such a thing, I will accept it, but your missiles touch no spirit in me that pleases Tohil."

"You mean Tohil's talking to you now, telling you he doesn't like the idea of using missiles?"

"No, Senor O'Hara, he does not talk to me now. But I would know, I would feel resonance of the earth if such a thing were pleasing to him. Tohil will choose a natural form to help you destroy the comet, not an artificial one."

The more I questioned Reyes, the more convinced I became that he thought he was telling the truth. He really did believe Lana's comet was going to crash into the earth unless I stopped it. He tried to recite huge lumps of the history of his people and their gods, asked me twice if I had read any of the English translations of the *Popol Vuh*, which was a book that told part of that history, and through all of that convinced me of only two things. He was going to catch hell from Security, and I would have to protect him.

I got my water jug and a rope from the truck cab, then carried the jug to the table where I poured for both of us. A quick glance around detected no one within eyesight.

"One more thing," I said, walking behind him toward the truck. Uncoiling the rope, I dropped a loop over him, tightened it and dropped two quick half-hitches over his body, completely pinning his arms to his side.

"What do you mean by this?" he asked without struggling.

"I'm trying to save your butt. Open your mouth."

He did and I stuffed my bandana in. Only then did I wonder where I was going to hide him.

The alcove ruin in the canyon wall caught my eye. After checking to see that no one was in sight, I dragged Reyes the seventy-five meters to the little ruin, taking the water jug with us.

The walls of the ruin formed a double-*U* shape with the open ends facing the back of the alcove. I made Reyes sit in the second *U*, tied his feet together with the end of the rope, and set the water jug next to him.

"You ought to be able to work loose in five or ten minutes. When you do, get out of here." Then I walked out of the ruin as casually as I could.

Forcing myself to take every step slowly, I walked back to my campsite, emptied the water cups, and put them in the truck. With the same artificial patience I strolled to the monument headquarters and arrived only a few moments before I heard the distant sound of helicopters.

Chapter Four

"Gee-zus Martinez O'Hara," the agent said, holding a pink, wallet-sized card, "my name is Agent Torelli, and I will read you your civil rights under the U.S. Constitution. You have the right to remain silent. You have the right to have an attorney present for all interrogations. If you understand these rights and choose to speak without an attorney present, anything you say can and will be used against you in a court of law."

He looked up at me with an almost bored expression on

his face. "Do you understand these rights as I have read them to you? If so, please sign this affidavit to that effect." He held out a cheap ballpoint pen. On the radio in the background, Grilled Cheese sang "Whiteout Rock 'n' Roll."

I took the pen, then looked carefully at the affidavit. It was a page-and-a-half long and reminded me of a book I had seen once that was set in a typeface called Flyspec. After bringing the affidavit close to my face and squinting to bring the words into focus, I finally shook my head. For some reason, my encounter with Reyes had made me feel bolder than usual. "I can't read this thing—and I'm not signing anything I can't read. Sorry."

"That is understandable," Torelli said, handing me another piece of paper. "Please sign this statement saying that you refuse to sign the rights affidavit."

The statement was just as long as the affidavit and printed in the same small type. I dropped it on top of the other one. "Like I said, I'm not signing anything I can't read and understand. May I call a lawyer, now?" It didn't matter to me that I didn't have a lawyer. It seemed pretty obvious by then that I was going to need one.

"You can't call your lawyer until you sign this statement saying that you understand your rights," Torelli said. His face remained impassive.

"Suppose you and I just sit down and talk about what happened to me?" I said.

"We can't do that until you sign this statement."

I looked around the chief ranger's office where we were sitting, felt the presence of the agent standing at the door behind me, and had a certain feeling deep in my bones that there was no way this was going to work out in my favor. "Do you have a magnifying glass?"

Much to my surprise, he pulled one from his briefcase. I accepted it and picked up the rights affidavit again. No matter how I moved the magnifying glass or the affidavit, I still couldn't get the words into focus. "What does this say, Agent Torelli?" I asked finally. "What does all this small print add to what you read to me?"

Agent Torelli grinned. That was the first sign of emotion I had seen from him.

"It says your ass is in the grinder, smart mouth, and if

you don't tell us everything we want to know, we'll grind your bones so fine that only a sand lion could tell the difference between you and the dust."

I took a deep breath, let out a sigh, said, "What the hell," and signed the rights affidavit. The affidavit itself was a form of coercion, and if we ever ended up in court, maybe a good lawyer could use that in pleading my case. With a quick squaring of my shoulders, I rejected that negative idea. It was too damned early in the fight to give up.

"Do you want to call a lawyer?"

"How long would it take to get one here?"

He squinted. "Oh, a day or two."

"And what would I be doing during that day or two?"

"Nothing, if you didn't want to, Mr. O'Hara."

"Forget the lawyer for now," I said, hoping their delaying tactics would prove to be another mistake on their part that my future lawyer could use.

"Good," Torelli said. "Where is this Mr. Reyes who made contact with you?"

"In the canyon, somewhere," I said. "He told me he came here a month ago by bus and today's bus hasn't come yet, so I doubt if he's left."

"We're checking the whole canyon out, but we haven't found him yet. Where would he have run to?"

I met Torelli's stare eyeball to eyeball. He would have to blink first, because without giving anything away, I was going to avoid lying at all costs, and I knew telling the truth would keep me steady. "Senor Reyes told me he wasn't going to leave, and I think he meant it."

After a long, uncomfortable moment he said, "All right, Mr. O'Hara. For subjective reasons that are somewhat irritating to a professional like myself, you have led me to believe that you are telling the truth." He pulled a battered tape recorder from his briefcase. "So suppose you start from the beginning—when you decided to come here—and tell me everything that happened up till now." After turning on the recorder he said, "First interview with Gee-zus Martinez O'Hara, Chaco Canyon, New Mexico, code number"—he looked at his watch—"delta-bravo-seven-six-one-one-four, twenty-eight June. You may begin, Mr. O'Hara."

"Well, I decided to take two weeks vacation."

"Which you falsely swore would occur in and/or within fifty miles of your home in Weatherford, Texas," Torelli added.

"Correct. Anyway, after a day or two I was feeling rather restless, and while I was digging around on my bookshelves for something to read, I came across an old book I had on the Indians of the Southwest. Then I remembered a trip my ex-wife and I had taken out here years ago, and I decided to come see Chaco Canyon again."

"For the record, did you tell anyone where you were going?"

"No, I did not."

"Not even your neighbors?"

"No one, Mr. Torelli. I just told the neighbors I would be gone and asked their son to pick up my mail and newspapers."

"You had no contact, written or verbal, with Mr. Cacabe Campos Reyes at that time? Is that correct?"

"His name, according to him," I said, "is Cacabe Reyes Campos, his surname being Reyes. And I had never even heard of Mr. Reyes at that time."

"You just said his last name was Campos."

"It's a tradition in Latin American countries," I said, "that the mother's maiden name is placed after the father's surname."

Torelli frowned. "That's stupid."

"It's certainly a pain in the butt here in America. I finally had my name legally changed because of that." The words were still coming out of my mouth when I knew I shouldn't have said that.

His frown deepened. "You telling me your name's not actually O'Hara?"

"I was christened Jesus O'Hara Martinez. O'Hara was my father's surname. Martinez was my mother's maiden name."

"And you had it changed to . . .?"

"Jesus Martinez O'Hara." If Reyes had made me feel bolder, Torelli's attitude had reinforced that feeling.

"What happened to Gee-zus?"

"They crucified him."

"Don't get smart with me. The records say your first name is Gee-zus."

"J-e-s-u-s," I said, "pronounced *hey-soos*."

Torelli shook his head. "Never did understand you Hispanic people. Anyway, get back to Reyes. Wait a minute. Spell his name for me."

"I can only guess."

"That will do."

I spelled it for him and he wrote it down.

"Can you prove your relationship?"

His question was like a blindside thump on the head. "Can I prove what?"

"That you neither knew nor had contact with this Mr. Reyes prior to coming to Chaco Canyon to meet him?"

"Please be careful, Agent Torelli. I'm trying to tell it to you like it happened, because I don't have anything to hide. The purpose of my trip to Chaco Canyon was relaxation. I neither knew nor had contact of any kind with Senor Reyes. I did not come here to meet him."

"Whom did you come here to meet?"

"No one."

"Whom did you contact after you left Weatherford?"

"No one."

"Where did you stop?"

"Well, let's see. I ate in Seymour and got gas in—"

"Name of the restaurant?"

"I don't remember. It was a big place full of locals."

"If you remember, tell me. So you got gas there, too?"

"No, I didn't gas up until I got to Crosbyton."

"Name of the gas station?"

"I don't remember. I just picked the lowest price I saw."

"And you paid cash?" He sounded skeptical.

"Yes."

"But you don't remember the name of the station?"

"No."

"Who is your contact in the R-U-G?"

"The rug?"

"The United People's Party of Guatemala. Who is your contact?"

"Agent Torelli, I don't know what you're talking about. I've never heard of the Rug or the United People's Party."

"All right, we'll get back to that. Did you talk to anyone when you ate or bought gas?"

"Of course." A husky unfamiliar voice on the radio grumbled in a song about being, "too damned old to dance."

"What did you talk about?"

"The weather. Road conditions. I don't know. The usual traveler's babble."

"You sure of that?"

"Yes! What do you think I was talking about?"

"That's what I'm here to find out, isn't it, Mr. O'Hara?"

I tried very hard to calm myself. My new self-confidence was slipping fast, and I knew there was nothing to be gained by irritating him.

"Where did you go after you gassed up at Crosbyton?"

"I drove straight to Palo Duro Canyon and camped for the night. I talked to a park ranger about the fee, and made passing conversation with several of the people also camped there."

"Did you get their license numbers?"

"God, Torelli, why would I get their license numbers? They were just people camping in Palo Duro."

"Only trying to help your case," Torelli said. "If you had gotten their license numbers, that would have been useful to us."

"Ask the rangers. Everyone had to sign in there, just like here. They'd have the license numbers."

"Did they check your license number when you registered?"

"No, I don't think so, why?"

"If the rangers didn't check, those people could have given fake numbers."

His statement was so absurd, there was nothing I could say.

"All right, so you didn't get their numbers, and we can't be sure the numbers at the park were good ones, but we'll check them out. What did you do next?"

"I cooked myself some dinner, read for a while by lantern light, then climbed into the truck and went to sleep. Oh, I went to the restroom and took a leak before I climbed into the truck."

"Don't get smart with me, O'Hara. You'll pay for it if you do. Just answer my questions. Did you sleep all night?"

"Yes."

"What time did you get up?"

"Six-thirty or so. I made coffee, then I went to the rest-room, showered, and put on clean clothes." My voice trembled and I fought to calm myself. "I left there around eight."

Torelli arched one eyebrow. "Continue."

"I drove from there to Amarillo where I picked up the interstate and headed for New Mexico. I stopped to eat and gas up at some little town named Santa Rosa, or Santa Anita, or something like that. There's a book of matches I picked up at the restaurant in with my camping gear that will tell you."

"Did you talk to anyone there?"

"No more than the day before."

"And no one from the R-U-G or any other Communist organization contacted you there?"

With a sigh I said, "No one contacted me about anything—certainly no Communists." But I wondered if Reyes . . .

"You know you'd better tell me if you talked to anyone, don't you?

"Yes. If I think of anything out of the ordinary—"

"I'll worry about what's ordinary. You just tell me what you remember, okay?"

I nodded.

"Good. Go on with your story."

"I stopped in Albuquerque to eat, and decided to stay there overnight. It was a Motel Twenty-One, I think. You'll find matches from there, too."

"And who did you talk to?"

"The desk clerk, the waitress . . . nobody else."

"And the next morning?"

"That was this morning. I got up about five and jumped straight into the truck. Got here about eight, eight-thirty, registered, put the truck in the campground, and walked back up the canyon to the ruins of Pueblo Bonito."

"To meet Mr. Reyes," Torelli said.

Chapter Five

I took a very deep breath and counted to five by thousands before I said, "I did not go to Pueblo Bonito to meet Mr. Reyes, or the Rug, or Communist spies, or anyone else. I went there because it is the pueblo I remember best from my last visit."

Torelli cocked an eyebrow. "So, you were here before? Did you meet Mr. Reyes then, too?"

"No. That was a visit my wife and I made out here several years before we were divorced. We were only here for a day and a half and we didn't meet anyone."

"We'll talk more about that later," Torelli said. "Right now, tell me what happened this morning when you walked from the campground to Pueblo Bonito. Did you see anyone suspicious looking? Anyone following you?"

"No, not that I noticed. I was too busy enjoying the clean air and the ruins to pay much attention to the people—except that there aren't many people in the monument now. It's too early in the season—one of the reasons it's a good time to come here. Should I have been on the lookout for Commies?"

He ignored my sarcasm. "So you walked down the road to Pueblo Bonito acting like a tourist, not paying enough attention to the few people around you, and then what happened?"

"I was following the self-guided tour across the main plaza of Pueblo Bonito when this man, Reyes, accosted me and said—"

A staccato knock behind me was followed by someone entering the room. I didn't turn around to look.

"Hate to bother you, sir," a female voice said, "but Agent Sergeant McSpadden wants you to know that so far we haven't turned up anything but this."

A hand and arm passed me on the left, handing a photograph to Torelli and lacing the air ever so faintly with a fine perfume. Unfortunately, that gentle musk couldn't distract me from knowing that if she had given him the photograph Reyes had shown me, it was going to cause big problems.

21

"Thanks, Lankford. Tell McSpadden to keep me up to date—and tell him to find out if the office has O'Hara's complete dossier yet."

"Will do." The woman left.

Torelli stared at the photograph for almost a minute before he turned it around and showed it to me. "Is that you?"

I held out my hand, but he didn't release the picture, so I leaned forward and what I saw surprised me more than it must have surprised him.

The photograph showed the same Mayan wall, but the figure standing in front of the wall was wearing a colorfully elaborate costume of feathers, shells, and leather along with a plumed headdress trimmed in jaguar skin. Under that headdress, a face that looked surprisingly like mine smiled back at me.

"Well? Is it you?"

"No."

"It looks like you."

"I can't help that, Agent Torelli. I've never been any place that looks like that, and I've certainly never *worn* any *thing* that looks like that."

He turned the picture around again and shifted his eyes from it to me, and me to it, several times. "Maybe it's you. Maybe not. Hard to tell. A blowup should show whether or not you're lying."

"Dammit, Torelli! A blowup isn't going to prove anything."

"Now we're getting somewhere."

"No, we're not. Suppose you enlarge the picture and the face you see there looks like me? What does that prove? Nothing. Absolutely nothing. I'm telling you, Reyes had a very similar picture, and I told him the same thing. A picture of a man who looks like me standing in front of some Mayan temple, or on a movie set, or whatever it is, doesn't prove a damn thing."

"The hit dog howls," Torelli said. "Why are you so upset about this?" He waved the picture at me. "Could it be that here in my hand I hold hard evidence against you?"

Angry and indignant, I drew myself up in the chair. "Agent Torelli, you may badger me all you wish. You may try your shoddy word-tricks to the satisfaction of yourself and your mas-

ter. However, I will admit to being no more a dog than you
—and even then, I would hesitate to admit being a dog."

Torelli's smile moved like a lizard across his face and then
was gone. "Well, well, well. I believe we are getting somewhere after all, Mr. Fancy Words. If you're not very careful,
you might even start telling the truth."

"You wouldn't know the truth if it pinned you in a corner."

"And what would the truth *be* about you and Mr. Reyes?"

"That he's crazy and I never saw him before today."

"I said the truth."

"That is the truth, Torelli. You can bring in a doctor and
question me under drugs and hypnosis for all I care. Reyes is
a crazy man who claims to be from Guatemala. He thinks I'm
the descendant of somebody called Great True Jaguar, and he
thinks Lana's comet is going to hit the earth and he thinks I
can help stop it before it does. That's the truth. Why the hell
do you think I called you guys?"

"Would you take a polygraph exam?"

"No. Absolutely not. They're too inaccuate. I don't—"

"I don't agree with that."

"Then you're either ignorant—which means you don't
know enough about the subject—or you're stupid for putting
your faith in a machine. I have a file full of information
showing—"

"Let me get this straight," he said. "You'd volunteer to
be questioned under drugs and hypnosis, but you refuse to
take a polygraph exam. Is that correct?"

"Correct."

"Then you're the one who's either ignorant or stupid.
Don't you know that under those conditions we can find out
anything we want to know about you?"

"Of course. That's why I said I'd do it."

Torelli stared at me. "You really think you're telling the
truth, don't you?"

"Unless I've been unconscious part of the time and missed
something, I am telling the truth. Why is that so hard for you
to understand?"

"Because your story sounds so phony. It sounds like you
were in the process of making some kind of information deal
with a foreign national and turned chicken. We see your kind
of case once or twice a month. But nobody's ever concocted a

story as bizarre as yours before. Complete with picture," he said, tossing the photograph across the desk.

"May I look at it again?" I asked.

"Go ahead."

I picked up the photograph by the edges. As I stared at the improbable scene, I had a flash of another scene in that same jungle clearing. "Listen to me, Torelli." I glanced up to make sure I had his attention. "I told you Reyes had a picture something like this? Well, when I looked at his picture and when I looked at this one just now, I got a flash—an image in my mind—like I'd seen this place before, in pictures, maybe."

"Don't take no trash from the garbage man. Just hug your woman and fug your man," the radio growled.

Torelli leaned back and turned the radio off, but his eyes never left me.

"I don't know if the picture of this place is in one of my books at home, or one of the books in the libraries, or where, but if I saw the other pictures again, I'm sure I'd recognize them and then you'd know where the hell this place was."

"In your books at home?"

"Maybe. Could have been something I saw in one of the libraries I've been using. Look, you're going to check out my house, aren't you?"

Torelli arched an eyebrow. "We might."

"Of course you will. You think I'm some kind of spy. So when you check out the house, go through all the books I have on Indians—or take me home and I'll go through them."

"O'Hara, the only place you're going anytime soon is the office in Albuquerque."

"You mean jail?"

"No. You'll stay at the office. We have facilities."

The way he said *facilities* sent a shiver through me. "So you can interrogate me twenty-four hours a day?"

"We are open for business around the clock. Security never sleeps."

"And neither do its guests?"

He laughed—a real laugh, so full and genuine that I was startled by it.

"You're quick, O'Hara. I'll give you that. But no, we won't question you around the clock. First of all, it's against the law,

24

and second, there's no need. Not in a case like yours. Not yet. However, if that need should arise, we are—"

A quick knock on the door was followed by several people entering the room. "The office has his dossier," a man said.

I turned in my chair and saw three people behind me, the silent male agent who had been at the door the whole time, plus another man and a woman.

"And the suspect, McSpadden?"

"Nothing so far, sir. Nothing in O'Hara's truck, either."

"But, we believe we found the suspect's clothes, sir."

"His clothes, Lankford?"

"Yes, sir," she said. "We found a blue seersucker suit and a blue and white polka-dotted tie in one of the ruins near the campground. Pockets were all empty."

"Any other clues?" Torelli asked.

"Not much. The suit came from Sears, Roebuck in Panama City, Panama. The tie doesn't say."

"Shoes?"

"None."

"All right. Starnes," Torelli said to our door guard, "tell the A-chopper pilot I want to take off in fifteen minutes. And then find Watters. You two will come with me to help guard Mr. O'Hara."

"Will do, sir," Starnes said as he left the room.

"McSpadden, you'll take over here, and I don't want you back in Albuquerque until you've searched every acre and every building and every ruin within fifty miles of this place."

"That's a lot of ruins, sir. Can I have a few more people?"

"I'll try to get you some from Phoenix. I've already ordered a supply chopper loaded out of Gallup so you'll be able to set up camp by nightfall. Lankford, take Mr. O'Hara outside, please."

She had her hand on my arm even before I could stand up, and I heard metal clicking in time to see her bringing out her handcuffs.

"Not necessary, Lankford," Torelli said. "Mr. O'Hara has no place to run from here."

"Yes, sir." She guided me out of the office by using my left arm as a steering lever.

"Can we go outside?"

"Sure."

Once outside, I felt a little better—less confined. Agent Lankford didn't offer any conversation, and neither did I. My thoughts were occupied with wondering what had happened to Reyes. Why had he shucked his clothes? How had he gotten away? Or had he? Maybe he was hiding somewhere in the canyon. A ripple of guilt swept through me as I thought about tying him up like I did, but if that had convinced him to hide from Security, then it wasn't such a bad thing after all.

A loud whine rose from behind the headquarters building. One of the choppers was warming up.

"All right, O'Hara," Torelli's voice said from over my shoulder, "let's get going."

With Lankford by my side, I followed Torelli to the chopper where Starnes and the agent I assumed was Watters joined us.

The chopper wasted no time taking off, and as it rose over the canyon, I wondered where among those rocks and ruins Reyes could be hiding, and what would happen to him if they caught him. Then I wondered what was going to happen to me.

Chapter Six

The flight to Albuquerque went all too fast. It seemed like one minute we were circling Chaco Canyon as we gained altitude, and the next minute I was watching the brown, broken land pass underneath us, and the next minute the pilot was flaring the chopper's nose up for a landing on the broad roof of a building on the outskirts of the city.

Starnes and Watters rushed me from the chopper to an elevator. With one holding each of my elbows we rode down three floors in silence. They hustled me through an office with at least one computer terminal on every desk. It looked like the tech writer's center at GenDARF. Then we went down a short hall and into a small room that I immediately identified as an interrogation room.

What other kind of room would be brightly lit in its center and dark around the perimeter? I sat in the chair under the light like a obedient prisoner on a TV show. If we were going to keep playing these kinds of games, I knew I had to play along.

"Wait here," Starnes said.

"Certainly." It seemed like I waited hours before Starnes returned to the room with a glass of ice water and a sandwich of cheese and bologna. I ate it and then it seemed like a few more hours before Torelli came in with a dark-skinned woman whose features looked vaguely familiar.

"This is Agent Velasquez," Torelli said. "She is going to be your case officer. From now on, if you have anything to tell us about your case, you tell her. Understand?"

"Yes," I said, looking carefully at her. Her features were almost classic Meso-American Indian with her rounded hawk-like nose, deep-set eyes, and an expression set on her full lips that made her look like pictures I'd seen of Mayan queens. Only her modest navy blue suit broke the image.

"When can I talk to a lawyer?"

Agent Velasquez smiled. "One is being appointed for you—one with Top Secret clearance." She rattled some kind of gibberish at me in a language that wasn't English or Spanish.

"Pardon?"

When she spoke again, it was in Spanish, but her words came so quickly in that rolling, unaccented way native Latinos have, that I could make no sense of them and shook my head.

"Do you not speak Spanish, Senor O'Hara?" she asked.

"*Poquito*—some phrases, a few words, some slang—but then only very slowly."

"So we will talk to one another in English." Her phrasing was very formal, but she had only the slightest trace of an accent that wasn't quite Spanish. "Tell me first about this man, Reyes, whom you met at Chaco Canyon."

"Like what? I mean, where do you want me to begin?"

"When was your first contact with him."

"This morning—that is, if it's still today, uh—"

"It is still Wednesday. When was your first contact with the man, Reyes—before today?"

"Never. I told you that, already. I never met him before today."

"But you have talked to him before," Torelli said from the shadows.

Velasquez's head swiveled in his direction, and I couldn't see her expression, but I was sure she wasn't pleased. Did she outrank him, I wondered?

"No. I never heard of him, talked to him, met him, or anything else before today."

"I believe you," Velasquez said.

The brief relief I felt was quickly followed by suspicion. Were they pulling the good-cop-bad-cop routine? Did people really do things like that?

Velasquez cleared her throat and sat down across the table from me. "Mr. O'Hara, I want you to tell me again everything that happened from the time you left GenDARF to begin your vacation."

"But Torelli taped the whole thing," I said.

"Yes, but I would rather have you tell me yourself."

I closed my eyes and sighed before I opened them again and met her gaze. "All right. I had a month's vacation coming, so I decided to take two weeks of it and just work around the place and enjoy not doing anything I didn't want to do. But after a couple of days I got restless. Sunday afternoon I was prowling through my bookshelf looking for something to read, and when I reached my books on Indians of the Southwest, I had a sudden urge to go to Chaco Canyon."

"Why?"

"Well, I had been there once before, and it's my favorite of all the Anasazi ruins. That other visit had been too short, so I decided to go spend a week or so there. I threw every-thing—"

"Can you tell us more about why Chaco Canyon was your favorite Anasazi ruin?"

"Is it important? I mean, sure, if you want to know."

First I told her about the variety of building styles rep-resented in Chaco Canyon, then about how nice it was to be able to walk through the ruins anytime I wanted to without having to take a controlled tour.

Velasquez interrupted to ask me how much I knew about the Anasazi, and I began sharing with her some of the inter-esting things I had learned about them. Her eyes never left my face as she asked questions. She seemed particularly in-terested in the puzzles of how such an organized civilization as the Anasazi had been could apparently have no written language and why they built straight, paved roads with curbs when they had no wheeled vehicles and no beasts of burden.

Without warning, Torelli said he thought it was time to quit for the day. Velasquez agreed. "Your lawyer will be here tomorrow," she said. Much to my surprise, she held out her hand before she left and I shook it.

An agent I hadn't seen before escorted me down a floor and to a windowless room that contained a neatly made bed, two chairs, a table, and a full bookshelf above the bed.

"The bathroom," the agent said, pointing to a door in the corner. "There are some of your clothes in there, plenty of towels, and your toilet kit. You need anything else, you ring that buzzer on the wall. Okay?"

"Sure, fine," I said. "Thanks."

He left and the door locked with a gentle *thunk*.

Why had I thanked him for locking me in a cell? No matter how nice the room looked, it was still a cell. However, I was sure it was much nicer than any jail cell would have been, and since I had violated the Security Act, I didn't think I had a right to complain about the accommodations. All at once I felt totally deflated and knew the false bravado I had felt wouldn't last. Soon I'd be the passive little me I always was.

The books on the shelves over the bed were a real surprise to me. Every one of them was about Indians of the Southwest, or of Mexico, Central and South America, dozens of books whose titles I was familiar with, and probably two dozen more whose titles I wasn't familiar with. There was also a translation by Tedlock of the *Popol Vuh*, the book Reyes had asked me about. I didn't want to know what was in that book.

I took a long shower, put on a clean tee shirt and my old jogging shorts, and selected T. R. Fehrenbach's *Fire and Blood: A History of Mexico* to read, and made myself comfortable on the bed. Somewhere in the middle of the first chapter I fell asleep.

When I awoke it was to the sound of a pinging alarm and it took me several seconds to realize that the sound was coming from the bathroom. I stumbled out of bed to find the source and the pinging stopped.

A man's voice from the ceiling said, "Good morning, Mr. O'Hara. You have thirty minutes to get ready for breakfast."

With a startled shake of my head I sat back on the bed.

The pinging started up again, and I figured it had to be weight-activated and I understood how much of a prisoner I really was. I got up, took a shower, and dressed in the best jeans and shirt among my camping clothes. Just as I finished combing my hair in front of the bathroom mirror, someone knocked on the door. "Come in," I yelled, knowing they would whether I wanted them to or not.

"Ready for breakfast, Mr. O'Hara?" a young man asked from the bedroom.

"As ready as I'm going to get."

He took me to a cafeteria where people were already eating. I chose *huevos rancheros*, and even though the eggs were a little overcooked, the chili that covered them was much better than I would have expected in a government cafeteria. As I was cleaning my plate with a *tortilla*, Agent Velasquez sat down at our table.

"*Como dos y dos son cuatro*, your man Reyes has escaped us."

"As sure as two and two are four, he's not my man."

"*Sea lo que sea*, in any case, we cannot find him."

"Good." I wanted to smack myself for saying that, but there was something secretive about her, something hidden that rubbed me the wrong way.

"Do you desire to brush your teeth before the session of this morning?" she asked.

"Yes, *gracias*."

"*Por nada*. Take him, Potter."

After I had brushed my teeth, Potter advised me to bring my toothbrush and toothpaste with me—something I was grateful for later when lunch and dinner were both served to me in the interrogation room. Its adjoining bathroom was the only other room I was in the rest of the day.

My court-appointed lawyer, Miss Stovall, showed up after lunch and quickly informed me there was nothing much she could do until formal charges were filed against me—and under the Security Act, the government had sixty days to file formal charges. She also said that since I had already confessed to breaking the law, she didn't hold out much hope for me. I didn't hold out much hope that she was going to help.

She stayed the rest of the afternoon while agents Velasquez and Torelli questioned me repeatedly about what had happened with Reyes, and why I had decided to go to Chaco Canyon, and what I knew about *La Raza Unida de Guatemala*, and who else I might know from Central America. Then they switched unexpectedly to asking questions about why I had applied to work at GenDARF.

Not once during all that time did Miss Stovall counsel me. She left before dinner, but the line of questioning Velasquez and Torelli were pursuing continued until Potter took me back to my cell many hours after dinner. I took a long shower to help relax me, and as soon as I hit the bed, I fell asleep.

But sleep brought distorted dreams in which I was pursued by demon agents, trapped in cold, narrow tunnels by faceless Communists, and attacked by mad Guatemalans who kept shoving me through tiny holes into awful darkness.

Once I woke up sweating, but I couldn't remember what was chasing me. When I finally slept again, I dreamed about a river full of talking catfish, and voices that whispered powerful secrets in my ears before calling me by name to get up, get up—

"Mr. O'Hara, it's time to get up."

Chapter Seven

Potter rushed me through breakfast, and I was barely seated beside Miss Stovall in the interrogation room, still feeling more than a little angry, when Agent Velasquez said, "Senor O'Hara, this is CIA agent Bjornson."

"We have some questions for you, Mr. O'Hara," Bjornson said. His blue eyes actually seemed to sparkle.

Mine narrowed. "Surprise, surprise, Mr. CIA. I thought you'd come for a social visit."

"Is he always sarcastic?"

Velasquez looked down her perfectly hooked nose at me from where she stood across the table. "No, but do not worry," she said. "When we finish working with Senor O'Hara, there will be no sarcastic muscles left in his tongue."

I stared up into her black, unreadable eyes. "What the hell do you want from me?" I asked. "Hugs and kisses for your charity?" All my frustration from the previous two days boiled over. "I may have been an hour or two slow in reporting Reyes to you, but damn it all, I did report him. And what do I get—"

"That is quite enough from you, Senor O'Hara."

Bjornson looked amused and Velasquez looked so self-satisfied that I hated them both. "Go to hell, Malinche," I said to her.

Velasquez leaned across the table and slapped my face, all in one swift motion. She hit me so hard I thought she'd broken my neck. But I couldn't blame her. Malinche, the slave girl who helped Cortez defeat Montezuma, was also known as the Great Whore.

Miss Stovall stood and picked up her briefcase. "I'm due in court soon, Mr. O'Hara. I will talk to you later."

Somehow I wasn't surprised when she left.

"I am sorry for you," Velasquez said.

"I'll bet. I shouldn't have said that, Ms. Velasquez, and I apologize, but . . . well, you guys keep treating me like I'm some kind of contemptible criminal, and I've about had it with your idea of due process under the law."

"You have only had the beginning of our process," she said, her black eyes boring through me, her torso over the table, her weight resting on her palms, her breasts moving ever so slightly in a pendulous sway under her pale blue blouse. "We will teach you patience and a decent tongue, Senor O'Hara, regardless of what you tell us."

"*Primero Dios*," I said. "God willing."

The look on her face was as surprised as I felt. Where in the world had I heard that expression before? That wasn't what my grandmother O'Hara always said. Her expression was always, *Si Dios nos da vida*, wasn't it? When had I ever heard anyone say, *Primero Dios*?

"I thought you only spoke *poquito* Spanish," Velasquez said. "Now I hear you talking like someone from Central America, from Guatemala, maybe?"

With a shrug of my shoulders I tried to dismiss what I couldn't understand myself. "Get serious. It's just something left over from my childhood. Or something I heard. I don't know."

"Maybe you know some other things you haven't told anyone," Bjornson said. "Perhaps if Agent Velasquez left the room, you would share some of those things with me."

"Like what?" I asked, surprised when Velasquez actually did leave the room.

"Did you have a great many Hispanic friends in high school, Mr. O'Hara?"

"I suppose I did, why?"

"Is it possible that you are still acquainted with some of those friends?"

"Sure. What's your point?"

Bjornson sat across from me and leaned earnestly across the table. "Mr. O'Hara, we have reason to assume that some of your Hispanic friends have underground connections to several Central American Communist regimes—including *La Raza Unida de Guatemala*—and we believe that you are familiar with some of their activities."

"Well, I don't believe it. And I don't believe this is happening to me. And I don't believe you're saying these kinds of things."

"You'd better believe it, buster," Bjornson said, "because you're going to hear a lot of questions from me about those *friends* of yours, and I expect straight answers."

Straight answers. I thought of Wycyzcski, my boss, and suspected that he was glad to have me gone. He was always asking for straight answers, too, and was rarely pleased with mine. But words were my only real defense.

Bjornson and four other agents from the CIA, plus two people whose affiliations were never identified, questioned me for the better part of ten days, interrupted only by meals, sleep, and an occasional visit from Agent Velasquez with her own list of questions.

Miss Stovall showed up occasionally, but never stayed for very long. She seemed convinced of only two things—that there was nothing she could do for me until formal charges were filed, and that her caseload was too heavy.

What had that shrink, Dr. Bessle, said about me? That I was passive aggressive? Well, Miss Stovall reinforced every bit of my passive aggression as I kept forcing all my anger deeper and deeper into myself.

Somewhere near the end of the week an auditor from the IRS showed up demanding that I call her Mrs. Wilkerson and demanding to know where the receipts were for my four-year-old computer. Where were the receipts for every book in my library? Why had I claimed seventeen dollars less refund than I was entitled to on my previous year's tax return?

My interrogators began working me in relays, each agent with his or her own agenda, each with his or her own prejudices and suspicions. Somewhere in the middle of it all I lost track of days and weeks. Miss Stovall quit coming to see me, and I quit caring what happened to me next. The more questions they asked, the more numb I felt, until I was going through the motions like a robot.

The DSA had literally torn my house apart looking for evidence against me. They told me they'd done it after badgering me into signing a form giving them permission to do so. I wasn't surprised, and I knew I couldn't let it matter. If I let down my defenses for that, God only knew how else they might hurt me.

The CIA had apparently questioned every Hispanic and Irish resident of Weatherford, Fort Worth, Parker, and Tarrant counties, and every present and past employee of General Dynamics Aerospace whose last name was even faintly Irish or Hispanic, and read me page after brain-numbing page of those names asking if I knew them. They made me wish I hadn't so purposefully ignored so much of my heritage.

Finally I said, "Why don't you ask me if I knew Mexico's President Obregon? He was an Irish-Mexican—O'Brien was the family name before his father changed it. Just because he died before I was born, doesn't mean that he might not be implicated."

Bjornson looked confused by that, but Velasquez laughed.

The IRS had reviewed my tax returns for the last fifteen years, found errors in all of them, and was prepared to sue me for hundreds of thousands of dollars in back taxes, penalties, and interest, but was willing to settle out of court if I would reveal my hidden sources of foreign income and the location of my foreign bank accounts. No matter what I said, Mrs. Wilkerson was convinced that I had great amounts of cash either in Swiss bank accounts or Cayman Island bank accounts, but for some reason, not in both. After a while I rewarded her persistence by telling her I had buried it all in a lead-lined box on Padre Island. She was not amused.

Agent Olsten from the Bureau of Alcohol, Tobacco, and Firearms wanted to know the exact date and place I had purchased my pistol, my deer rifles, my shotgun, and every round of ammunition stored in my safe. When I obviously couldn't provide that information, he assured me that BATF would prosecute me to the fullest extent of the law.

Even NASA got in on the questioning, sending an Air Force colonel who wanted to know anything I could tell NASA about Lana's comet, as though I had some magic observatory or something, and if Reyes had mentioned the Russians and Chinese preparing rockets to intercept the comet.

One night in the middle of all that, Potter woke me from a dead sleep, forced me to get dressed, took me to the roof, and put me aboard a helicopter. The chopper took me to the airport to a waiting jet. The jet took us to Fort Worth, a place I recognized by its skyline outlined in lights and because I recognized the terminal at Meacham Field where they put me on another helicopter that took me to the DSA building in Weatherford outside the GenDARF plant where I worked.

Once inside that building, I might as well have been back in Albuquerque. The layout and the color scheme were slightly different, but the routine interrogation resumed after breakfast that morning without a pause. Velasquez was there, and Bjornson, and Mrs. Wilkerson, and Potter, and Torelli, NASA's Colonel Mears, and even agents Starnes and Watters whom I had only seen in passing since they escorted me from Chaco Canyon.

Occasionally my mind would wander and I would think about Mama, and the people at work—besides Wycyzcski— and my neighbors and the few friends I'd made outside of GenDARF. And Miss Spiegel. God, I wondered who she had gone to the Fourth of July picnic with, but as soon as I caught myself doing that, I shut those thoughts off. I couldn't afford them.

All day, every day, seven days a week they interrogated me, asked me the same questions they'd already asked a hundred times before, then variations on those questions. Then they had new questions asking for the same information, then trick questions, which were always too obvious, but which most of them asked in a way that suggested they were assured of some special answer, which I didn't have to give them.

The only things I learned out of all those sessions were that they were all paranoid to the nth degree about Russia and the Central American Communists, and that Lana's comet might indeed be on some kind of near-miss course with earth. From myself I learned what a passive ball my life could shrink into and I began to understand that retreating into myself was my only real defense against them.

Then one morning after breakfast, Potter took me back to my cell instead of to the interrogation room. I sat in my cell for hours waiting for him to come back and get me, but he didn't.

Agent Lankford brought my lunch on a tray, and she gave me a strange look when she said, "Don't worry, Mr. O'Hara, I think you're going to be all right."

I had a feeling she was wrong.

Chapter Eight

I waited for hours after lunch for someone to come get me and was surprised by how angry I was with them for not coming. They were messing with my day—messing with my mind—forcing me to cope with uncertainty, and after all the routine questioning, leaving me alone in my cell was a minor form of psychological torture that got worse day after day with no one but Potter or Lankford coming to my cell, bringing my meals, refusing to tell me what was going on.

Then one day Torelli showed up. "I have more bad news for you, O'Hara. Your mother died last week."

My brain went numb. "When?"

"Last week. September seventh."

"The funeral?"

"It's over. I'm sorry."

He left without saying anything else, and for the longest time I just sat there staring at the door, wondering how in God's name my life had come to this. Mama dead? Already buried? September seventh? How could it be? A great, cold numbness clutched my heart.

Potter and Lankford continued to bring me food, and Lankford especially tried to coax me into eating more. I poked at it. I put some of it in my mouth. I chewed. I swallowed. But mostly I counted.

Three meals a day. Two days. Three days. Four days.

On the fifth day I cried every few minutes.

By the seventh day I had accepted that Mama really had died and tried to take my mind off her death by searching two or three times through every book on the shelf, looking for a picture that matched the Reyes photograph, but I found nothing and couldn't concentrate on reading, and after a while I just sat curled up in a chair and screamed occasional obscenities at the walls.

Twelve days after they told me Mama died, the interrogation resumed. Even though I tried to keep track of the days again with a homemade calendar, sometimes I would forget and then not know if a day had passed since I last marked the calendar, or two days, or a week. I was sure months passed before I finally gave it up. Nothing else was real to me anymore, so why should time have been different?

Without warning, with no noticeable change in the questions I was being asked, the interrogation stopped again, and the empty days of waiting returned. On the fifth morning, instead of breakfast, Agent Velasquez showed up at my door.

"I have good news for you, Senor O'Hara. You were correct about Lana's comet. We and the Russians have launched rockets to intercept and destroy it, and you can go home now."

"Pardon?" I stared at her blankly. "Go where?"

"Home, Senor O'Hara—back to work, of course. You have been cleared of all charges."

"Everything? The IRS, too?" I couldn't believe—

"Well, the IRS may still present you a problem, but you have been cleared of all security charges."

"What about my house?"

"We have restored it to its original condition and returned all your possessions, of course."

"What's the catch? Why the sudden change?"

She cleared her throat. "We believe you are innocent of everything except failure to report, and we have dropped those charges. There is no catch. You will, of course, report any and all future contacts with foreign nationals, such as Senor Reyes, directly to me, at this phone number." She handed me a card. "I will remain your case officer."

I put the card in my pocket and nodded slowly. "So, I'm not really cleared, just set loose to mingle with the loyal citizens. Aren't you all afraid I'll contaminate—"

"You are cleared. I promise you. Come, there is a car waiting to take you home. You will have to return to your job after the first, but you are truly lucky. You still have four days of Christmas vacation left."

"Christmas? But . . . but . . ." There were no words for my shock. I had gone to Chaco Canyon in June, Mama had died in September, and now it was already past Christmas.

She took me by the elbow and led me from my cell through the gray halls to the car waiting for us in the underground garage, assuring me all the while that she would send my clothes and things in a few days, and that I would readjust in no time.

The car with two agents in the front seat and me alone in the back took me home, and I stared out the window the whole drive without really seeing anything that looked familiar. Weatherford might as well have been a foreign country. When we got to the house, the agents escorted me to the front porch, then left.

As soon as I pushed the door open, I smelled an offensive trace of ammonia like old cat urine. I turned the light on and saw leaning stacks of books near the center of the living room floor, large unpainted patches in the walls, carpet torn loose from the corners of the room, and roaches skittering away to only they knew where. In one corner stood someone's poor attempt at holiday cheer—a twisted little cedar tree, its needles turning brown, its dry limbs hung with a dozen cheap ornaments, a handful of tinsel, and one blinking red light.

Some old habit clinging to my brain told me the light was not on the tree. It was on my answering machine. The same habit carried me to it, pushed the rewind button, then set it to play back its messages.

A soft voice spoke to me from the tape. "Senor O'Hara, now that you have been released by your *federales*, we must get together very soon. I will contact you later this week because we do not have much time to—"

I stopped the machine. The voice on the tape belonged to Cacabe Reyes Campos.

Chapter Nine

At three-thirty the next morning someone knocked repeatedly on my back door.

I was already half-awake, unused to sleeping in my own bed, but I hesitated before going to answer it. Under normal conditions, I would have taken my pistol along with my flashlight in order to answer the door at that time of night. But if the boys from the BATF had left my pistol, or my shotgun, I hadn't seen either of them, so I took my Crain Predator machete and my flashlight to the back door. Not quite sure how to set myself for defense with a machete in the narrow hallway, I was nevertheless reassured by the Crain's forty-two-ounce weight and the fit of its curved, finger-grip handle.

Expecting to see Reyes, somehow I wasn't surprised that the face squinting in the beam of my flashlight belonged to Agent Velasquez.

"Let me in," she said. It was an order, not a request.

I unlatched the screen and let her in, keeping the machete's fifteen-inch blade close to my leg, more for psychological support than any use it might be at that moment. The urge to jab her with its double-edged point was only a passing one. After she squeezed past me very cautiously and headed for the living room, I latched the screen again and locked the door.

"*Cabrónes!*" she said as I turned on the living room light. "They swore to me that this had all been taken care of." She turned and looked at me. "I am sorry for this, Mr. O'Hara." There was a look on her face, different, softer maybe, than any I had seen on her, but after six months under her thumb, it was easy enough to ignore.

"Sure you are," I said, leaning the machete against the wall and flopping into my armchair, "and you're sorry to have to come here in the middle of the night and wake me up, but unfortunately my interrogation isn't quite over. Did I get it right?"

Velasquez stood in the middle of the room facing me, eyes hooded, hands shoved into the back pockets of her faded jeans, shoulders back, breasts thrust forward under a tight sweater. An erotic rush through my gut made me sit up straighter in my chair and look away from her.

"I am here for another reason," she said.

Careful, careful, a voice whispered in my ear, *she's nothing but danger for you.* The voice couldn't stop me from seeing how nicely her jeans fit around her hips. "So what do you want from me?" I asked, forcing myself to look her straight in the eyes.

"Reyes contacted you, did he not?"

What was left of my erotic rush drained away and a wave of embarrassment took its place. I hadn't realized what six months without sex had done to me. My imagination had gone loco. Velasquez was just here for more interrogation. "I figured you guys had the phones bugged, so I didn't bother to call you. So what?"

"Listen to me, Senor O'Hara. You must understand that I am your friend. I want to help you."

"Help me what? Go to prison?"

"I want to help you find Reyes."

"Well, you can just hat up and get out of here then, because I have absolutely no intentions of making any contact with Mr. Reyes, by phone, in person, or any other way. The next time he calls me, you trace it. You go out and track him down. You find out what kind of crazy man he is, and you deal with him however you want to. But whatever happens, leave me out of it. I've had all the aftereffects of meeting Reyes that I can stand."

"It is not that simple," she said. "I know about Reyes. He is *chuchcahau*, and must be respected."

I remembered the word. "You mean he's some kind of pagan priest, don't you?"

Velasquez smiled. "Only pagan if you do not believe in the god Tohil."

"What?" I shook my head in frustration. "Just tell me what you want from me at this ungodly hour of the morning and then get out of here."

"Mr. O'Hara, you must let Reyes make contact with you, and you must arrange a meeting. Then tell no one but me— no one else in the DSA, you understand?"

"Only the what, not the why. But I guess you squeezed the why's out of me. Except why can't you just trace him?"

She squatted down in front of my chair, elbows resting on her knees and looked up at me. "Because, Jesus, your phone is not bugged—not exactly. The devices monitoring your telephone shield it from bugs. Your conversations are protected."

The fact that she had called me Jesus was almost lost in the midst of her claims, but I had noticed it. What was she after now? "Why should I believe you?" I asked, my eyes locked on hers. "What have you ever done to make me trust you for more than a second?"

"Nothing," she said without blinking, "but you must trust me. It is most imperative. You are needed and so am I."

"By whom?"

"By the world."

"Again?"

"By the world, Jesus. The world needs us."

I looked at her and looked at her, and suddenly a thought came to me that I surely didn't need. "Don't tell me you . . ."

Her face had those classic Meso-American features.

"You don't mean to say . . ."

Her dark eyes smoldered with a light of their own.

I closed my eyes and shuddered and wrapped my arms around myself. When I opened my eyes the odd light was gone from hers. "You want me to help you trap Reyes?" I asked without expecting an answer. "All right, I'll do it. But I want my house repaired and fumigated, and I want my guns and the rest of my books back, and I want my name cleared in writing with copies registered in the courthouse."

"Yes, that can all be done."

"Then I'll help you trap Reyes."

"You must help now. If you don't, he could act on his own and we might never be able to catch him."

"First the clearance and the house repairs, then I'll help."

Her face set itself in an expression that matched the pictoglyphs she reminded me so much of. "There is insufficient time. You must help immediately."

"Why can't you just leave me alone?" I asked with a sigh.

"You are as essential in this as Reyes."

"But you said you believed I'm innocent."

"That is true. There is no evidence to prove you seriously violated security regulations."

"Then what the hell are you talking about?"

"I am talking, Mr. O'Hara, about your life and my life and the life of the world. We have to find Reyes before it is too late."

"If I help you do this will you please agree to—"

The phone rang.

"—leave me alone?" I picked up the receiver. "Hello?"

"I have called to warn you," that soft, one-of-a-kind voice said in my ear, "that you are being closely watched. Your *federales* are very frightening."

"Where are you?" I asked without thinking.

"You will know soon enough. The time is short and the fourth year approaches, the year of your day. Be prepared. You will know the time."

"Listen, Reyes, would you please . . ."

The dial tone buzzed in my ear.

"What did he say?" Velasquez demanded.

As accurately as I could I recited it to her.

"Do you have cold weather camping gear?" she asked.

"I did before I left here six months ago. Who knows what's left of anything I own?"

"Find what you can and get it ready. Make a list for—"

"Like hell I will."

"Make a list of what you don't have that you need, and I'll make sure you get it."

"Look, Velasquez, I don't know what the hell you've got in mind, but if you think—"

"Shush!" She held her hand up, but stayed in her squat in front of me. "Listen to me, O'Hara, and listen carefully. I need your total and unequivocal cooperation in this matter, and if I do not receive it, I know how to arrange for you to be a permanent guest of the government—and I do not mean a residence in that padded room you have been living in. I mean in a prison, in a cell. Is that where you want to rot the rest of you life away?"

I could only shake my head.

"Then do as I tell you. Get your camping gear packed. Make me that list. And be ready to leave whenever Reyes wants you to. Understand?"

42

"Yes, but can I ask one question?"

She stood up in a sinuous motion of her whole body that ended in the rotation of her shoulders. "Ask."

"Whose damn side are you on, Velasquez?"

"The winning side, I hope. Whose side are you on?"

"My own. It's the only side I have."

Velasquez smiled. "Do not hold onto that too tightly. You might find other sides worthy of your support. Now, turn out the light and I will leave by the front door. I want that list by tomorrow night, O'Hara."

I turned out the light, and after a long moment's delay, she slipped into the darkness. I went back to bed and fell asleep almost immediately. When I staggered downstairs in the morning it was almost as though I had dreamed the whole thing—but not quite.

My Crain Predator machete was still leaning against the living room wall, but tied through the hole in its handle was a buff-colored, pelted thong with black rings and spots. My big desk encyclopedia had a picture of a jaguar with a pelt marked in exactly the same pattern.

Suddenly I was awake. What had she said about the god Tohil? I couldn't remember, but I knew it was important.

Chapter Ten

I spent all that day in an argument with myself as bit by bit I dug my camping gear out of all the heaps the feds had left lying around in every room of my house. The more I dug, the angrier I got, and the angrier I got, the more foolish my thoughts became.

No, I couldn't jump in the truck and drive away from all this. But even if I wanted to, would the truck start and run? How long had it been since anyone had driven it? If not the truck, what? My bicycle? How far would I get on that?

No, I couldn't call some other government agency and ask for their help. What agency with any power hadn't questioned me? And what chance would I have that any government official—city, county, state, or national—would believe me rather than Case Officer Velasquez of the DSA?

No, I couldn't catch the airport limo and fly to Arizona to see my aunts or visit Mama's grave. If the feds didn't catch me at the airport, they'd be waiting for me when the plane landed, and Velasquez would really wrap the rules around me when I got back.

No, I couldn't put on my backpack and hike my way out of trouble. It was too far to any place that might be remotely safe, and my experience didn't exactly prepare me for that.

No, I couldn't say to hell with them all and barricade myself in the house.

No, I couldn't escape. I was a pawn again, like I always was—the obedient pawn, verbally aggressive, but nothing more.

I screamed until my throat hurt. Sometime in the middle of it all I sat on the floor and cried. What else was there to do?

When I finished crying I went back to work getting my camping gear together. There was a new jar of peanut butter and a new jar of jelly in the cupboard and, surprisingly enough, a loaf of fairly fresh bread on the counter. I made myself several sandwiches and ate while I worked.

By six I had all my gear gathered, checked, and packed, and a short list of what was missing—mostly food, toilet articles, and stove fuel.

At seven Velasquez called. "You have my list?"

"Yes."

"Good. Seal it in an envelope and give it to Potter when he gets there. Have you heard from our friend?"

"No."

"But you will call me after he contacts you?"

"Yes."

"*Bueno.* Do not rabbit on me, O'Hara. I am depending on you to get me to Reyes."

"I understand."

She hung up and I was glad. After sealing the list in an envelope, I sat down to play some records. The stereo didn't work. A few minutes investigation showed that it had been taken apart, and whoever put it back together had screwed something up. The only problem was that I probably didn't know any more about stereo equipment than they did. Fiddling with it had me totally frustrated when someone knocked on the door.

"Mr. O'Hara, it's me, Potter."

"Do you know anything about electronics, Potter?" I asked as I opened the door.

"No. Why? You having trouble?"

"Not me," I said, handing him the envelope. "Why would I be having trouble? But some of your *compadres* had trouble putting my record player back together."

"Uh, well, do you want me to take a look at it?"

"No, Potter, it's not your fault. You take the precious envelope to Senorita Velasquez and I'll worry about this."

Five minutes after he left I regretted sending him away. At least he would have been someone to talk to. The television didn't work, either. None of its wires were connected to anything. Once it was plugged in and its antenna and signal booster wires were hooked up to the video recorder and the video recorder was plugged into the TV, I got a decent picture. Unfortunately, none of the channels were showing anything worth watching.

In the cabinet beside the stove I found a half-full bottle of Beam's black label and fixed myself a stiff highball. Then I sat down on the living room floor to begin sorting the stacks of books. An hour later I had managed to pull all the physics and engineering books from the stacks when the phone rang.

I didn't want to answer it. I didn't want to hear from Reyes, and I didn't want to talk to Velasquez. My answering machine was on, so I let the machine answer it on the third ring. It was Reyes's voice that followed my message.

"Senor O'Hara, I know you are home, and I hope you are listening. I will come to your house tomorrow afternoon at three o'clock. Please be home."

In the middle of the day? He was going to come in the middle of the day? Why in the world would he do something so foolish? Did he want to get caught?

What did it matter? I asked myself. Why should I care what Senor Reyes did? If he wanted to walk into a trap at my house at three o'clock tomorrow, that was his business. Besides, the sooner DSA caught him, the better off I'd be.

With perverse delight I punched Velasquez's private number into my phone. She answered almost immediately.

"He called. He'll be here at three tomorrow afternoon."

"Are you sure it is tomorrow afternoon he will come, not tomorrow morning?"

"That's what he said."

"Do you have everything packed?"

"Everything except what's on the list—but I won't need it now, will I? You can arrest him right here."

"You just leave it packed," she said. "I will get to your house around nine or ten tomorrow morning. I had your truck serviced the day before you came home, so it is ready to go."

"Now wait a minute, Velasquez. If Reyes is coming here, why does my truck have to be ready? Why does my gear have to be packed? What the hell are you trying to tell me?"

"Only what I told you last night. You have to trust me, Jesus. Please? I cannot do this alone."

"Why? You never gave me a reason."

"I cannot tell you on the phone. It will take time. *No gano Toledo en un credo, eh?*"

"I don't know what that means."

"It means you must give me time to explain later. Toledo wasn't built in a day. For now, Jesus, I put my faith in you, and *primero Dios*, it will all come clear in the morning."

"And if I don't want to give you time?"

"Do not force my hand, my friend."

Silence hung on the wires between us.

Finally I said, "All right, Velasquez, I'll give you time— but not because I want to, and not because you want me to, but because I really don't have a choice."

"*Gracias.* I will see you tomorrow."

"Yeah, well, *de nada* and good night to you, too." I put down the phone, looked up at the ceiling, and screamed, "Bitch!"

Then I laughed.

It was all so stupid. Because I had been too recalcitrant to tell the DSA I was going to Chaco Canyon, I had lost six months of my life to a meaningless interrogation. Consequently, I was about to be dragged into some new mess by a woman who looked more and more like a renegade agent— and I didn't have the backbone to stand up to her. Why? What did she want, anyway?

Did Velasquez think Reyes was going to lead her to some secret Commie organization or something? Did she think he was a spy for the Russians? Or the Chinese? What did she want from him? Or me, for that matter? Why couldn't she just take Reyes and my truck and go wherever her scheming heart led her?

I smiled suddenly and felt much better. There was the answer. Velasquez could arrest Reyes, take my truck—and my camping gear—and go wherever she damn well pleased. She couldn't make me go anywhere.

With that solution safely tucked away in my head, I finished off my highball, fixed another, and with a lot of patient fiddling and tongue-biting, managed finally to get the record player rewired and working again. The second highball was gone, so I fixed a third, stacked five Asleep at the Wheel records on the turntable, put on my headphones, and lay down on the floor to listen. Chris O'Connell sang her sweet self out in the middle of my head, and primitive pictures from Meso-America played through my mind.

The next thing I knew, my body was vibrating. The headphones were dead, and as I slipped them off I realized that it was daylight outside. The vibration was Velasquez pounding on the front door.

"O'Hara! You had better open this door before I break the glass and come in there after you."

"I'm coming!" I shouted as I climbed groggily to my feet. "Hold your damn horses!"

"What is the matter with you?" she asked when I opened the door.

"Nothing. I fell asleep on the floor last night listening to music, and I couldn't hear you for the headphones." I looked at my watch. "Besides, you're early."

"That is quite beside the point. I do not suppose that if Reyes had called you would have heard the telephone ring?"

"No. But the machine would have picked it up. No blinking light, no phone call. Relax, Senorita," I said with a forced smile. "I will put some coffee on to perk, and you can enjoy it while I take a shower and get dressed."

She wrinkled her regal nose. "You were drinking last night."

"So what's it to you?" The solution I had celebrated was perfectly clear in my otherwise muddled mind.

"Nothing. I apologize for yelling at you."

"Accepted. Now sit down and make yourself at home. I'll get the coffee on and head for the shower."

After I had showered and dressed and joined her in the living room for coffee, I said, "I've been thinking about what you said last night and there's an answer—"

"So have I, Jesus. I have decided to give you as much explanation as I can before Reyes arrives."

Chapter Eleven

"You can arrest Reyes and take my truck and all my camping stuff and go wherever you want to," I said. Despite my best efforts to calm my voice, I knew I sounded overeager.

"Such a proposal will not work, Jesus," Velasquez said. "I asked you to trust me, but I did not trust you. Now I must do that and give you the reason for trusting me that you deserve." The look in her eye spelled trouble.

"I don't want a reason to trust you. Just take the truck and go. You can have it. You don't ever have to bring—"

"Your truck is not what I want, Jesus. It is you who are needed."

My mouth opened, but nothing came out, and I didn't even know why it opened. What in the world could she mean?

"Listen to me, Jesus, and during the time we have before the arrival of Cacabe Reyes, I—"

"If you're going to keep using my name, call me Martin. Only Mama and my aunts ever call me . . ." I couldn't finish. Now it was only my aunts who would call me by my given name.

"If that is what you wish, that is what I will call you, Martin, although I must say that I think the name—"

"Maybe you could save telling me all this until you and Reyes get back from your trip? I can wait."

"Please, Martin, make yourself comfortable and listen to my story. Then we can settle everything else."

With a deep sigh I sat back in my chair. "All right. I don't know why, but all right."

"All my grandparents grew up together in the same village. They immigrated to the United States together with their children, my parents, and even though I was born here in

Texas, I spent almost every summer living in the village that was my grandparents' home in Guatemala."

"Guatemala? You're from Guatemala?" Suspicion rose in me like a flash flood.

"My parents are—or they were. They are dead now."

"So what's your connection to Reyes?"

"May I tell the story my own way, please?"

"First tell me what your connection to Reyes is."

"He is my cousin, the son of my mother's cousin."

"Of course he is. Why didn't I figure that out? Dammit, woman, what the hell is going on here?"

"*Por favor*, let me tell you. I was born Shirlito Ramona Velasquez Lopez y Campos, but on my birth certificate my parents put my name in the American fashion, so I was always known as Shirlito Ramona Velasquez. Cacabe Reyes Campos is the son—"

"The world shrinks. The circles tighten." I didn't know what to make of what she told me, but I felt very uncomfortable and even more wary of her.

"He is the son of my grandmother's niece. But the world is even smaller than you think, Martin. Cacabe and I were taught stories that make me now believe your great-great-grandfather once lived in the same village as ours did."

"You mean you think we're related, too?" A new anger shaded my suspicion.

"No. No. But it was our great-grandfather who first suspected yours was a descendant of Great True Jaguar."

"Now wait a minute. You knew all this stuff *and* the Mayan mumbo-jumbo, and still you let them put me through all that crap for the last six months? Why? . . . Why?"

"Because when it started I did not know what was happening, and only by accident did I hear Torelli laughing with someone about True Jaguar. That was when I assigned myself to the case to find out who you were. Since I am the DSA's resident expert on Central American affairs, they would have assigned me, anyway. However, I wanted to hear your story while it was fresh—before they got you too confused to tell it."

"But why didn't you get me out of there?" I felt betrayed without knowing why. She didn't owe me anything.

"I could not. Once I had checked your background and was sure you were telling the truth, the investigation had gained its own momentum—mostly because of Lana's comet, and because of the recent gains by the Communists in *La Raza Unida de Guatemala*. I could not stop the investigation then. I could only try my best to control it."

"But . . . why . . . I guess I just don't understand. Why couldn't you just tell them about this crazy cousin of yours?"

"First, Martin, I do not think Cacabe is crazy. His life is in greater harmony with the world than the lives of any Americans I know. Second, if I had told them I knew Cacabe, they would have begun investigating me. Then I would not have been in any position to help you or Cacabe. Thus, third, I knew that if Cacabe had said what you claimed he told you—and I doubted you could have made it up—then I knew you had to be protected at all costs."

"But what took so long?"

"So long?" She sounded defensive. "Do you know that some investigations like yours often go on for years? It took all of my persuasion and power to conclude this case as quickly as I did."

"Well, it may have seemed quick to you, lady, but it seemed damned slow to me. It was long enough to kill Mama."

She looked at me from under the shadows of thick eyebrows, and her voice trembled ever so slightly when she spoke. "I am sorry about your mother."

I waited, silently resenting her presence and all she represented.

"Do you know what day is coming, Martin? It is the leap year day, the twenty-ninth of February, the day of the Great True Jaguar, and of his son, Seven Jaguar."

"Listen, don't start in on that Jaguar stuff like Reyes did. I didn't understand it then, and I'm not going to understand it now, so don't bother."

"That Jaguar stuff, as you call it, is the making of your fate and the fate of the world."

I wasn't sure if she was being sarcastic or if she really believed what she had just said. When I finally accepted the full seriousness of her expression, I didn't know what to think.

"Come on, Velasquez. We're civilized citizens of the United

States of America. Leave all that Mayan mumbo-jumbo for the *brujos* and the *campesinos* and the anthropologists."

"It is true that the Mother Church frowns upon the teachings of the daykeepers like Cacabe, and God forgive me, if what I believe is a sin." She crossed herself. "But what Cacabe told you is part of what he and I were taught as truth. *A son of Great True Jaguar and Macaw House will be called from his hiding place in the north to travel the road to Xibalba like Hunahpu and Xablanque did, and save the world.*"

"And you can believe that . . . you can believe that kind of thing and still be a good Catholic?"

"It is what I believe, yes."

I shook my head. "She-it. I'm in big trouble. Velasquez, what happens if I call Torelli at DSA right now and tell him what you just told me about you and Cacabe Reyes?"

"We would share your troubles. Torelli would like nothing better than to bring charges against me. He thinks Indians like you and me and Cacabe are not fit for—"

"What does my Indian heritage have to do—"

"Can you look in the mirror and deny it?"

"No. But I'm an American citizen who happens to have Indian blood, not an Indian who happens to be a citizen."

"Not in Torelli's eyes. He has that New Mexico attitude toward Indians—do not trust them, do not respect them, and do not run over them if you can help it. They stink up your car. As far as he is personally concerned, you and I do not deserve equal rights with his kind—"

"He can't just deny—"

"He can do whatever he wishes within the framework of the Security Act, and that is more than you want to know. He would not admit his prejudices, of course, because that is against the law. But nothing can stop him from using the law to satisfy his prejudices." Her tone was angry and tired.

"So he wouldn't mind getting us both under the lights?" It was a statement more than a question, but I waited for her response anyway.

"Yes, Martin. Torelli would most like having you, me, and Cacabe, all under his control for interrogation. What he would do to us, would make your last six months seem like a vacation."

I shook my head. "Damn, Velasquez. You know how to put the squeeze on, don't you?"

She looked down at her hands and her voice softened. "It is not I who squeezes you."

"Then who is it?"

"That I do not know, Martin. I am only Shirlito Velasquez who would be a friend to help you in what you must do."

"Yeah. Well, what I want to do is get the hell away from all of you."

"But that is not your *obligación*."

"What is my obligation? To listen to you and some crazy Guatemalan *brujo*? When things got tough for my family and it looked like they were going to get worse, my maternal grandmother always said, '*De Guatemala en Guatepeor*.' Now I know why."

"I have never heard it before. What is *Guatepeor*?"

"It's a pun, Velasquez, a joke. *De mal en peor*? From bad to worse?" She was frowning at me. "You understand puns, or don't they let you make jokes in the DSA? From Guate*mala* to Guate*peor*? From Guate-bad to Guate-worse?"

"Yes, I understand it, but I do not find it amusing that such a word play is made on the good name of Guatemala."

"Forget I said it. Forget the whole thing. It's a bad joke. As soon as Reyes gets here—if Reyes gets here—you take him and the truck and forget me. Please? I don't need all this, Velasquez."

"Would you call me Shirlito?"

"No. Absolutely not. I don't want to be on familiar terms with you or Reyes. In fact, I wish you'd go back to calling me O'Hara, okay?"

"We cannot leave you here," she said. "If Cacabe thinks you must go to the seven canyons of Weatherhill in Mesa Verde, that is where you must go, and where I must go with you."

"There's no way out of this for me, is there?"

"No, I do not think so. Can you not—"

The doorbell interrupted her.

We exchanged glances as I got up to answer it. It was too early to be Reyes, but who else would it be?

Chapter Twelve

Reyes stood on the porch wearing faded blue jeans and a blue windbreaker zipped to his chin. His eyes shifted restlessly under a battered brown fedora. The sky hung over him like a silver grey tent.

"You're early," I said, opening the door. "You told me you'd be here this afternoon."

He stepped past me into the house. "Only the gods keep perfect time, Senor O'Hara."

"Cacabe? *Que tal?*"

"Shirlito!"

Velasquez and Reyes stepped quickly into each other's arms, jabbering like disk jockeys. For a full minute I listened to them as they talked so fast I couldn't understand a thing they were saying. The way they kept glancing at me prickled the hairs on the back of my neck.

When they finally stepped back from the embrace and their tongues slowed down a little, I could only comprehend stray words and phrases and realized their babble wasn't pure Spanish. I didn't know what Indian language or dialect they were speaking, but there was no doubt in my mind who was the main subject of their conversation.

"Ask him why he's early," I said. The anger in my voice didn't surprise me. "Ask him if he isn't worried about getting caught. Ask him why the—"

"You forget I speak English, Senor O'Hara. Tohil taught me, remember?"

He paused, but I ignored his question, and thus ignored his pagan god.

"Please forgive me, Senor O'Hara, for coming early to your house. The time of my arrival was decided by the fact that I had to evade several of your aggressive *federales* who appeared to have—"

"They're not my *federales*, Reyes. They're hers. Why don't you ask her about them? The Defense Security Agency," I said. "You remember them, don't you?" I took a sideways step toward the kitchen and could not see his reaction. For once I hoped I had forgotten to lock the back door.

Reyes put his hat on the dining table and unzipped his windbreaker as he said, "*Si*, of course I remember your *Security*. Why do you work for such people, Shirlito?"

She said something long and unintelligible, then added, "Maybe I should finish this in English for Mr. O'Hara's benefit." Velasquez glanced at me, then turned back to Reyes. "I felt like I could best serve my country, the United States, and my Hispanic heritage by working for the DSA. Now I am not so sure."

He asked her a question in their native tongue and she answered before he turned to me with a smile. "Do not worry, Senor O'Hara. It is a sign from Cristos and Tohil. As always, Shirlito is a true daughter of our people."

"What the hell's that supposed to mean?"

"It means she has the pure blood of Quitze. It means she will help us find the seven canyons of—"

"Not us, Reyes—you." I shook my head, stepped away from them, and held up my hands. "You two can help each other all you want to—in a thousand canyons for all I care. I'm out of it, now. *Terminado. Finis. Kaput.* I've done my part."

They shared a look and smiled. I slid my foot another step closer to the kitchen.

"Is your camping gear in the truck?" Velasquez asked.

"Yes. Take it and get out of my life. You can keep it for all I care. And the truck, too."

Velasquez gave me a thin smile. "As Torelli would say, 'No way, Jose.' Cacabe cannot complete the task without you because you cannot complete it without him." Her eyes were alight.

"What the hell is that supposed to mean? Oh, never mind." I backed away, distrusting them both, wanting nothing more than escape from them and all their crazy ideas. "You all go on, and if we're lucky, we'll never see each other again."

"*Que no!*" Reyes said, motioning me away from the kitchen door with several jerks of his hand.

His hand was filled with a big automatic pistol—a 9 mm Taurus by the look of it. The hammer wasn't cocked, but I couldn't remember if the Taurus was single-action or double-action. It didn't matter. I wasn't about to move.

"Now, wait a minute." My eyes saw nothing but the pistol. "There's no need to let this problem get out of control."

My legs were locked in place. My hands were up, like in the movies. My heart raced. My mind cursed the creeps from the BATF who had my guns.

"Indeed, Martin, that is true," Velasquez said, "we need not let these little difficulties get out of control." Her smile was gone, but she looked almost sympathetic. "You have only to come with us as Cacabe wishes."

"I would rather you came because you understood the need for it," Reyes said, still holding his aim on my chest, "but *sin falta*, one way or another, you must come. *Cometa Xibalba* will not wait for us."

My eyes focused on the gun as I slid down into one of the chairs at the dining table. There was something important here that I was missing, and if only . . . Then I knew. My mind latched onto it and I felt as though someone had just released the tension from my muscles. Slowly I lowered my hands.

"You won't shoot me," I said, looking from the gun to Reyes's face. "You don't dare. If I'm so damned important to you, you've got to have me alive and well."

He shifted his aim slightly. "Perhaps a wounded arm will not keep you from doing what must be done. In fact, Senor O'Hara, such a wound might make you easier to control."

I saw the pistol wobble and his thumb move, and I heard the double click as he pulled the hammer back. Single- or double-action, it was ready to fire.

"No, Cacabe," Velasquez said. "That is not fair."

"If it is necessary, it is fair, Shirlito."

"But it is not necessary. Mr. O'Hara will come with us, won't you, Martin?"

I forced myself to look at her, still seeing the black gaping barrel, steady now in Reyes's hand. My hands shook. "Sure," I said. "You bet. *De acuerdo!* You want me to take a truck ride with you? Fine. No sweat. Let's go."

She stepped between me and Reyes.

"Shirlito!"

She held out her hands. "Come, Martin. I will not let you be hurt."

My hands came up of their own accord and she grasped them warmly. "I'm afraid." The words left my mouth on their own.

"That is good," Reyes said, tucking his pistol in a holster under his windbreaker. "Fear will keep us alert."

"I don't understand."

"We have a great distance to go," he said. "Did you pack food in the truck?"

"No. Miss Velasquez was supposed—"

"I have it out back," she said.

She released my left hand and held my right in both of hers. Her dark gaze locked onto my eyes and sent a small shiver up my spine.

"Promise me you will not do anything foolish," she said.

"I don't know."

"Please, Martin, promise me that you will help us load the truck without trying to escape, and that you will help me drive to Mesa Verde. Promise me that much for now?"

There was a special pleading in her voice, a softness about her face, a warmth from her hands, and a sudden realization that something deep inside me was responding to her—and not for the first time. "All right," I said, without knowing why, but without knowing where else I could turn. "In for a penny, in for a dime."

Velasquez leaned toward me. "Trust me, Martin. Trust Cacabe."

I smelled gardenias, but her words snapped the spell. "No way," I said, pulling my hand from hers. The chair was behind me and I had no place to back away, so I shoved both hands in my pockets. "I'll do what you ask me to because I figure I don't have a choice, and I'm headed back to jail anyway. At least this way I'll stay out of jail for a little while longer."

"Would you rather fight to save the earth, or stay here and die when *cometa Xibalba* arrives?" Reyes asked.

"Neither," I said. "If Lana's comet is going to hit the earth, there's certainly nothing *I* can do to stop it. I just don't want to go to jail, that's all." My eyes shifted from him to Velasquez. "Who are you people, anyway?"

She smiled and offered me her hand again. In her other hand she held my Crain machete. "Come. We will load your truck and begin our drive to Mesa Verde. Perhaps by the time we arrive we will have convinced you that we are who we say we are."

With less reluctance than I expected to feel, I took her hand and let her lead me to the back door, as though it were her house instead of mine. As we came out of the house I saw a small blue car parked in my shed. "Yours?" I asked.

"Yes." She opened the hatchback to reveal several sacks of food and camping supplies.

"Why not back your car up to the truck? No sense in hauling all that stuff all the way out front."

"Perhaps you should bring the truck back here."

I looked from her toward the front of the house and back to her. "You'd trust me to do that?"

"Yes, Martin, I would trust you to do that."

"What would keep me from just driving away?"

"Nothing."

"But you're not worried about that?"

"No."

"Why?"

"Because if I expect you to trust me and Cacabe, we must trust you. Will you go get your truck and bring it back here?"

There was a look on her face that I didn't understand, and a tenseness in my chest that followed it. "Yes. I'll get the truck."

"Then our adventure begins."

"Sure," I said, walking toward the driveway, "our adventure begins." Me and two Commie lunatics, I thought. To my surprise, I felt eager to get started—or maybe eager to get it over with.

Chapter Thirteen

I don't know what I expected as we headed west out of Weatherford on Interstate 20—maybe a fleet of highway patrol cars rushing to surround us with their lights blazing, or DSA helicopters landing in front of us, or someone else rescuing me from the crazy game Reyes and Velasquez had entangled me in. But nothing like that happened, and as I drove along under the stormy grey skies, my sense of anticipation began to fade.

All the way from the house, Velasquez and Reyes had been talking softly in their native tongue, and the longer we drove without some sign of rescue, the more I resented being locked out of their conversation. Besides, Velasquez had chosen to sit in the middle, and in spite of myself I was acutely aware of the scent of her gardenia perfume and the warmth of her body. That only heightened my resentment of their rudeness.

"You two enjoying the trip so far?" I asked. "I'm not bothering you, am I? I mean, if I am, one of you could drive and I could crawl in the back where you wouldn't have to pay any attention to me at all."

"Are you angry?" Velasquez asked.

"Yes. You're damn right I am." I glanced at her, then brought my attention back to the road. Light rain spattered the windshield. "Between the two of you, you've put me through six months of hell, then dragged me out of my house and into God only knows what kind of trouble, and now you're rude enough to sit there talking to each other like I'm not even here, in some language I don't understand."

"We were talking about you."

"Oh, great. That's just great. Didn't either of you have parents to teach you any damn manners?"

"You *are* angry," she said, laying a hand on my arm.

"Me, angry?" I turned on the windshield wipers and kept my eyes straight ahead, wishing she would let go of my arm, hoping she wouldn't, confused by the conflict. "Not me. I'm not angry. I'm just trying to keep from being bored to death."

"Please, Senor O'Hara," Reyes said, "the fault is mine, not Shirlito's. It is easier for me to speak our Queche than in your English, but such is not fair to you. Your pardon, please?"

"Sure."

"You must be fair with us, too." Velasquez gently squeezed my arm before removing her hand. "Cacabe's apology is sincere."

She shamed me and I didn't know why. "All right. I'm sorry. I accept Senor Reyes's apology. Sincerely. But I do wish that instead of jabbering to yourselves you would take the time to tell me what we're going to do next."

"We will drive to Mesa Verde," Reyes said simply, "to the seven canyons of Weatherhill's mesa."

"The park's bound to be closed this time of year."

"We will get in. We must get in."

I took a deep breath and let it out in a long, noisy sigh. Whatever else Reyes was, he was certainly persistent. "Okay, so we get into the park somehow. Then what?"

"We seek the entrance to Xibalba."

"Right, like there are going to be signs saying *This Way to the Mayan Underworld. Form a Single Line Right.*"

"The true signs will be there." There was no hesitancy or doubt in his voice.

"So maybe you find this entrance. What do you do then?"

"We enter Xibalba, the underworld, and challenge the lords to a ballgame for the stake of—"

"Whoa-whoa, whoa. First of all, I don't believe there's any such place, but just for the sake of conversation, let's suppose there is. What makes you think I'm going down into some cave in the mountains with you?"

"It is you who must go. Only you can defeat them."

"Perhaps you should tell him the stories from the Council Book," Velasquez said. "What you and I take for granted must sound very strange to him."

I nodded. "It's going to take us at least three days to get there—if we don't run into snow—and we don't have anything else to do for entertainment. I'm willing to listen to some new fairy tales." Maybe he'd slip and give me some clue to their true affiliations—like agents of *La Raza Unida de Guatemala*.

"Three days will barely start the story, but I will tell you what I can of it, beginning with One Hunahpu and Seven Hunahpu."

"Am I going to have to remember a lot of strange names?"

"Such is not necessary for now."

"Good."

"This happened one day, long before humans were created. The gods One Hunahpu and Seven Hunahpu, sons of Xpiyacoc and Xmucane—Grandmother of Day, Grandmother of Light—were playing ball in the great abyss on the road to Xibalba. The lords of Xibalba were annoyed by the sounds of the game, which came to them as though coming through their roof."

"Go slowly for him, Cacabe."

"*Si. Por consiguiente*, One and Seven Death, the great

lawgivers of Xibalba, the foremost lords of the underworld, challenged One and Seven Hunahpu to come to Xibalba and play ball with the lords there."

"Sounds exciting," I said. "They play for fun or for money?"

"They played for their lives, Martin." Velasquez touched my arm when she spoke.

"They played for their lives," I repeated.

"Yes," Reyes said. "Their lives were at stake and they lost them."

"And you've got some crazy idea of a repeat performance starring us? No thanks."

"Let him continue. The story has just begun."

I hoped she was wrong. I hoped for my sake that the story was about over, but I held my tongue.

"Guided by messenger owls sent by the Xibalbans, One Hunahpu and Seven Hunahpu passed safely through the roaring canyon, passed the River of Many Spears, across the Blood River and the Pus River until they came to the crossroads. There they made their first mistake and met their first defeat at the four roads, Red Road, Black Road, Yellow Road, and White Road."

I shook my head, but Reyes didn't seem to notice.

"Black Road said to One and Seven Hunahpu, 'Follow me,' and they followed Black Road, and this was a mistake and a defeat, because Black Road was the road the Xibalbans had chosen for them. They followed Black Road until they came to the ruling circle of the lords of Xibalba where One and Seven Hunahpu greeted wooden statues of the lords, thinking they were talking to the lords themselves.

" 'Good morning, One Death. Good morning, Seven Death,' they said in turn.

" 'Good morning, House Corner and Blood Gatherer.'

" 'Good morning, Pus Master and Jaundice Master.'

"With each 'good morning' the Xibalbans laughed harder, but One and Seven Hunahpu did not hear the laughter and continued greeting the wooden statues of the lords of Xibalba.

" 'Good morning, Bone Scepter and Skull Scepter.'

" 'Good morning, Trash Master and Stab Master.' "

"Delightful names," I said.

"Shhh, Martin. Let him tell his story, please?"

"Sorry." The rain washed across the windshield in weak gusts.

" 'Good morning, Wing and Packstrap,' they said at last. Only then did One and Seven Hunahpu hear the laughter of the Xibalbans and know they had made a second mistake and met defeat.

"The Xibalbans kept laughing until One and Seven Death said, 'We are glad you came. Here, sit on this bench.'

"One and Seven Hunahpu sat down, then immediately shouted and jumped up and started waving at their buttocks because the bench was a red-hot rock and they had burned themselves. Again the Xibalbans laughed." Reyes chuckled. "It is funny, no?"

"If you say so." Didn't seem very funny to me.

" 'You will be all right,' the Xibalbans told One and Seven Hunahpu. 'Just go into this house we have prepared for you and we will bring you torches to see by and cigars to smoke.' "

"Surely they didn't go in," I said.

"But they had no choice," Velasquez answered. "They were in the domain of the Xibalbans."

"She is right." Reyes laughed again.

I glanced at him and when I looked back at the road saw flashing lights in front of us, and eased my foot off the accelerator. "Uh-oh. Look up ahead."

"Police," Velasquez said.

"Could be a wreck," I offered.

"Or a roadblock. Look for an exit."

"I think we just passed one."

"Back up to it."

I pulled off the road and brought the truck to a stop on the shoulder. My head told me to keep going, to turn the three of us over to the police, and stop this craziness, but my gut said no. The lights looked like they were at least a mile ahead of us in the slackening rain. Whatever they were doing, cars and trucks were passing them. "No way I'm going to try to back up. We'll keep driving and act like everyone else. Look for a semi to screen us as we pass them."

Velasquez and Reyes exchanged a few quick Indian words. "You are not going to try something foolish, are you?" she asked.

"You've already got me in the middle of something *foolish*. No, I'm not going to turn us over to the cops, if that's what you mean." I signaled to pull out into traffic and accelerated along the shoulder. In the mirror I could see a big truck bearing down on us. "Here we go," I said as the semi pulling two trailers swept past us behind a wall of spray.

I stomped on the gas and within ten or fifteen seconds had almost caught the semi. Easing through its blinding spray into the left lane, I guided the pickup almost by feel until our cab cleared the spray from the semi's front wheels. The driver probably wouldn't like me hanging that close, but at least I knew he could see me and wouldn't accidentally try to pull into the left lane. Holding our speed even with the semi's we raced down the road toward the blinking police lights.

Chapter Fourteen

The semi slowed as it approached the lights and we slowed with it. I figured as long as I kept the eighteen-wheeler between us and the police, the less chance we had of being spotted. That was assuming that someone was looking for us. Maybe the DSA was on Christmas vacation, too. Maybe Torelli and his crew didn't care what happened to me.

For some reason the thought that Torelli might not care cheered me up.

A sudden gust of wind and rain shoved us toward the semi.

I fought the wheel, felt the rear end slide, and turned hard into the skid, foot off the gas, no brakes. A split second after the rear end stopped sliding, I nudged the accelerator down. The tires grabbed and suddenly we were driving in the midst of a hurricane of wind and rain somewhere close behind the semi's lead trailer.

There was no telling where we were in relationship to the police lights, so I took a chance and eased off the accelerator enough to drop farther back.

Red and blue flashes jumped out of the spray. A gleaming shadow crossed the road. Then the lights were behind us and staying put. I let out a shuddering sigh.

"A wreck," Velasquez said. "Three cars at least. They are not interested in us. Relax."

Her hand patted my leg. My leg tensed.

"Sure. Relax, like pull yourself together—seldom said to anyone in a position to do it. Go on with your story, Reyes. I need the distraction. You were talking about torches and cigars."

"Yes, I was telling you that One and Seven Hunahpu went into Dark House, for that is what it is called. One and Seven Death sent them a torch and two cigars—all three of them already lit—and a messenger told One and Seven Hunahpu that they had to return the cigars and torch in the morning in the same condition they had received them."

While he was talking I accelerated around the semi and took possession of a patch of road between bunches of traffic.

"Again One and Seven Hunahpu knew they were defeated because the torch burned out, and the cigars burned out, and there was no way to return them."

"Correct me if I'm wrong," I said, "but are One and Seven Hunahpu the dumbest two gods man ever invented, or are they acting so stupidly for a reason?"

"Perhaps," Reyes said.

"What kind of an answer is that? Perhaps what?"

"Just perhaps, Senor O'Hara. One should not be too quick to judge the early gods. Was Cristos foolish to allow Himself to be crucified? I think not. Perhaps One and Seven Hunahpu were stupid on purpose and perhaps not. It is too early in the story to tell."

I blinked and shook my head. "That's the strangest thing you've said yet."

"Continue, Cacabe, and help him understand."

"Si?"

"Yes," I said. "Go ahead. Give me the whole party line."

"One and Seven Hunahpu failed the test of Dark House because their torch burned out and their cigars burned out. Later when One and Seven Death asked what had happened to the torch and cigars, One and Seven Hunahpu admitted that they were all used up. So One and Seven Death ordered that One and Seven Hunahpu be sacrificed."

"You're crazy. Even if I believed you, which I don't, there's no way I could—"

"There are many tests in Xibalba," Reyes continued, staring straight out the windshield as though I hadn't spoken. "There is the Chattering House, which is filled with the worst possible cold. There is Jaguar House filled with jaguars, and Bat House, and Razor House, but One and Seven Hunahpu didn't have to face any of these tests, because they failed in Dark House and were sacrificed."

I started to say something, then decided to let him go on. His voice had gained an interesting timbre, and despite my disbelief, the story at least kept me from wondering what I was actually going to do when we got to Mesa Verde.

"The Xibalbans killed One and Seven Hunahpu and cut off One Hunahpu's head. They buried the bodies by the Sacrificial Altar of the Ballgame, but One Hunahpu's head they stuck in the crook of a tree. Before that time the tree had no name and did not bear any fruit, but as soon as One Hunahpu's head was stuck in its branches, it bore fruit that looked like One Hunahpu's head. So the tree got its name, *head of One Hunahpu*, which we call calabash tree today." He paused. The rain was falling harder.

"Interesting," I said, feeling like I had to fill the silence.

"*Si.* The Xibalbans thought so, too. They stared at the tree and could not tell the calabashes from One Hunahpu's head, and so One and Seven Death ordered that no one was to go near the tree or pick the fruit. Everyone obeyed except one virgin daughter of Blood Gatherer, whose name was Blood Woman.

"When no one was looking, she sneaked up on the tree and said, 'I want to try the fruit of this tree.'

" 'No, you don't,' one of the calabashes replied.

" 'Yes, I do,' Blood Woman said."

"You must remember that Blood Woman was a virgin and not very wise, yet," Velasquez added.

The temptation to ask Velasquez if she was also a virgin passed as Reyes started speaking again.

" 'Very well,' the calabash said. 'Hold out your right hand with your palm up so you can receive the fruit of this tree.'

"Blood Woman did as the calabash told her, and the calabash spat its saliva squarely into the middle of her hand. She jerked her hand back and looked at it, but the saliva was gone.

" 'That is my sign,' the calabash said, 'for I have passed

64

my life on to you. And now you must go up to the surface of the earth and seek out my mother, Xmucane.'

"The virgin Blood Woman was afraid, and went home, instead, but already life was growing in her belly. By the time she got home, her father, Blood Gatherer, could see the life in her and denounced her child as a bastard.

" 'Make her tell who the father is,' One and Seven Death said, for even in Xibalba a father will be punished for not marrying the mother of his children. 'If she doesn't tell, then sacrifice her and her child, too.'

"So, Blood Gatherer demanded that his daughter tell him who was the father of her child, but Blood Woman said, 'There can be no child, Father, for no man has seen my true face.'

" 'Sacrifice her,' Blood Gatherer said with tears in his eyes. Pointing to his servants, the owl messengers, he said, 'Take her out with White Dagger and sacrifice her. Bring back her heart in a bowl for the lords of Xibalba to see.' "

"Everyone needs a father like that," I said. "She should have gone to the surface of the earth like the calabash told her to." I had the oddest feeling for Blood Woman, a kind of sympathy for the poor virgin. Mythology was overloaded with virgin mothers, but it was hard not to sympathize with them.

"We are coming up on Roscoe," Velasquez said. "We want to take Highway Eighty-four north from there to Lubbock."

"Right. North on Eighty-four. So the owl messengers killed Blood Woman because a calabash got her pregnant."

"No. Blood Woman convinced the owl messengers not to sacrifice her, but the owls did not know what they could take back in the bowl in place of her heart. 'Take this red tree sap,' she said, gathering the sap from a croton tree in the bowl, 'and let them burn no more true hearts, but burn only the sap from the trees. For doing this you owl messengers will be blessed by the surface of the earth.' "

"I thought you were only going to hit the high points of this story?"

"The high points? Yes, Senor O'Hara, that is what I am doing. I am telling you only that part of the story that has meaning for what we will soon face."

The light was beginning to fade, and the rain showed no signs of slacking up. Suddenly I was hungry. "Either of you interested in eating?"

"There are sandwiches in the back," Velasquez said, "and coffee in the thermos."

"No, I mean a hot meal, in a restaurant, and a restroom to wash up in before we eat."

"Yes, I could eat," Reyes said, "but that does not mean we can stop to do so. We have many miles to travel before we stop."

"We're going to have to stop for gas, and I'm going to have to stop to use a restroom, so why not get hot food while we can? By the time we roll into Lubbock, everything decent will be closed down."

"Is there no Denny's in Lubbock?" Velasquez asked.

I laughed. "I don't know. Probably."

"Then we eat sandwiches now and look for a hot meal when we get to Lubbock."

The finality in her voice dimmed the brief humor I felt. "The driver and owner of this truck says we stop and eat."

"No. Please? Only for the restroom, then we go on."

"We stop."

"Do not make me force you, Senor O'Hara."

For the first time since we had hit the road I thought about Reyes's pistol. "Can you drive?" I asked.

"No, but Shirlito can drive."

"A stick shift?"

"Yes," she said.

"All right," I said with a sudden realization. "There's the Roscoe exit. We stop for gas and restrooms only, and to get the food out of the back." And maybe I can shake you two, I thought. "Then Senorita Velasquez can drive for a while."

As long as I could break free, they could drive all the way back to Guatemala and *La Raza Unida*, for all I cared.

Chapter Fifteen

The gas station was one of those convenience stores that only uses gasoline to lure customers off the road in order to sell them motor oil and junk food and beer and gimme-caps with crude slogans printed on them. Like most of those stores, it had a sign in the window that read, VIDEO TAPES FOR

SALE OR RENT. ADULTS ONLY. Probably sold them to truckers with VCRs in their sleepers. One day I fully expected to see a road sign reading SAINT FRANCIS OF SALES, MONASTERY AND WINERY AND VIDEO RENTAL.

The entrance to the restrooms was in the store itself and Reyes stayed with me as I made my way back there. I had the definite feeling that he wasn't going there for the sake of his bladder. By the time we walked out of the restroom, after I had taken the opportunity to wash my face and brush my teeth, Velasquez was paying for the gas.

"I moved the food up front," she said. "Would you rather have a soda? Or the coffee?"

I looked from her to the skinny girl in the stuff-fronted western shirt behind the counter and wanted to scream. Reyes stepped close to my side. "A root beer," I said.

The girl behind the counter gave me a lopsided grin, then held out her hand. "That'll be another dollar."

Velasquez paid without flinching, so I went back to the refrigerator case and pulled a root beer out of the rack. Good old Reyes stuck right with me. Maybe I'd have a better chance to get away from them in Lubbock.

Once we were back in the truck with Velasquez behind the wheel and me in the middle, I popped the top on the root beer and said, "Don't wind the engine too high in first. She doesn't like it. And watch out when you down-shift not to let the clutch out too soon."

She started the engine and eased us past a pickup with a trailer and out into the rain and onto Highway 84. "I have driven your truck before, Martin."

"When?" I asked. Reyes handed me a sandwich and I took a bite. Ham and cheese. Not enough mustard.

"Several times after we all returned to Weatherford. I wanted to be familiar with it and to make sure it ran well."

"That doesn't surprise me. I don't think anything you two do can surprise me. In fact, nothing can surprise me, anymore." Except the bitterness I heard in my voice. "Are you both *Raza Unida*?" I took another mouth-filling bite of the sandwich.

"What?"

"*La Raza Unida de Guatemala*. Are you Commies?" I asked around the wad of food in my mouth.

Reyes jabbered in Indian.

"Why do you ask such a thing, Martin?"

"Because I can't figure out any other reason for us to be going through this masquerade. Look, I'm not stupid. I've been putting up with all this mythology stuff because I figured that sooner or later you were going to tell the truth."

"We are not *Raza Unida de Guatemala*," she said.

"They are bad people," Reyes added.

I looked from her to him and back to her. "Then who in the hell are you?"

For a long moment the cab was silent except for the noises of the truck and the rain and me finishing off the sandwich.

"We are who we say we are," Velasquez said finally. "We have not lied to you." She sounded a little offended.

"This is true, Senor O'Hara. I do not understand why you will not believe us."

"Is he really True Jaguar?" Velasquez asked.

"I am sure of it," Reyes said. "True Jaguar, descendant of Seven Jaguar, unknown son of Bearer, Begetter, Great True Jaguar. Tohil revealed him to me. And Cristos confirmed him."

A chill ran through me. Somehow it was more frightening to think that I was in the hands of pagan fanatics than Central American Communists. "You're serious, aren't you? You're both really serious? I don't believe you. I can't."

"You must, Martin. It is all true. If you do not believe, how will you defeat the Xibalbans and stop the comet?"

"Dammit! You're crazy!"

Reyes grabbed my right wrist with his left hand and clenched it so hard my fingers felt numb. I was startled by his strength.

"Senor O'Hara, this is no game. This is no craziness. The world will depend on what we do, especially on what you do. If we fail, if you refuse to believe and help us win against Xibalba, then *cometa Xibalba* will surely strike the surface of the earth in revenge for the destruction of One and Seven Death."

My head shook on its own and words refused to form on my tongue. It was a dream—a bad dream. It had to be. There was no way I could accept all their Mayan mumbo-jumbo.

Suddenly I relaxed and let out a loose shuddering sigh. I had lied. There was something that could surprise me. Some part of my weary mind believed them. Some shadowy bundle of nerves in my brain was still tangled in those webs of myth and legend I had loved as a child and as a student. Those nerves responded and sent a shiver down my spine.

"You are all right?" Reyes asked, releasing his grip.

"Yes. I'm all right." My trembling body gave the lie to my words. "I'm okay."

"You're shaking, Martin."

"It'll pass." I held the can of root beer in both hands, willing my cold fingers to hold onto the reality of the moment.

"What is it, Martin? Tell us what it is."

"I can't. It's too scary."

"Can we help?"

"Yes. Let me out of the truck and disappear from my life."

"It is wet out there, Martin. You are not prepared for the weather. You are not—"

"I'm not prepared for any of this." My hands shook as I put the can down in the holder on the hump.

"That is why I am telling you the story," Reyes said, "so you will be prepared when the time comes."

I tucked my hands into my armpits and shivered. "This is crazy and we all know it. All right, I'll accept the fact that you're not *Raza Unida*. Who are you working for? Boeing? Lockheed? Martin Marietta? What kind of secrets do you think I know, anyway?"

Neither of them answered and I sat there, eyes closed, listening to the engine and the rain and the wipers, and felt like I was shrinking down into the seat, into myself, until I saw an image that made me flinch. Then another.

"Martin?"

And another. Words I didn't understand came out of my mouth as yet another all too familiar image flashed before me. "The wall, Reyes. The wall of carvings. The one you had the picture of. Where is it, Reyes?"

"Kaminaljuyu."

"Where's that?"

"It is an old Queche city in Guatemala. No one lives there now, except the gods."

"But I've never been to Guatemala!"

"Be calm, Martin," I heard Velasquez say. "Breathe deeply and try to relax." Her saying that and several deep breaths soothed me down from hysteria to simple insanity.

"I know you have never been there, Senor O'Hara. Tohil made the pictures for me."

"Whatever you want from me, I'm not going to be any good to you," I said. A strange gutteral sound escaped my mouth. "I'll be crazy and worthless and then what are you going to do? Where will you find *Iquibalamdez?*"

"You will be all right, Martin, but you must control yourself and try to relax."

What had I just asked them? What did it mean? My arms wrapped themselves around me. Why were the images so real in my mind? Closing my eyes, I arched my neck and forced myself to take a deep, long breath and let it out slowly.

The images brightened. I heard something tap the root beer can and then felt Reyes put it in my hand. I trembled.

"Drink a little," he said. "It will help."

Nothing was going to help, but I did as I was told. Maybe if I went through the motions the nightmare would end. I took two long shaky swallows before I tasted the bitterness.

"What?" I said after a hard swallow. "What did you put in there?"

"Relax," Reyes said. "Breathe deeply."

"Relax," Velasquez crooned. "Relax."

My body wouldn't cooperate. I tried to let go, but instead of feeling relaxed, my body began to go numb—especially the end of my nose. "Drugs. You drugged me."

"Only something to help you relax."

"Feel bad." Bad was the wrong word. I felt detached. I felt unplugged.

Disconnected.

Sleepy.

Quiet oceans murmured in my ears.

Voices tiptoed around me.

Pictures drifted past. Familiar pictures. Frightening pictures. Carved walls. Feathered costumes. Old pictures.

"*True Jaguar*," the voices whispered. "*True Jaguar, True Jaguar, True Jaguar.*"

I turned away with a moan.

"*True Jaguar*," they repeated.

"True Jaguar," Velasquez said.

I opened my eyes. The rain had stopped. The night was dark. On my right, Reyes snored softly. Velasquez drove hunched slightly over the wheel. The speedometer read seventy-five. My stomach felt queasy.

"Could you slow down a little?"

"Of course," she said, easing back on the accelerator. "I guess I was not paying close attention to the speed. How do you feel?"

"Okay, I guess. I don't know. Reyes drugged me, didn't he?"

"Yes. He was afraid for you."

"Why?"

"He thought you were seeing a vision."

"Why?"

"You kept repeating *Iquibalamdez*."

"What's that mean?"

"It means Son of True Jaguar."

I opened my mouth, but nothing came out.

Chapter Sixteen

"Is there something you should tell us, Martin? Did you see something? Did you hear voices?"

"Uh, uh, I don't know." I couldn't admit what had happened. Not to her. Not yet. "Tired. Feel a little nauseous."

"Cacabe," she said sharply.

"*Por que?*" He sat up with a jerk.

"Martin feels *mareado*."

"I will give him something."

"Oh, no. No more of your drugs."

Cellophane rustled as he pulled something out of his shirt pocket. "Pepto-Bismol?"

A weak chuckle escaped me as I tore two of the pink tablets out of their cellophane pockets. I popped them into my mouth and chewed them thoroughly, reassured by the familiar taste, wanting a cigarette. Six years since my last cigarette and I still wanted one any time I tasted Pepto-Bismol. There was something about those combined flavors that meant comfort and relief.

"Better?"

"*Poquito*. Thanks . . . I think."

"You must forgive me for the *nartico*, senor. I feared for you. A man needs room to have a vision. I feared you would hurt yourself or hurt us. I am sorry."

The lights from the dash were enough to show the expression of concern on his face, and I liked him at that moment even though I couldn't believe him. "Why are you doing this to me?"

"I do nothing. Tohil acts for the other gods."

"Gods, Reyes? You never give up, do you?" Even as I spoke I could still see the wall half-covered with vines and smell the dusty feathers of the old costume. I shook my head and tried to block it out.

"Who would give up when the world is at stake?"

Turning to Velasquez I was struck by the nobility of her profile in the dim light. She really did look like a Mayan princess, like one of those—I stopped that thought. It was dangerous. So was she. I had to remind myself that they were lunatics or worse. "How far are we from Lubbock?"

"About ten miles, I think."

"And we'll spend the night there?"

"Yes."

I leaned back, closed my eyes, and concentrated on the sounds of the truck and the road, the monotonous rhythms of the sounds. Only moments later, it seemed, we slowed to a stop.

"Motel," Velasquez said.

She opened the door and let in a cold gust of wind as I opened my eyes.

"Wait here. I'll register us."

"Who sleeps with whom?" I asked Reyes as we both watched Velasquez enter the motel office. "Or do we get separate rooms?"

"Only one room, but no one sleeps with no one." His voice was as sharp as his gaze in the orange glare of the motel neon. "Shirlito and I discussed it. You will each take a bed and I will sleep on the floor as I am accustomed to."

"Right," I said. "Of course. How foolish of me to think otherwise. You're going to sleep in front of the door so I can't escape?"

"Yes. Of course," Reyes responded with a sudden smile. "How foolish of you to think otherwise."

I looked at his expression and laughed. "A sense of humor? You actually have a sense of humor?"

"Yes. Of course," he said again. "How foolish of you to think otherwise."

I laughed even harder and was still chuckling when Velasquez returned to the truck.

"You feel better, I see?"

"Reyes has a sense of humor. Can you believe that?"

"Of course."

"How foolish of you to think otherwise," Reyes said.

It shouldn't have been funny. It should have been stupid by that time, but occasionally stupid is funnier than funny, and I laughed all the way to the room, much to the amusement of Reyes and Velasquez. I decided it was the aftereffect of the drug he had given me.

"You can use the bathroom first," Velasquez said after Reyes had locked us into the room with two security latches and a chain.

"I can wait."

"You go first."

She was ordering me and I responded like a good little soldier, too weary to resist. There was no window in the bathroom for me to climb out of, so I contented myself with a quick shower, and a change into fresh underwear. I had no pajamas, and after a moment of modesty, I walked out into the room in my underwear.

Even though I tried to act like it was perfectly normal for me to parade in my underwear in front of strangers before I jumped beneath the covers, I avoided looking at them. Yet I had the sneaking suspicion that Velasquez was watching me, and self-consciously pulled my shoulders back and my stomach in. All in all it was embarrassing and as soon as I got in bed, I shut my eyes.

"You feel better?" Reyes asked.

"Yes."

He used the bathroom next and when he came out, I opened my eyes and saw he was wearing a long red nightshirt.

The covers were warm. My eyes were heavy. My bed was just firm enough to feel good after a long day. I felt my body growing leaden and my brain sliding toward sleep, but I blinked and forced myself to keep one eye open with a kind of primitive lechery. I was determined to see what Velasquez would wear to bed.

Chapter Seventeen

Several blinks later I saw light streaming around the edges of the curtains and realized it was morning. Reyes was wrapped in a blanket, his knees up, leaning against the door. Soft rumbling snores rose from under the blanket. Velasquez's bed was empty. I heard water running in the bathroom.

When the bathroom door cracked open, I pretended I was still asleep, but opened an eye just enough to see Velasquez tiptoe naked to her little suitcase on the dresser. She stood in a ray of light from the window, her breasts full, her thighs firm, her skin dark like polished persimmon wood.

Reyes snorted and moved.

Velasquez snatched something out of the suitcase and dashed back into the bathroom.

I thought it was a very exciting performance and I rose to the occasion. "Bravo!" I shouted, clapping my hands. "Bravo!"

Reyes woke up with a start and jerked to his knees with his pistol in left hand. *"Por que?"*

That made me laugh as I called, "Bravo," again.

"You should be ashamed of yourself," Velasquez said from the bathroom.

"I am ashamed," I called back with unexpected playfulness. "I am ashamed for looking upon your wonderful nakedness." I actually did feel a little ashamed, but I wasn't about to admit it. *"Perdona me, senorita,* but you have nice . . . conformation."

Reyes muttered something unintelligible as he stood up and peeked out the edge of the drapes.

"Thank you," Velasquez called through the door. "So do you. Like a thoroughbred."

"How would you know?"

"Your DSA rooms were monitored by camera twenty-four hours a day. And then there was last night."

Whatever shame I felt was replaced by embarrassment at

her having seen me. It took a full minute before I thought to get angry about it. Then it was too late. Even if the DSA thing wasn't true, she had seen me in my underwear last night, and that didn't leave much of my conformation a secret.

"Shall I begin today's story?" Reyes asked.

"What?"

"I have much still to tell you, Martin."

It was the first time he had called me Martin, and I think he was waiting for a reaction. I sighed. "Can it wait till after breakfast and a few cups of coffee?"

"If you wish. But there is much to tell, for now that you know the background, the most exciting part of the story is yet to come."

"I can hardly wait."

Velasquez checked us out of the motel and we walked across the street to a pancake house for breakfast. They *let* me sit on the inside part of the booth next to the wall. She sat next to me and Reyes sat opposite us. We all ordered the $2.99 Special with eggs and pancakes and bacon and fruit, and to my surprise they both crossed themselves and said a silent prayer before eating. Reyes had ordered two of the specials for himself, but he was finished eating before either of us.

Several times during the meal I thought about how I should be planning my escape from them, but I pushed that concern to the back of my mind and concentrated on the delicious food and coffee. After all, if I refused to leave the restaurant with them, how would they force me to go in front of the thirty or forty customers?

What could Reyes do, pull his pistol? That would bring the cops down on us for sure, and if he truly was intent on getting to Mesa Verde, the last thing he needed was cops. An Hispanic alien—even one with a valid visa—carrying a 9 mm automatic was not going to endear himself to the Lubbock Police Department.

As soon as Reyes finished eating, while I was still working on the last three pancakes and a couple of strips of bacon, he gave me that intense look I had seen before, and I would have bet a hundred dollars on what he wanted to talk about.

"Do you remember what I told you yesterday?" he asked.

"Sure. I remember." Much to my surprise, I actually did remember most of it.

"Then I will begin where we stopped, with the story of Blood Woman who carried the seed of One Hunahpu."

"She's the one the owls were supposed to kill, but she talked them out of it?"

"Yes. The messenger owls had the White Dagger, but they did not use it against Blood Woman. Instead she carved into the bark of a croton tree and filled a bowl with red sap for them—"

"Which was supposed to be her heart. The lords of Xibalba must be fairly stupid if they cannot tell a heart from a lump of tree sap."

"Do you know what a lord's heart looks like?" Reyes asked.

"Of course not."

"Blood Woman was the daughter of a lord. Perhaps the lords of Xibalba did not know what the heart of a daughter of a lord looked like, either."

"Okay," I said. "I'd forgotten that I'm not supposed to be logical about this."

"My words tell you the truth, Senor O'Hara. The world began with nothing more than the words of the gods, the words of Bearer Begetter-Bearer Begetter. Their words were their genius and their genius made the world."

With a nod of my head I stopped resisting and went back to eating. He was determined to tell me more, and I was actually curious to hear where all his mumbo-jumbo was headed.

"The four messenger owls—who are called Shooting Owl, Macaw Owl, One-legged Owl, and Skull Owl—took the resin from the croton tree that Blood Woman had collected in their bowl, and carried it back to the lords of Xibalba.

"One Death looked at it, felt its red surface, which was sticky like drying blood, and said, 'Good. Hang it over the fire to dry so that it will be a warning to all virgins to protect their faces.' "

"I love the euphemisms," I said, giving Velasquez a wink. A blush spread through her cheeks and she dropped her gaze.

Reyes paid no attention and continued. "The lords of Xibalba were fascinated by the smell of the drying heart and gathered around the fire. While they were inhaling the smoke, the messenger owls guided Blood Woman out of Xibalba and to the home of Xmucane, the mother of One Hunahpu. That is how the virgin Blood Woman defeated the lords of Xibalba."

It took me a few seconds before I completely understood why Velasquez had blushed. It had something to do
with her virginity. Either she was a virgin, and the mention
of it embarrassed her, or she wasn't, and that embarrassed
her.

Under much different circumstances I might have tried
to find out which of those alternatives was true. As we were,
there was no temptation, but I still had to remind myself that
she was a threat to me.

"Now when Blood Woman presented herself to Xmucane,
she said, 'I am your daughter-in-law, and I am your child, and
I carry the children of One Hunahpu.'

"The old woman, Xmucane, screamed at her, 'Go away!
Go away! Leave me alone! Is it not bad enough that my lastborn
sons One and Seven Hunahpu died in Xibalba? Why must you
come here to mock me?'

" 'One and Seven Hunahpu are alive, Mother-in-law,' Blood
Woman said, honoring Xmucane by calling her mother-in-law.
'You will see that their genius is alive when you see the children
I bear, for those babies carry the genius of One and Seven
Hunahpu.' "

I shook my head as I chewed my last piece of bacon. "What
do you mean by genius? Do you mean that One Hunahpu
passed his intelligence to his children?"

Reyes looked at Velasquez. "Yes and no," she said. "The
Queche word is *naual*, which means, uh, which means things
that do not translate very well in one word. *Naual* is spirit,
and animal spirit, and soul, and complete essence, and—"

"Kind of like the German *Geistes*?" I asked, displaying
ten percent of my German vocabulary.

Reyes was following the exchange with quick turns of his
head.

"Yes," she said without hesitation, "except that *naual* can
also refer to the spiritual character of places and things."

Since *Geistes* had always been a word whose meaning was
suspect to me, I put *naual*-genius in the same category. "Okay.
I think I've got it."

"Are you ready to leave?" Velasquez asked.

I looked at her and I looked at Reyes, and I knew that if
I was going to break away from them, this was the time to
do it.

Chapter Eighteen

I truly wanted to escape them, yet, for the first time since that day in Chaco Canyon when Reyes accosted me, I felt like I was a part of what he and Velasquez were trying to do. I was caught up in a spirit of camaraderie that felt comfortable without reason.

Along with the camaraderie came confusion. The cross currents of my emotions, like those of a river, swirled and eddied, but were still headed relentlessly downstream. Frightened or not by the approaching gulf, I knew something inside me had given over to the natural flow.

I looked across the table at Reyes, then at Velasquez sitting beside me, and knew that my future—my near future, at least—was tied to those two. "Yes," I said. "I'm ready to go anytime you are."

Velasquez had the waitress fill our thermos with fresh coffee, and paid the bill while Reyes and I used the restroom. Then he and I ran across the street through the cold and started the truck so that the heater was just beginning to put out warm air when she joined us. Reyes got out and let her sit in the middle, and I was glad he'd done it. The warmth of her thigh next to mine was comforting.

"Something in you has changed," Reyes said.

"I noticed that, too. What is it, Martin?"

"Well," I said as I squeezed the truck into traffic, "I'm not exactly sure, but let's just say you've worn away some of my hostility."

"But you still do not believe what Cacabe has tried to tell you?"

"No. Not yet. But I don't believe you're Commies or spies for Boeing, either, and maybe you've convinced me that I'm not in any immediate danger from you. However, we have a long way to go before I can begin to accept Senor Reyes's tales of the gods."

That wasn't quite honest, and I knew it. Part of me already believed what Reyes was saying. The last thing he needed, though, was encouragement, and the last thing I needed was to believe in something that only the primitive part of my brain accepted. I kept my eyes on the road. "Sorry."

"No matter," Reyes said. "The time will come when you will understand. Then you will believe."

"Go on with the story, Cacabe."

"Si. Blood Woman tried to persuade Xmucane, mother of One and Seven Hunahpu, of the fact that she carried One Hunahpu's seed. Xmucane would not believe her and sent Blood Woman to get a netful of corn to feed the bastards she was about to bear.

"When Blood Woman got to the garden, she found only one stalk of corn and she cried and wept until she heard voices speaking from her belly. After listening to the voices, she called out to Harvest Woman, guardian of the corn.

" 'Oh, Harvest Woman, come face to face and look at me, for I am a sinner and a debtor, and my only good waits in my belly.'

"The stalk of corn crackled and Blood Woman grabbed an ear by the silk and pulled it out. Another ear took its place and she pulled that out, and soon her net was full of corn, which she took back to Xmucane, her mother-in-law.

" 'You have destroyed our garden!' Xmucane cried when she saw all the corn Blood Woman was carrying. Xmucane ran off to find the destruction, but instead she found the one cornstalk, and standing beside it she found Harvest Woman who smiled at Xmucane, then turned and walked away.

"Xmucane ran back to Blood Woman crying, 'It is true! It is true! You are my daughter-in-law! Let us prepare for the birth of my grandchildren, for they are truly the genius of my sons One and Seven Hunahpu.' "

I whistled softly. "You sure I'm not going to have to remember all this?" I asked. "I mean, it's interesting, but it's an awful lot to absorb, much less remember."

"Just listen, Senor O'Hara. Listen with your heart. Then you will remember what you need to remember when the time comes."

"When is the time? Didn't you say something about February 29 and leap year?"

"Yes." He smiled and looked pleased. "The last day of February, this coming year that you call leap year, is a day of great importance to mother-fathers of the Queche people. Such a day does not come for us every four years. It comes for us only every 37,960 days, at the end of every great cycle of Venus."

I did some rough division. "That's about every hundred years, isn't it?"

"Every one hundred four of your years. It is the only day in the cycles of days that has no number, for it is called the day of True Jaguar. The following day is the day called One Hunahpu, and the great cycle of Venus begins again."

I waited, but he didn't add anything. "Just what does that mean?"

"It means that the day of True Jaguar is a day that is hard to see," he said. "Very few people live long enough to see it twice, and no one who has seen it once wants to see it twice. It is not like the week of Seven Jaguar that comes every seven cycles—"

"About every five years," Velasquez said.

"*Gracias*, Shirlito. The week of Seven Jaguar is a week of secret celebrations for the daykeepers, for the mother-fathers, during which we praise Seven Jaguar, the unknown son of Great True Jaguar."

Out of the corner of my eye I saw him shake his head.

"No," he continued, "the day of True Jaguar is a day of earthquakes and storms, a day of beginnings and endings. It is a day to be prepared for and then a day to be forgotten as quickly as possible. From the time when my father first trained me as a daykeeper, I knew I would face the day of True Jaguar."

"And you're afraid of it," I said, hearing for the first time the undertone of fear in his voice.

"I fear what will happen if we do not act properly."

I shivered and turned up the heater. "So all this day-keeping is based on astrology and signs and portents?"

"Astronomy, Martin. The daykeepers study the cycles of the planets and the days of the earth. In our calendar we have certain special—"

"You mean the Mayan calendar?"

"The Queche calendar," Reyes said.

"We have special days based on astronomy just as leap year is based on astronomy. They are the days when the calendar is brought into harmony with the universe."

A weary groan escaped my lips. "How did I ever get into

this?" Neither of them answered me, and I was paying too much attention to traffic as I put us on Highway 84 to look at them. If the DSA ever caught up with me again, they were going to lock me away in some federal loony bin, because— God help me—the more I heard, the more I believed that Reyes and Velasquez were telling the truth.

"Listen with your heart," Reyes said.

"Right." The urge to say something sarcastic was quelled by a fear I couldn't name, and suddenly I felt very exposed and vulnerable.

Velasquez put a hand on my arm. I kept my eyes on the road and the traffic under the cold grey sky, knowing I dared not look at her now. A lump had formed in my chest, the same kind of lump I got when they played the national anthem at a baseball game, but at least that patriotic lump made sense.

"Listen carefully to me, Martin, because you must understand. Cacabe has wagered the fate of the earth on what he believes—and what he believes is that you are the only living male descendant of Great True Jaguar. If Cacabe is right, then on the day of True Jaguar, you and only you will be able to defeat the lords of Xibalba and stop Lana's comet from destroying life on earth."

"Oh, no. Oh, no. You can't lay that on me. You can't just say, 'Here you go, Martin. The fate of the world is in your hands. All you've got to do is go down to Hell and fight some gods you've never heard of before.' You can't do that."

"They're not gods. The stinking lords of Xibalba are not gods."

"Gods or not, it's not fair." My feet were still cold and my teeth were on the verge of chattering. "Turn up the heat, will you."

Velasquez moved the heater lever. "Life is not fair," she said. "Life is only life. Fair has no meaning except as we put meaning on it. It is not fair that you were not prepared for this all your life as Cacabe has been. It is not fair that you do not know the gods and the stories so you can understand whom you must face. Although, as Cacabe said, you will not have to face gods—only the stinking lords of Xibalba. But even that's not fair to you, just like it wasn't fair that Cristos, Who was without sin, died for everyone's sins."

"Oh, no. Don't go comparing me to Christ. That's pushing things way too far."

"I am sorry. You are not like Cristos. You are Jesus O'Hara Martinez, and life has been unfair to you as it has been unfair to thousands of others throughout history."

She was angry, and I could hear it.

"Was life fair to the early Christians? Was life fair to Judas Iscariot, whose reward for completing the prophecy was to burn forever in Hell? Was life fair to Joan of Arc when she revealed that our Lord spoke directly to her? Who is life fair to?"

"Most people aren't asked to sacrifice themselves on the altar of some pagan belief," I said. "I mean, there's unfair and there's *unfair*. You two expect me . . ."

Again the cab was filled only with the noises of the engine and the road. The ultimate irony was that I knew I would go along with them as far as I could—farther than I realized only five minutes before. Their game was contagious, and I was infected, and behind all that was going on, I had a rising fever of curiosity. How could I ever go back to writing tech manuals for GDA? I had to see how this would play itself out.

"All right, Reyes," I said as we left the Lubbock city limits behind, "tell me some more."

Chapter Nineteen

I drove, Reyes talked, and Velasquez amended and explained parts of the story.

Reyes told about the birth from Blood Woman of the twins Hunahpu and Xablanque, about the jealousy of their older stepbrothers One Monkey and One Artisan, and how Hunahpu and Xablanque tricked their stepbrothers into climbing a yellowwood tree, then made the tree grow so that One Monkey and One Artisan could not get down.

I wasn't much impressed with Hunahpu and Xablanque, but I didn't interrupt Reyes. Something more immediate was bothering me. A brown sedan had been hanging behind us a half a mile or so since we left Lubbock.

I eased our speed up to seventy and the brown sedan

stayed the same distance behind us. Reyes was still talking about One Artisan and One Monkey, but what he was saying didn't seem very important.

In the middle of a cruel episode about their grandmother, Xmucane, laughing at One Artisan and One Monkey who had gotten as ugly as the monkeys living in the tree tops, I let off the accelerator until we slowed to fifty. The brown sedan slowed with us.

"What is wrong?" Velasquez asked.

Reyes stopped in the middle of a sentence.

"We're being followed." I said.

"Are you sure?"

"The same brown car has been staying the same distance from us since we left Lubbock. What kinds of cars does the DSA use?"

"The usual government issue—stripped down sedans, single color, no vinyl tops."

"That fits our escort, I think."

Velasquez turned slowly and looked back through the camper shell. I eased us up to sixty again.

"You are right," she said. "That is a government car if I ever saw one."

"They must know by now that we've spotted them."

"Yes, but their only job may be to follow us whether they are spotted or not."

"So what do we do now?"

She turned back around. "We keep going. Somewhere between here and Mesa Verde we'll find a way to shake them if necessary."

"Like where? Unless you're planning a route you haven't told me about, we're going to drive right past the DSA regional office, aren't we?"

"We must stop at Chaco Canyon, first, if we can."

"What?"

"Yes, Cacabe, I know that."

"Chaco Canyon? When were you going to tell me?" I asked.

"Soon."

"God. Here we go right back into Torelli's hands."

"Not necessarily."

"Why?"

"Because," she said, "I left two surprises for Torelli. I told my Washington agency chief that I was going undercover on this operation and asked her to keep Torelli off my back."

Was this all some kind of DSA trick to get Reyes to reveal some Communist operation they thought he was part of? I couldn't believe that. "Then why are we being followed?"

"Because whoever is behind us is probably from Washington."

"You mean they don't trust you?"

"I mean they are paranoid just like every other security agency in this country."

"What's the other surprise you left for Torelli?"

She smiled. "I left a message telling him exactly where we were going and that if he interfered, I'd have him busted back to a GS-2 sweeping floors."

"And that's a surprise?"

"Yes."

"Whoopee," I said flatly. "That would certainly scare me off if I thought I was about to bust one of my superiors in the agency for being a Communist spy."

"You just drive and let me worry about Torelli."

"Yes, ma'am. Anything you say, ma'am."

"Cacabe, maybe you should skip the other stories for now and tell Martin about Hunahpu and Xablanque's journey to Xibalba."

"Save it," I said, slowing the truck and pulling off on the right shoulder.

"What are you doing?"

"I'm stopping. And if the government car stops"—I checked the rearview mirror and saw that it had—"then I'm going to walk back there and turn myself over to the DSA."

She grabbed my arm.

"Martin! You cannot do that. Do you still not—"

"Dammit!" I said, turning to face her, my left hand poised on the door handle. "You two twist my brain and feed me all this Mayan mumbo-jumbo until you have me believing it, then you don't even trust me enough to tell me where we're really going or what's going—"

"Please, Martin. You are saying—"

"Don't tell me what's going on, but you tell the government so they can keep an eye on us every step of the way, and all the time your ass is covered because you told them—"

"Do not shout at her, Senor O'Hara."

Reyes had his pistol in his lap, but I didn't care anymore and tried to stare Velasquez down. "You told them you were working undercover on this case, so that when the shit hits the fan, Reyes and I will catch it all. Thanks a whole helluva lot, but no thanks. I'll take my chances with the DSA on my own."

"No, Martin. I did not intend to treat you badly. You must remember that despite what you think, I have never done anything like this before, either. But I have to trust my heritage and what Cacabe tells me."

"And," Reyes said, "there is something both of you should know at this very moment. Even you, Shirlito, do not understand all that is happening."

He spoke so softly that I bit off the words that were rushing toward my tongue and waited to hear what he would say. I wondered as we sat there what our DSA tail was thinking.

"Speak, Cacabe," she said, turning toward him.

"Do you remember the legend of the cactus star?"

"Of course—that an evil yellow star like the flower of the prickly pear will shine upon the Queche, and on that day, Hunahpu and Xablanque will return to . . . what are you trying to tell me, Cacabe?"

He looked at her and then shifted his gaze and stared out the windshield. "I have read the seeds and stones many times since our childhood. I have looked for other interpretations for what I have read. I have traveled the circle of the great—"

"Bye," I said, pulling the door handle and opening—

Reyes's hand shot in front of Velasquez and grabbed my wrist. He yanked me back into the truck and the door slammed shut.

"No," he said, with a crazed look in his eyes. His right hand clutched the automatic, pointing it straight at my gut.

"You must listen to this, now—both of you, together. Then if you want to give up, Senor O'Hara, I will let you go, and try to do your job with Shirlito to help me."

"And if she wants to go with me?" Suddenly I felt protective of her, although I couldn't think why she would need my protection.

"She and I can talk about that. But please drive while I

am talking. If you stop again, they will stop again, and you will have your chance to run away."

"Do as he asks, Martin, and if Cacabe tells us the wrong thing, perhaps I will leave with you. Perhaps we are both at risk here. For now, please drive."

With a nod I put the truck into first and started accelerating down the shoulder before pulling back onto the highway. As long as Reyes looked crazy and sounded crazy and was crazy enough to point his pistol at me, I was just as happy to let Velasquez argue with him if she wanted to, but not me.

Reyes waited until we were back up to cruising speed before he said, "Tohil and Cristos have been working together since I was a little boy in preparation for what we have to do. When our great-grandfather read the stones and seeds that told him about your lineage from Great True Jaguar, he also saw something else that he passed on to my grandfather, and my grandfather passed on to my father."

I was keeping my eyes on the road, but out of the corner of my eye I could see he was addressing Velasquez.

"The stones and seeds our great-grandfather read, told him that in his lineage two children would be born who would carry the genius of Hunahpu and Xablanque. You and I were born on the same day, in the same year, Shirlito."

"That is not what my parents told me."

"No. They did not. Everyone who understood feared the signs and the omens. But it is true. An hour after your mother bore you in Texas, my mother bore me in Guatemala."

"And what have your interpretations told you this means, Cacabe?"

"The stones and seeds only point in certain directions, Shirlito. You know that. But every generation since our great-grandfather when the daykeepers of our family have read the seeds and stones at the end of the week of Seven Jaguar, the seeds and stones have said that a girl and a boy would be born within an hour and they would possess the genius of Hunahpu and Xablanque."

"And you think we are those two?" Velasquez asked.

"Yes. The reading of the stones and seeds has never changed. I think you possess the genius of Hunahpu and I possess the genius of Xablanque."

"That cannot be," she said, shaking her head over and

over. "As Martin said, I am a modern woman living in present-day America. There is no way I can be what you say."

"Now you know how I feel."

"It cannot be, Cacabe. The seeds and stones must be wrong." Her statement was made in a pleading tone.

"Four generations they have not changed, Shirlito."

"But why? Why do you tell me this now?"

"Because we must live the roles of our spirits when True Jaguar faces the lords of Xibalba."

Chapter Twenty

I almost whooped for spite when Reyes told Velasquez that she was going to have to play a god if we all ever got to Xibalba. What a great idea. Let her cope with the problem of having to be someone else, of having to play some role she didn't like or understand. I bit my tongue to keep from saying anything, but damn, it felt good.

Twice she opened her mouth, but only sounds came out—no words. She was in the same predicament I was in, only she should have been more prepared for it. Maybe now she would be a little more sympathetic with how I felt.

"Cacabe, this is wrong," she finally said.

"No, Shirlito, it is neither wrong nor right. It is only true."

"But this was nothing I was taught. How could this be? How can a woman carry the genius of a male god?"

"Am I not mother-father, she-he, daykeeper? Have you forgotten, living here in this sterile country, that we are all half female and half male?"

Left and right I am my parents, mother-father in myself. No, Cacabe, I have not forgotten. Yet where before us has gone a woman with the genius of Hunahpu?"

We were entering Muleshoe.

Reyes rattled something in Indian. She rattled back. After a while they were going at each other verbally at the top of their lungs, both gesturing, Velasquez growling when she interrupted him, Reyes snarling in reply.

I laughed. As soon as we left town, the road ahead was clear and straight, and except for our DSA escort, there was no one within sight on our side of the highway. I hit the gas. The speedometer was creeping past ninety-five when they finally stopped shouting.

"Martin? What are you doing?"

"Just driving down the road with two crazy passengers, giving the DSA a racing thrill, seeing how fast this old red truck will go. Why? Aren't we having fun?"

"Martin, I don't think you should be—"

"You know," I said, glancing in the mirror as the truck found the bouncing rhythm of the road. "I'm not sure that government heap will go as fast as R.D. They're falling back."

"R.D.?"

"The truck. I named it Ramses the Second, but that took too long to say, so I called it Ramses Deuce. R.D. Get it?"

"*Por favor,* senor," Reyes said. "This is too fast for my stomach."

Reluctantly I let up on the gas and we slowed to sixty. "Ah, here come the feds."

"What is the point of all this, Martin?"

"I just got tired of listening to you two jabber at each other." I flashed her a smile. "Besides, Senorita Velasquez, I am most pleased to see you find yourself in a position similar to mine."

She looked at me, then said, "I must do what is expected of me—as you must. *Que sera.* It is our fate. We have no choice. If this is how God intends for me to serve, this is how I will serve."

"Well, hell. You give in too easily. Looks like you win again, eh, Reyes? Two conscripts for your plot."

"The winning and losing must take place in Xibalba."

The tune from *The Wizard of Oz* came to me and I couldn't resist the temptation. "Ohhh, we're off to see Xibalba, the underworld of the gods, to fight the dirty devils there, no matter what the odds. We'll fight the old Xibalbans there, because, because, because, because, becauuuse—because of the nasty things they does. Da-dum da-dum da-dum da-dum, da-dummm. Ohhh, we're off to see Xibalba, the underworld of the gods!"

"Truly, Martin, that is terrible."

"Yeah. Don't you love it?"

"What is this song?" Reyes asked.

"Nothing. Just something I made up on the spot from *The Wizard of Oz*. Don't they run *The Wizard of Oz* down in Guatemala every Easter?"

"What is he talking about, Shirlito?"

"It is a movie for children, Cacabe. Never mind."

"*Perdona me, senorita*. It is movie for adults. It is the first blatantly existential movie ever to capture the hearts and minds of America. Do you know what that means?"

"I do not think so."

"It means that if we ever get to this Xibalba of yours, we're going to be just like Dorothy and her motley crew in the movie. The wizard didn't do anything for Dorothy or Tin-Man or Scarecrow or the Cowardly Lion. They had to do it for themselves. All the wizard did was recognize what they'd done— and in Dorothy's case he couldn't even do that, and he couldn't get her home."

"This is confusing to me," Reyes said.

"It is confusing to me, also, Cacabe, and I have seen the movie several times."

"Remember how Dorothy got back to Kansas? The Good Witch told Dorothy how to do it herself, and she did. That's existentialism. You've got to do it for yourself."

"But we will have the help of Tohil."

"And Cristos," Velasquez added.

They had me there. I'd never been much of a believer in any gods, and now they were saying two of them would help us out. "Maybe so, but *God helps those who help themselves*, Mama always said."

"How far are we from New Mexico?" Velasquez asked without warning.

"Oh, I don't know. Ten, fifteen miles. The town you argued your way through was Muleshoe, and it's about twenty miles from the border if I remember the map right."

"We should buy gas before we cross. It will be cheaper."

"Right." I looked at her and she turned her eyes away. "Doesn't this whole thing about being Girl Hunahpu rub you the wrong way, like you were . . . I don't know . . . like you were being used?"

"Yes, it bothers me, but not for those reasons. I was arguing with Cacabe only because I do not feel worthy of this burden, and do not want him to depend on me if I cannot serve properly."

"I don't think either of us gets a choice."

"*Así es la vida, tango.*"

"Yeah, that's life, all right. You have any more surprises, either of you? Why don't we get all of our cards on the table right now?"

"No," Velasquez said.

"I do not know, Senor O'Hara."

"What do you mean, you don't know?"

"Only that there must surely be things that I will say or do that will surprise you, but I have no method of making such a list for you now."

"What about in the story? Are there any surprises in the story?" I asked.

"Yes, of course."

"How foolish of me to think otherwise."

Suddenly all three of us laughed and the tension between us shattered. Even after we stopped laughing, we rode for a while in contented silence.

"Well, then," I said finally, "on with the story, Senor Reyes."

"Start with Hunahpu and Xablanque's ballgame."

"Very well, but in telling the story from there I must leave out some parts of great humor and instruction."

"Save those for later," Velasquez said, "when we have more time to listen and appreciate them."

"Tell you what, Senor Reyes. Why don't you just save them until after we get gas. That way you won't be interrupted and it might be easier to follow—if you know what I mean."

"Oh, but yes. *Sí.* Certainly. Do you feel better now about our *obligación*, Senor O'Hara?"

"I don't know what you mean."

"Does it sit more comfortably in your mind?"

"Yes. In a way, I guess it does. But there are still an awful lot of gaps that have me worried. Like, what are we going to do in Chaco Canyon? And how are we going to get into Mesa Verde if it's closed? And if February 29 is the magic date, why are we hurrying to get there so early?"

"In Chaco Canyon I left many things that may help us on our way to Xibalba."

"Don't you think the DSA found them? They supposedly combed the whole canyon and the outlying ruins as well."

"No, I do not think your *federales* found what I left there. They would not know where to look for them, and would not know what they were seeing if they found them. Only another daykeeper would recognize the things I left."

"Okay, so we go pick up your things at Chaco Canyon, and—assuming DSA manages to let us get that far—we drive up to Mesa Verde, and it's closed. Then what?"

"Then we must pass whatever barriers are before us, or find another way in. That is why we need so much time. First we must get there, then we must be purified, then we must enter *ube Xibalba* and make our way to the circle of the lords of Xibalba, and pass the tests that Hunahpu and Xablanque passed, then arrange for the ballgame to take place on the day of True Jaguar. I do not know how much time that will take."

"You're the daykeeper but you don't—Okay, I can see that. But suppose, just suppose, that we cannot get into Mesa Verde. You have some kind of backup plan?"

"Yes. We will return south and stop at what your park service wrongly calls Aztec Ruins National Monument."

"Why can't we stop there on the way up?"

"Because it is in the town of Aztec, and I do not believe that we would be allowed to search for *ube Xibalba* there."

"What about Chaco Canyon? Can't we find the road to Xibalba from Chaco Canyon? Didn't you tell me something about that?"

"Yes. There was once an entrance there to *ube Xibalba*, and that is why our people left no writing that would give the lords of Xibalba power over them. But I searched Chaco Canyon before you came, and the entrance is well hidden and deep and probably very small, and I do not think—"

"Gotcha. It's Mesa Verde or bust."

Chapter Twenty-one

After stopping for gas at Farwell, we crossed into New Mexico and headed for Santa Rosa. Velasquez broke out the coffee, and Reyes began telling the part of the story that Velasquez thought was most important.

"Hunahpu and Xablanque were playing ball in the Great Abyss of Carchah, in the same ballcourt where their fathers had played over the roof of Xibalba. The lords of Xibalba heard them, of course, and knew who was making all that noise. They sent the messenger owls to summon the boys to a ballgame in Xibalba in seven days time. The messenger owls went to the home where Hunahpu and Xablanque lived with their grandmother, Xmucane, and their mother, Blood Woman, and delivered the summons to Xmucane, who agreed to deliver it to her grandsons."

"I'll bet that really made her happy," I said before taking a noisy sip of my coffee. Reyes ignored my comment.

"Grandmother Xmucane accepted the summons, but after the messenger owls left, she wept and tore at her hair and cried that she could not give such a message to her grandsons, because surely it meant that they would die in Xibalba like One and Seven Hunahpu. Then she thought of a way to keep her word without delivering the message to her grandsons in time for them to arrive at Xibalba in seven days.

"She gave the message to a louse and said, 'Little louse, you tell my grandsons that the messengers of Xibalba came and have summoned them to a ballgame seven days from today. Now, I know it is a long way to the Great Abyss of Carchah, so you must pace yourself so you do not run out of energy.' Then she set the louse down on the doorstep and smiled, knowing the louse would never make it to the Great Abyss in time to deliver the message.

"Hours later the louse had only reached the middle of the road behind the house when he was greeted by a toad named Tamazul. 'Where are you going, louse?'

" 'To the Great Abyss of Carchah to deliver a message to Xmucane's grandsons.'

" 'It is a long way to the Great Abyss. Why not give me the message and I will deliver it for you?'

" 'I cannot do that. The message is in my belly.'

" 'Then ride in my belly,' Tamazul said, 'and you will get there much faster.'

" 'Thank you,' the louse said, and with that Tamazul swallowed him.''

"Excuse me," I said, "but I assume that a stupid louse letting a toad eat him is all leading to things we'll need to know when we get to Xibalba. Am I right?" I took another sip of my coffee, surprised by how fast it was cooling.

"Of course, Senor O'Hara."

"How foolish of me to think—oh, never mind. I'm sorry I interrupted." The grey sky seemed to be lowering on us.

"Now because the toad Tamazul had a full belly, he could not hop very fast, so he did not make much progress toward the Great Abyss before he met a big snake named Zaquicaz.

" 'Where are you going, Tamazul?' Zaquicaz asked.

" 'I am carrying a message to the grandsons of Xmucane,' the toad said.

" 'Tell me the message and I will carry it for you.'

" 'I cannot,' Tamazul said. 'The message is in my belly.'

" 'Then ride in my belly and we will get there faster,' Zaquicaz said, and when Tamazul agreed, Zaquicaz swallowed him and began slithering his way as fast as he could toward the Great Abyss.

"Laughing Falcon spied the snake Zaquicaz hurrying toward the Great Abyss and swooped down on him. After the snake explained what he was doing, Laughing Falcon swallowed the snake and flew to the Abyss where he circled overhead crying, 'Wak-ko! Wak-ko!' ''

As I finished off my coffee, I silently thanked Reyes for not repeating the dialogue again.

"Well, the boys, Hunahpu and Xablanque, saw Laughing Falcon and Xablanque grabbed his blowgun and shot the falcon in the eye. Laughing Falcon wobbled down to the ballcourt in the abyss and cried, 'You have wounded me, when all I did was bring you a message from your grandmother.'

" 'Name the message,' Hunahpu demanded.

" 'Heal my eye first and I will name the message that lies in my belly.'

93

"Hunahpu took some sorrel gum off the ball they had been playing with and put it on Laughing Falcon's eye, and soon his eye was healed again. 'Now name your message,' Xablanque said.

" 'All right,' Laughing Falcon answered and spit up the snake.

" 'Name the message, snake,' they demanded.

"And the snake spit up the toad and the toad spit up the louse and the louse said, 'Your grandmother Xmucane said to tell you that a message has come from the lords of Xibalba, a message from the lords One and Seven Death, summoning you to a ballgame in seven days from today.'

" 'Okay,' the boys cried. 'This is what we have been waiting for. Now we will face the lords of Xibalba and defeat them.' "

"That's the part I'm waiting for," I said.

"Be patient, Martin."

"Only if you pour me some more coffee."

She poured for all three of us, emptying the last drops into her own cup. "Cacabe tells the story the way his father told it to him, and his grandfather told it to him. It is a complete story and you must let him tell the whole thing."

"I'll try to be more patient," I said, shifting down to begin the climb up a long hill. A glance in the mirror showed the DSA car still behind us by about a half a mile, but I had quit worrying about it for the time being.

"After Hunahpu and Xablanque received the message, they rushed home to say goodbye to their grandmother and mother, both of whom wept for them. 'You will die if you go to Xibalba,' Xmucane cried. 'You will die like your father and uncle died before you.'

" 'No,' Hunahpu and Xablanque said together, 'we will not die. To prove it, we will leave you signs of our word.' Each of them planted an ear of corn in the center of the house. 'Look, Grandmother. Look, Mother. When these ears of corn grow, you will know we live. When they die, you will think we have died, also. But when they sprout again, you will know that we have not died and that you shall see us again.'

" 'We will try to believe,' Xmucane and Blood Woman said.

" 'Try hard,' Hunahpu said as he and his brother hugged the two women goodbye. Hunahpu and his brother then grabbed their blowguns, left the house, and ran to the place where they had hidden their ball and playing equipment.'

"Is that an airplane or a helicopter?" Velasquez asked, pointing out the window at the nine o'clock position.

"Helicopter," I said as soon as I saw it. "What do they think we're going to do, run and hide in this desert?"

"We do not know that it is a DSA helicopter," she said.

"And we don't know that it isn't. I've got five dollars says that it is."

"May I continue?" Reyes asked. "We are coming to the part of the story you both have been asking for."

"Yes, Cacabe, please continue."

"Well, Hunahpu and Xablanque went quickly down to Xibalba, through Neck Canyon with its rapids and the spears, across Blood River and Pus River, which were all supposed to be tests for them, but which they crossed easily. Soon they came to the same crossroads their father and uncle had come to. Hunahpu and Xablanque also took the Black Road, but before they did, they summoned a mosquito, which at that time lived on the juices of fruit, not the blood of people.

" 'Come, little mosquito,' Hunahpu said. 'Go down this road ahead of us to the circle of the lords of Xibalba and bite each one of them in turn. If you will do this thing for us, we promise you some blood from every traveler on the roads of earth above.'

"So the mosquito flew ahead to the circle of the lords of Xibalba, and Hunahpu and Xablanque followed close behind him. Now mosquito could tell which of the seated figures were wooden statues because they were cold, so he flew straight to the first of the lords, who was One Death, and bit him on the back of the neck.

" 'Oww!' One Death cried.

" 'What is the matter, One Death?' asked House Corner, who was seated next to One Death.

"Mosquito bit House Corner next. 'Oh,' said House Corner, 'something has bitten me.'

" 'What is the matter, House Corner?' asked Pus Master from beside the wooden statue between them. Then he, too, cried, 'Ow!'

" 'Ouch!' cried Bone Scepter and Wing and Bloody Teeth, each in turn as mosquito bit them.

95

"Hunahpu and Xablanque were hiding in the shadows to see who cried out when bitten, and listened to them ask each other by name what was wrong so that they could identify each of the lords of Xibalba.

" 'Yeow!' cried Bloody Claws and Packstrap and Skull Sceptor, Jaundice Master and Blood Gatherer and Seven Death when mosquito bit each of them in turn, so that soon Hunahpu and Xablanque knew which were the lords and which were the statues.

"The boys walked out of their hiding place and into the middle of the circle saying, 'Good morning, One Death. Good Morning, Seven Death. Good morning, House Corner,' and so on until they had greeted all the lords in turn, and the lords of Xibalba knew that the boys had beaten their test."

"I hate to interrupt again, but isn't this list of the lords different than the first list?"

"Yes, it is," Reyes said, "but no one knows why. Perhaps Trash Master and Stab Master were no longer in favor with One and Seven Death, and Bloody Teeth and Bloody Claws took their place. Or perhaps the lords decided to change names. Whatever the reason, it is not important to the story as far as—"

"Except," Velasquez said, interrupting him, "that we might have to face lords of Xibalba whom we know nothing about. Should we not be concerned about that, Cacabe?"

Chapter Twenty-two

"I cannot say whether the lords of different names should concern us, Shirlito."

"Then I'll give you a question, Reyes. Are we going to have to cross the Blood and Pus rivers and all that?"

"Yes."

"Do you have any idea how?"

"I have brought rope and tools."

"That's encouraging. What about the mosquito? Have you hired a mosquito to bite the lords so we can tell which ones are real and who's who?" I felt silly asking those questions—

96

or was it that the questions seemed silly? Whichever, the silly got overruled by that primitive, believing part of my brain.

"Tohil and Cristos will provide for our needs."

I bit back the sarcasm I wanted to use in response to that. "Okay, so we manage to cross the nasty rivers, get down the Black Road to the circle of the lords, determine which of them are real, and which of them are not, greet them, and then what?"

"What will happen to us, I cannot say. All I can do is tell you what happened to those who went before us. After Hunahpu and Xablanque greeted the lords of Xibalba, they were invited to sit on the hot stone bench.

" 'No, thanks,' they said. 'That is a cooking bench, not a sitting bench. Is that all the hospitality you have?'

" 'We have prepared a guest house for you,' the Xibalbans said. 'You can rest here, and tomorrow we will play ball.'

"So Hunahpu and Xablanque entered Dark House, and a messenger brought them one torch and two cigars. 'You must return these to the lords in the morning and they must be just as they are now.'

" 'Fine,' Hunahpu and Xablanque said. As soon as the messenger left they put out the torch and substituted the bright feathers of a macaw's tail for the flame, and because the boys were from the surface of the earth, the feathers shone with light and fooled the messenger who was spying on them. They put out the cigars and substituted fireflies for the glow, and again the messenger spies were fooled. In the morning when the messenger came to take the torch and cigars back, they were not consumed.

" 'Who are these boys? Who bore them?' the lords cried when they saw the unburned torch and cigars. 'How have they done this thing to us? Where do they come from?'

"The lords called Hunahpu and Xablanque before them. 'Where did you come from?' they asked. 'Name the place!'

" 'We came from Xibalba,' the twins answered.

" 'This cannot be,' One Death said, 'but we will find out the truth later. Now it is time to play ball.' "

"And for us, it's time for a bathroom stop, and maybe some lunch," I said. "We aren't too far from Santa Rosa. You'll have to make a decision there anyway about whether we're going to take the short way to Chaco Canyon through Albuquerque, or the long, long way through Santa Fe."

"The short way," Velasquez said. "Since they are so blatantly following us, there is little to be gained by taking the long way."

"Okay. If we fill up with gas in Santa Rosa, we can make it all the way through Chaco Canyon and on up to Aztec without stopping again. But it's going to be eight or nine tonight before we get to the canyon. You know that, don't you?"

"That does not matter," Reyes said. "I can find my supplies in the dark."

"Yeah, but will it matter to the rangers?"

"That remains to be discovered, Martin. It worries me, too."

"Aw, hell," I said, "we'll be all right. With Girl Hunahpu and The Xablanque Kid, who's going to dare challenge us?"

"Please, Senor O'Hara, this is not a funny game. It is the most serious *obligación* of our lives."

"I thought you had a sense of humor, Reyes?"

"Yes, but this is not to be laughed at."

"Well, you stay sober and somber. Me, I'm going to laugh. Because it's either laugh or scream. What about you, Girl Hunahpu?" I could see she was fighting a grin.

"It is amusing to think about, Cacabe," she said. "Would not laughter be one more weapon we could wield against the lords of Xibalba?"

Reyes did not respond. I returned my attention to the road, not wanting to think about the fact that this Mayan madman I had agreed to follow couldn't laugh at himself. Overhead pale grey waves of clouds skudded along under the heavy grey clouds. Something inside me said we were going to see snow before too long.

"Very well," Reyes said finally, "I do not understand this new humor of yours any more than that song you sang, but I will not complain if you use the humor to help us."

"Whoopee. Now we can laugh all we want to, eh, Shirlito?" I nudged her arm with my elbow.

She broke out laughing and both Reyes and I looked at her like she was crazy. "It wasn't that funny," I said.

"No," Reyes said.

"*Ya lo creo,*" she said, "I should have known better."

That made me laugh, and with both of us laughing, Reyes laughed, too. When we pulled into the restaurant parking lot a few minutes later, I thought we were all going to race each other to get to the restrooms.

Lunch was delicious and plentiful, and we didn't talk much except about the possibility of snow, which I was worried about, but which Reyes seemed to think would help us. "Why?" I asked as we were leaving the restaurant.

"Because we will look for places where the snow melts because of the heat rising out of Xibalba," he said. "One of those places will be our entrance to *ube Xibalba*."

After we filled the truck with gas, Velasquez offered to drive and I was more than willing to let her. Lunch had made me sleepy and seemed to have made them quiet. I closed my eyes shortly after we got up to cruising speed on I-40, and when I opened them, I was surprised by how dark it was. Beside me Reyes snored softly. "Hi," I said. "You've been driving for a long time. Where are we?"

"We are almost to Prewitt—eleven miles from the road to Chaco Canyon, the sign just said."

I looked at my watch. "Sure is dark out there."

"It is six-thirty."

"How are you doing?"

"*Así, así.*"

"So-so, huh? You want me to drive?"

"Yes. When we get off."

I was content to wake up slowly as we rode along without talking until two snowflakes hit the windshield followed by half a dozen more. "Ah, yes, snow. Just in time for me to drive."

"You do not have to drive, Martin."

"It's only fair. Besides, I've driven in snow many times."

"As you wish."

Reyes was still asleep when we stopped, so Velasquez climbed into the middle of the seat from the driver's side, and for the first time I got a close-up look at her rear end in those tight jeans she was wearing. It was shaped exactly the way I think a female rear end ought to be shaped, and I had to resist telling her so. The snow was falling steadily by the time we passed Crownpoint and I switched on the yellow fog lights to cut the glare off the snow.

Only when we hit the unpaved washboard road to Chaco

Canyon a mile or so later did Reyes wake up. "We are close, no?"

"Just forty miles of bad road to go. We'll be there in an hour and a half or so. And you know what? I haven't seen our friends from the DSA in almost an hour."

Two hours later we drove up the west side of Chaco Canyon with only the parking lights on. Reyes looked for signs of the park staff, but could see nothing through the falling snow except a bright security light. We stopped at the ruin of Kin Kletso. I turned out the lights, and Reyes and Velasquez got out and told me to keep the truck running. I felt like the getaway driver at a bank holdup—like they were Bonnie and Clyde.

They were back in less than five minutes. Reyes was carrying a large burlap sack that smelled of dust and something old when he dropped it on the floorboard and climbed in.

I pulled back onto the road with just the parking lights on and headed for the northern exit from the monument. "That's it? That bag is all we came for?"

"Yes."

"Must be damned important stuff in that bag."

"It is. You may drive us to Mesa Verde, now."

"Right, boss. All we have is another twenty-five miles of bad desert road out of the canyon, and then another hundred and forty or fifty miles to the park. Why, we can probably be there by three or four in the morning."

"That is good."

"Are you serious?"

"Yes. Do you not think we will have an easier time sneaking past your barriers in the dark?"

"That depends on a lot of things, my friend. I'm not sure I want to drive that park road up the mountain in the dark, in the snow, without being able to use all our lights. And if we use our lights, we're going to be fairly easy to see."

"Not if it is snowing hard enough," Velasquez said. "Then no one would be able to see us very well."

"Oh, you're a big help. If they can't see us, we can't see the road, remember. Look, it's already snowing harder. Why don't we just pray to Tohil and Cristos for a blizzard?"

"That would be too much, I think, senor."

"You're damn right it would," I said, shoving the shift

lever into first and creeping up the narrow dirt road out of the canyon. "You're damn right."

Chapter Twenty-three

As soon as we got out of the canyon, I turned the heat higher and opened my wing window.

"Why do you turn up the heat and then let in the cold?"

"To warm my feet and keep me alert," I said.

"I could drive, Martin."

"No way, lady. I don't want anyone else but me pushing R.D. over these roads. Once we hit the blacktop, I just might let you drive on up to the park, 'cause I want to be wide awake driving in. Until then, you just get what rest you can. We may have to do some pushing before this is all over."

She didn't say anything, but she leaned against me and put her head on my shoulder. I liked that, but couldn't say so because I didn't want to risk a negative reaction from her. Yet the moment gave me a flash-memory of her standing naked over her suitcase, and I smiled.

Somehow Reyes went back to sleep and his snoring gained an irregular vibrato from the bouncing of the tires on the washboard road. When we finally reached the real highway and turned north, Velasquez was asleep, too. I didn't have the heart to wake her, so I drove on.

I couldn't remember what the town of Bloomfield looked like, and when we drove through it, only a dozen little circles of light declared that Bloomfield existed at all behind the falling snow. Aztec was a little brighter, but it didn't look like much either, and I called up the memory of wandering with Denise among its amazing ruins on a bright May day years before to remind me of what lay muffled in the darkness.

The images I recalled were sandstone and blue. The stonework was of mixed styles reflecting the various stages of occupation. The man on the side of the road staring back at me through the snow was some Meso-American warrior out of the past. Feathers and skins, scales and shells covered him in an elaborate costume crowned by a headdress of red, yellow, white, and orange feathers that stood two feet or more over his head. Hanging from his belt was a shiny sword with a drop-step point. His face looked all too familiar.

"It is you."

I nearly jumped out of the truck.

Velasquez had spoken and now the man was gone. She crossed herself and blew into her closed hand like my mother used to do.

"Damn. You scared the hell out of me. I thought you were asleep."

"I thought I was, too, when I saw that man."

"*Por que?*"

"Go back to sleep, Cacabe."

"*Si.*"

"You saw him, too? You mean he was real?"

"I do not know if he was real, Martin. I only know that I saw a man standing beside the road, dressed in a costume of the ancient kind, and his face was yours."

With a shiver I said, "That's scary."

"Tell me why."

"If we're both so tired we're seeing things, who's going to drive?"

"That is not what you meant when you said you—"

"I know. Doesn't it frighten you a little to see visions in the middle of the night?"

"Not if I recognize them."

"Oh, great. You see a vision and you think it's me, so it's okay. Right?" I shifted down into second and the back of my gloved hand rested on her thigh as though my hand had a mind of its own. It stayed there until I shifted up into third again. "I think we should have stopped in Aztec and put the chains on."

"There is not enough snow on the road, yet."

"For a girl from Guatemala, you sure know a lot about snow."

"A girl from Texas."

"That's right."

"Is there anything I can say to lessen your worries, Martin?"

"Yeah. You can tell me this is all a crazy dream—that the DSA drugged me to learn the truth and the drugs are causing this dream. That would lessen my worries a bunch."

"There is no reason to lie to you."

"Well, in that case, lady, I don't know anything you can do. We're just pawns in the games of the gods." There should have been more humor in my voice. "But who cares about us."

"I do. I care about all three of us," she said, "you most of all."

"Don't talk like that."

"Why?"

"Because I don't think I can handle it. We have enough on our hands already without adding . . . well, you know."

"No, I do not know," she said. "Perhaps you should tell me."

"I'm serious, Velasquez. I don't think—"

"Call me Shirlito."

"No. That's too familiar."

"We will be very familiar with each other before all this is over, I think."

"What's that supposed to mean?"

"Oh, nothing. But there is another part to the legends of our people."

"So tell me."

"You will listen?"

"Well, I don't have the radio on, do I?"

"Very well, Martin, but you must let me tell the whole thing. It is not very long."

"You're on. It's your play."

"A good word, play. The legends of the Queche tell of some time in the future when the gods will touch the people directly again and a new leader will rise up to make life better for everyone."

I sure hoped she wasn't talking about me. I didn't need any more heroic fables laid on me.

"The legend is like the fantasy books that people read. The readers know the fantasy stories have never happened and never will, but they read them anyway. So it is with the legend of Seven Jaguar, the son of Great True Jaguar. Seven Jaguar was never supposed to have existed. Yet in the legend he does exist and he falls in love with a woman from the Queche people and she bears him a son, and the son fathers a son, and each son fathers a son of his own until many great cycles are repeated, and finally True Jaguar is reborn."

"And you and Reyes think that's me."

"Yes. But there is more. In the story, True Jaguar, the descendant of Great True Jaguar and Seven Jaguar, meets a Queche woman who carries the genius of the gods, and she bears him a son named Hunahpu Jaguar, who is half man and half god, and who leads the Queche people to a new and better life."

Suddenly I understood what she was getting at, as though it hadn't been right there in front of me the whole time. "And Reyes believes that you two carry the spirit of Hunahpu and Xablanque, which means . . . Are you propositioning me, lady?" I dared not take my eyes off the road to look at her.

"This morning when Cacabe and I argued, it was over this. Until I met you, I did not believe the legend of Seven Jaguar. Until today, I did not believe in a woman carrying the genius of the gods. Do not forget that for most of my life I have lived as a modern American woman, a good Catholic, a tithing member of my parish, and—"

"So what's the point?"

"The point is that I believe what Cacabe has been saying about our lives—all three of us—because what he says touches nerves in me that run below all of my modern feelings. And I think that you and I have been thrown together for a reason. I also think that whether or not you want to admit it, you have feelings for me as a man has for a woman."

"You mean that I'm hot for your bod? You bet I am— ever since I saw you naked this morning. But that only means that I'm a horny man and you're a beautiful woman." She had touched something that I didn't want any part of messing with. "It doesn't mean anything else. Period."

"So you will not admit your own feelings?"

"I just did."

"No, you did not."

"Look, Shirlito, I think you're a beautiful woman, but my thinking that doesn't imply anything more."

We rode a long time after that without saying anything. I found a decent country music station on the radio as I drove us up into the mountains, past the Colorado border and on into Durango. By then the road was well covered with snow.

I stopped at a triple-A service station and the three of us took the opportunity to go to the restrooms while they put the chains on and gassed R.D. up. The man who took Velasquez's money suggested that we look for a room in Durango for the night because the road west had been receiving snow all day. When we got back in the truck I repeated to Reyes what the man had said, but he insisted that we go on.

Velasquez offered to drive, but I knew I wouldn't have been comfortable with anyone besides me at the wheel. After filling our thermos with coffee at Durango's one all-night store, I drove us west toward Mancos. A program called Honky Tonk Night on the radio kept the cab filled with plaintive music that fit my mood.

Even with the chains the driving was tough. I was constantly shifting up and down, searching for the right combination of speed and traction. Every half mile or so we passed cars off on the side of the road, and the more of them we passed, the more worried I became until finally we rolled into Hesperus doing fifteen miles per hour.

I looked at my watch. "That's it. No more driving tonight."

"But we have to go on," Reyes said.

"It took us almost an hour and fifteen minutes to drive the last eleven miles, Reyes. We're still a good forty, fifty miles from Mesa Verde. At the speed we've been traveling—"

"He's right, Cacabe. There is a motel sign over there."

"We must go on," Reyes said. "We must."

Chapter Twenty-four

"No, Cacabe," Velasquez said gently. "We have come a great distance. Let us rest now, and tomorrow we will be better prepared to go on."

He sighed. "Very well. Let us rest here, then."

The motel had a vacancy, one room, two beds, and we split up as we had the night before—Velasquez and I each in a bed and Reyes on the floor. I didn't realize how tired I was until I finally snuggled down into the covers. It seemed like only seconds later that a warm, naked female body slipped in bed behind me and curled up against my back.

"I sent Cacabe to breakfast—even though his moral instincts told him to stay," Velasquez whispered. "He is a terrible prude. But he said he would wait for us at the cafe."

"Uhhh . . . I don't . . . I mean . . ."

"It is all right, Martin. We do not have to make love. I only wanted to feel your skin against mine. It is nice."

My expectations rose, and every male impulse in my body wanted to turn over and hug her to me. My skin tingled against hers. Yet even though she had initiated this, I felt reluctant to take advantage—

"Did you know I am a virgin?" she asked.

My expectations fell as swiftly as they had risen, except that I knew from the way she was stroking my thigh that there was carnal hope. "No, I didn't. I only guessed it."

"It is true. I have never known a man face to face."

"Here," I said, turning over, "now you see me face to face."

She smiled and twined her fingers in the hair at the back of my neck. "But I still have not known you."

I let my fingers trace her ribs, my body ready, my mind hesitant. "I do not want to hurt you, Shirlito." Her skin had a fine texture like Japanese silk paper.

"You will not hurt me." She pulled me closer until we were touching from knees to chest.

I trembled. "If you're a virgin, there will be some pain."

"Only a little. It will be a joyful pain."

"Do you have . . . uh, I don't have any protection."

"It is not necessary."

"Are you . . . you're sure?"

"Yes, I am sure."

We kissed.

No sparks flew. No electric tremors ran through my body. No raging passion roared through my blood.

But her lips seemed exactly fitted to mine. Our kisses pressed, paused, pulled away, and pressed again with a sweet urgency that drew our squirming bodies together. We moved with the same rhythm as our hungry kisses, until we forced our way past her virginity and raced with the animals to a ragged, gasping conclusion. In that instant before nothingness, the bright image of a feathered headdress flooded my mind's eye, then dissolved in the sky of dark stars.

As I opened my eyes, I raised myself higher on my elbows and saw written in the contours of her face the lineage of kings. "You are beautiful," I said, starting to tremble.

"Thank you, Martin. You are beautiful, also."

106

I laughed softly. "Right."

Still locked together, I rolled us over on our sides so that her left thigh fitted under my waist and her right one rested atop mine. My trembling stopped. Her smile seemed ready to break into laughter.

"There," she said, "now I know you face to face."

We kissed. "It will be better the second time," I assured her. "We'll go slower and pay more attention—"

She stopped my words with another long kiss. "I liked the first time. Fast was fun."

"So is slow."

"You have a great deal of experience, don't you, Martin?"

There was that question no man wants to answer to a woman he cares about—and I knew that I cared about Velasquez far more than I ought to. "Yes. I have had much experience. I was married, remember."

"But you have made love to many women."

"Yes," I said after a hesitant pause. "Face to face. But I've certainly never known a woman like you."

"I will take that as a compliment."

"It was meant to be." Her eyes were so dark I thought I could see my reflection in them.

"There were pictures for me at the climax."

That surprised me—and bothered me. "For me, too."

"Do you know what this means, Martin?"

I didn't want to know. I didn't want any Mayan mumbo-jumbo tacked on to lovemaking. "It means that Reyes won't have to sleep on the floor."

She giggled. "Yes, though I doubt he will sleep in a bed. It also means that we are compatible."

"I'd agree with that."

"No, I mean truly compatible, in harmony."

We lay smiling at each other until I had a sudden suspicion that she meant something more than—"You mean compatible as in the rest of our lives?"

"Yes."

"Don't do this to me, Shirlito. Making love doesn't mean getting married."

"I said nothing about marriage, Martin. Do not panic. What we have discovered is one more thing in our lives that connects us. That does not imply that we should—"

"Shhh." I laid a finger on her lips and kissed her nose. "Let's not spoil this by talking it to death. Just hug me."

We hugged. Then kissed. Then got up and showered together before going to meet Reyes for breakfast. As we crunched through the snow to the restaurant, I thought about Mesa Verde and the myths of Xibalba for the first time that day.

Chapter Twenty-five

While we were eating, someone turned up the television in the corner and shouted, "Listen to this!"

"—and announced an unprecedented and historical effort that took place last month. State Department spokeswoman, Margaret Marie, confirmed that China, Japan, and the European Space Agency combined their resources to launch a third rocket in an effort to destroy or divert Lana's comet before it can threaten the earth."

Reyes shook his head and went back to eating.

The more the man talked, the more unsettled I felt. If China, Japan, and the E.S.A. could work together on something like that, it must really be serious. But did that—

"Ms. Marie would not divulge the megatonnage of any of the warheads now on their way, but said each rocket was capable of independently intercepting and destroying Lana's comet. National Science advisor, Kim Krugh, and ex-astronaut, Ivan Michaels, both said that while there is still insufficient evidence to prove that Lana's comet is a threat to earth, these precautionary steps taken by the many nations should guarantee our safety."

Reyes snorted and looked at me. "They will not succeed. We must go on."

For some reason I believed him and nodded. Under the table Velasquez squeezed my hand.

It didn't take us long after breakfast to check out of the motel, load R.D., and head up the highway toward Mancos. The seventeen miles through light snow flurries took less than an hour. The three of us didn't talk much, but Velasquez— for some reason I found it awkward to think of her as Shirlito—sat close, often with her hand on my right thigh.

From Mancos to the entrance to Mesa Verde National Park took another thirty minutes. Much to my surprise, the park gate was open and showed recent evidence of a snow plow.

"Must be something going on up at the lodge," I said.

"Can we avoid this lodge?" Reyes asked.

"No. We have to drive right past it to get to the main part of the park. Maybe we should stop there and act like tourists."

"The DSA knows we are coming here. What good would it do us to act like tourists, Martin?"

I'd almost forgotten about the DSA. "I don't know. But if they know we're coming, what's the point? What's to keep them from arresting us before we ever find this secret entrance to Xibalba?"

"They will not be able to stop us," Reyes said, "because Cristos and Tohil are watching over—"

"Well, you'd better get to praying. Somebody's following us again."

"That is to be expected."

"We will drive straight to Square Tower House."

"That's it? Drive to Square Tower House and jump out of the truck and get arrested? Why not just stop now and avoid the long mountain drive?"

"Because they will not arrest us," Velasquez said. "They have been sent to observe us until they are sure they have evidence. Only then will they ask for permission to arrest. By the time they think they have evidence, we will be on the road to Xibalba."

"And what's to keep them from following us?"

"They can follow if they wish," Reyes said, "but I do not think they will wish to."

I knew from his tone of voice that he was smiling, and I was glad. One of us needed to be content with what was happening. I kept thinking about those three rockets rushing toward Lana's comet, and wondering why I was going on with this.

Much sooner than I expected to, we could see the lodge perched high on the mountain above us to our right. Ten or fifteen buses sat in the parking lot, and as I drove past I had to resist the impulse to pull into the lot and denounce this whole adventure.

But a glance at Reyes revealed a kid getting close to his

favorite amusement park, and Velasquez had her head on my shoulder and her hand on my thigh, and I knew that as much as the rational centers of my brain might shout for me to stop, my heart and my gut were committed to following these two strange people who had altered my life.

We passed the road to the park office and drove straight through the fresh snow down to the parking area on the mesa above Square Tower House. As soon as I parked the truck and opened the back, I looked around expecting to see dozens of federal agents closing in on us, but no one came. It took Velasquez only ten minutes to divide the gear among the three of us, and when we got our backpacks on—me with the Crain machete strapped to the pack frame—Reyes said, "This way," and started walking south on the road. We followed, our breath forming little clouds of fog in front of us.

After about a hundred yards, Reyes left the road and cut through the brush to the edge of the mesa. "Down here," he said.

I looked where he pointed. "You've got to be kidding. That's almost straight down."

"There are steps."

Sure enough, there were steps of a sort, steps chipped out of the rock by people with feet or shoes smaller than ours, but steps and handholds nonetheless. We backed down the Indian trail—Reyes first, then me, then Velasquez—for the better part of an hour until my lungs burned with the cold and my gloved hands ached from the strain.

"We have . . . to rest," I gasped. "I can't . . . go on." My nose was almost numb and my cheeks were stinging in the wind.

"But Senor O'Hara . . . we are only . . . twenty feet from the bottom."

I looked down, and sure enough, he was right. "Did you . . . hear what Reyes . . . said?" I called to Velasquez who was at least twenty feet above me.

"Yes. Be careful."

"Of course."

"How foolish of you to think otherwise," Reyes said.

I would have laughed if I hadn't been afraid of falling down the cliff. When the three of us finally sat on the narrow trail at the base of it, all I could concentrate on was getting air in my lungs and warming my face in my hands.

"It is the altitude," Velasquez said.

"Nothing to do with . . . the exertion would it?"

"Too much . . . in one day," she said with a grin as she patted my leg.

"There is much more to go," Reyes said, looking up. "I think they are coming down after us."

I looked up and didn't see anyone, but forced myself to my feet anyway. "Then let's go."

The trail stuck close to the base of the cliff, then became a ledge about three feet wide that finally led to the base of the Square Tower House ruins. The broken walls stood tall under an overhang of the cliff a hundred feet above us. Square Tower, with its windows making it look like a watch tower, hugged the cliff face and dominated the ruins. It had been impressive when I had seen it from above years before, but now under a dusting of snow, it was more than impressive. It was spooky.

Reyes ran to the first wall of the ruin. "We are close," he said. "I can smell it."

I sniffed the air, but couldn't smell a thing.

Voices echoed in the distance.

"Hurry," Reyes said.

"There is no need to hurry, my friends," a deeper voice said.

Standing in front of Reyes was an Indian wearing a blue down jacket and a cowboy hat. "You have come to challenge the devil. I can see it in you. I am Henry Great Bear, watcher of Square Tower House."

Reyes made the introductions while I just stared stupidly at Henry Great Bear. Then in an instant I understood. "You're a Ute Mountain Ute, aren't you?"

"Yes. I've been watching for you three. In fact, the whole tribe has been watching for you in a way. The legend said you would come."

"What are you talking about?"

"The legend of She Blank Man and Hundakoo Shirt Woman and Mountain Lion Man. The legend says you would come and be lost, but a watch of the people would find you and lead you to the gates of the Road to Beginning." He grinned. "That's a long way from my job as a computer programmer, but you can never tell about legends. Every once in a while one of them comes true."

"So are these the gates?" I asked with a sweep of my arm.

"No. Well, little gates, maybe. In the kivas of the Old Ones there are *sipapuni*, holes that the elders say go all the way down to the underworld. Can you smell them?"

"Yes," Reyes said.

I tilted my head back and took a deep breath. "No. My nose must be too cold."

Henry Great Bear looked back up the trail. "Well, we'll get you warm in a little while. Right now we need to leave here, because I think I hear the cops coming."

Reyes shook his head. "We must find the entrance to the underworld, Henry Great Bear."

"We'll get you there. And you won't have to squeeze through some little *sipapuni*, either. Come on."

In single file we headed down the canyon away from the Square Tower House ruins—Henry Great Bear, Velasquez, me, and Reyes. I had a whole head full of questions I wanted to ask, but the trail was narrow and rocky and sometimes not a trail at all, and it was all I could do to keep my footing and hold the pace.

"This is Navajo Canyon," Henry Great Bear said when we stopped for a short rest, "and we are out of the national park. The cops won't follow us onto the reservation."

I nodded and looked at Velasquez and she smiled just as Henry Great Bear stood up and started walking again. Two hours later we reached a dirt road with an old International Harvester Travelall parked beside it.

"From here we ride," Henry Great Bear said.

After we put our packs behind the seats, my legs were so weak I could barely climb in the backseat beside Velasquez.

Reyes sat up front. "Where are we going, now?"

"To Alan Lodge's house. We'll hold the purification rites there, and tomorrow we'll take you to the gates of the Road to Beginning." He turned on the engine, then picked up the mike for his C.B. radio, and said something unintelligible. He got an answer back in the same language and laughed. "There's going to be a celebration at Alan's tonight."

Chapter Twenty-six

After two hours of bouncing east along a network of unpaved roads, we reached Alan Lodge's house. A dozen pickup trucks and station wagons were parked along the road, and a group of men waited in the yard to greet us.

They talked and laughed and asked questions all at the same time, and generally treated us like long-lost relatives. In the house we were fed stew and hot chocolate, and afterward, our host broke the seal on a liter bottle of Wild Turkey and poured everyone an ounce or more, which we drank in toast to each other.

In the corner by the door the pile of coats and jackets grew to a mound as more and more people arrived by the carloads until the house throbbed warmly with the happy noise of them all. Reyes and Velasquez and I were each surrounded by shifting groups of people eager to see us and touch our arms, or shake our hands. My eyes kept threatening to close even as I tried to answer questions that were thrown at me about how we had come, and how long we had been on the road, and if we wanted something more to eat and drink. No one said anything about where we were going, but their attitude left no doubt about the pleasure of the whole event for them.

Somewhere in the middle of the afternoon I sat in a leather covered chair and put my head back.

Velasquez woke me with kisses on my nose and forehead. "We must eat now," she said when I opened my eyes. "Then Cacabe says the purification ceremony begins."

I followed her to the kitchen where more hot stew awaited us, and homemade bread and a thick block of cheddar cheese. Reyes was already eating, and one of Alan Lodge's daughters stirred something on the stove. The house was very quiet.

"Where is everyone?" I asked as I sat down.

"Eating in the barn," the Lodge girl said. "We have a community room with a big fireplace out there, and that's where you'll get the cold wash."

113

"The what?" Velasquez asked.

The girl giggled. "The purification ceremony."

Two hours later Reyes, Velasquez, and I stood in front of the fireplace in the barn wearing only cotton nightshirts that had been beaded and embroidered, but which gave us no protection from the cold even with the noisy fire at our backs. My feet felt frozen to the floor, and my body trembled, but I tried to stand in as dignified a pose as I could. After all, we were the guests of honor.

An old couple—the man, heavy set; the woman, skinny to the bone—stood in front of us holding hands, wielding rattles, and led the chanting of the sixty or seventy people who half filled the room. Several times either the old man or the old woman would pause and touch each of us with their rattle before resuming the chant with the other. They all chanted until my feet were numb and my legs vibrated from the cold.

Without warning the chanting stopped. The old couple backed up. Buckets of freezing water poured down on the three of us.

I shuddered and yelped. The audience clapped and whistled, cheered and cat-called words I didn't understand, but when I saw Velasquez's wonderful body plastered by the wet cotton gown, I'd have whistled myself if I hadn't been gasping for breath through my chattering teeth. Only the strategically placed beadwork on her gown kept her from looking totally naked.

Three young boys presented us each with a large, heavy wool blanket. "Th-th-that's an odd-d-d purification r-rite," I stuttered as I wrapped my shaking body in the blanket.

"We must honor it," Reyes said.

"I'll feel better about honoring it when we've got some warm clothes on."

"You may go and put your own clothes on, now," the old man said. "You're as pure as you're going to get." He grinned and vibrated his dentures at us.

Reyes held out his left hand to the old man and in it were three blue kernels of corn. "Plant these for us," he said. "If they sprout after February 29, you will know we live. If they do not, you will know we have died."

The old man accepted the kernels with a nod of his head.

The three of us hurried to a small side room to dry off

and put our clothes back on. Whatever modesty we felt was shoved away in our hurry to get warm, although Cacabe seemed to be dressing with his eyes closed.

When we returned to the community room, dressed but still cold, we were given another round of cheers and applause, then people broke up into groups, talking to us and each other, the young people manning the record player, and Henry Great Bear's prediction came true.

The whole occasion turned into a party. New people arrived, greeted by shouts and hugs. Some of the ones who had been there for the ceremony left, departing through hugs and laughter. We drank and talked and snacked and laughed, and I even persuaded Velasquez to dance a few slow dances with me when the young people started playing music I knew how to dance to.

Later she and I found Reyes telling stories off in a corner with a diverse audience of attentive listeners. We waved goodnight to him and bundled up in our jackets and hats, but it seemed like everyone at the party wanted to shake hands with us or slap our backs or hug us before we finally left the barn and walked the hundred yards to the house through the snow and freezing night air.

Back in the house Velasquez led me to a bedroom filled almost side to side by a king-size bed. The walls that didn't have shelves on them were covered with posters of singers and actors, and a banner over the window read, GOOD LUCK, CORDY!

"This is the Lodge's oldest daughter's bedroom. She's away at college, so it's ours for the night."

The bedroom was too chilly to spend a lot of time fiddling with each other's clothes, so we got undressed as quickly as we could and burrowed under the covers. For some reason we made love without much foreplay, then spent a long time afterward kissing and touching.

When I awoke, pale light filled the low window. My left arm was under Velasquez, and both she and my arm were asleep. As gently as I could, I eased my dead arm out from under her, and tried to work some sensation back into it.

A knock on the door was followed by Henry Great Bear's voice. "Time to get up."

Only after some intensive kissing would Velasquez agree to get up and get dressed. We ate a breakfast of ham and eggs and cornbread and lots of coffee with Henry Great Bear, the old couple from the night before, and Alan Lodge. To my surprise when we went outside, many of the people from the night before, men, women, and children, were lined up from the front door to the road.

They weren't laughing, then, and some of them looked like they were still feeling the alcohol, but they all stood there waiting with great dignity to touch our hands, crossing palms to palms, before we climbed into the Travelall and Henry Great Bear drove us away. Velasquez and I both turned and waved as we bounced down the road, and our friends, the Ute Mountain Utes, waved back until we were out of sight.

"Special people," I said as I turned back around.

"You are the ones who are special," Henry Great Bear said. "You have brought life to the legends and given us reason not to forget and our children reasons to learn."

We rode in silence for a while before Reyes asked, "What is the name of this place you are taking us to?"

He chuckled. "It is called No Name Place, and its canyon has no Ute name. Only its kiva has a name. It is called Gate to the Road of Beginning."

"And what will we find there?"

"The ladders down into the heart of the earth."

I heard a helicopter overhead and moments later saw it sweep up the canyon ahead of us. "You said they wouldn't follow us here."

"That's a BIA chopper—Bureau of Indian Affairs. I'm sure it's not looking for us."

"What if it is?" Velasquez asked.

"It can't go where we're going anyway. We're going to leave the road in another mile or so, and after that it's a two-hour hike up No Name Canyon. The only way anyone could get close to us is to come behind us on foot. I wouldn't worry about—"

"Henry, this is home," a voice said from the C.B. "We've got winter mosquitos and they want to bite you."

"Thanks, home. Out." He leaned forward and switched channels. "X-ray Alpha, this is Halo. Do you read me?"

"We read you, Halo."

"Time to beat the drums."

"Roger, Halo. Time to beat the drums. X-ray Alpha, out." Again he changed channels.

"What does all that mean?" Reyes asked.

"Oh, I just called for a little help. Home said the BIA is looking for me—us, probably—and X-ray Alpha said they'd find some people to cover our backs."

"Why do you transmit in English?" I asked.

Henry Great Bear laughed as he slowed the Travelall down, made a hard right across a rocky stream, and eased us up a narrow track into a side canyon. "Sometimes it's fun to transmit in English and drive the BIA and the Raspberry Twinkies crazy."

"Raspberry Twinkies?"

"Sure, red all around and white in the middle." He braked the Travelall to a stop under a low, overhanging ledge. "Time to switch to ankle express."

"Henry this is home," the C.B. squawked as we got out. "Do not acknowledge. Spiders on the way. Out."

"So, they think that if they find us they can rappel down on us, do they?" Henry said. "We'll see about that."

Velasquez and I put on our packs as Henry opened a storage compartment and pulled out a long-barreled, scoped rifle. I turned to see Reyes's reaction and was surprised to see him holding his automatic pistol out to me. The pistol was holstered and he also held some spare clips, and a box of ammo.

"Just in case," he said. "I have one for each of us."

I took all of it, and he pulled another set from his pack and handed it to Velasquez. Suddenly I was frightened again. "Hey, you never said anything about shooting at people in this deal."

"Perhaps we will not have to."

"Yeah," I said, fastening the belt around my waist but under my jacket, "let's sure as hell hope we won't."

Chapter Twenty-seven

We hiked up No Name Canyon behind Henry Great Bear, and every time we heard the helicopter, we pressed ourselves against the canyon wall or huddled down in the rocks. Several times I saw Velasquez and Reyes cross themselves. I would have crossed myself, too, if I'd thought it would do any good. But I didn't, for fear of offending someone upstairs. I'd been an unbeliever too long.

For hours we hiked up the continually narrowing canyon and hid each time the helicopter flew over, until without warning Henry Great Bear said, "There it is."

I looked up and saw a deep wind-sculpted hollow in the east wall of the canyon. In the hollow sat an old style pueblo in such wonderful condition, it wouldn't have surprised me at that moment to see Anasazi walking around in it.

"*Maravilloso*," Reyes whispered.

"Amen to that."

Velasquez led the way through the deserted pueblo up to a mound covered with layers of shells and feathers and little talismen and lengths of braided cloth and hair. Even I could tell how holy this place was. A ladder poked through the top of it and I realized it was a kiva.

"Come smell this, Martin," she said, stepping her way carefully to the top.

I joined her beside the ladder and smelled warm air filled with strong scents of life and decay that rose from the kiva through a curtain of eagle feathers. I could feel the strong old magic that guarded the entrance.

"Like home," Reyes said. "It smells like the jungle."

The noise from the helicopter echoed into the canyon, but instead of passing as it had before, it seemed to get louder.

"On your way," Henry shouted, running out from under the overhanging cliff with his rifle at the ready. "Get going."

"We must burn the copal," Reyes said.

"Burn it down there. Come on, Shirlito," I said. As soon as she carefully parted the barrier of eagle feathers and climbed down the ladder into the kiva, I followed. Reyes was right behind me. From outside we heard the distinctive echo of a high-powered rifle.

When Reyes's feet hit the floor, he pulled a lighter out of one pocket and a small stoneware bowl out of the other. He dropped something in the bowl, lit it, mumbled a few words, and moved around the ladder to one side of the kiva where a slab of stone rose six or more feet in the air. Behind that stone was another hole with a ladder poking out of it, and without hesitation Reyes started down the second ladder.

Velasquez followed him, and I followed her, expecting any minute to hear someone coming into the kiva. I thought I heard more shots, but I couldn't be sure, and when I thought about Henry Great Bear up there by himself, I didn't wait to find out. The second ladder went down much farther than the first one had, and when I finally came to the bottom of it, I realized we were in a natural cave. The air smelled heavy and old.

Reyes moved his flashlight beam in a slow circle around the cave. Velasquez and I brought out our flashlights, and she located the next ladder. Across the cave from us it leaned against a large boulder. When we reached it, we saw it wasn't a ladder at all, but rather steps cut into the face of the boulder.

"Well," I said, "is this where the Road of Beginning starts? Do we have to go up to go down?"

"Yes," Reyes answered, already up the third step. There was no mistaking the excitement in his voice.

We followed him up the boulder steps to a wide path marked by fist-sized stones at its borders, and we hardly paused as we walked along that downward-sloping path into a natural tunnel. "Wait a minute," I said, stopping after we had walked some hundred steps or so into the tunnel. "Turn out your flashlights."

Without a word we all turned them off. The rough ceiling fifteen or twenty feet above us glowed with phosphorescence. Once my eyes adjusted to the change of color and brightness, I said, "Looks like we can save our batteries for now."

"What is it?" Velasquez asked.

"I don't know. Some kind of lichen, maybe."

"*Lampara Dios,*" Reyes said. "God's lamp. It grows in the caves at home, also, and that is what it is called."

"Might as well take advantage of it as long as it lasts."

We continued down the sloping, sometimes twisting path, our way lit by the glowing ceiling, our pace set by Reyes, whose eagerness I couldn't share. Passages split off, or opened up suddenly on one side or another, but we stuck to the path marked by the border of stones. The farther we went into this cave system, the more doubts I had, and the more reluctant I became to rush on.

119

"Slow down," I called ahead, "or go on without me. I'm not running to Xibalba. Besides, I'm hot." Reyes stopped and Velasquez came back to join me as I shrugged off my pack and removed my jacket. I wadded the down jacket up and stuffed it into one of the pack's outside pockets, then put the pack back on, and buckled up the hip belt in time to help Velasquez into her pack after she'd taken off her jacket.

"I am worried, Martin," she said, taking my hand.

Her statement and tone caught me off guard. "Why? What are you worried about?"

"I do not know. I have this bad feeling."

"Wait," I said, stopping again and taking her other hand in mine so that we stood facing each other. Bringing her hands to my lips I kissed each of them in turn. "You know all the rules have changed for us, don't you?"

"I think so, but tell me what that means to you." Her eyes glowed in the phosphorescent light.

"It means that I can't just shrug you off. That if you're worried, so am I. That if you want to go back to the surface, we can turn right—"

"No, we must go forward."

"Then tell me what has you worried."

"I do not know. Truly, Martin, I do not know, but I will tell you as soon as I have words for it."

"That's fair enough. Shall we join cousin Cacabe?" We shared a quick kiss before we went on.

Reyes was sitting on a rock, waiting for us. "Are you hungry? Do you want to stop to eat?"

"Not me. You, Shirlito?"

She squeezed my hand. "No. How far down do you think we are, Cacabe?"

He stood up. "Two hundred feet? Three hundred feet? Who can tell? All I know is that this is the right road."

"How do you know that?" I asked.

"The stones tell me, but also I can smell it—the odor of life and the odor of death, each weighing the same in the nose—and the heat. This is *ube Xibalba.*"

A brief shiver ran up my spine. "You know, you never finished telling me what happened to Hunahpu and Xablanque."

"Then as we go, I will tell you."

He turned and the three of us began walking down again—Velasquez and I holding hands. "It's just a stroll down the road, Ma."

"*Perdone?*"

"Never mind. The twins were about to play ball with the lords of Xibalba. Does that sound right?"

"Most certainly. That is where we stopped, where the lords of Xibalba told the boys it was time to play ball, and the boys agreed. 'We will use this fine ball of ours,' One Death said. But the ball he was referring to was actually White Dagger rolled up in bone dust to look like a ball.

" 'We brought our own ball,' Hunahpu said.

" 'A good gum-rubber ball with lots of bounce in it,' Xablanque added.

" 'But you must play with ours,' One Death insisted. 'We made it just for you.'

"The twins agreed, but they knew the Xibalban ball was actually White Dagger in disguise and said so.

"The Xibalbans threw their ball into play and Hunahpu hit it with his yoke. That knocked White Dagger out of the ball of bone dust, and White Dagger went bouncing from wall to wall. The boys stayed out of its way and cried, 'Call off your stupid dagger or we will go home. It wasn't our idea to come here in the first place.'

"White Dagger was supposed to kill the twins, so when it failed, the Xibalbans were very angry because they knew they had been defeated again. 'All right,' they said, 'but why don't we bet on this next game?'

" 'What shall we play for?' the boys asked.

" 'Four bowls of flowers,' Seven Death said, 'one of red petals, one of white petals, one of yellow petals, and one of whole flowers.'

"The boys agreed and the game started. They played very well against the Xibalbans, then lost on purpose."

"I know better than to ask why." The air got even warmer and it smelled fresher.

Velasquez squeezed my hand and smiled.

"The Xibalbans were very excited that they had defeated the boys after only one game, so they said, 'You may rest in Razor House and pay your wager in the morning.' But as soon as the boys entered Razor House, One Death rushed to his flower garden and told the macaws guarding it to stay awake all night and keep the boys from stealing flowers.

"Hunahpu and Xablanque entered Razor House and found themselves surrounded by knives thirsty for blood. 'You may take what little blood we have,' Hunahpu said, 'or you may spare us and we will let you drink of the blood of every animal on the face of the earth.'

"The knives immediately dropped their points and the boys sent the smallest knives out of the house to instruct the ants on how to secretly cut flowers from the Xibalban garden and bring them back to the boys. The knives did this, and the ants joined them and by morning, the boys had filled the bowls.

"When the messenger owls discovered that Razor House had not killed the boys, they ordered the boys to present the prizes to the lords of Xibalba. And when the lords of Xibalba saw the bowls of flowers the boys carried, they knew—"

"Look, there," Velasquez said.

The passage ahead widened into a brighter area—too bright for light coming only from phosphorescent lichen. Sitting on the path in the middle of the brightness was a one-legged owl.

Chapter Twenty-eight

Forty feet before we reached the owl, we stepped into the back of a large cave. The owl sat in the entrance to the cave and beyond it we could see green mountains—jungle green mountains.

"I have been sent to warn you not to come any farther," the one-legged owl said. We stopped when it spoke. "Go back to the land you came from."

"We came to challenge the lords of Xibalba to a ballgame," Reyes said. "Are they afraid to play ball with human beings?"

"You have been warned," the owl said. With three or four great flaps of its wings, it launched itself into the air.

"Tell the lords of Xibalba that Hunahpu Woman and Xablanque and True Jaguar have come to challenge them," Reyes shouted as he ran to the cave entrance.

Velasquez and I ran to join him and the three of us watched

the owl fly up and away. "Go home," it called. "Go home. Go home."

"Shit," I whispered.

"What is it, Martin?"

"I just heard an owl talk."

"We all did."

"Yeah, but I don't believe it—I mean I don't believe it's possible."

"It is very possible," Reyes said, "but now I think we should make some tea and eat some food, because we're going to need our energy."

Only when I got my backpack off did I realize how good it felt to be free of the weight. I readjusted my gun belt and hung my Crain Predator machete on the left side of it for balance.

Reyes poured water from his canteen into the lid of his little camp stove, and Velasquez and I got out the sandwiches Alan Lodge's daughters had fixed for us. I surprised Reyes and Velasquez with a sealed bag of chocolate chip cookies. "Juanita Great Bear," I said. "She gave them to me yesterday."

Soon we were sitting in the entrance, munching on roast beef sandwiches and sipping Reyes's oddly sweet but very delicious tea. "What is this?" I asked him as I held out my cup for more.

"It is a daykeeper's tea. We use it when we know we will be facing a long day, or a hard day filled with many readings."

"It's drugged," I said.

"Yes, in your sense, you would say it is drugged. It contains caffeine and several other mild stimulants—altogether the same strength as a cup of coffee."

"All right, I get the point. One man's coffee is another man's drug. Besides, I rather like it. . . . Do you see what I see out there? I mean, that looks like regular jungle and mountains, and the sky looks like any overcast sky, and somewhere near here there's a waterfall or some fierce rapids, because nothing else makes a sound like that."

"The canyon of rapids?" Velasquez said with an arched eyebrow.

"Yes, but why the hell do I have this terrible feeling we're not in Kansas, Dorothy? Or Colorado, either."

"We are not in Colorado, True Jaguar. I do not know Kansas, but I do know that we are in Xibalba."

I wanted to tell him not to call me True Jaguar, but all I managed to do was open my mouth.

"Martin, I think Cacabe is telling the truth."

"That's what scares the hell out of me," I said. "Where's Edgar Rice Burroughs when you need him?"

"What do you mean?"

"I think he wrote about this place and never knew that it was really here. There is a Pellucidar."

Reyes closed up his stove and arched an eyebrow at Velasquez.

She said, "No, Martin. Pellucidar is a fantasy. Xibalba is real."

"If it looks like it's real and smells like it's real and sounds like it's real and feels like it's real, it must be real," I said, "but I'm waiting to hear it quack."

"Sometimes you say the strangest things, True Jaguar."

Velasquez grinned. "He makes another joke, Cacabe."

I looked at him. "You call me True Jaguar. Why don't you call her Hunahpu Girl?"

"Because she is my cousin Shirlito."

"Well, I'm your buddy O'Hara," I said, holding out the bag of cookies. They each took several. "Senor Reyes, you can call me O'Hara. You can call me Martin. You can even call me Jesus. But I'd just as soon you didn't call me True Jaguar. Makes me very uncomfortable."

"Very well, Senor O'Hara."

"Just O'Hara will do fine. And I'll call you Reyes."

"And you can both call me Shirlito. Now, what do we do next, Cacabe?"

"We follow the road." He put a cookie in his mouth, then pointed to the wide ledge running from the cave.

The following minutes were filled with the sound of eating cookies. Finally I put the rest of the cookies in my pack, stood up, and brushed off my pants. "Well, it's"—I looked at my watch and shook my head—"ten P.M. according to this. That's wrong. It was only about noon when we reached the ruins."

Velasquez looked at her watch. "Mine says four-thirty A.M."

"Mine says midnight," Reyes offered.

"Oh, that's great. That's just great. We set out to accomplish something on a very particular day, and now our watches are screwed up and we don't know what day it is."

"The stones and seeds in my bag will tell us the day," Reyes said. "That is how we will know."

"And what do we check the stones and seeds against?" He didn't answer, and I looked up into the overcast sky. "Something tells me we won't have sun and stars to give us help, either." I jerked my backpack off the ground and shrugged it on. "So do we go forward or backward, daykeeper?"

"Forward, of course," Reyes said as he repacked his stove and teapot.

"How foolish of you to think otherwise," Velasquez added.

None of us laughed, but we exchanged sympathetic looks. We were all in this together. "Forward it is. Anything else in the twins' story we need to know?"

"*Mucho.*"

"Then you'd better walk and talk at the same time."

The ledge was wider than it looked, and there were stones marking the trail that led us slowly down the mountain from where we had come out of the cave. We were walking toward the noise of the water, though, and I wondered exactly what we were going to find ahead of us. Somehow I was more ready to meet Guatemalan guerrillas with machine guns at the bottom of the trail than to see gods from Mayan mythology.

"The lords of Xibalba were amazed that Hunahpu and Xablanque were alive and presenting them with flowers, and they were all ashamed that the twins had defeated them again. However, they were sure that they could defeat the boys in another ballgame, so they invited Hunahpu and Xablanque to play again. The boys agreed, but they played all day and the game ended in a tie."

"Do you know how to play this game?" I asked.

"I think so."

"That's a lot of help. How are we going to win a game we don't know how to play?"

"If we can, we will challenge them to something else, like basketball."

"Three-on-three basketball?" I shook my head. "Of course. Go on."

"That night the boys were put in Chattering House, and

125

the lords of Xibalba were sure the cold in there would kill them. But the boys huddled together to save their warmth and in the morning came out alive. That day they played ball again and tied again.

"The next night they were led to Jaguar House, but when they saw what it was, they asked a passing ant to get his friends to gather all the bones they could find, and soon the jaguars were chewing on the bones brought by the ants rather than the bones of Hunahpu and Xablanque."

"How many more of these nice houses are there?" I asked. The sound of roaring water was getting closer.

"Only Fire House and Bat House. Hunahpu and Xablanque survived Fire House, but in Bat House Hunahpu lost his head and Xablanque had to make him a new head out of a squash. When they went to play ball that next day, the Xibalbans rolled Hunahpu's real head onto the court in place of the ball.

" 'You're defeated! You've lost the game before it starts. Give up! Give up!' the lords of Xibalba shouted, and all around them the Xibalbans laughed.

"But Xablanque kicked the ball, which was really Hunahpu's head, out of the court. The lords of Xibalba ran after it, but a rabbit took the head and ran in a circle around the court and brought it back to Xablanque who put it on Hunahpu's shoulders in place of the squash and kicked the squash down to the end of the court and scored.

" 'No fair! No fair!' the lords of Xibalba shouted."

The roaring sound was getting so loud that Reyes almost had to shout.

" 'This is the ball you gave us,' Hunahpu said. 'That seems fair to us.'

"There was nothing the Xibalbans could say, so they sent their players onto the court and they all played as hard as they could until the boys suddenly gave up and—"

"Son of the great whore," I said. "Will you look at that?"

We stopped and looked down into a canyon three hundred feet wide and as many deep. At its bottom a river of churning water and rocks and great splintered trunks of trees roared up at us like a hungry animal.

"Neck Canyon," Reyes shouted. "The River of Many Spears."

"And we have to cross that?"
"Yes."
"How?"

Chapter Twenty-nine

"I do not think I have enough rope!" Reyes shouted.

"Even if you did, how would we get it across the canyon?"

"Come back away from the noise," Velasquez hollered.

We all walked back along the trail until we didn't have to shout at each other to be heard. Even there Neck Canyon still roared at us.

"We must go down into the canyon," Reyes said.

"Is that the way Hunahpu and Xablanque did it?" I asked.

"The story does not say. It only tells us that they crossed without getting hurt."

"Great. Just great."

"Maybe we can find a narrower place," Velasquez said. "Why not follow it upstream?"

"Won't cost us anything but time and energy. I'm game."

"Yes. We should try that."

We walked down the trail again, past the point where we had stared down into Neck Canyon. The trail weaved back and forth from the canyon rim for several hundred yards before it opened out onto a wall of grass eight feet high. We all walked over to the rim and looked down, then across. The canyon was still two hundred feet wide at least at that point and showed no signs of narrowing upstream.

"Now what?" I shouted.

Reyes pointed upstream, then led us back to where the trail entered the grass. I pulled out my machete and took the lead, hacking away the grass that overgrew the trail. Ten steps in and I was sure we were lost. A look over my shoulder showed that the grass had closed behind us and I couldn't see any trail at all. Thirty minutes later I had the terrible feeling we were walking in circles, and I wondered if the grass grew right up to the canyon rim and if suddenly we could walk—

"Whoa," Velasquez called.

"What?"

"Get beside me."

Reyes and I fought our way to her side. She pushed back some of the grass and pointed. "What about here?" she asked. "Do we have enough rope, Cacabe?"

Two jagged fingers of land stuck out from opposite sides of the canyon, and from where we stood it didn't look more than seventy-five feet between them. I hacked us a trail out of the tall grass, and we walked as far out on our side of the canyon as we could. The view wasn't as encouraging up close. One hundred fifty feet was a more accurate description of the distance.

"How are we going to get a rope across that?" I shouted.

"I have grappling hooks," Reyes shouted back.

"Yeah, but you have to find a way to get one of them across, *and* hooked onto something that will hold our weight."

"Can we climb down and cross at the bottom?" Velasquez asked.

"Maybe," I said, peering over the edge, "but I'd hate to try it wearing this." I shrugged my way out of my pack at the same time Velasquez shrugged her way out of hers. "Oh, no," I said.

"Yes. It will be easier for me. I will carry the rope across."

"Down, maybe, but how are you going to get across?"

She pointed. "See that line of rocks? That could be a way. Closer I might see others."

With a shake of my head I looked at Reyes and said, "What we need is some lightweight line one of us can carry over."

"We have only two hundred feet of one-half-inch rope," he said. "I thought it would be enough."

"That's not going to cut it." I took a deep breath and rolled my head back, as though loosening my neck muscles would lead to an idea. High overhead I saw a flying speck moving across the sky. I bent over, took my binoculars out of my pack, and searched the sky until I found the speck again.

"What do you see, Martin?"

"A scissortail, I think. You look."

She took the binoculars. "Yes, a scissortail."

"Look there," Reyes said pointing low over to the other side of the canyon.

"Hawks," Velasquez said when she found what he was pointing at. "Three of them. Big ones. Might even be eagles."

Each of us took a look through the binoculars, and after Reyes spent several minutes looking from the hawks to the scissortail and back again, he handed the binoculars to me with a shake of his head. "The scissortail is safe from those hawks. They are the atomic missiles, O'Hara. But they will not catch the scissortail comet."

I smiled. It was a nice interpretation of a natural . . . But what was really natural here? The canyon? The high grass? "If you say so, Reyes, I'll take your word for it."

The grass. Maybe . . . Drawing my machete from its sheath again, I went back to where the tall grass began and chopped off a bunch of it as close to the ground as possible.

"What is it?" Velasquez shouted as I rejoined them.

"I hope it's the answer to our rope problem." Where I'd cut them off, the grass averaged half an inch wide on either side of the stiff central petiolule. Using my teeth to find a break, I stripped half of one side, then the rest of that side, and two strips from the other side, and repeated the operation for five of the long blades of the grass. Each strip was a quarter of an inch wide and six to seven feet long.

"Hold these," I said, giving the cut-off ends of four strips to Velasquez. With some quick twists learned in my childhood at the YMCA, I began a four-strand braid of the grass and soon had five feet of green line dangling from her hands. Reyes stood and watched us, shaking his head. I braided in four of the new pieces, and worked that down until I had almost ten feet of grass line.

"You ready to test it? Let's see if we can break it."

On the third tug it gave way on one side of the interweave.

"Well, hell. It looked like a good idea."

"Could you try it with whole blades?"

"Sure, but if we do it that way, it's going to be heavier than the rope we already have."

"How long will it take to make three hundred feet of this narrow line?" Reyes asked.

I looked at what was in my hands and saw the little cuts as well as the line. "Say we average five feet per section at five minutes per section, a minute a foot equals three hundred minutes. Five hours. Maybe more. We're going to have to do it with gloves."

"If we all work together, it will not take as long. Show us how, please."

"But what are you going to do with it?"

"Use it to pull the other rope across."

"How?"

"You will see. Show us how to do the braid, please."

My glance at my watch registered 2:17 A.M. before I remembered the new time problem. What the hell did we have to lose? "All right. Let's get some grass."

After cutting enough grass with the Crain to keep us busy for a few hours, I taught Reyes and Velasquez the basic braid, and how to roll the strands around in the process so that the braid stayed smooth. It was slow work with the gloves on, but the skin on our hands would been shredded without them.

The next time I glanced at my watch it said 1:22 P.M., and I ignored it after that and concentrated on making line, using most of my time to splice ends together while Reyes and Velasquez made the sections. The roar from Neck Canyon kept us from talking much, and after a while we worked in the privacy of our own thoughts. A long time later we finished braiding and had three hundred feet of green grass line that weighed about fifty pounds.

I was about to suggest that we eat when I saw Reyes working with a little pile of stones. "What is that?"

"An altar. I will burn copal and pray for a bird to carry our line across," he said.

Sitting down next to Velasquez I took off my gloves and leaned against her. "Reyes is going to pray for a bird to help us get the line across."

"Good."

"You think he'll get one?" I asked in surprise.

"Yes, Martin. At least I believe it is possible."

I shrugged my shoulders and waited—too tired at the moment to argue. Reyes quickly had a little fire going and I could smell the sweet incense. He crossed himself, prayed, crossed himself, and prayed again. No matter how much I doubted that anything would come of it, I dared not say anything.

Suddenly I heard a loud cry overhead and a giant macaw with a gorgeous tail swooped down and landed beside Reyes. He leaned close and spoke to it, pointed across the canyon, then held out one end of the grass line. The macaw grabbed the line and took off, flying straight across the canyon with the line uncoiling behind it like a mad snake.

When it reached the other side, it circled the trunk of a low tree and started flying back. Reyes struggled to attach a folded grappling hook to his climber's rope and the climber's rope to the end of the grass line, but I was so dumbfounded by what I was seeing that I never thought to help him.

Velasquez did, and together they had it fastened before the macaw returned. It landed beside Reyes, let him take the end of the line from its claws, then flew away.

Only then did I get up and join them. "That's the damnedest thing I ever saw."

"Not damned, O'Hara. Holy. We must pull now."

I could only nod as the three of us hauled our grass line back and it pulled the rope and grappling hook across the canyon. Once we got it set, all we'd have to do was go hand over hand on the climber's rope for a hundred and fifty feet across certain death if we fell.

Chapter Thirty

When the grappling hook reached the tree on the other side, we sawed the line and rope back and forth until the hook opened, caught, then dug into the tree. The three of us jerked the rope with all our weight and it didn't budge. Reyes took out the other folding grappling hook, tied it to our end of the rope, opened it, and set it solidly between two boulders.

Looking at the rope sagging down into the canyon made my stomach roll over. This wasn't going to work. It couldn't work. "Now what?" I shouted.

Reyes smiled as he took carbiners out of his pack, then took straps out that he attached to our pack frames with clevis pins.

The noise from the canyon was too loud for him to explain as he went along, but as I watched him move our waist belts higher on our pack frames and turn our shoulder straps upside down, I finally understood how we might be able to get across using his system. We could hook the pack frames to the rope

131

with the carbiners, sit in our waist belts with our arms through the pack straps, and pull ourselves across. It would be scary as hell, but at least we would be secured to the rope.

"Who goes first?" I shouted. "You want me to?"

"Me," Reyes answered, motioning us back away from the edge. He stopped fifty feet back where the noise was a little less intimidating. "I am the lightest," Reyes said. "You two can hold the line to keep pressure on the grappling hook while I cross. When I get there, I can make sure the hook is set properly in the tree, and then Shirlito can come across."

"No." I shook my head. "She can stay here and wait for us."

"I cannot, Martin. I am the next lightest and I will go after Cacabe. Then you can follow us." She squeezed my hand.

"Okay . . . but I'm worried."

"Have faith," Reyes said.

"Sure." What else could I have said?

Reyes went first. Velasquez and I braced ourselves against the line, trying to keep tension on it without putting it under a strain. It wasn't much of a safety line, and it certainly wouldn't hold Reyes if the grappling hook gave way. But it did make us feel like we were being of some use.

As soon as all Reyes's weight was on the rope, it sagged even deeper into the canyon. To my surprise he made quick progress until he was about thirty feet from the other side. The rope from him to the edge of the canyon went steeply up from there, and he fought to hold every inch he gained on the canyon wall.

"He's not going to make it," I shouted to Velasquez.

"Yes, he will. Be patient."

I glanced at my watch before remembering that it couldn't tell me anything. We should have waited. We were all too tired to be attempting something that difficult. Reyes seemed to be hanging still and was probably exhausted. Looking sideways at Velasquez, I shook my head. She nodded and pointed. I looked back across the canyon as Reyes climbed up over the edge.

"Faith," she shouted. "You have to have faith. You have to believe." She climbed to her feet and walked out to where our packs were hooked to the rope.

"Velasquez," I shouted as I caught up with her, "I don't like this. It's too dangerous."

"Think positively. Believe." She slipped her arms into the pack straps and stood up. "See? Cacabe signals that the rope is set. I will be safe."

Indeed, Reyes was waving. "Maybe so, but . . ." I wanted to kiss her and hug her, yet I was afraid. "Be careful."

"Of course." Taking my hands, she kissed me, then released me quickly. "Here I go." She stepped to the edge and, holding the rope, eased herself over.

If I could have jerked her back at that moment, I would have. The rope went taut. Velasquez slid twenty feet down the rope without effort. I gasped.

She smiled, then shouted something lost in the roar, and began pulling herself sideways toward the other side.

It was agony for me, watching her move across Neck Canyon. All I wanted to do was pull her back and hold her and tell her—tell her what? That I loved her? Could I say that to her? Maybe not, but that was what I wanted to do. Instead I squatted on the rim of the canyon, one hand on the rope that was her lifeline, and never took my eyes off of her until she reached the other side and Reyes pulled her up to safety.

They both waved at me. I waved back, reluctant to follow them. Regardless of the fact that both of them had made it across with no serious difficulty, I had no confidence in my ability to do the same. Suddenly I wanted to go back, to follow the trail up the mountain, through the cave, and out into the kiva in the No Name Ruins. There was no way Reyes could stop me this time. Or Velasquez, either.

But there was no way I could leave her. Not now. No matter how much I was frightened by everything that had happened, I couldn't turn my back on Velasquez. Maybe it wasn't love I felt for her, and maybe she didn't need my protection, and maybe I couldn't explain what I felt even to myself. None of that mattered at the moment.

All that mattered was that if she was going on with Reyes, I had to go with her. Xibalba hadn't quacked for me yet, and if it ever did, I wanted to be there to hear it. And if it didn't, I wanted to know how *La Raza Unida* had found this place, and just where the hell it was.

I waved to Velasquez and Reyes, then checked the strap and carbiner that attached my backpack to the rope. It seemed solid enough. After slipping my arms through the shoulder straps, I sat on the waist belt and buckled it over my thighs. With great trepidation I crawled to the edge of the cliff, forcing myself to look across the canyon, not down into the churning river full of rocks and broken trees.

Nothing prepared me for the feeling I had when I finally let go of the cliff and hung in my backframe harness as it slid down the rope toward the center of the canyon.

The bouncing sway turned my stomach over and over.

The roaring sound overwhelmed my brain.

The twisting river below kicked my fear up into my throat.

I gasped for breath. The waistbelt squeezed the circulation out of my thighs. The pack straps cut into my armpits. The pain stopped everything else.

When I looked back to where we had started, I realized I was already halfway across the canyon. When I looked to where Reyes and Velasquez waited, I saw them gesturing for me to join them. In either direction I had to go just as far on the swaying rope, so I clenched my teeth and grabbed the rope. Pulling myself a few feet the first try wasn't much of a triumph, but it reassured me for the second pull and the third, until I realized I was actually getting closer.

And each pull was getting harder.

My shoulders ached. My biceps burned. My arms sagged under their own weight. The shoulder straps cut into my armpits, and I knew they were cutting off the circulation.

Still I had twenty yards to go—sixty feet that might as well have been sixty miles. It was too far. Too damned far. I grabbed the rope with both hands and tried to chin myself on it to take the pressure off my armpits.

My fingers slipped.

I fell.

The jerk of the straps sliced into pain. A vision of blood spewed past my face.

I screamed.

That saved me. I heard myself scream. I felt the panic running rampant in my mind, and I stopped it. I had no choice—if I wanted to live.

Forcing myself to breathe deeply stilled the last tremblings of my panic. With a wave of my hand to let Velasquez and Reyes know I was all right, I began again to pull myself toward them. Each inch seemed like a foot, each foot, a yard, each yard like ten yards, but finally I had worked myself to a point where I was hanging almost within reach of the cliff.

I looked up into the face of a grinning Reyes. He lowered an end of our grass line to me, and even though I wasn't sure it would bear any of my weight, I grabbed it. With Velasquez and Reyes pulling, I got close enough to grab a vine with my other hand. My fingers ached, but I pulled myself even closer until I got a foothold, and finally climbed the last eight feet up to join them.

After I crawled over the rim, I collapsed into a blur of rainbow images.

Velasquez and Reyes freed me from the pack, then rubbed my arms and legs. Velasquez was saying something, but between the ringing in my ears and the roaring of the canyon, I couldn't hear her. But I could still see the images.

Feathers and headdresses, shells and bone, masks and jaguar skins swam just behind the shifting patterns of Velasquez and Reyes above me. "Help," I whispered, feeling all too much in need and too foolish at the same moment. "Please?"

She leaned down and kissed me on the forehead, then put her lips close to my ear. "You will be all right, Martin. Cacabe thinks we should sleep."

"Not here," I shouted.

"No. Not here. As soon as you can walk we will search for a quieter place."

"Now."

"Soon." She continued to rub my arms and I closed my eyes and let her. For the moment at least, I didn't care if we ever went anywhere else.

My rest didn't last long. Velasquez helped me to my feet and then into my pack. It felt like it was full of stones. Reyes led us away from the canyon along a narrow trail bordered by fist-sized rocks. Velasquez walked behind me. I walked because I had to. Six months of interrogation had turned my muscles to jelly, and the trip across the canyon had wiped out any energy I had to overcome my poor physical condition. But I kept walking anyway until my thighs burned with pain.

Looking up I saw that the trail headed up a ridge, and

Reyes was already fifty yards ahead of us. "This is it," I said. "Tell him no more." With that I sat down.

Chapter Thirty-one

"You cannot sleep on the trail," Reyes said.

"I can. Watch me."

"You do not understand. It is not safe. I must find us a safe place to sleep, a place where we will be sheltered from the lords of Xibalba."

"Screw the lords of Xibalba. I'm exhausted." Overhead I could see the hawks rising toward the scissortail, which seemed to be flying down to meet them.

"He cannot go far, Cacabe."

"*Como no!* Of course, I will find a place."

I closed my eyes and leaned against my pack, too tired to wonder what Reyes was looking for that would indicate the kind of place he wanted for us. All I wanted to do was sleep.

How long had it been since we had slept? It felt like days, maybe weeks. How could we—

"Martin, while Cacabe looks for a place for us to rest, there is something I must tell you."

I opened my eyes and looked into hers where she knelt facing me. I couldn't read her expression.

"When you were crossing the canyon, I made an important discovery," she said. Her voice told me things still hidden in the mysteries of her face.

"You don't have to say anything."

"Yes, I must. There are things between us, feelings I have, that cannot be explained by legends and fate."

"It's all right. I know what you mean." I did know, and I also knew my fatigue wouldn't help me face it.

"No, you do not know," she said. "You think I am going to tell you that I love you, but that is not what—"

"You mean you don't love me?" The question jumped out of my mouth.

"Yes, I love you, but that is not what I was going to tell you. The problem is that I do not know how to tell you this thing that I feel deep inside me."

"Can it wait till I'm more awake?"

She looked hurt. "Yes, I suppose it can."

"It's just that I'm too tired to think straight," I said, "and that isn't fair to you."

Her face brightened. "You are a special man, Jesus O'Hara Martinez."

"Not special. Exhausted."

"I have found a place," Reyes called.

With Velasquez's help I got to my feet, and together we trudged another hundred yards up the trail. The place Reyes had found for us was little more than a wide spot in the path, but he was busy putting a ring of rocks around it—the fist-sized rocks that had lined our trail since we entered the big cave at Mesa Verde. While I struggled out of my pack and fought to keep my eyes open, Velasquez shrugged her pack off in one sinuous movement and began assisting Reyes.

As soon as I unrolled my sleeping bag, I jerked my down jacket out of the pack, folded it up for a pillow, and stretched out on my back on top of the bag.

Velasquez said something I didn't understand, but when I opened my eyes to look at her, she and Reyes were lying beside me and Reyes was snoring noisily. I smiled even as I fell back asleep.

The long trail was hot. The jungle was close. The shadows were thick. The protruding root of a tree formed a seat with a back where a weary man could rest for a moment.

The first owl landed on a branch in a tree across the trail and balanced on its one leg. "I am Onelegged Owl," it said. "Who are you?"

"True Jaguar."

"True Jaguar is dead."

"Great True Jaguar is dead. I am the son of the grandsons of his son, Seven Jaguar."

"You must go back to where you belong, True Jaguar. This is the land of the lords of Xibalba, and no place for a mortal man like you."

"I cannot go back."

"Go back!" it screeched as it launched itself into the air. "Go home, human! Go home!"

The scissortail circled overhead. The hawks flapped their way higher and higher toward it. There was no sun.

The second owl was shaped like an arrowhead, pointed and sharp, and its eyes were pink, and its feathers were black. "I am Shooting Owl," it said. "Who are you?"

"I am True Jaguar."

"Are you the son of Seven Jaguar's sons and grandsons?"

"Yes."

"Why do you bring the infants with you?"

"I bring no infants."

"You lie, True Jaguar. Turn back. Go away." It launched itself into the air screaming, "Go away! Go away, liar!"

The hawks seemed no closer to reaching the scissortail.

The third owl circled once revealing its red back and its golden horns before it landed on the branch. "I am Macaw Owl," it said. "Who are you?"

"Go away. I have answered your brothers. That is enough."

"You are the one they call True Jaguar."

"Leave me alone."

"You are a foolish liar whose seed will die in this place."

"Go to hell."

"You should go to hell, True Jaguar. There you will be more welcome than you are here. Go to hell," it cried as it took off from the branch. "Go to hell."

The hawks had stopped flapping and were riding the thermals. The scissortail still flew a long way above them.

The fourth owl had no body or legs. It only had a skull-shaped head and short, narrow wings that it moved like a hummingbird's to hover in front of the branch where its brothers had perched. "I am Skull Owl," it said. "You are True Jaguar. Do you have a message for the lords of Xibalba?"

"No, I have no message."

"Then go home, True Jaguar. Go back to the lands of mortals where you belong."

"I cannot go home."

"Then I will return, and you must give me a message for the lords telling them how you want to die."

Laughter.

"Until we meet again, True Jaguar."

More laughter.

Skull Owl broke from its hover and silently flew away.

The scissortail appeared to be climbing away from the hawks high above the jungle.

Vines grew visibly longer in just a few seconds. Tendrils searched for purchase on the rocky trail. Jungle thickened. Light faded.

Shooting Owl returned and swooped around me. Before I could turn to protect myself, he jabbed his pointed head into my shoulder blade again and again. Pain throbbed through me, but my body hung suspended in thick air, muscles paralyzed, unable to move. My bladder screamed for relief. My hip wept with a pain of its own.

I opened my eyes.

Overhead the hawks climbed up toward the scissortail.

Underneath, the small rocks that had cushioned my fatigue had grown to jagged boulders fighting their way into my body. With a groan I rolled to my side on an aching hip, then pushed myself to a sitting position. Someone must have beaten me while I slept, because I hurt all over.

Beside me, Velasquez slept on her back with a contented smile caught on her lips. Beside her slept the snoring Reyes. Welcome to Xibalba, I thought, land of the twisted reality, where the needs of a Guatemalan nut-case rested on the aching body of an unbeliever like me. The grin I felt didn't quite make it to my lips.

First I needed to relieve my bladder. Then I needed to do some stretching exercises to work the kinks out of my body. After that it was up to Reyes. I looked at my watch, then unfastened its strap and took it off. Its bizarre time would only drive me crazy, so I stuck it in my shirt pocket even as I caught myself looking at the bare spot on my wrist above my slightly swollen hands.

Only as I stood up did I realize how truly stiff and sore I was. From my shoulders to my feet, every joint protested my movement with persistent signals of pain. But as much as my body hurt, I knew that moving would help reduce the pain, and I began rotating my shoulders and flexing my hands as I walked across the trail to find a place to relieve myself.

"Who are you?" a voice asked.

Looking up, I was surprised to see Onelegged Owl sitting on a branch of a tree. "I'm Jesus O'Hara Martinez, terror of the underworld. Who the hell are you?"

"I am Onelegged Owl, messenger from the lords of Xi-

139

balba. Go back to your own world, Jesus O'Hara Martinez. Go back to the land of the mortals."

"We've already had this conversation, Oneleg. I can't go back, so why don't you and your brothers just save yourselves the trouble and leave me alone." To emphasize my point, I started urinating.

"You are a fool, Little True Jaguar," it said.

"Maybe so, and maybe not."

"If you do not leave now, you will never be able to leave."

"And if you'll just fly down here, I'll piss on your feathers. Now leave me alone."

"You are a fool."

I fumbled with the flap on my holster and pulled the 9 mm automatic Reyes had given me. "I'll give you three seconds to leave me alone," I said.

Old Oneleg laughed, so I aimed carefully and pulled the trigger. The pistol bucked in my hand as it fired, but Oneleg never moved. He just kept right on laughing.

Chapter Thirty-two

Reyes shouted something I didn't understand. I stared at Oneleg for a long second, then stopped urinating and pulled the trigger again.

Oneleg squawked and fell. The branch fell away from the tree. Oneleg flapped furiously, rising toward me.

I ducked.

"You will die!" it screamed as it flew past my head. "The lords of Xibalba will chew your bones to dust."

A pistol barked three times behind me.

I spun around in time to see Reyes fire twice more.

"Meet us at the crossroads, you flying son of the great whore," he said. Then he lowered his pistol and laughed as Onelegged Owl flew quickly out of sight.

"Damn," I said, tucking myself back into my jeans. "I don't believe all this crap. I dream about that blasted owl and then he shows up."

Velasquez had walked over to me, then put an arm around my waist. "You dreamed about him, Martin?"

"Tell us."

As simply as I could I described the dream and the visit by the four owls.

"And Skull Owl asked for a message?" Reyes asked.

"That's right. Why, does that mean something?"

"It means only that we should prepare a message to send to the lords of Xibalba, a question to ask them that they cannot answer."

"You mean a riddle?"

"Is that your word?"

"Yes, Cacabe. *Acertijo*."

"*Si, acertijo*."

I looked at them both. "Well, I don't know any riddles except why that owl isn't dead. Surely one of our bullets hit him."

"Perhaps," Reyes said, "and perhaps not. *Un acertijo, eh?* I think I know the one they cannot answer."

"Well, Cacabe, are you going to tell us?"

"No. If you know the answer, they might trick you into telling. If I am the only one who knows, they will have to trick me, and then only I will carry the blame if I fail."

"What's so damned important about this riddle business anyway?"

"It is a test," Velasquez said. She kissed my cheek. "You know how the lords like tests."

I returned her kiss and ignored her comment. "So what's next, Reyes? Does this trail take us to the magic crossroads?"

"*Que si!* It must."

"Then let's get on with this, okay?"

She squeezed my waist and grinned. "Do you not want to eat first, Martin?"

The press of her body against mine made me want to do something besides eat. "No. But if you two want to, I'll eat a little."

"Let us walk for an hour or two," Reyes said, "and then—"

"Right. Who can tell us when an hour or two has passed? Or even what day this is?"

"When we stop to eat, Senor O'Hara, I will build an altar and read the stones and seeds so we will know what day this is."

141

I walked over to my sleeping bag and began stuffing it into its sack. "Maybe we haven't missed the Twelfth Night fireworks yet."

They both looked at me as they started getting their own gear together.

"You know, the night before Epiphany? The night when you shoot off fireworks to celebrate the coming of the wisemen to Bethlehem? . . . I guess you don't know."

"It sounds like fun, Martin."

"Yeah, it was. Our priests didn't much like children having fun, but at least on Christmas and Twelfth Night they tolerated the idea that kids could have fun in church without being sacrilegious," I said, cinching the stuff sack on my sleeping bag.

Velasquez shuddered. "What about your parents? Did they not encourage you—"

"Papa died when I was thirteen. Mama used to say, *Play at home, pray at church.* She wouldn't even let us go to Twelfth Night until we had taken our first communion." I tied the sleeping bag to the top of the pack frame. "Papa always said, *Your mother is right. Listen to her.* So," I said, slipping my stiff arms into the shoulder straps, "Twelfth Night was something special for me. Guess they won't have it here, though."

"I suspect not," Velasquez said. She already had her pack on, and Reyes was ready to go.

"Next year in Jerusalem," I said as I stood up.

Velasquez laughed. Reyes looked very puzzled. "It is a joke, Cacabe, a play of ideas about hope for the future." She rattled something to him in their Indian dialect and a smile spread across his face.

"So are we going, or not?"

"I will lead," Reyes said, starting up the trail.

"What about our pistols?" I asked, falling in behind him. "Are they going to do us any good against the lords of Xibalba?"

"I do not know."

"Wouldn't it be nice to have some idea before we come up against them?"

Velasquez took my hand. "Why does it matter if the pistols work or not?"

"Because it would be nice to be able to shoot our way out if we have to."

"Yes, of course. How foolish . . ." She looked at me, and we both chuckled.

Overhead I saw one of the hawks rising faster than the others. I pointed. "Looks like someone's about to score."

Reyes glanced up without breaking his stride. "They will fail," he said. "We must not."

I looked up again, and with all my heart I rooted for the hawks.

Chapter Thirty-three

We hiked up the trail for what seemed like more than an hour or two, pausing once to fill our canteens in a crystal clear spring, then continuing to the top of the ridge. By the time we got there, I had worked out all but the deepest soreness in my joints and was beginning to feel human again.

On the edge of the horizon I thought I saw pyramids rising darkly above the jungle, but the light was too poor for me to be certain. Even so, I felt a shiver of apprehension. Lowering my gaze to the valley between the ridge where we stood and the next ridge, I could see flashes of red in the valley bottom.

"Blood River," Reyes said.

"Another of the fabled tests?"

"Yes. We must cross it and then Pus River to get to the crossroads that lead to the circle of the lords."

"We going to eat here?"

He looked around. "Yes. This is a suitable place."

We all shucked our packs and Velasquez and I set about putting water for coffee on the camp stove to boil, and making cheese and bologna sandwiches. Reyes worked off to one side, pushing rocks with a stick into a half circle, then starting a fire. As the coffee water started to boil, I could smell the incense burning, and hear Reyes saying the Lord's Prayer.

Taking a bite of my sandwich, I turned to watch him. He followed the Lord's Prayer with a Hail Mary, then dumped a pile of crystals and seeds on a flat rock and began sorting them according to some system that made no sense to me—all the while muttering unintelligibly to himself.

Velasquez handed me a cup of coffee as I finished my

143

sandwich, and sat down beside me. Reyes was still going strong. Then unexpectedly his muttering turned into another Hail Mary and another Our Father, and he looked up and smiled at us.

"Tonight is Twelfth Night," he said.

The twelfth night after Christmas? "Impossible," I said. "We haven't been gone that long."

"The crystals and seeds do not lie, Senor O'Hara."

"Then I guess we'll see if the lords of Xibalba like fireworks, won't we." I meant it as a joke, knowing we weren't going to set off fireworks to celebrate, but none of us laughed.

"If this is Twelfth Day," Velasquez said, "that means that time is going three or four times faster than normal. Is that correct, Cacabe?"

"It means even more than that. Our first day here equals five days above. It also means that I will have to consult the name of the day on a regular basis, so that we can strike the comet at the perfect time."

A silence settled over us as Reyes started eating. I ate another sandwich and drank another cup of coffee, enjoying that silence, feeling at once closer to Reyes in spirit and farther away in reality. As though sensing my need for quiet, Velasquez leaned comfortably against me the whole time without saying anything. I liked her closeness.

When I realized that Reyes was finished eating, I said, "Time to get going." Ten minutes later we were back on the trail headed single file down the other side of the ridge, Reyes, Velasquez, and me.

The slope was easy. The trail was in good condition, and in what seemed like less than an hour, we reached flatter ground where the trail ran through towering stands of bamboo and where we were immediately set upon by mosquitos.

Velasquez rubbed some Skeeter Stop on each of us, and that kept the mosquitos from lighting on us, but we still had to walk through clouds of them until a little while later we reached the bank of the river. The clouds of mosquitos around us immediately flew to the edge of the river where they joined black swarms of their sisters feeding in the eddies.

"Blood River," Reyes said proudly.

What struck me most about Blood River was the smell, an intense version of that living odor that rises from a deer when you first slit it open to gut it. It was an internal smell, a visceral smell that made my stomach roll. There was no doubt in my mind that it was blood flowing down the river, not water. Across the river I could see the trail as it continued into the jungle, almost as though there had been a bridge or a ferry there once. "How do we cross?" I asked.

"We could build a boat," Velasquez said.

"A boat?"

"Or a raft, really. There is plenty of bamboo around here to build one with."

She was right, and it didn't take Reyes or me more than a second to recognize it. We all dropped our packs, then I got out my Crain machete and started looking for the biggest, thickest bamboo I could find. Chopping it down was fairly easy work, made difficult only by the necessity of stopping every once in a while and putting on more Skeeter Stop to replace what I'd sweated off.

Velasquez and Reyes hauled the bamboo to the river bank and there confronted the problem of how to bind the bamboo together. By the time I joined them, dragging in the last bamboo pole I thought we would need, Velasquez had figured out that we could tear strips of bamboo off the greenest I had cut, and use those strips for lashings. Her method worked quite well. In short order we had what looked like a serviceable raft about six feet by ten feet sitting on the bank of the river, and three long bamboo staffs to pole it with.

"Now comes the big question," I said. "Will it float?"

"Of course it will float, Martin. It is bamboo. The question is, will it hold all of us up?"

"There's only one way to find out."

"I will pray for us, first, and ask a blessing for our boat," Reyes said.

"Raft," I said, correcting him. "Wouldn't want to confuse the gods."

He and Velasquez both knelt and crossed themselves and I felt too self-conscious not to kneel, also. I bowed my head for the same reason, and caught myself reciting the Lord's Prayer silently and automatically. Perhaps most surprisingly, I felt comforted by it. Maybe Mama had managed to pound some faith into my bones after all.

When they crossed themselves again and stood up, I stood

up, and with the two of them on one side and me on the other, we lifted one end of the raft and dragged it into the gently swirling blood. The raft rode higher in the blood than I expected it to.

"Looks all right," I said. Grabbing one of the poles, I stepped out onto the raft and bounced a little. "Feels all right, too. Get the packs and we'll put them on first."

Three packs and three people didn't seem to bother our little raft at all. When we were all loaded, we pushed away from shore and out into the current.

A lashing popped loose. Its broken end flopped uselessly into the bloody stream.

"No problem," Velasquez said, setting her pole and trying to push us toward the other side of the river. "It will hold."

A second lashing popped, spattering blood on my arm.

The three of us pushed together with our poles, but the current held the raft in the middle of the river. The swift current pulled us downstream against all our efforts.

"Faster!" I shouted. "We have to pole faster."

The third lashing popped loose, then the fourth.

We poled faster.

The current pushed harder.

"Go! Go!" I shouted. More lashings popped loose.

A third of the raft began to split off. The raft spun as we poled. Reyes growled in anger. He threw himself flat on the raft, holding the two parts together with his bare hands.

"We're almost there!" Velasquez shouted. "Push, Martin! Push!"

Two more lashings broke.

I pushed. She pushed. Reyes growled. The current swirled. Suddenly we slowed. She and I poled even harder, away from the current, toward the shore and safety.

"Hurry," Reyes said in an unnaturally calm voice. "I cannot hold on much longer."

We slipped out of the main current as an eddy swept us toward the mosquito-covered bank. As soon as we bumped the shore I set my pole as hard as I could in the river bottom and pushed.

"Get off! Get off! Both of you!"

Velasquez threw the packs ashore, then jumped herself, landing in the middle of a black swarm of mosquitos. She immediately turned and grabbed the side of the raft. Reyes crawled off to join her.

The split widened as the rest of its lashings gave way.

"Look out!" I shouted. Releasing the pole I jumped to the side of the raft, felt it give under my foot, and jumped from there to shore.

The raft, suddenly freed of its burden, bumped gently against the bank.

"Pull it ashore," I said. "We're going to need it to get back."

By the time the three of us managed to haul the raft all the way up on the bank, it was in two separate pieces, and a third of the lashings holding those two pieces together had come loose.

"I do not understand what happened," Velasquez said, examining the lashings. "They should not have torn loose like that."

"Don't worry about it." I put my arm around her shoulders. "We'll fix it when we come back, and at least this way we won't have to cut new bamboo."

She shook her head. "It still does not make sense."

"Let's get away from all these mosquitos, and see if we can get back upstream and find the trail."

"The trail is right here," Reyes said. He was already wearing his pack.

We picked ours up and joined him where he stood by a trail leading into the jungle. It was bordered by fist-sized stones. I turned around and looked back across the river, then pointed without saying anything. The trail that had brought us to Blood River was directly across from us. We hadn't gone downstream at all. I could even see the marks where we had dragged the raft down the bank. A long sigh escaped my lips.

"Welcome to Xibalba," Velasquez said softly.

"Amen. Let's get out of here."

We put on our packs and started hiking along the trail, going up again, up a new ridge whose other side no doubt contained our next obstacle—the Pus River. I could hardly wait.

Chapter Thirty-four

The top of the new ridge was flatter and less rocky than the one before it had been, and a cool breeze blew over its crest. We decided to eat there and rest. Once we ate, none of us felt like going anywhere, so I pulled my sleeping bag out of its stuff sack and fluffed it out onto a soft-looking piece of ground covered with low grass. Velasquez brought her bag over to mine, and zipped the two of them together.

I didn't need a formal invitation, and quickly took off my boots and socks. Velasquez stripped to her bra and panties before sliding down into the double sleeping bag. A glance at Reyes showed him already in his bag on his side, with his back to us. Even though I felt suddenly exposed, I took off my shirt and jeans, rolled them into a pillow, then slid in beside Velasquez.

She greeted me with a fierce embrace and chewed the kisses from my lips.

"Easy," I finally whispered. "Gently, gently." I knew that Reyes wasn't asleep, but I didn't care.

Longer, slower kisses led to a sensitive union that was quickly overrun by our bodies thrashing for relief. I peaked first, but she was close behind me, and we tumbled down into panting exhaustion together.

Velasquez put us on our sides this time, and even though I wanted to talk, to tell her how special I felt in her arms, my brain couldn't seem to reach my tongue.

When I woke up we were curled up together on our sides, spoon-fashion, with her head resting on my right arm. The ground beneath us felt like a rocky washboard. The light was the same uniform grey as when we had fallen asleep. Reyes's sleeping bag lay empty, and I looked, but couldn't see him. High above us the scissortail circled in wait for the hawks climbing their way up to it.

"Good morning," Velasquez said softly.

"Good morning to you," I replied, stroking the compound curves of her waist and hip with my left hand. "I didn't know you were awake."

She turned over to face me. "I have been for a little while . . . though I'm not really sure it is morning."

We kissed. "Does it matter?"

"No."

"Wonder where Reyes is?"

"Praying, I suspect," she said. "I smell copal burning."

Only when she said that did I detect the scent. "Maybe we should get dressed before he comes back."

"Maybe we should make love again."

We kissed again.

"Maybe you're right," I said, taking her fully into my arms.

For reasons I didn't understand, we had a very awkward time coupling and never quite found a rhythm that was good for both of us. That struck me as funny, and as I climaxed a long twenty or thirty seconds behind her, I giggled.

She giggled, too.

We looked at each other and giggled some more—and were still giggling when Reyes walked back into camp clearing his throat.

"It is all right, Cacabe," Velasquez said. "You will not embarrass us."

"But you embarrass me," he said, sitting on his sleeping bag with his back to us. "You have no sense of decency."

She looked at me, and I looked at her, and we both giggled again. Our amusement only tapered off as we broke apart and searched the depths of the sleeping bag for our underwear. Reyes had the camp stove going, and as we dressed, I smelled coffee perking. All of a sudden I felt very positive about everything.

"Well, Reyes, what's on today's agenda?"

Without turning he pointed down into the valley. "First we must cross the Pus River, then find *el cruce de los señores Xibalba.*"

"The cross roads"—I dug my cup out of my pack—"that's where we have to pick one of the colored roads, right?"

"All roads here lead to *la plaza de los señores.*"

"Why are you calling them *los señores?*"

"Because they are *los señores*, the lords of Xibalba."

"Of course. How foolish of me to think otherwise."

Reyes grunted.

Velasquez slapped me on the butt. "Get off the bags, comedian, so we can roll them up."

I spun around and grabbed her, pulling her tight against me and covering her nose and cheeks with kisses.

"Martin!"

"Shirlito!" I said before covering her mouth with mine.

"You waste our time," Reyes said.

"That's a matter of viewpoint," I replied after I released Velasquez and began unzipping the bags. "All a matter of viewpoint, eh, Hunahpu Woman?"

She gave me a nod and a lopsided smile, but there was a questioning look in her eyes.

In a few minutes we had restuffed our bags and joined Reyes around the stove to share in the coffee and some oatmeal he had made. We ate mostly in silence, and it wasn't until we were cleaning up that Reyes said, "I have read the seeds and stones. It is your January 9 above. Three more earth days have passed."

"Just because we slept?"

"No. Because that is the way of Xibalba—to confuse us."

"But we still have sufficient time, Cacabe?"

"Yes. I believe that is so. While you lay in your lust, I prayed to Tohil and Cristos and even Dios Mundo, the god of earth, for answers. I received no sign, but I learned nothing bad, either."

"That is good, is it not?"

"Yes. Even though Xibalba plays *la tracalera* for us, I cannot believe otherwise."

"So, let's hit the trickster's trail," I said, "and see what else this place has in store for us." A few minutes later we were on our way down the trail and I was humming to myself.

"What is that song?" Velasquez asked.

"Uh . . ." I had to pause for a second to remember the lyrics. " 'Six Jolly Coachmen.' We sang it at camp when I was a kid."

"I can tell it is a happy song. Are you happy, Martin?"

"Yes," I said, skipping ahead several quick steps and patting her on the butt. "I'm happy."

She swatted my hand away and flashed me a grin at the same time. I fell in behind her again, humming the song, realizing as I did so that I'd probably be humming it all day. It was one of those tunes that was hard to get out of my head.

"There," Reyes said.

The trail ahead of us leveled out for thirty or forty yards, then stopped at the edge of a yellowish-green mire. Pus River. All of a sudden I could smell it and wanted to throw up my breakfast. By the time we reached its edge, I could at least tolerate the odor.

"How will we cross that?" Velasquez asked. "It's as thick as tapioca pudding."

"Yuk. I'll never eat pudding again."

"No raft will work here."

"Maybe not," I said, "but we could probably build a floating bridge—if there's enough bamboo around here."

Velasquez pointed upstream. "There? Is that bamboo?"

It was, so I shucked my pack and took up my Crain machete, cutting while they hauled the bamboo to where we wanted to cross. It took almost fifty pieces of bamboo and hours of work to construct six sections of bridge each about two feet wide and twenty feet long.

"Think that's enough?" I asked.

"We can only lay them across and see," Reyes answered.

The first section was easy. We stood it on end, then let it fall with a sickening splat onto Pus River. A terrible stench rose around us, then drifted away. Velasquez turned away and vomited. I didn't blame her.

If there was a current in that river, it wasn't noticeable, and I walked out to the end of the section and back with no trouble. Getting the second section down was trickier. I carried one end and Velasquez carried the other, but as she got past the halfway point, the first section started to sink and the bilious odor rose from the river again. I had to manhandle the second section into place by myself. The same with the third.

When I got back to land after putting the third section into place, I sat and rested for a minute or two. Reyes went out on the bridge and fastened the sections together with some bamboo hooks he had cut.

"Perhaps Cacabe and I can lay the next section, Martin."

"No," I said, shaking my head. "I don't think so. You'd both have to get out on the end, and then you'd sink. Let me rest for a minute more, and I can do it."

When Reyes finished hooking the sections together and came back to shore, I grabbed the fourth section and marched out to the end of the bridge. Barely pausing to plant my feet, I heaved section four out in front of me and danced backward.

It flopped into the pus a foot or two in front of section three. I came back for number five and Reyes went out and hooked four and three together.

When I threw five into place, I could see that the last section was going to reach the opposite bank with length to spare. "Help me pull this end up on shore a little," I said. "Maybe that will help anchor it."

After pulling the end up on shore a yard or so, then wiping the disgusting pus off our hands onto the grass, Reyes went out and hooked the fifth section to the fourth, while I waited beside the sixth section. He came back all too soon for my tired muscles.

I had been right about the distance. The free end of six landed on the bank, and despite the nastiness of our chore, I felt good about the bridge.

Reyes had his pack on and the last of the hooks in his hand and barely let me get off the bridge before he went across. Velasquez followed him once he stood on the other shore, and I followed her. It had taken us the better part of four or five hours, I guessed, but we'd—

"Go back! Go back!" a vaguely familiar voice cried.

There above us hovered the Skull Owl of my nightmare—wings and head, but no body or feet.

"Go back!" it cried. "There is nothing for you here."

Chapter Thirty-five

"We have come to challenge the pitiful lords of Xibalba," Reyes said. "Tell *los señores* we are coming." He almost sneered the command.

"No!" the owl screamed.

"Yes!" Reyes screamed back. "Take our message to your weak, stupid, and incompetent lords. You have no choice, Skull Owl, for I know who you are and I order you by name."

Skull Owl hovered lower. "Then give me your death message, surface fools. You will die for your arrogance."

Reyes smiled and his face shifted into an expression of great strength—an expression like those carved on many a stone wall in the jungle. "I will give you a question for *los señores.*"

A detached voice whispered, *Be careful, Xablanque.* Several seconds passed before I realized the voice was in my head.

"Ask them this," Reyes-Xablanque said. "What has two heads and two tails, walks on two legs, and signals the defeat of the lords of Xibalba?"

"Fools!" Skull Owl screamed as it climbed swiftly over our heads. "Be gone before I return. Go home. Go home."

"What does all this mean, Cacabe?" Velasquez asked.

I wondered the same thing without fully wanting to know the answer. But I did want to know the solution to his riddle.

"It means we have chosen correctly," Reyes-Xablanque answered. "Let us get away from here and clean the filth from our bodies. Then we can give thanks and offerings in our prayers."

"Yes. We must pray to Tohil and Cristos." The words came out of my mouth on their own, and a deep chill ran down my spine.

Velasquez spun around to face me. "What, Martin? What did you say?"

I struggled to keep her in focus. "N-n-never mind," I stuttered. "Uh-all I want to do is get cleaned up. Come on. Let's go." I was aware the whole time that another subtle shift had taken place in the world and I had shifted with it.

Velasquez wet a bandana and gave it to me. I wiped my hands as I walked, wondering what fate God had in store for us.

The path narrowed soon after we followed it into the jungle, so I took the lead with my Crain, hacking young bamboo and sticky vines out of our way. The more I hacked, the thicker they seemed to get and my arm ached with every stroke until I was swinging the Crain with willpower only. Eventually I chopped through to a wide, clear stretch of the trail bordered by thick, ankle-deep grass, and let myself collapse onto the soft ground. "You sure we're going the right direction?"

"Yes. The stones still mark the way," Reyes-Xablanque said, pointing to them. "This blocking of the path is only another trick from the lords."

Velasquez sat down beside me. "If Xablanque cannot find the way for us, who can?"

Xablanque grinned. "And so it begins. True Jaguar prays to Tohil and Cristos. Hunahpu Woman recognizes her brother. The lords of Xibalba must feel the earth trembling as we approach their enchanted circle."

I shook my head to clear away his words, but a bright mist lingered around my thoughts like a gauze mask that blurred everything except a central group of images.

Xablanque. Hunahpu Woman. True Jaguar. Those were our names before we had names. Without totally accepting it, I understood that. Those were our names when we lived in the myth. That, too, I understood. And those were our names for the confrontation with the lords of Xibalba.

Another chill raced down my spine. It was crazy. This whole thing was crazy. I knew who I was, and it didn't have anything to do with True Jaguar.

"Up and at 'em," I said, shoving myself to my feet.

"But Martin, you need the rest as much as—"

"Later. We can rest later." I walked quickly to where the vines closed in on the trail and started hacking again, forcing myself to concentrate on clearing the way. But the questions and the names swirled out of the mist until I started singing in time with the hacking.

> *Six jolly coachmen sat in an English Ta-a-vern.*
> *Six jolly coachmen sat in an English Ta-a-vern.*
> *And they deci-i-ded, and they deci-i-ded,*
> *And they deci-i-ded, to have another flagon!*

The more I hacked through the vines and bamboo, the more my singing sounded like growling until suddenly I broke out of the jungle and stumbled to a stop on a low grassy knoll. The ground sloped steeply away into the jungle again, but no more than two hundred yards in front of us, like a giant *X* sliced neatly out of the trees and undergrowth, four roads came together, one yellow, one black, one red, and one blue. I had the most awful feeling that I had seen them before.

""*El cruce de los señores.*"

"The son of Seven Jaguar's sons comes to the crossroad of The lords of Xibalba," Velasquez said, taking my hand. "The legends come true."

Deep in my gut I knew what she said was true on some primeval level. I had no idea of how to cope with it.

"Look," the man who had all too recently been Reyes said, "the trail widens for us."

I stared at him and saw as much old Mayan myth in his face as modern Queche daykeeper—as much Xablanque as Reyes. I jerked my head around and looked at her. "Hunahpu Woman," I whispered.

"True Jaguar," she responded.

My knees buckled and everything went black.

Beasts too frightening to remember charged through my head. Faces in agony split open, silently miming screams. Cold balls of light tumbled down the rocky hill to crush my unprotected soul. Seeds of darkness took root like mesquite to suck my heart dry of light and life. Voices rose out of the darkness.

Then the voices danced around me. The light flickered and shifted with them. I tried to move. Something pinned me to the ground. Something wet covered my forehead and eyes.

"True Jaguar?"

"Don't . . . don't call me that."

"But you are True Jaguar."

"No."

"*Que si.*"

"I am . . . I am . . ." Only one name came to me and I refused to say it.

"You are True Jaguar."

She took the wet cloth off my face, and I opened my eyes to stare into those dark windows of her soul.

"Hunahpu Woman."

It wasn't her voice.

It was mine. My body trembled violently and she held me in my arms as I closed my eyes.

"How is he?" I heard someone ask. *Xablanque.*

"I am . . ." My throat was dry.

"He is not yet coherent."

"Yes . . . yes, I am O' . . . uh . . ."

"Here, you are True Jaguar. You must be. It is necessary for you to accept that if we are to win."

"But you don't—" A cup touched my lips, and I raised my head and greedily swallowed the sweet tea.

"Not so fast. It is not good for you."

Reluctantly, I drank more slowly.

True Jaguar, a voice said in my head. *You are True Jaguar.*

"Jesus O'Hara Martinez," I whispered. "And you are Shirlito, and he is Cacabe Reyes."

"Yes. That is right. Just close your eyes and rest."

I did as I was told. Darkness stalked me with slow, sinuous steps, crept close, and sprang for my throat.

Screams.

Echoes.

Voices.

Owls. Four owls arguing over my carcass. I assumed my form and growled, cursed them with my deepest hate, and . . . they disappeared. In their place stood a priest holding an obsidian knife high over his head. Feathers covered his body. Red and black designs were painted on his face. His upper lip trembled in a fanatic curl. I growled again, and he, too, disappeared. Someone prayed.

"Lord Tohil, for the moment I borrow a second of your breath and a grain of your body as the blessing and the favor to shine your clear light—"

"Help me."

"—on my humble works, or my service, my pointing and mixing of the stones and the seeds. Please, Lord Tohil, join with Cristos to speak to me through the mothers, the fathers, the seeds and the stones. Please Lord Cristos, join with Lord Tohil to speak to me through—"

"Help me."

"—the mothers and the fathers, the seeds and the stones."

"Please help me."

"Converse dear lords, for this one question, in wind and cold, and bring—"

"I am here, True Jaguar."

"—us the answers of the moment and the answers for all every day."

Soft hands squeezed mine, and I felt a blister. The praying voice drifted into the background.

"You have slept a long time."

I opened my eyes. She smiled at me.

"Are you feeling any better?"

"What happened?"

"You collapsed from exhaustion. Xablanque said you entered the vision world. I think you were just worn out."

"Xablanque?"

"Yes. He is praying for us."

"Hunahpu Woman?"

She smiled again. "Yes. I am Hunahpu Woman for as long as you need me."

"He's praying for Cristos and Tohil to speak to him through his seeds and stones, isn't he?"

Her smile slipped away and her eyebrows arched in question. "Do you understand what he is saying?"

"Uh"—I listened for a moment, understanding his every word—"I guess I do."

"Then you are True Jaguar." She kissed my bewildered head.

Chapter Thirty-six

His words were as clear to me as though they were in English—but they weren't English. I knew they weren't. And they weren't Spanish, either.

He was speaking Queche. I don't know how I knew that, or how, how—"How?" I croaked.

"Listen to me," she said. "*I accept this task, my work, my service. You, lords, favor me, giving to my head the counting of the days.*" She looked at me. "Did you understand that?"

"Yes. Do you want me to repeat it?"

She kissed my forehead again. "Do you need to?"

"Well . . . I guess not." A shiver ran through me and I pulled myself closer to her. "But it scares me. I feel like I'm deep inside myself looking out through foreign eyes."

"Just let it happen, True Jaguar. The transition will be easier to accept and adjust to if you don't resist."

"Do we have to call each other by those names?"

"We are who we are. You may call me any of my names."

"Then I'll call you . . . I don't know." I gazed at her face, in that moment caught a glimpse of how much I loved her, and shook my head. "Maybe it'll come to me. How long have I been out?"

"We've all slept—you longest of all."

"I'm hungry."

"Suddenly I am, too. We can fix something while Xablanque is praying."

She climbed to her feet and only then did I realize that I was wearing only my underwear. "Where are my clothes?"

"Your pillow. What do you want to eat?" she asked, kneeling by her pack. "We have plenty of oatmeal, a little bit of bologna left that we probably ought to eat, two kinds of cheese, Swiss and cheddar, some peanut butter, trail food, raisins, nuts, chocolate bars, some smoked sausage I want to save, and—"

"Bologna and cheese—with lots of mustard," I said as I pulled on my jeans.

"That sounds good to me, too."

"It ought to sound odd, don't you think?"

"Why?"

My shirt smelled more than a little lived in, but I decided to wait another day before changing to the only clean one in my pack. "Well, if I'm True Jaguar and you're Hunahpu Woman and he's Xablanque," I said, buttoning the shirt, "shouldn't we be eating something besides bologna and cheese with extra mustard?"

"You mean Queche food? Have you ever eaten that stuff?"

"No, but shouldn't we—"

"Most of it's awful. You have to grow up with it to like it, I think. Too much chili pepper and cumin in everything. It was the worst part of going there in the summer. I used to take as much American food with me as I could."

"Doesn't sound very, uh, *patriotic.*"

She laughed. "Sometimes you say the strangest things."

I sat back down to put on my boots. "Look, Huna, the last thing I need right now is to be laughed at."

"Oh?" She rolled her shoulders back and leered at me. "Other than your bologna sandwich, what *do* you need right now?"

My eyes suddenly focused on her breasts thrusting against

her blouse. I blushed as I turned away and concentrated my attention on getting the seams of my clean socks straight on my feet.

"I'm sorry," she said with a giggle. "But you're so easy to tease. . . . And I like the way you look at me."

I pulled on my boots and jumped when someone moved—

"If you two are finished playing your sweetheart games I will tell you what the gods have told me." Xablanque's eyes glistened wetly.

"You are the one who brought us together," she said. "You must adjust to the results of that. So, tell us what Tohil and Cristos said."

"Huna's right," I added.

"Huna? Why do you call her—"

"I like it." She smiled.

"She is Hunahpu Woman."

"Maybe to you and the lords of Xibalba she is, but to me she's Huna—and if she likes it, it's none of your business, Xablanque. You got that?"

He stared at me for a long moment, then dropped his gaze with a frown. "Of course, True Jaguar, if that is what you wish from her."

"And I'll call you T.J.," Huna said. "Here's your sandwich."

I took it with a smile. "I like T.J."

"Do you want one, Xablanque?"

"Yes." His frown deepened. "In front of the lords of Xibalba, we must not use these childish names."

"Right."

"Ditto. What did the gods say?"

"That we are no longer in their provinces, and although they can give their opinions and advice, they can be of no direct help in what we have to do."

"So what does that mean to us?" Huna asked, slathering mustard on more bread.

"It's what I told you before," I said before he could answer. "It means we're not in Kansas anymore, Dorothy, and we're all alone on the yellow brick road, and we've got to save ourselves."

Xablanque frowned. "Tohil and Cristos are always with

us. We are never alone. But this is neutral land. Their power is limited here by their decisions."

"Then we're on our own?"

"Is he right, Xablanque? Are we on our own?"

Suddenly his eyes opened wider. "Do you know what tongue you speak?"

Huna shook her head. "I thought it was Queche, but now I'm not so sure."

"It is a tongue older than ours, a mother-tongue with no name known to me, but Queche, still." He crossed himself, folded his hands, offered up a muttered prayer.

Huna crossed herself, and so did I, bowing my head for a moment, sharply aware of what I was doing. But for the first time since I had refused to return to my catechism lessons when I was eleven, it felt comfortable to cross myself and bow my head.

"We must go on and find a hummingbird," Xablanque said. "We can eat as we walk."

"Do we have to rush? Can't we at least enjoy our breakfast before we trudge off to meet satan's helpers?"

"No," Xablanque said.

"Yes," Huna replied. "Eat your sandwich. Walking while you eat will do your digestion no good."

We sat and ate, Xablanque, Hunahpu Woman, and me, True Jaguar—three mythological characters sitting in the Mayan underworld eating sandwiches of bologna, mustard, and cheese. All the while I had the urge to say something, as though I should contribute some wisdom or knowledge or opinion about what we were doing in Xibalba. Nothing came to my mind.

"I have finished," Xablanque announced.

"Drink some water and relax a minute. Let your food settle," Huna said to him even as she looked at me. "In a few minutes we can go on to the crossroads."

He did as she ordered, and I followed suit before checking my pack and pulling it on. "I'm ready."

"Yes, I can see that you are. Now we can go, Xablanque."

"If you will give me the machete, I will lead the way."

I pulled the Crain out of its sheath and handed it to him, curved steel handle first.

After hefting it with an admiring smile, he said, "We go."

Xablanque led the way. Huna followed and I took up the

rear. The light over the jungle seemed to have brightened, and for the first time I saw flashes of red and yellow and blue flitting among the trees before the path wound once again into the thick of them.

Knowing there was life in the trees, probably macaws and parrots, cheered my soul. For all the uncertainty nagging at the back of my brain, I felt a sense of confidence that grew a little with each step deeper into the jungle. Maybe that was because I knew that we were not walking blindly into a trap set for us by the lords of Xibalba, nor would we be facing some wasteland of death where nothing grew.

Just the opposite was true. Every step the vines and underbrush and occasional stands of bamboo beside the trail grew closer and closer together. Every step required four, then five, then six hacks with the machete. Soon Huna had to relieve Xablanque at clearing the trail, and not long after that I had to relieve her. The bamboo grew so thick that even the Crain's full guard did not protect me from bruised knuckles. After thirty steps, I was totally exhausted and would have given the machete back to Xablanque except that I saw the crossroads through the trees.

"There it is," I said, the sight invigorating my arm. Another forty hacks and we were in the clear again with the trail splitting the junction of the red road and the yellow one at forty-five degrees from each.

No sooner were we all out of the undergrowth than a voice screamed, "Fools! Who are you?" Skull Owl circled over the crossroads.

"You know who we are," I shouted. "We are Xablanque, and Hunahpu Woman, and True Jaguar, come to destroy the lords of Xibalba, you half bird."

"Then hear this message from the lords," Skull Owl said as it circled lower and lower. "They command you to come to the great ballcourt and play a game for your lives. There you will die."

"Don't bet what's left of your body on it," Xablanque said.

"Follow Black Road to the circle of the lords," Skull Owl called as it began to climb again. "The lords await you."

Chapter Thirty-seven

Xablanque waited until Skull Owl flew out of sight before leading us up onto the crossroads. I was surprised to discover that the roads were some kind of cobblestone with an unevenly worn crystalline surface. The roads weren't colored. The stones were refracting light. Except for Black Road—its surface was made of black stones that looked like granite.

A bird called close to my back and I spun around in time to realize that Xablanque was making the sound. He repeated the call seven or eight times until it was answered from the jungle in the quadrant between Yellow Road and Blue Road. Moments later a flash of color darted with a buzz out of the trees.

"Who calls me?" a voice asked.

"Xablanque calls you," he said.

"Xablanque is dead. All the old gods are dead." The voice came from the flash of emerald and red buzzing around us— a hummingbird. It moved so fast, I found it difficult to keep track of. One second it was a shifting blur of color against the gray sky, and the next second it disappeared against the dark wall of the jungle.

"The genius of the gods never dies. The spirit lives forever. I carry the spirit of Xablanque. This woman carries the spirit of—"

"Now I know who she is," the hummingbird said, "and I know her secret. Who is this feeble mortal with you?"

It took me a long moment to realize that it was talking about me. "I am True Jaguar, descendant of Seven Jaguar and Great True Jaguar."

"And I am Hunahpu Woman."

"I said, I know who you are. Do they not teach women to listen anymore?" It zoomed closer to Xablanque. "What do you want from me? Why have you called me away from the flowers? What right have you to stand at the crossroads of the lords of Xibalba? Why was I—"

"We need your help," Xablanque said.

"Why should I help you?"

"Because we are in need," he answered simply.

"That is no reason. That is not even a—"

"We are in need," he repeated.

The hummingbird disappeared from sight and sound. Xablanque waited, staring at the jungle with shining eyes. Then after a minute or two, he whistled a different call, a shrill loud sound that hurt my ears.

"Stop it!" the hummingbird screamed as it zoomed out of the jungle straight toward us.

I grabbed Huna's hand and dropped to a crouch. Xablanque was already down on one knee.

Buzzing like a tiny saw, the hummingbird bounced off Xablanque's hat, knocking it from his head. "Talk to me, you stupid bird, or I will do it again." He grabbed his hat by the brim and stood up.

"Stay down," Huna said, squeezing my hand. I didn't need any encouragement.

The hummingbird zoomed in again. Xablanque swatted at it with his hat. A thump was followed by an angry scream.

"Talk to me, hummingbird," Xablanque said. "I have no quarrel with you."

"Do you know who I am?" the hummingbird asked as it darted back and forth over Xablanque's head. For the first time I could see how large it was—as big as two fists held together, probably the biggest hummingbird that ever existed. Its throat was scarlet and its body was iridescent emerald green.

"I am Huitzilopochtli, Lefthanded Hummingbird, god of Anahuac and all the Nahuatl, god of the Toltec and the Mehica, god of the Aztecs and—"

"The god of bloody death," Huna said.

"No," Hummingbird said. "I never demanded the blood and never wanted it. The Mehica corrupted my name. The Aztec minister Tlacaelel corrupted my name. He started the bloodthirsty cult and ripped my heart from the body of eternity."

Xablanque dodged another attack and swung his hat at the bird again, but missed. He stuck two fingers in his mouth and whistled even louder.

Without reason, I stood up.

"T.J., be careful."

"Why are you attacking us?"

"Because your idiot friend whistles to pierce my ears."

"It hurts mine, too. Stop it, Xablanque."

He looked at me, and I thought I saw a little uncertainty in his face before he turned away. "As True Jaguar commands," I heard him say.

Huna stood beside me, one hand on my arm, the other held out with fingers closed. "Please come talk to us," she said.

To my surprise the bird flew straight to her and perched on her wrist. It was a full nine inches tall. "I thought hummingbirds had to fly all the time?"

The bird ignored me and seemed to be addressing Huna. "My name is Huitzilopochtli. I am Lefthanded Hummingbird, first god of the Mehica, above all other gods—even Quetzalcoatl. I was shamed by Montezuma Illhuicamina and his three sons. I was shamed by his grandson, Montezuma Xocoyotzin, who some call Montezuma the Great. I piss on Montezuma the Great. I am Lefthanded Hummingbird, shamed by the lords of Xibalba. What do you want from me?"

"How did they shame you?" she asked.

Lefthanded Hummingbird fluttered its wings, but stayed on her wrist. "The lords of Xibalba told the minister Tlacaelel to demand that the Mehica make bloody sacrifices in my name. I fought back with the Michoaca and others, but even so, my true power was eventually drained away. Then the lords brought me here and made me king of the hummingbirds of Xibalba so they could laugh at me. Even the puny lords of Xibalba have more power now than I do."

"We need your help," Xablanque said.

"I have nothing left but my pride, thoughtless one," Lefthanded Hummingbird answered. "There is nothing I can give you. I have no powers. Besides, your reasons are not enough to make me help you."

"We go to fight the lords of Xibalba," I said.

"To help us would be to gain revenge."

"I have already gained all the revenge I can."

"How?"

"I sent my daughter Malintzin to help the false god Cortez defeat the Mehica."

"Malinche, the great whore," I whispered.

Lefthanded Hummingbird chirped. "Some call her the

great whore, but those who lived should have thanked her and me for putting an end to the blood cult that would have sacrificed them all. Malintzin was the best of my creations."

"But you got no revenge on the lords of Xibalba."

"I am too old for any more revenge."

"Too old and too weak," Xablanque said. "We must look for another."

Hummingbird disappeared from Huna's hand with a violent buzz. An instant later it flashed past Xablanque's head.

"Ow!" Xablanque said, grabbing his ear. "If you're not too old to do that to me, why can't you do that to the lords of Xibalba?"

"Is that what you want from me?" Hummingbird asked, moving back and forth in front of us like a shuttlecock.

"Yes. You know the circle of the lords?"

"Of course."

"Then go with us there, and do to each of them what you just did to me. Poke them each in the ear."

"Why?"

"So we can learn which are real and which are statues. Can you tell them apart?"

"Not when they sit still."

"Do you know them by name?"

"No," Hummingbird said as it lit once more on Huna's wrist, its curved, pointed beak pointed at Xablanque.

"Then perhaps if you poke each of them in the ear, they will give away their names."

"Perhaps, but what good will it do?"

"It will help us take the first step toward defeating them," I said, feeling a sudden need to be a part of the conversation. "Wouldn't you like to see the lords of Xibalba defeated?"

"Don't be stupid. There's nothing I would like more than that except to get my powers back. You three couldn't do that, too, could you?"

"No, we have no such ability," Huna said. "I am sorry." With her free hand she stroked Hummingbird's head and back.

It stared up at her for the longest time before it said, "All right, but not just for revenge. I do it because Hunahpu Woman carries a hope I cannot deny."

"What do you mean?" I asked.

165

"She carries your children," Hummingbird said, "the son and the daughter who will lead the Queche to greatness again. Do you know nothing?"

My mouth fell open, but nothing came out. Huna pregnant? With my—our children? Twins?

"I am not so sure," she said.

"Be sure." Hummingbird tilted its head back until she started stroking it again. "I have seen them and they are both beautiful."

Her eyes met mine—her glistening eyes—and her face radiated an unearthly light. "Our children, T.J."

With Lefthanded Hummingbird between us, there was no way I could take her into my arms, yet in my uncertainty, that was the one thing I needed most to do. "Uh, our children? Are you—"

"The prophecy speaks only of one child," Xablanque said.

"So what?" Hummingbird followed its question with a warbling that sounded almost like laughter. "Prophecies have been wrong before."

"I do not believe," Xablanque said with a shake of his head, "that you can know so much about—"

"Look!" Hummingbird pointed his beak at the sky.

We all looked up and saw a falcon tumbling down from where the barely discernible scissortail circled above us. One of the falcon's wings flapped for control while the other flopped around its body. After falling for what seemed like forever, it plunged into the jungle.

"The first rocket has failed. *Cometa Xibalba* still flies."

For the briefest instant I saw Cacabe Reyes, the Guatemalan *brujo*, in place of Xablanque, but the instant passed and he was Xablanque once again. "That's only one," I said with more confidence than I felt. "That's still leaves two rockets to destroy the comet."

Xablanque shook his head. "The comet comes."

Chapter Thirty-eight

"Let's go poke the lords," Hummingbird said as it launched itself off Huna's wrist.

She took my hand and gave me a quick kiss. "Yes," she said, "let's go poke some life into the lords of Xibalba."

"We will take Red Road," Xablanque said.

"How do we know that's the right one?"

He smiled. "There are no right and wrong roads in Xibalba. They all lead to the circle of the lords, but some lead there more easily than others. We will take Red Road."

Then I remembered. Cacabe meant red road. "Lead the way."

Lefthanded Hummingbird flew ahead as we walked down Red Road toward the circle of the lords, Xablanque almost marching, me and Huna walking quietly in step, holding hands.

"Are you excited, T.J.?" she asked, breaking the silence. "About this?"

Huna grinned. "About our children."

"Yes," I said without hesitation.

"You don't sound excited." The disappointment was heavy in her voice.

"I think I'm in shock." I tried to smile at her, but my face wouldn't quite cooperate. "A month ago I didn't even think I had a future at all. Now all this, and you, and you're carrying our babies. That's a lot to absorb—and hard to get too excited about when we're headed for a showdown with the lords of Xibalba."

"Are you happy that we're going to have children?"

"With you I'd be happy doing almost anything." There were so many things that had changed between us that I wasn't sure about much except how I felt about her. Even the way she talked was different. But then, so was the way I talked. I tried to sound positive. "Huna, I think I can cope with this if you'll give me time to adjust to it all."

She still looked disappointed, but something else changed the shape of her mouth. "We have even more reason to defeat the lords, now."

An image of her swollen in pregnancy and swinging a war club flashed through my mind. "You'll have to be careful."

"I'm not sick, T.J. I'm pregnant."

"You'll still have to be careful and let me and Xablanque handle the physical part of—"

"T.J.!" Huna grabbed my arm and forced me to stop and face her. "Listen to me. We're in this together—you, me, and

167

Xablanque, equal partners in this fight. I'll do what I have to do, when I have to do it, and you can't interfere. You have to promise me that. If the lords discover dissension between us, they'll try to use it against us. Now, stop worrying about it. We'll be all right."

Anger, love, and concern roiled through me.

"Hunahpu? True Jaguar? Why do you stop?"

I waved to Xablanque who had stopped fifty yards or so ahead of us and stood staring back at us with his hands on his hips. "Be there in a minute," I called. Then I looked straight into Huna's wonderful eyes. "It won't be easy—not with . . ." The right words wouldn't come. "I'll try to stop worrying, but I can't promise anything. I, uh, well, that's just the way it is. That's how I feel."

Her eyes flashed with amusement and affection. She tilted her head sideways and we kissed.

"That's how I feel," Huna said with her lips still very close to mine and her body pressing against me.

"She is already pregnant," Hummingbird said, circling close overhead. "Leave her alone."

His voice startled me, but Huna only held me tighter, and her mouth fought to keep my lips on hers.

"Hurry up," Xablanque called. He looked nervously up at the sky, then back to us. "There will be time enough for wallowing in your lust, later."

I pulled back from her enough to see her whole face and grinned. "Do you have any idea what he and Hummingbird are talking about?"

Her grin was crooked, as though something else was trying to take its place. Her eyes flicked toward Xablanque before they met mine again. "Not a clue," she said.

"Should we pay any attention to them?"

"Only after you kiss me again."

I obliged her, but out of the corner of my eye, I could see Xablanque. His arms were folded across his chest and his head was thrown back. When Huna's lips and mine pulled apart after a series of tiny kisses, I looked up, too. The pleasant mood was broken by the sight of the scissortail and the two remaining hawks. "They're gaining on it, don't you think?"

"You saw what happened to the first one," she said.

"It takes more than one fallen bird to make a pile. Just because one failed doesn't mean that the others—"

"What about the lords of Xibalba?" Hummingbird asked as it circled close to us again. "How will you fight them with your bodies locked together? A beast with two backs is no match for a lord of Xibalba. Let's go. Let's go." Hummingbird flew over Xablanque's head and back down the road.

"Come on." Huna took my hand and led us off toward Xablanque. "We have to assume the other two rockets won't succeed, that it's up to us to destroy the comet."

"Heroes to the end," I said. "Will you marry me?"

"What?"

"I said, will you marry me?" The words surprised me. The feeling behind them did not. I had just never before allowed myself to think about getting married again. Once had seemed like more than enough, but if I was ever going to take that risk a second time, I wanted to take it with Huna. "When this is all over, I mean. Will you marry me when this is over?"

She smiled and squeezed my hand. "Yes, T.J., I'll marry you. As soon as we have accomplished our task, I'd be delighted to marry you."

"We must go faster," Xablanque said. Without waiting for us to close the thirty-foot gap between us, he turned and started his purposeful march again.

Only then did I notice the low stone walls flanking the sides of the road. "Look." Hand in hand Huna and I walked to the side of the road and squatted in front of the wall. Rows of elaborate carvings, no glyph more than two inches high, covered the face of every stone in the wall.

"Ancient," she said.

"Can you read them?"

"No. Xablanque," she called. "Can you read what is written here?"

He stopped, turned, and looked at us with frustration written all over his face. "It doesn't matter."

"But what does it say? How do you know—"

"It doesn't matter, True Jaguar, not to us. Please come with me."

"Can you read it?" We stood as I asked the question and walked to join him. "Well, can you read it?"

Warren C. Norwood

"I read a small part while you two were doing the dance of heat. It is the story of the creation of Xibalba."

"You'd better stop talking about True Jaguar and me like that, cousin Xablanque."

"So how was it created? What does—"

"Don't make fun of our feelings. You helped bring us together."

"—about Xibalba?"

Xablanque snuffled like he was clearing his nose. "Hunahpu Woman, if you must act out your lust, please keep it away from my presence."

Huna took three quick steps and slapped Xablanque on the arm, hard enough to knock him off balance. "Don't talk to me about lust. Don't tell me what I can and can't do in your presence. Don't belittle the feelings I have for True Jaguar. What do you know of feelings and love?"

Xablanque stood back from her, anger and defiance scrawled on his face, and something unreadable written in his eyes. I didn't know whether to be proud of Huna or upset with her. She was overreacting, but I sensed there was something much older than his words, some sticker from their past between them that was the real cause of this outburst.

"I had my duty," he said.

"Yes, and Carlita had your baby."

He looked down at his feet. "It was Eight Batz, the holiest of days. You know that. There was nothing I could do."

"You could have been with her when she died. You could have loved her enough for that."

"You're an American," he said, raising his eyes to meet hers. "You are a foreigner who only visited us. You have no right to criticize me."

"I am a woman. I have every right. Carlita loved you, but all you wanted was her body—and when her body died giving birth to your son, you didn't care."

There was their problem laid out for me to see, and I was embarrassed by my presence, and embarrassed for them, too. This was the wrong time and place to be opening old wounds. They should have known that, both of them. "Why are you two—"

"Of course I cared," he said, ignoring me and stepping

170

closer to her, "and she knew it. When I sent up my prayers, they were for her and—"

"Carlita cursed you as she gave birth to your son. She screamed—"

"Stop it! Both of you." They stared at me, and I knew I understood something that they didn't. "This is what the lords of Xibalba want. Can't you see that? Isn't that what you said? That they would use dissension to divide us?"

"Stay out of this," Xablanque said. "The lords have nothing to do with Hunahpu's blame and anger, and nothing—"

"Yes, they do," Huna answered, laying her hand lightly on his arm. "We settled this argument long ago, Xablanque. But we both forgot that. I am sorry."

He looked away, down the road for a long moment before turning to face her. "You are right," he said, putting his hand on hers. "You are both right. The lords have already started their work against us."

Chapter Thirty-nine

"Are you three coming, or not?" Lefthanded Hummingbird asked. "Or is this all some trick you are playing on me?"

"It is no trick, Hummingbird," I said, taking Huna's hand. "The lords are already reaching out to distract us, but now that we know that, we can—"

"Oh, shut up and let's go," Hummingbird said.

Huna made a brief laughing sound. "Ordered around by a hummingbird. What have we come to?"

"*Ube Xibalba*," Xablanque said, looking up at the ever-present drama overhead.

"Well, whatever it is, it's time to get on with it. Lead kindly, bird."

Lefthanded Hummingbird zoomed in a circle around us, then darted down the road and paused, waiting. We were already walking, Xablanque in the lead again, Huna and I hand in hand behind him. I was content to walk without speaking, and so, apparently, was Huna. As we walked several miles deeper into Xibalba, the carved walls bordering the road gradually rose from knee high to waist high, then higher. As they rose, so did a disquieting tremble within me.

Beyond the walls, the jungle appeared to grow thick and heavy. Monkeys chattered as they moved through the canopy. Macaws and parrots and other brightly colored birds sat watching us pass, or left their perches to cross the road overhead.

"It's like they're judging us."

"Of course they are, True Jaguar," Xablanque said. "They are gathering information for the lords."

"How foolish of me to think otherwise."

Huna squeezed my hand. "How much farther, Hummingbird?"

"As far as we have come and that again."

I shook my head in annoyance at that thought but kept walking, concentrating on the pace and our steps, trying to ignore a growing disturbance I felt. After another thousand steps or more, I glanced at the wall on our right, read the sign, and almost tripped over my own feet. "Stop."

"What's the matter?" Huna asked.

"Why are you—"

"Just stop a minute," I snapped as I walked over to the wall bordering the right side of the road and dragged Huna with me. "The lords will wait for us."

"So they will," Hummingbird said, buzzing close to my head, "but I will not wait for you all day."

I ignored him. "This wall, I can read it. It says, *'This is the beginning of the end.'*"

"T.J., are you sure?"

"Yes, I'm sure."

"Even I can read only a few of these glyphs," Xablanque said. "They are from a time before time."

"It says," I continued, "*'After the beginning, after the coming of Maker-Modeler, their other names of joining were listed. They are called Bearer-Begetter, Bearer-Begetter, and Matchmaker-Midwife and Xpiyacoc-Xmucane. Bearer-Begetter recognized the balance made by word and not-word, and their word was the creation, and their not-word created a dark hole under their feet.'*"

"I see the names of Plumed Serpent and Heart of Sky," Xablanque said, his voice rising.

"Yes. It lists the names of all the gods." I took several

steps down the wall, filled with an excitement that was edged with something darker. "Here it says, *'Bearer-Begetter gave the word and the earth appeared out of nothing, and because of the genius of the word, groves of pine and croton and cypress sprang from the new soil of earth, and with the trees came the animals.'*" I took another step down the wall, Then another. "Look. These are all lists of plants and animals *'born of the genius of their word.'* It's a roll call of the Mayan Eden."

Huna squeezed my hand with great urgency and pulled me farther down the wall past the list of animals and plants.

"I can read it now, too," she said. Her voice trembled. "*'From the not-word came the underworld called Xibalba. Then came the lords of Xibalba: One and Seven Death, the lawmakers of Xibalba; House Corner and Blood Gatherer, whose task it is to draw blood from people; Pus Master and Jaundice Master, whose task it is to make people swell with pus and turn yellow with sickness—'*"

She shivered. "Yuck. They're all here, Xablanque."

"I see their names." He shook his head. "But I was never told that Xibalba came from the not-word."

Scanning ahead I could see that the text changed again at a major glyph, and I knew that Huna was reading it with me.

"Look, T.J., it says here, *'Only the word of the gods, the genius of their words can control Xibalba.'*"

"What does that mean for us, Xablanque?" I asked as a galloping chill raced up my spine. "And what does that mean about me and the comet?"

"I don't know, True Jaguar." His voice sounded small and bewildered. "This is older than everything I learned in all my years as a daykeeper."

"Here! Here!" Hummingbird called from farther down the road. "Come read this, you idiots! I should have known you fools didn't know what you were doing. But this is the end of it, I can tell you that."

The three of us ran to where Hummingbird hovered in front of the head-high wall on the other side of the road.

"Sweet Maria," I whispered as I came to a stop. Under the glyph for death were three names—Xablanque, Hunahpu, and True Jaguar.

"*'Long after the One and Seven Death are gone,'*" Huna read while I forced my eyes to follow the glyphs, "*'three will*

*come to Xibalba to challenge the lords, and those three will
be called Hunahpu Woman and Xablanque and True Jaguar
and death will rule over them.' "*

"What'd I tell you?" Hummingbird said. "This is the
end for you. And for me, too. When the lords find out I
agreed—"

"Shut up," I said. "Go on, Huna."

*" 'Those three who come to Xibalba will be weak and full
of doubt. They will show their weakness and doubt when faced
by the lords, and the lords will have dominion over the changes
in those who come. Two of those who come will die. One of
them will be banished from Xibalba. The remaining lords will
have dominion over Xibalba, and new lords will spring from
the not-words to—"*

"That's enough for me," I said, squeezing her arm. "We
can turn around, right now. No matter how you divide it, that
means that either you or I or both of us aren't getting out of
here alive, and I'm not willing—"

"T.J., you're hurting my arm."

"I'm sorry," I said, releasing her. My whole body trembled.

She quickly took my hand. "It is all right. But you must
not give up so easily. We don't know that—"

"I know. I know I'm not willing to take a chance on losing
you and our . . . and our . . ." The words wouldn't come, but
tears did.

"You did not let Hunahpu read far enough." Xablanque
smiled. *" 'This is the word of the lords of Xibalba,'* it says.
Just because they carved it on their wall, doesn't mean that it
will come true. Their word is not genius."

"Then you take the chances. Huna and I are going back."

"No, T.J. We have to go on."

"True Jaguar is right. Go home! Go home to where you
belong!" Hummingbird screamed.

His screams set a dark chord vibrating inside me, but the
voice wasn't Hummingbird's. It was a deeper voice, a voice I
recognized all too clearly—the voice of Skull Owl.

"Go to hell!" I shouted back.

Hummingbird zoomed at me.

I screamed and ducked.

"Go home!"

"Go to hell," I shouted as it swooped again.

Huna swatted Hummingbird with a hard swing of her hat.

Hummingbird slammed against the wall and fell to our feet.

Skull Owl's voice laughed from the jungle. "Go home! Go home! Or you will die."

Xablanque fired his pistol over the wall into the trees.

Skull Owl screeched.

"You go home!" Xablanque shouted. "And tell your masters we are coming!"

When Skull Owl didn't answer, I looked around. Huna was on her knees with Hummingbird in her lap. Tears rolled down her face. "I killed him," she said.

I knelt beside her. "It wasn't your fault."

She bent further over and stroked Hummingbird's still body. "But I killed him."

"He's still breathing. Look at his neck."

"We must go on," Xablanque said. "We cannot stay here."

"But Hummingbird is dying."

"Maybe he's only stunned," I said, lifting him carefully from Huna's lap. He was cool to the touch, almost cold, but I could feel his heart beating. "Take your bandana," I said, "and make a sling around your neck. You can carry him while we head out of here."

"No," Xablanque said. "We have to go forward."

Huna tied her bandana in a sling and took Hummingbird from me. "Xablanque is right. It is even more important now that we go and defeat the gods." Tears still ran down her face.

I stared at her in disbelief. "What's the matter with you two? The sign says we're going to die. Hummingbird's already dying. . . . Can't you see that we have to get out of here?"

"We have to stop *cometa Xibalba*," Xablanque said. "That is the only thing we can care about. That is our *obligación*, remember?"

As Huna climbed to her feet holding the unconscious Hummingbird close to her breast, her eyes met mine. "We have to go forward, T.J."

"We can't. Not after all this. Not after everything we know now."

"We must. You know that."

I did know it. And looking in her eyes, I knew she was

175

going on—which meant I had no choice except to go with her. But I sure as Xibalba didn't have to like it.

Chapter Forty

Xablanque led the way again down Red Road, but Huna set the pace, refusing to walk any faster than she had to, so as not to jostle Hummingbird who rode in the sling, cushioned by her breasts. Huna walked with one hand holding him pressed gently against her. Had there been a way, I would have gladly changed places with him.

"Why this special concern over Hummingbird?" I asked. "A little while ago he was a mean-spirited old ex-god calling us fools, and now you're treating him like he's your long-lost child or something."

She arched an eyebrow, giving her face an odd, unbalanced expression. "He deserves no less from me, and as much from you, I would think. Or have you forgotten so quickly that he only agreed to help because of our children?"

The look on her face forced me to think before I spoke. I *had* forgotten why he agreed to help us. "I guess I got so caught up in everything else, and just the idea of the children, that I didn't waste too much attention on why he was helping us. But I'm still not sure why you are . . . I mean, he's only . . ."

"You know he is more than whatever you want to reduce him to," she said, "because you know much more than you are willing to admit, T.J." Her expression softened. "Let go. Cut your restraints. We can't afford to have you crippled by doubt. You read the wall. It's too late for you suddenly to become reluctant again."

I couldn't meet her gaze, so I looked ahead. On either side of the road the walls now stood ten or twelve feet tall, and their tops leaned away from the road. The walls appeared to rise and curve away from the base as far into the distance as I could see where it looked like the road ran between great stepped pyramids. Whatever else the road was, it was now a trap from which we couldn't easily escape—even if we turned back.

"So now what?" I said. "With Hummingbird hurt, how do we figure out who's who in the circle of the lords?"

"We'll find a way. Have faith." She hooked her free hand into the crook of my left arm.

The smile I gave her was a weak one, and my eyes darted from hers back to Xablanque as we followed him down Red Road.

Have faith, she said. Have faith in who? Or what? Have faith in Tohil and Cristos?—who both told Xablanque we were out of their range? Have faith in the genius of the old gods? In Hunahpu and Xablanque? I had more faith in myself than in either of them.

Maybe that was it. Maybe that was what she was trying to tell me—to have faith in myself. But, dammit, how could I have faith in myself when I was no longer sure who I was? How could I have faith in some *me* I didn't even know?

Or was there a greater faith involved here?

Suddenly Huna's simple statement meant much more. Should I have faith in Tohil and Cristos and the old gods, and myself? Could I? Could I blindly give myself over to that? Was faith what this whole journey was all about? Faith in something greater than all of its components?

Without understanding why, I sensed that I had made a breakthrough and crossed myself. Then I grinned when I realized what I had done.

"All right," I said aloud. "I'll try to have faith."

"That is an odd way of—"

"Let me go," Hummingbird said from Huna's breast. "What do you want from me, you wretched woman?"

"Xablanque!" I called. "Wait a minute."

"You've been hurt," Huna said, easing the sling from around her neck.

"You should know. You hurt me."

"Only after Skull Owl possessed you," I said. "He made you attack us."

Huna slid her hand under his body and took him out of the bandana. "I didn't mean to hurt you."

"Skull Owl? That wretched slime? That putrid scum? That stinking puddle of rancid nectar? He could never—"

"What's the matter?" Xablanque asked as he stopped next to Huna. "Oh, it's Hummingbird."

Hummingbird turned to look at him. "Of course it's me, you idiot. Now make this pregnant wench let me go."

She opened her grip so that he lay on his back across her right palm and she offered him her left wrist. "Can you perch?"

With a blur of wings, he jumped from palm to wrist. "What a stupid question. Now tell me what happened."

Quickly and efficiently Huna described the series of events that led to his falling unconscious. As she spoke, tears trickled from her eyes.

"You cry for me?" Hummingbird asked.

"I was afraid I had killed you."

"You can't kill a true god—even a weak old god like me. Lords you can kill. Gods, never." He looked around. "How far have we come?"

"Miles," I said, "thousands of steps, anyway."

"Read the wall, stupid."

I read it aloud. " *This is the final warning. Go back to where you came from, or prepare to meet the lords of Xibalba and give yourself in offering.*' That's cheery."

"That's death. Go back, you three. Forget your plans and get out of here."

"What about revenge?" Xablanque asked. "Don't you still want your revenge?"

"That's my worry."

"We can't go back," I said. "We have to meet the lords and destroy *cometa Xibalba* before it destroys the earth." The conviction in my voice startled me as much as the words themselves, but even as I spoke, derisive laughter filled my head.

Chapter Forty-one

"T.J., do you hear what you're saying? Did you—"

"It is true, Lefthanded Hummingbird," Xablanque said as a smile stretched his lips. "We cannot go back."

"Xablanque, did you hear what T.J. said?"

"Of course I heard. Why are you surprised? True Jaguar only stated the obvious."

"Well, *I'm* surprised," I said.

"You should not be."

"You are crazy—all three of you. Your names were on the wall—under the glyph of death. Death. Death! Can't you hear?"

"We hear you," I said, "but we have to go on. You listen to me. We *have* to go on. We have *no choice*. Why can't *you* understand *that*?" I wished my head believed what I was saying as much as my gut seemed to.

For a moment no one spoke. With her free hand, Huna stuffed her bandana into her jeans pocket, then took my arm. Still perched on her other wrist, Hummingbird turned his head away from us and stared down the road. Xablanque shifted his weight back and forth, rocking on his heels. His smile had taken over his whole face.

"If you can still fly, will you help us like you promised?" I asked.

"I can fly," Hummingbird said, turning his head back to stare at me with beady eyes. "And I will help you. But not for revenge. I told you, I'm too old for revenge. I will poke the ears of the lords of Xibalba because I believe that one of you —this Hunahpu Woman carrying your children—will escape from Xibalba. For her sake and for the children's future, I will help you." He shook his head in a most human gesture and looked down the road again. "In the thousand-thousand years of my godhood, I cannot remember greater fools than you three."

"Fools or not, we thank you," Huna said.

"Thank me after you escape, woman." Hummingbird flew off her wrist in a buzz of wings. "Follow me, then."

He darted down the road and we followed—the three of us side by side, marching to meet the lords. I was eager and anxious, excited and frightened, knowing that I had crossed another line I didn't understand. Hummingbird's assurance that Huna would live to escape Xibalba bucked up my morale. However, my fear of the death undercut that same morale and battered the young growth of faith I thought I had felt.

What good was faith against the certainty of death that kept closing in on me? I didn't believe in heaven and hell, didn't believe in any afterlife populated by souls or spirits of the dead. I didn't believe in souls and spirits. At least I hadn't before we came to Xibalba. But even if there were souls and spirits, death was death. When I died, even if there was some surviving residue of the inner me—of my personality and

179

being—that lingered on, I suspected that the cosmos would efficiently absorb that singular bit back into itself. The mysterious *I* would slowly disintegrate, along with my potential energy, until I was indistinguishable from anything else in the universe.

So, faith in what? Not in getting out of Xibalba. I believed Hummingbird when he said only Huna was going to escape. Yet even as we marched into the heart of Xibalba, closer and closer to where death awaited us, on some gut level I did have faith in something—if not in a life beyond this one, then in the living of this one to—

"You are very quiet, T.J."

"Thinking. Worrying. I don't know." I smiled at her as best I could. "Remember how I told you I felt like I was looking out at the world through alien eyes? Now I'm beginning to have alien thoughts and impulses and . . ."

"And that makes you wrinkle your brow?"

"Yes. At least partially that—and also the fact . . . well, uh, I think I'm beginning to feel as though all this is natural, as though this world and these thoughts are real and my other life was some kind of dream before I woke up here." Until I spoke those words, I hadn't realized what was actually digging at me. I was beginning to feel like True Jaguar.

"You shouldn't let that worry you."

"Why not? You don't think a total change of identity should worry me?"

She squeezed my arm and smiled, even as she forced me to keep pace with her and Xablanque. "You are who you are, T.J. You know who that is, and I know who that is, and Xablanque knows who that is. Your identity has only expanded. It has grown to meet the circumstances. But you are still you, inside."

"And who's that? Who am I?"

"You are Jesus O'Hara Martinez True Jaguar, grandson of grandsons of Seven Jaguar and Great True Jaguar. That is who you always were. But now, you can see this other part of yourself."

My birth name almost sounded like someone else's. I shook my head. "You know those little wads of paper from Taiwan that are all flattened out, but when you put a few drops of water on them they expand tenfold into flowers? I feel like

I've got one of those things inside me, and it's filling me with strange ideas faster than I can understand them."

"Like what?"

"Like suddenly I'm worrying about what I have faith in. I haven't had any real faith in anything since before I reached puberty. I just figured the world ticked along, and we ticked with it, and *que sera, sera*. Now it's like something's opened up inside me, or maybe it's because I've crossed into this new world. But whatever it is, I'm suddenly wondering, what do I really believe in, and what does courage mean, and is faith in living this life to its fullest enough for me?"

"I'm not sure I understand the last part."

"Me neither. Except that I think I have a faith in myself that I didn't have when we started this odyssey. And I think that's growing into something else."

"My prayers are answered."

"What do you mean?"

"I have prayed that you would come to an understanding like that, that Cristos would open your heart, and He has answered me."

"Don't tell me about that. I don't want to hear it. Talk like that makes me more uncomfortable than I already am."

She rested her head on my arm for a second before straightening up. "Very well. But you must promise not to resist what you feel."

"I don't think I can."

"This is good," Xablanque said.

He had looked so intent on marching down the road, I didn't think he had been listening. "Why do you say that?"

"Because we will need all the faith we can hold on to when we come face to face with the lords."

I looked down the road, expecting to see the circle or plaza or whatever the lords of Xibalba had created for their greeting grounds. Carved walls curved so high up and away from Red Road that I realized these crumbling walls were actually the walls of buildings that bordered the road. I also saw high doorways choked with loose stones and vines where the jungle had worked its way through the decay like the photographs I had seen of Mayan ruins. And for the first time since Pus River I smelled something truly awful. "What is that?"

Xablanque wrinkled his nose. "We're getting close. That is their odor."

"The lords of Xibalba smell like that?"

"No," Hummingbird said.

He startled me. I hadn't heard him fly back to meet us. "They only surround themselves with that odor to keep everyone away from them."

"Didn't bring any deodorizer, did you, Huna?"

She returned my smile. "No, but I wish I had."

"Xablanque is right," Hummingbird said. "We are getting close to the circle of the lords."

"I don't see anything," I said, looking down Red Road again.

"The road you see, True Jaguar, is illusion. You are less than five hundred of your steps from the circle."

"So now what?"

"Now I must find a way for you to spy on the lords while I poke them in their ears as Xablanque requested. Wait here."

I watched him fly high up the left building wall until he disappeared. Far above I could see one of the two remaining hawks rising to meet the scissortail. "There goes another one," I said, pointing.

Xablanque and Huna both looked up. "It will fail," Xablanque said, "as the first one failed."

For some reason I didn't argue with him. Maybe I believed he was right. "I'm hungry," I said, looking away from them.

"Me, too."

It didn't take very long to get our packs off and make some sandwiches. "That's the last of the bread," Huna said.

"What about sleep?" I asked before taking my first bite. "Think we ought to try to get some sleep before we go on?"

"We don't have time," Xablanque said.

"How do you know? When did you last read the seeds and stones, brother-cousin?"

"She's right. Better read them when you're finished eating."

He looked hard at me before nodding. We finished up the last of the cookies, too, then Huna and I stretched out while Xablanque began his timechecking ritual. Huna took my hand, and I meant to say something to her, but the next thing I knew Hummingbird was screeching at us.

"Get up. Get ready. The lords of Xibalba are all there. They're waiting for you."

I pushed myself up on one elbow and rubbed my eyes. "So? We knew they were expecting us."

Hummingbird zoomed back and forth across the road. "They are angry," he said, "very angry."

"Good."

Seeing Xablanque rub his eyes made me realize that we had all probably slept while Hummingbird was gone.

"Perhaps anger will make them careless," Xablanque said.

I shivered. "Let's pray for that or something better."

Huna crossed herself and I followed suit, then our eyes met and we both smiled. As I leaned over to kiss her, a deep voice rumbled up the road.

"Five and Thirteen Death welcome you to Xibalba."

Chapter Forty-two

I laughed. I didn't know why, but I laughed.

"Is death so humorous?" Hummingbird asked.

"No," I said, finally making the connection, "but that voice is. Sounds like one of those TV preachers. *Fiii-ev and Thirteeeen Dea-eth well-come you to Xibal-ba.*"

Huna giggled and squeezed my arm.

Xablanque frowned. "Mocking the lords will only make them angry."

"They're already angry," Hummingbird said, "but I have found a place where you can spy on them."

"It is a good thing you and I have a sense of humor," Huna said, "because this place needs some laughter."

"Amen."

Xablanque frowned again. "I have told you before that I do not see how such laughter can be——"

"Quit talking like humans and follow me," Hummingbird said, flashing fifty or sixty feet down the road.

As soon as we got close to where he hovered, he darted

into a narrow doorway. Huna got Xablanque's flashlight out of his pack for him and mine for me. Then I took hers out and handed it to her, and we gave each other a quick kiss.

"Come in," Hummingbird called.

With a nod, Xablanque drew his pistol, and ducked into the darkness. Given what had happened with Skull Owl, I didn't have much faith in pistols, but I drew mine anyway as Huna followed him. When I stepped in behind her, the stench of ammonia almost knocked me back out. I held my breath and looked around.

We were in an empty room, a large empty room that seemed eerily silent. The floor was coated with slippery muck, and a play of Xablanque's flashlight on the ceiling revealed the source of the muck. Thousands of bats hung from the ceiling. We were walking through their guano.

Hummingbird darted through a doorway on the opposite side of the room without giving us time to think about the bats. That doorway led into a low tunnellike hallway, pleasantly without droppings on the floor, where I gratefully gasped for breath.

Dark shapes scurried scratchily away from Xablanque's flashlight. Distant trilling sounds stopped as we zigzagged our bent-over way deeper into the building. The walls of the hall were as covered with glyphs as the walls outside, but I had no desire to stop and read them.

In fact, they were closing in on me. I could feel them. The air smelled old and dead. Dust filled my nose.

Stone grated against stone. The whole building was about to collapse on top of us. I couldn't breathe.

"Help," I gasped, dropping to my knees. Why wouldn't my lungs work? Why couldn't I get enough air?

"Xablanque, it's T.J.! Something's wrong."

"Help," I choked.

"What is it? What's the matter?" I heard her ask from some distant place.

Something heavy rested on my shoulders. The building. It was coming down. I fought for air.

Hands covered my face. I couldn't get them away.

The darkness spun around me. My arms trembled underneath me. I was drowning. I was dying. I knew it.

"Breathe slowly. Breathe slowly. You're hyperventilating."

I fell.

Mmmmmm. Mmmm. Hummmmm.

Cloth covered my face. My head rested on something soft.

"Stupid human. How can *he* fight the lords of Xibalba?"

Who was that?

"He'll be all right. He just hyperventilated—got too much oxygen in his system. . . . See, he's coming around."

"Stupid. Stupid."

"True Jaguar? Can you hear me?"

"Mmmm."

A light shined in my face. I could see it through my eye-lids, but my eyes didn't want to open. "I can hear."

"Just relax, T.J. Breathe easy. Relax. Move that."

The light went away. "What happened? It closed in on me."

"Don't worry about it. You're all right now."

"You sure?" I asked, forcing my eyes open. My head rested in Huna's lap and I looked up at the planes of her face brightly lit on one side, dark on the other.

"Yes. Just don't breathe too fast."

"But I couldn't get enough air."

"No, you got too much."

"As soon as you are ready, True Jaguar, we have to go on. Lefthanded Hummingbird doesn't think we're safe here."

"Me neither," I said. "Help me up." They helped me roll to my knees, first, and then to stand. I bumped my head.

"Be careful," Huna said. She stuck my pistol in my holster and handed me my flashlight.

"Hurry," Hummingbird said.

"We're coming. Go on, Xablanque. I'm all right."

"I'll take the drag."

"I can do it."

"No, T.J. You take the middle for a while."

"Hurry," Hummingbird said again.

"Right." I nodded to Xablanque and felt a little light-headed. Maybe it would pass.

Single file again we zigzagged through halls and rooms. Every step made me want to scream. Several times I caught my breath coming faster and forced myself to slow them. When I finally saw light coming from the outside, I almost pushed past Xablanque to get to it.

Hummingbird perched on a vine just inside the wide doorway waiting for us. "Be quiet," he said, "and look."

Xablanque, Huna, and I each stepped into the doorway. Through a thin veil of vines we could see a small circular plaza where the four roads of Xibalba came together again in an X. Each of the three quadrants of the circle that I could see had concentric stone stairs up from the plaza to a platform where six people in complete Mayan regalia sat on benches. Vines grew around the ends of the platforms and between some of the stones, as though even in Xibalba the jungle was trying to reclaim the land and cover the artificial organization forced upon it.

I leaned into the open and looked to my right. We were standing in a doorway at the end of our quadrant, and the closest figure to us was no more than ten feet away. I motioned with my hand as I stepped back and squatted down. Huna and Xablanque squatted down beside me, and Hummingbird flew from his vine to perch on Huna's wrist.

"There are twenty-four lords out there," I whispered.

"Only twelve of them are real," Hummingbird said. "The rest of them are carved from wood."

"Okay. So you're going to fly around the circle and poke them in the ear, one by one."

"Yes, for Hunahpu Woman's sake."

"You've made that clear. The hard part for us will be watching the lords in our quadrant."

Huna stroked Hummingbird. "Start on the quadrant to our left," she said. "Perhaps that will distract our lords enough so that when you get to them they will not notice if we step out of hiding to watch their reactions."

"I can do that for you."

She looked at me and nodded.

"Well, then, let's do it."

Xablanque dug a pad and pencil out of his pack and handed it to me. I sketched the quadrant and numbered the positions where the lords and mannequins were sitting, one through twenty-four. Hummingbird waited until we had settled ourselves in the doorway before he flew out and turned left. We had to lean forward to see him poke the first lord in the ear.

Nothing happened.

He flew to the second lord and poked him in the ear.

186

"Ow," the second lord cried.

"What is the matter, Bloody Teeth," the fourth lord asked.

"Something poked me in the ear," the second lord answered.

I marked number two as Bloody Teeth.

Hummingbird poked the third lord and again nothing happened. But when he poked the fourth one, the lord cried out.

"What is the matter, Pus Master?" Bloody Teeth asked.

"Something stabbed me, too," the fourth lord answered.

I marked number four as Pus Master.

"What are you two crying about?" the fifth lord asked.

"Something poked both of us in the ear," Bloody Teeth said.

"Owww!" the fifth lord cried. "Something bit me!"

"It got Bone Scepter, too," Pus Master said.

Number five was Bone Scepter.

One by one Hummingbird poked all twenty-four of them, some of the real lords several times after they cried out, and I thought that maybe Hummingbird was getting a little revenge after all. As one would cry out, another would ask him by name what was the matter until finally I had them all identified and marked on the chart.

Hummingbird flew into the doorway, said, "Good luck, fools," then flew out again and disappeared from sight.

I started to stand up, but Xablanque laid a hand on my arm.

"Something is wrong," he said.

"What's wrong?" I asked. "We've got all the real lords located. That means we pass this test, doesn't it?"

"Yes. But there is something wrong about the lords."

"These names don't all match," Huna said, "but we knew we might run into that. You said it shouldn't matter."

"But there's something else, something about the way they answered that bothers me."

"What?"

"I do not know."

With a sigh I said, "Well, either we go out and face them or we go out and face them. If there's something out of kilter, we'll find out soon enough." I climbed to my feet. "Okay?"

"Okay," Xablanque said.

Huna smiled as she led the way out the door. "Here we go."

Chapter Forty-three

"Greetings, lords of Xibalba," Huna shouted as she stepped clear of the vines. "We have come to see you as we promised in our messages."

"Who are you?" a booming voice asked.

"Let us greet you first," I answered, stepping out beside her, "and then we will tell you whom we are."

Xablanque joined us, and we climbed down the steps, then walked together to the middle of the plaza. All the lords wore scaled vests, feathered headdresses, and jaguar skin capes with pearls and pieces of turquoise and bone sewn on them in patterns. I had to admit to myself that they were a pretty impressive-looking lot—impressive enough to make me tremble inside. But I refused to let them know that I was frightened.

"Greetings, Bloody Teeth," I said, bowing with a great flourish to where he sat.

"Greetings, Pus Master," Huna said, bowing to where Pus Master sat.

"Greetings, Bone Scepter," Xablanque said with his own bow. Then he whispered, "I know what is wrong. Half the lords are female. I never heard of such a thing."

"Maybe they got horny," I whispered back, turning toward Bloody Claws so we could address them in order of rank, lowest to highest.

Thus we ignored the mannequins and greeted each of the lords by name, Bloody Claws, Jaundice Master, Skull Scepter, Trash Master and Stab Master, Soul Burner and Mind Burner, and, finally, Five and Thirteen Death, whom the three of us greeted together.

"How do you know our names?" Five Death asked.

"It was we who stabbed you in the ears," I lied.

"What is wrong with women lords?" Huna asked.

"Who are you?" Five Death demanded.

"Nothing's wrong with women lords," I whispered to Huna, then said as dramatically as I could, "My esteemed companions

188

on this journey to Xibalba are called by names familiar to you, names that recall the destruction of One and Seven Death."

The lords growled and mumbled to each other.

"But it isn't written," Xablanque whispered. "There are no female lords in the stories of Xibalba."

"There are now," Huna whispered back.

I let the lords growl to each other for a moment before I continued. Since they already knew who we were, I figured there was nothing but dramatic effect left to us, anyway. "It is my most humble privilege, my honor, and my joy to introduce to you Xablanque, genius of the god Xablanque, and—"

"Imposter!" someone shouted. "Xablanque's dead."

"Shut up!" another voice said.

"Both of you be quiet."

"Stick it in your ear."

Laughter.

"Up yours!"

"Between your legs!"

"Out yours!"

"Sew it shut! You don't know how to use it."

"And my special privilege," I shouted, "my very special privilege, to introduce to you, Hunahpu Woman, the genius of the god Hunahpu."

More laughter.

"And who are you?" Five Death demanded.

"He is another imposter!"

"A joke!"

"A twit!"

"Kill him!"

"Silence!" Thirteen Death roared. She looked pretty fierce when she did it, too, and I had to remind myself that she was just a lord, not a god.

All the other lords fell silent.

Thirteen Death looked around the circle and gazes dropped away from hers. Finally, she nodded slowly, which made her macaw-feathered headdress look almost regal.

"Now," Five Death said, "tell us who you are."

"I am True Jaguar, grandson of the grandsons of Seven Jaguar, who was son of Great True Jaguar." My voice dropped when I said that, because suddenly the plaza was still and I was sure I could hear the lords breathing. Or was it me breathing?

After a long pause, Five Death said, "We have heard stories of a True Jaguar, but we did not believe them. We have heard stories of grandsons of grandsons of Seven Jaguar, but we did not believe them. Why should we believe you?"

I drew myself up to my full height, aware, somehow, that what I answered at this moment was all-important to us, and having no idea what to answer.

"True Jaguar has come to challenge the lords to a ball-game," Xablanque said.

"A ballgame?"

"We don't play with mortals."

"Kick his ass back to the surface."

"Kill him."

"Screw him."

"You wouldn't know how."

"Kill them all."

"Find out what the stakes are, first. What would we play for?"

This time I knew the answer and turned toward Soul Burner, who I thought had asked the question. "Our final wager would be for *cometa Xibalba.*"

"*Cometa Xibalba?*"

The lords hooted and laughed.

"You want to bet the comet?"

They guffawed and cried.

"Are you crazy?"

They pointed and giggled and fell off their benches.

"Crazy! Crazy!"

They clutched their sides and moaned.

"Kill them before we all die laughing."

None of us were prepared for that—especially Xablanque, who looked distressed. Amusement was the one reaction he couldn't understand, but then, in this case, Huna and I didn't understand it, either.

"Good," I shouted. "Good. Die laughing."

All at once they stopped, and silence filled the plaza.

"Come sit here so we can talk to you without shouting," Five Death said, motioning to a low bench in front of his.

Huna took me on one arm and Xablanque on her other,

and strolled us over to the bench. We had barely stopped before she spat on it and a cloud of steam hissed up from it.

Several lordly voices moaned in dismay.

"Must be the wrong bench," Huna said. "That bench is for cooking, not sitting."

"How stupid do you think people from the surface are?" Xablanque asked.

I shook my head. "Maybe the lords of Xibalba have such cold rear ends that they have to sit on hot benches."

One of the lords behind me giggled for a second or two, then stifled it. I glanced at Thirteen Death and saw her eyes narrowing. Whoever had giggled was in some kind of trouble.

"The lords of Xibalba have no problems with their rear ends," Five Death said as we turned to face him, "and because you are our guests, we will overlook your rudeness. You are tired. You have come a long way. We will give you a place to eat and sleep and provide whatever comforts you desire. Then tomorrow we can discuss this ballgame you wish to play."

"How will we know when it is tomorrow?" I asked. "We have never seen it dark in Xibalba."

"You will know. We will tell you." He whistled.

A man walked out of the doorway closest to Five Death's bench, a man wearing mirror shades and jungle fatigues, and carrying a rifle that looked like a Kalishnikov—one of the AK models. The man's face was dark and weathered, and his black moustache drooped down past his chin.

I was more surprised to see someone like him there than if he had shown up when we first entered Xibalba's jungle.

"Our messenger will show you to the guest house," Five Death said. "If you need anything you can't find in the guest house, tell him, and he will see that you are taken care of."

Xablanque's hand rested on the butt of his pistol, but Huna put a cautioning hand on his arm. Three pistols were no match for an automatic rifle, and we all knew it. I shook my head slightly and Xablanque dropped his hand.

The man motioned with the rifle, not pointing it at us, but letting us know that he would if he needed to. We walked out of the plaza on Black Road with him behind us, and I could hear the lords talking to each other as we left. They did not sound very happy.

The messenger pointed with his rifle to a low, stone building beside the road. Beyond it, peasant women dressed in bright-colored skirts and embroidered blouses tended a cooking fire. In the distance someone sang a slow song in a language I didn't recognize.

It was no surprise to read the series of glyphs over the door of the building when we got close to it. DARK HOUSE. "This is where they came before, isn't it?"

"Yes," Xablanque said. "This is the next test."

"So now what?"

"We go in," Huna said with a glance at the messenger.

"I will bring you torches," the messenger said.

We stooped through the doorway one by one, and Huna guided us with her hands so that once we were inside, we turned and faced the lighted doorway. The messenger was nowhere to be seen.

"We must be careful in here," Xablanque said.

"I thought that was the law of survival in Xibalba."

"We must be careful with everything from now on, True Jaguar. There is too much here that is different from the stories, too much I do not understand. One of us must always be awake. We cannot depend on what happened before. We have—"

"Take these," the messenger said from the doorway. In his hands were three burning torches. We each took one.

"And these." He handed us three foot-long cigars already lit. "All that the lords require in return for their hospitality is that you return these things exactly as they were given to you," the messenger said.

He stepped back and a stone fell into the doorway, sealing it from the outside.

Chapter Forty-four

Dark House wasn't totally dark. Horizontal slit windows up close to the ceiling of the small room let some light in, but I suspected they were there so someone could spy on us.

"Get your flashlight out, Hunahpu," Xablanque said.

As soon as she had it out and turned it on, Xablanque extinguished his torch and we followed suit.

"Now the cigars," Xablanque said.

We stubbed out the cigars. Xablanque took off his pack and rummaged through it for a moment before triumphantly pulling out a small roll of red tape. "Help me cut this up, True Jaguar."

I took out my pocket knife, Huna shone the light, and Xablanque held the tape for me to cut it—reflective tape.

Once I cut off three two-inch pieces, Xablanque put one piece over the burnt end of each cigar. "There," he whispered, leaning the cigars, taped ends up, against the back wall. "Now when the light shines on the tape, the cigars will look like they are lit. I'll burn a little tobacco every once in a while so the messenger will smell it when he spys on us. The flashlight will make him think the torches are still burning, and that's how we'll trick the lords."

"Now what?" I asked as I took off my pack. "Do you think the three flashlights will get us through the night?"

"They have to. I think now we should rest as much as possible, but one of us needs to be awake at all times in case the lords have some other surprises for us in their hats."

"You and Huna can sleep if you want. I'm not tired, yet." I wasn't tired, but I was nervous. Being locked in that room was worse than being trapped in the pyramid earlier. The air was too close—too stuffy in there.

As though sensing my feelings of confinement, Huna took my hand and squeezed it gently. "Me neither," she said.

"Listen to me, you two," Xablanque said, his face in the shadows out of the flashlight beam. "If I go to sleep, you have to stay alert—one of you does—and you have to burn a little of this tobacco occasionally." He set a palm-sized drawstring bag and an unglazed bowl on the floor in front of the flashlight. "You two can't get so involved in each other that you don't pay any attention to—"

"We understand, cousin."

The way Xablanque had said *involved* made me want to laugh, but my throat was too tight for laughter to escape.

"I am serious. Our lives are at stake here."

None of us said anything as Xablanque unrolled his sleeping bag and made himself a pillow. I concentrated on slowing my breathing. "We know that, Xablanque. You rest. Huna and I will stay alert."

He grunted and lay down on top of his sleeping bag beside

the outside wall. After Huna took her pack off, she and I moved to the other end of the room. We spread out my sleeping bag, and I was breathing heavily by the time we sat side by side.

"Try to relax, T.J.," she said softly. "You must try to relax. Think about all the air coming in those windows."

I took in a slow breath. "Good, stinky Xibalban air."

"No, not bad air. Fresh, clean Weatherford, Texas, air, blowing up from the Gulf."

"Smelling like fish." I tried to call up a picture of Weatherford in my mind, but nothing came. A shuddering sigh escaped me.

"You're not helping."

"I'm sorry. It's hard to breathe in here."

"Let's talk about something else." Her right hand traced aimless patterns on my thigh.

My throat tightened again. "What should we talk about?"

"I don't know? How about . . ."

"Let's talk about the guy who brought us here."

"Xablanque?"

"No, not to Xibalba—to Dark House. The guy in the camo fatigues, let's talk about him." Anything to take my mind off the stuffiness.

"Why? Why does he interest you?"

"Aren't you curious about how a guy dressed like that, and carrying a Kalishnikov rifle, ended up as a messenger for the lords of Xibalba?"

"You think the Russians are selling them arms?"

The sound that escaped me was more of a snort than a laugh. "I like that. I really do. But given that you can buy AK-47's and AKM's from almost any arms dealer in the world"—I paused to suck in air—"and given that ten or twenty countries make copies of Kalishnikov's, it's hard to point at the Russians."

"So where do you think the messenger came from?"

"Well, I think Xibalba probably has some connection with the South American cocaine and marijuana business. Maybe the guy's a Peruvian or Columbian or Bolivian mercenary."

"Bolivian coke mercenaries working in the Mayan underworld? Now it's my turn to like it. A little preposterous, though, don't you think?"

"Any more preposterous than our being here?"

There was a long moment of silence between us. Across the room Xablanque snored in a gutteral rumble. The flashlight had lost its brightness and I wondered again if the batteries in the three flashlights would last the night. Maybe there were some extra batteries in our packs. Had I thrown any in? I couldn't remember.

Huna yawned and squeezed my leg. "You are a very special man, T.J., but I wonder if you will ever realize how special."

"No. I've never had any reason to think of myself as special—and I still don't. Why don't you try to get some sleep?"

"I'm not tired. I want to stay up with you."

"You sound tired."

"Well, maybe I am tired, but I'm not sleepy."

A shadow moved across one of the slit windows over the opposite wall, and I saw it pause before I heard faint laughter from outside. "Listen to that. They sound happy with what's going on."

"You think Xablanque's tricks are working?"

"I hope so. Let's burn a little tobacco to keep the deception going."

"You know," she said as I retrieved the bowl and tobacco from the middle of the room, "I don't think those cigars were just tobacco."

"Marijuana," I said, crumbling a piece of tobacco leaf from Xablanque's bag into the bowl. "The old Mayan priests used to smoke pot to get instructions and visions from the gods."

"That fits. Some of the Queche daykeepers still smoke it on holy days."

"Makes you wonder if pot and tobacco are all that those cigars are made of." I lit the tobacco. "What would keep the lords from lacing them with hashish or cocaine or heroin?"

"That's scary." She shivered and leaned against me.

I let myself laugh softly as I put my arm around her shoulders and noticed with some relief that my breathing was close to normal. "With all the other threats to us here, you're frightened by the possibility of drug-laced cigars?"

"The drugs, not the cigars. Suppose they keep trying to drug us? How will we protect ourselves?"

"As best we can."

"We won't be able to eat or drink here."

"Until we run out of food and water of our own. But don't worry. We'll figure something out."

She turned and snuggled against my chest. "I love you, T.J."

"I love you, too," I whispered.

"Mmm . . . do you know that's the first time you've told me that?"

"Yes. It wasn't that I didn't want to tell you, but, well, those words are so loaded that I was afraid that you might—"

"Shh," she said, putting a finger to my lips. "Just hold me and quit worrying."

I did as I was told, content for the moment just to sit there in that stone room, cradling this very special woman in my arms, and thinking about nothing in particular. But as she relaxed, she grew heavier, until finally she was asleep and her body felt like lead. I had to lower her shoulder into my lap.

Her head rested in the crook of my elbow like a dead weight. Her shoulder dug into my right thigh. Her ribs pressed heavily on my left thigh. My legs were going to sleep. My toes began to tingle.

I shifted. She moaned.

A tear ran down my face.

What am I doing here? I wondered. How can we possibly hope to survive this insanity? Forget the comet. Forget Xablanque's plans to save the world. Why are we really here? Is this a drug dream? Is the DSA causing all of this to happen? Or is this Hell? Am I paying now for my sins?

Black questions thumped through my brain followed by the leaden knowledge that we were going to die—all of us— me and Xablanque and Huna and the babies. The babies, our babies were going to die. Why?

Because you are a coward, a voice said.

No. Why? I tried to see who it was, but my vision was blurred.

You should have returned to the surface.

Yes. No. I can't. I don't understand. Darkness chased tears down my face.

You will all die here.

Let us go. Please? Let us go.

You must leave now, mortal. You must leave—

Pain shot through my leg and I screamed.

"*Que? Que?*" someone shouted.

"T.J.? Wake up!"

I screamed again.

"Wake up!"

I opened my eyes to the darkness. I tasted salt and tears. Somewhere in the distance I heard derisive laughter that sounded all too familiar. But what shook my body and frightened my mind was the inhuman scream escaping my throat.

Chapter Forty-five

All I knew was that I couldn't stop screaming and I couldn't let go of Huna. How long I clutched her in my arms and screamed I don't know. It felt like forever.

Then without warning I realized everything was quiet in the room and Huna was holding me in her arms. A headache banged on the back of my skull like a hammer on a large bell. My face was wet with tears. I heard someone outside laughing in maniacal pleasure.

"Did you have visions?" Xablanque asked. "What did you see? What happened to you?"

I tried to answer him, but my thick dry tongue was stuck to my palate.

"Give him some time," Huna said sternly.

"And water," I croaked.

Huna held the canteen to my lips and let me drink in little sips. My mouth tasted like it was lined with salty ashes and the water didn't wash the taste away. The pounding in my head eased a little. "Voices," I said, forcing myself to sit up. "I heard voices telling me we were going to die." I sipped more water. "And telling me—telling us—to leave Xibalba."

"Dark House," Xablanque muttered.

"What are you saying?" Huna asked.

"The real darkness of this place," he said, "is in our heads, in our minds—not this physical darkness." His arm waved through the fading beam of the flashlight. "The threat of Dark House is what they can do to our—"

"You mean they attacked"—I shuddered—"you mean they *can* attack my mind directly?"

"Perhaps, yes." He sniffed repeatedly like a dog following a faint scent. "What do you smell?"

"Tobacco," I said.

"Something else, too." He sniffed again. "I do not know what it is, but we must get out of here."

"But don't we have to wait until they—"

"Not if we can move that stone door ourselves."

There was room in the doorway for all three of us, but no matter which way we pushed on the stone, it wouldn't budge—not up, not down, and not to either side. After a few minutes of pushing without results, we gave up and sat panting on the floor. The exertion had made my headache worsen. "That was a stupid idea," I said.

"Maybe it was," Xablanque said, "so now we must do the next best thing to escaping. We must fight smoke with smoke. Get me the bowl and tobacco."

I crawled across the stone floor to where we had left the bowl and tobacco, and brought them to him. Then I took my flashlight out of my pack and turned it on so he could see better. Huna turned hers off.

Xablanque took five small leather bags out of his pack. From several of the bags he poured powder into the bowl. From one, he took dry leaves and crumpled them on top of the powder. From another, he took some large seeds and laid them around the edges of the powder and leaves. Finally he took out a piece of copal, which I recognized from his day-keeping rituals, and placed the copal in the center of the bowl.

"Are you going to check the time?" I asked. "Boy, that's really going to put the lords of Xibalba in their places."

"No, I am not daykeeping. I will merely try to purify the air in here."

He lit a match and gingerly touched it to the bowl.

A foot-high blue flame shot up, followed by a cloud of sweet-smelling smoke that quickly filled the room.

"Idiot!" Panic clutched my lungs. I gasped for air.

"Relax!" Xablanque commanded. "This will not hurt you."

To my surprise I relaxed and let out a long breath. Time floated. My lungs felt clear. My headache eased. The panic passed. I took deep breaths and felt even better.

Xablanque had almost disappeared as the flashlight beam reflected off the swirling blue smoke, but I could feel Huna beside me. "Are you all right?"

"Yes."

"This won't hurt the babies, will it?" I asked, suddenly angry at him for just the possibility.

"No," Xablanque said. "Just relax and breathe naturally."

"What is all that?"

"Do not worry, True Jaguar."

I let out a long sigh, but it didn't help the irritation I felt. "Easy enough for you to say. You weren't the one who heard the voices or felt the pain or did the screaming." Huna squeezed my arm, and her presence so close beside me was most annoying. "What happens next?"

"We wait and see."

"No, I mean after they let us out of here."

"Then we challenge the lords to a ballgame."

"Basketball?"

"Yes, if they will accept that."

"And if they won't?"

"Then we must play the game they propose."

"I don't like it."

"Neither do I."

Xablanque muttered something unintelligible, then said, "We have no choice."

"You should have made them name the game before they locked us up. Why didn't you do that?"

"I never thought of it."

"Well you should have," Huna said. "You're the one who got us into this mess. Why didn't you think of it?"

"Because he's too much *brujo* and not enough leader."

"What are you two trying—"

"Stop this!"

"Who's going to make me, *concha*."

"Why you scum-sucking little pig, you can't talk to her like that." I rose to hands and knees. "I'll make you eat your tongue and that bowl of blue—"

"Eat this!"

The color of steel swished past my eyes through the smoke. I fell backward to get away from it and grabbed at the handle of the Crain. I'd show that little sonuvabitch some real steel.

199

"Stop it! Stop it!" Huna shouted. "Xablanque! T.J.! Stop it, both of you!"

I had the machete in my hand, but I didn't move. I could see Xablanque squatting in the smoke, holding his camp knife. He wasn't moving either. If I lunged forward, I could get him.

"It's the lords. They're doing this," Huna said. "They're using us against each other."

"Screw the lords." I spat in Xablanque's direction. "Screw him, too. I won't let him—"

"Listen! Listen to yourself. T.J., please?"

"He started it."

"I will finish it, too, gringo."

"Cacabe!"

Her word—his name—cut the swirling blue smoke between us, and for a brief moment I saw Cacabe Reyes Campos squatting in front of me. Then he became Xablanque again. I sat down suddenly as the smoke swirled around him. Stillness held the smoke and the smoke held us.

"She is right," Xablanque said finally. "The lords are doing this."

I sighed and slipped the machete back in its sheath on the side of my pack. "I know. I know."

"This should not . . . I mean, I am sorry."

"Me, too. But more than that, how do we fight them? How do we keep them from making us kill each other?"

"Who can say? Who can know what tricks they will use on us?"

"Well, we'd better figure something out or we're not going to beat them."

"Do not talk like that, T.J. We will beat them."

"You, maybe. Hummingbird said that you'd live."

"We'll all beat them. We can."

I glanced up away from her and saw the outline of a head in one of the slit windows. Lowering my head as casually as I could, I whispered, "We're being spied on."

"There has probably been someone watching us the whole time," Xablanque said.

"Great. Then they know about all of this, don't they?"

"Of course they do."

"How foolish of me to think otherwise."

We didn't laugh, but I yawned and felt better. "I think I'm sleepy now. How about you, Huna?"

"I could sleep. Will you stay awake, Xablanque?"

"Yes."

Huna and I curled up together on my sleeping bag, but after a long time of restless shifting, I realized that there was no way I was going to sleep. I was too afraid of what might happen—to me if I went to sleep, and to us if the lords got ahold of Xablanque's mind.

From the sound of her breathing, I guessed that Huna had fallen asleep and was glad for her. By concentrating on counting her breaths, I was able to relax, and drifted in and out of the world of half sleep until I heard a loud scraping sound.

"The lords of Xibalba await your presence this morning," a voice called from the doorway. "Will you come to the great ballcourt and greet them?"

"We will," Xablanque answered.

"First you must hand out the torches and cigars the lords so graciously provided in the condition they were given." The voice laughed.

I was on my knees by then and crawled to where the torches lay beside the back wall. Huna sat up. Taking my lighter out of my pocket, I lit the first torch and passed it to Xablanque.

"Here they come," he shouted before tossing the first torch out the door.

We sent the second and third out in quick order after the first while Huna began stuffing the sleeping bag into its sack.

"What about the cigars?" the voice called.

"Coming," Xablanque said, lighting each of the cigars in turn. "We'll be out in a minute."

Instead of tossing them out the door, he handed one to me and one to Huna, then grabbed his pack by the straps. As soon as we had all our gear in hand, we walked out of Dark House into the dull grey light of Xibalba smoking our lordly cigars.

Chapter Forty-six

The armed messenger-guard waiting for us was not the same one who had brought us to Dark House, but he wore the same uniform of jungle fatigues and mirror shades. He stood close enough to the door that I could see his rifle was one of the Chinese versions of the AKM. His unarmed assistant held the three torches and two cigars.

"Nice gun," I said as I handed the messenger my cigar.

He frowned and didn't say anything as he passed it to his assistant, so I turned my back on him and knelt beside Huna to finish closing up my pack.

"Where are you from?" the messenger asked.

"From the canyon with no writing," Xablanque answered. His pack was closed, and he was pumping up a basketball with a small hand pump.

"The lords wish to know the exact place."

Xablanque laughed. "Tell them to figure it out themselves."

The messenger motioned to his assistant who trotted out onto Black Road toward the circle of the lords, carrying the burning torches and cigars. "You will wait here."

"Anything you say, boss," I said. "Tell the lords we're practicing our slam-dunks."

"What does that mean?"

Xablanque dribbled the basketball a few times, then passed it to me. "It means jump shots to you."

The messenger's face lit up. "Ahhh. Max Zaslofsky. Bob Cousy. Bill Russell. Wilt Chamberlain. Elgin Baylor. Jump shot!"

I passed the ball to him and he did a lay-up on an imaginary basket over the door to Dark House. His rifle sling slid from his shoulder to his elbow, and the rifle swung between his legs causing him to trip and fall on his face just as he released the ball. It went straight up in the air and bounced down on his back. Xablanque took the ball on the second bounce.

"Better try it without the rifle," I said, helping the messenger to his feet.

He shook my hand off his arm with a frown.

"Who were all those people he named?" Huna asked.

"Old basketball players. Very old. Where did you learn about Bob Cousy and Wilt Chamberlain?" I asked him.

"On the LV."

"What's that?"

"The LV." He outlined a triangular shape with his hands. "The lordsvision."

"You mean the television?"

He looked confused. "What is the tell-a-vision?"

"What is lordsvision?"

"Are you so ignorant," he asked, "that you have never seen the pictures on the great triangle of the lordsvision?"

"That's where you saw Cousy and Chamberlain?"

"Yes. Every holiday we watch basketball on lordsvision. Last holiday Syracuse beat Fort Wayne in the playoffs."

I whistled through my teeth. "When was your last holiday?"

"Chacalumne 24."

"That is no date I understand," Xablanque said.

"Me neither, but if I remember correctly, let's see . . . If he saw Syracuse beat Fort Wayne in the playoffs, his last holiday was 1955. At least, that's when the game was played. God only knows when they got it on lordsvision."

"Ask him some newer basketball names," Huna said.

"Okay. How about Patrick Ewing? Spudd Webb? Petey Case? Mark Aguire? Michael Jordan?"

His face stayed blank.

"Larry Bird? Julius Erving? Kareem Abdul-Jabbar?"

He shook his head. "Are these good players, also?"

"Yes. Let's try even older. How about Moses Malone? Or Bob McAdoo? Or Jerry West?"

"No," he said, "but I have seen Neil Johnston jump shoot."

"Who is Neil Johnston?" Huna asked.

"He was a hotshot scorer, or MVP or something. Played for Philadelphia, I think, back in the early fifties. Boy, I'll tell you, this place really is screwed up in time."

"Maybe just lordsvision is screwed—"

"Come to the ballcourt," a voice boomed down the road.

The messenger's face immediately hardened. "You must go, now, to meet your death."

"Thanks a bundle," I said, shrugging my pack on.

We marched down Black Road to the circle of the lords, bouncing the basketball back and forth between the three of us. I tried passing it to the messenger, but he only blocked it with his arm and refused to touch the ball. He pointed us down Yellow Road out of the circle, and a couple of hundred yards and some fancy dribbling later we arrived at the great ballcourt.

The lords were waiting for us in stone bleachers on one side of the court, flanked on each end by ten armed messengers—guards who looked bored, or sleepy, or both—or maybe drugged. The puzzle of who they were picked at the back of my brain.

The court itself was dug below ground level. Its sloping stone walls ended at a flat court not quite as wide as a basketball court, but longer, I thought. At each end, an iron hoop stuck out from the vertical end wall about eight feet up from the court. Also at each end, the court expanded into little wings no more than six feet wide that stuck out like the top and bottom of a capital I. Not exactly a NBA regulation court, but one that would serve if the hoop was large enough for our ball to pass through.

"You are late," Five Death said.

"We came when you called," Xablanque answered. "Stick your complaints in your elevator shaft."

"He doesn't have a shaft," one of the other lords said.

"Jaundice Master does."

"A big one!"

"You'd never get stuck in hers!"

"Up yours!"

"Silence!" Thirteen Death commanded.

The bleachers fell silent.

"So, you have come to play our ballgame, have you?" Five Death asked.

"No. We've come to challenge you to play some basketball," I said. "We understand you have seen it on lordsvision."

"Bring on Mikan. Bring on Coop. Throw that ball—"

"Our game first," Five Death said. "Deathball is the game we play here."

"Are the lords of Xibalba afraid of basketball?" Xablanque asked. "Are you afraid we can beat you two on two?"

"Three on three," I said.

"Hush. Let me do this."

204

"The lords of Xibalba are afraid of nothing."

"Then let's play basketball."

"Are you imposters afraid of deathball?"

"No," Xablanque said, "but it's not as good a game as basketball."

"Basketball," one of the lords shouted.

"Deathball, bitch," another said.

"Basket-ball! Basket-ball!" I chanted. With a nod, Huna joined me. "Basket-ball! Basket-ball! Basket-ball!" Half the lords seemed to be chanting with us.

"Deathball," Thirteen Death boomed, and the court fell silent once more.

"Compromise," Xablanque said. "We'll play basketball first. Whichever team wins can name which game we'll play next. Best three out of five wins the series."

"Four out of seven!"

"Ten of nineteen!"

"Fifty of ninety-nine!"

"Three out of five," Thirteen Death said. "The winner of three out of five games wins the series, but you play deathball first. Two against two."

"Only if we can name the stakes," Xablanque said.

"Your lives!" a lord shouted.

"*Cometa Xibalba!*" Xablanque shouted back.

"Booo! Booooo!"

"Fair enough," Five Death laughed. "When you lose, you forfeit your lives."

"If we lose."

"What about tie games?" I asked.

"If there's a tie," Xablanque said, "then the game being played stays the same for the next game."

"Agreed."

"How do we keep time?" Huna asked.

"An hourglass," Five Death answered.

"Fair enough."

"And if you lose, you destroy *cometa Xibalba* before it passes the moon's orbit," Huna added.

"Agreed. Now there is one other thing you must do," Five Death said. "You must tell us where you are from."

"We are from the surface," Xablanque said. "You know that."

"Exactly where on the surface? There are many entrances to Xibalba."

"From the place with no name."

A murmur went through the lords.

"Every place has a name."

"The place where we entered Xibalba has no name."

"Then what surrounds it?" Five Death asked.

"The canyon with no name," Xablanque said.

"Kill them now," someone shouted.

"And what is written there?"

"Nothing," I said. "There are no names and there is no writing so that the entrance to Xibalba is always open."

"Anasazi," a quiet voice said.

"The tribe of Seven Jaguar."

The court was so still, I could hear the lords breathing.

"Prepare to play the game," Five Death said.

Chapter Forty-seven

"Xablanque and I will play the first game," I announced.

Huna shook her head. "The fair thing to do is to draw straws, T.J."

"No. You've got the babies to think of. They call this game deathball, remember? I don't want—"

"We draw straws. Shortest straws play."

I could tell from the look in her eyes and the tone of her voice that there was little sense arguing with her, but I didn't like the idea of her playing the lords' game. A vision of her lying on the ground in a pool of blood flashed through my mind, and I shivered. I hated this place.

She broke a twig into three pieces and held them out to us in her clenched fist. Xablanque drew first, then I drew. When we compared pieces, Huna's was the longest, and I sighed with relief.

"That means I get to play the second game," she said.

"No, it doesn't. It means that we draw—"

"T.J., I won't argue with you, but I will play. Xablanque and I will play the second game, then you and I will play—"

"Who's going to be first to die?" a messenger-guard asked

as he and one of his companions approached, each carrying an armload of equipment.

"The lords are going to die," Xablanque said.

"Fools," the messenger said, grinning like he knew some big secret, "who's going to play deathball?"

"He and I are."

"Then you better get rid of those packs and things and we'll help you put your pads and paddles on."

The leather shoulder pads were like oversized football pads, but they flapped like the petals of a flower. The knee and thigh pads were also made of leather, but with the rough side out. The wooden paddles fastened at our waists with leather straps and stuck out on either side. The helmet was a gaudy thing of rough cloth and macaw feathers. The gloves were of the same cloth and had leather palms. The shoes were Converse All-Stars just like the ones I'd worn as a kid. By the time the messenger helped me get all that on, I was already sweating.

"Are you ready?" Five Death asked from the other side of the court.

"We will be when you explain the rules," I said.

"The rules are simple," Five Death said. "The first team to put the ball through the opponents' hoop twenty times wins the game. One member of each team must always stay back at his hoop, but that player cannot hold the ball. The other player can hold the ball, but only for ten steps. There is no time limit."

"That's it?"

"Yes. You may enter the court."

Xablanque and I climbed down the stepped sidewall to the court, and Five Death rolled a white ball down the wall on his side of the court. On each step the ball bounced and gave off huge puffs of dust.

"White Dagger!" Xablanque screamed. "Watch out!"

The ball flew to the middle of the court. Xablanque jumped sideways. His body curved into a C as the ball missed him.

"What is it?"

"White Dagger. It'll kill you."

The dusty ball bounced twice, hit the end wall, and zoomed toward me with a power of its own. I dodged and smacked it from behind with my gloved hand.

The ball exploded.

Dust blinded me.

Huna screamed.

The lords roared with laughter. "Die, fools!"

I stumbled backward out of the cloud of dust in time to see a large dagger with a wavy blade flying toward Xablanque. "Duck!" I shouted. "Duck!"

He ducked and White Dagger missed.

"Get out, Xablanque!" I clambered up the lords' side of the court without looking back. They were still laughing when I reached their bleachers and grabbed the first lord I came to by the throat. She struggled, but I pressed my thumbs into her windpipe.

"Call it off, Five Death!" I said. The lord began to turn mahogany red, her dark skin turning darker.

"Call off White Dagger," I heard Xablanque shout.

"I'll kill her." A terrible power surged through my hands and I knew I could break her neck. More importantly, I knew I *would* break her neck if I had to.

"Release Bloody Claws," Thirteen Death commanded.

"Call off White Dagger."

"Release her!" Thirteen Death roared.

"No," I said, pressing even harder. Bloody Claws's eyes bulged from her face.

"White Dagger, come!"

Something flashed past the corner of my eye into Thirteen Death's hand—White Dagger.

"Release her."

"No more nasty tricks," I said, keeping my grip on Bloody Claws's throat. "We play a fair ballgame or I choke the living breath out of you."

"Kill the scum!" someone shouted.

"A fair ballgame," Five Death said. "Now release her."

"Swear it," I said. "Swear that you'll play fair or I'll kill her and choke the rest of you to death one by one."

"Kill him, now! Now!"

Several of the lords surged toward me, but I swung Bloody Claws around between me and them. She dangled from my hands, terrible *awking* sounds rasping from her throat. "She dies," I said, raising her up off her feet. Her legs kicked wildly. Fury raged through me.

"We swear to play fair," Thirteen Death roared. "Now, release my sister!"

I dropped Bloody Claws and glared at Thirteen Death. "I swear by Tohil and Cristos that I will kill each and every one of you, beginning with you, Thirteen Death, if you ever try a trick like that again. Understood?"

Bloody Claws crawled away from me and was helped to her feet by several of the other lords.

"We will not be dictated to," Five Death said.

"Then maybe I'll kill you next," I said climbing up the bleachers toward him two steps at a time. My fingers itched to feel his pulsing throat in their grip. The lords scrambled over each other to get out of my way as I climbed.

"Stop it," Thirteen Death commanded. "I swore we would play the game fairly, and I am the lawgiver of Xibalba."

I paused three steps below Five Death and waited to see what he would do. Only then did I realize how angry I was, and the force of that anger frightened me almost as much as it seemed to frighten the lords.

"He can't dictate to us," Five Death said.

"Do you wish to test his hands?"

Five Death looked away from me and I felt a sneer curl my lip. I had crossed another line, and I knew it. "So, are two of you fit to play ball with us or not?"

"Yes. Soul Burner and Mind Burner will play the first game against you. Go wait with your friends."

I narrowed my eyes and stared at her for a full five seconds before turning away slowly and walking around the court back to where Huna and Xablanque waited. The looks on their faces startled me. "What's the matter?"

"We have never seen you like this," Huna said. "Even when the DSA questioned you, even when we told you weeks later that your mother had died, you did not show this kind of anger."

With a sigh I sat down. Suddenly I felt like all the energy had been drained from my body. "I've never been this angry before. I never knew—I never understood how anyone could be this angry." A glance across the court revealed two of the lords putting on their equipment.

"You would have killed Bloody Claws," Xablanque said. "That is good. That is the best part of your anger."

"Well, I don't think it's so damn good. I never even—"

"You have shaken the lords of Xibalba because they know you would have killed Bloody Claws. But worse for them, you revealed how weak they truly are."

"Great. Let's just hope they're weak on the ballcourt, because I don't trust them for a second, and I don't think they're shaken or scared or anything else—not really."

Huna sat down beside me. "You're wrong, T.J. Even as I feared for you, I watched with fascination how they shrank from your anger. The lords are afraid of you—truly afraid—because they have probably never had to deal with the kind of anger you showed them."

"Oh, I can't believe that. Watch out. Here comes one of their boys."

A messenger strolled up, his AK slung casually over one shoulder, a black ball smaller than our basketball in his hands. "Thirteen Death said to tell you that this is the ball you're going to use, and to show you there are no tricks."

Xablanque took the ball. "Heavy. Solid rubber, probably." He dropped it and it bounced back into his hands. "Not as lively as the basketball. We'll have to remember that."

"We are ready," a voice called.

I looked up and was surprised to see Soul Burner and Mind Burner already in the left end of the court. "Well, I guess we're on, Xablanque. Let's go play some ball."

Huna gave me a kiss before I stood up and a quick hug before she let me climb down into the court.

One of the messengers climbed down from the other side wearing only a tee-shirt and khaki shorts. Xablanque handed him the ball. Without warning the messenger threw the ball into the air. "Play ball!"

Xablanque jumped, but Mind Burner beat him to the ball, drove past me, and put the ball through the hoop three times before I got to the wall and blocked her next shot.

The lords screamed and cheered.

Chapter Forty-eight

I hit the ball with my fist toward the center of the court. Xablanque missed it, and Soul Burner hit it with one of his paddles. Mind Burner ran to the right wall.

The ball caromed off a step halfway up that wall, took a crazy bounce sideways, and ended up in Mind Burner's hands. She dribbled down court toward me with an odd gleam in her eyes.

With a sudden shift she threw the ball over my head.

Startled, I spun to see where it was just in time for it to hit me in the chest.

She took the rebound off my ribs as I fell down, and she put the ball through the hoop.

"Four to zero," someone shouted gleefully.

Xablanque appeared as I struggled to my feet and knocked Mind Burner out of the way as he took the ball from her hands. He began dribbling down the court, and when Mind Burner tried to follow, I spun around as hard as I could and caught her in the gut with my left paddle.

Unfortunately, her paddle caught me in the stomach at the same time and we both collapsed.

"Go, Xablanque," I heard Huna yell as I fought my way to my feet while trying to keep Mind Burner from getting up. My breath was coming in gasps.

"Foul," the messenger shouted. "Jump ball. No point." He ran to the other end of the court to get the ball just as Xablanque put it through the hoop.

"What foul?" I demanded, panting after him.

"Player down foul," he said, taking the ball from Soul Burner. "You can't hold her down."

"Who jumps?" I asked.

"You and Mind Burner will jump in your end of the court," he said.

I stayed close to him because I knew he wouldn't give any warning, and sure enough, as soon as he got to our end of the court, he threw the ball up. Mind Burner and I banged into each other as we jumped for the ball, and Xablanque got it. He immediately began dribbling down to the other end of the court.

Mind Burner ran after him. Soul Burner moved out from under the hoop to guard him. Xablanque faked a jump shot, drove past Soul Burner, and made a nice lay-up shot, made even nicer by the fact that he got the ball on the first bounce.

Xablanque spun, jumped, and shot again.

Suddenly the score was four to two, and I felt a little better. If they didn't wear us out, maybe we had a chance in this game.

Mind Burner took the ball and ran toward me. I threw out my arms just like a good basketball player, but she lowered a shoulder at the last second and rammed into me.

Breathless, I tumbled backward, listening for a cry of foul, but it didn't come. My head bounced off the stone floor of the court. I heard someone shout, "Five to two!" then, "Six to two!" by the time I got back to my feet. A deep ache burned into my side.

The lords cheered, then moaned.

I saw Mind Burner on her back under the hoop looking very dazed and Xablanque running down court.

Soul Burner was apparently ready for his charge, but Xablanque succeeded in knocking him down anyway and put the ball through the hoop three times, knocking Soul Burner back down in the process.

"Five to six," I heard Huna shout. "Go, Xablanque, go."

Mind Burner banged me hard from behind as she ran to help Soul Burner. I stumbled, but kept my aching legs under me.

Without warning, Xablanque threw the ball. I was so surprised to see it coming that I didn't react fast enough, and it bounced past me. Running after it, I had no idea what to do, but when I saw Xablanque and Mind Burner fighting each other and running side by side toward me, I kicked the ball back past them as hard as I could.

It hit halfway up the right wall, and bounced high. Mind Burner tripped Xablanque and took the ball off the second bounce before charging toward me again. This time I met her with a charge of my own and knocked her on her butt and the ball loose.

Xablanque grabbed the free ball, ran for the other end, and took a wild shot. It missed the hoop and went into one of the wing courts. He followed Soul Burner in after it, and I managed to bump Mind Burner before she could get around me to go help her partner. I gasped for breath and trembled with fatigue. My body ached and I wasn't sure how much longer I could go on.

The ball came out of the wing chased by Xablanque. Mind Burner beat him to it and charged back toward me, pulling up short before we collided again. Then she jumped, higher than I would ever have thought possible, and shot over my head.

"Seven," the audience shouted.

I spun as she took the rebound.

"Eight," they shouted as she jumped again.

Xablanque knocked the ball from her hands and I kicked it down the court. My knees threatened to give way.

Back and forth it all went until the game became an aching blur behind my desperate need for air. I moved through a strange world of muffled pain before a surge of energy lifted me beyond it. A sudden euphoria replaced the pain and I hit Mind Burner with the full force of my body, then stepped on her as I kicked the ball to Xablanque.

Soul Burner blocked the shot and kicked the ball high into the air. It fell almost straight down the wall at our end of the court and went through the hoop.

The lords erupted into screaming cheers, and as I collapsed onto the cold stone, I knew we had lost the game.

Chapter Forty-nine

By the time Xablanque and I summoned the energy to help each other climb out of the court, the lords had left, and so had the messenger-guards. As we struggled out of our equipment, I was too tired to be very surprised by that. The three of us sat alone beside the ballcourt under the dull skies of Xibalba without speaking. For the longest time I didn't have the breath to speak with, much less the inclination to say anything.

Finally I lay back, put my head in Huna's lap, and asked, "How much did we lose by?"

"Twenty to fourteen," Huna said.

"It is my fault," Xablanque said.

"It's nobody's fault," I snapped. "It was their game, and they knew what the rules were and what to expect, and we didn't. They suckered us the first game. We just have to win the next one."

"Xablanque and I play the next one, T.J."

"Like hell you will. You saw how rough they play. I won't let you take the chance that—"

"It's not your place to give me permission or *let* me do anything," she said. "It's my decision to make on my own, and I *will* play."

A sudden movement overhead distracted me from arguing with her for the moment. I pointed. "Look."

High above us the second hawk tumbled down the sky. From the way it fell, I guessed both of the hawk's wings were broken. We watched the hawk tumble until it disappeared below our horizon.

The scissortail circled still barely recognizable against the dull grey sky, and only one hawk remained to climb after it. Would any of the rockets intercept the comet, I wondered, suddenly aware of how much I didn't want the fate of the world on our shoulders.

"I told you they would fail," Xablanque said.

"So what do you want? A medal?"

"My only desire is to destroy *cometa Xibalba*," he said. "You should know that by—"

"Well, at the rate we're going, I'd say we have about as much chance as those hawks seem to have. Less, maybe."

"We have only begun our efforts, True Jaguar. You cannot surrender to the lords, now. What is one game, when we have four left? The important thing is not whether we win the first game, but that we win three games before the lords do."

"So run for office with your little speech. If we can't beat them down there"—I waved toward the court—"then none of that fancy thinking matters, does it?"

"You're tired, T.J. Don't let your fatigue lower your defenses against the lords. The first game is over. The lords of

Xibalba won. There is nothing we can do about that. All we can do is prepare for the next game, and if we can—"

"And figure out some strategy," I said before I realized what I meant. "Of course, Huna. I'm so tired I'm not thinking straight. Maybe we can put together a game plan that will give us a better chance tomorrow."

She laughed. "Tomorrow? Since when have we had tomorrows, here? Xibalba has been one big today. But you're right. Maybe we can work out a plan for the next game. What day is this, anyway, Xablanque?"

"I do not know. When we were on the road before we met face to face with the lords of Xibalba, the day was January 18."

"*Yesterday* was January 18? Maybe you should read the seeds and stones again before each game."

"I will read them now."

"Good." For a moment I thought I saw a frown cross Huna's face, but I closed my eyes, too tired to worry about it, and drifted into a hallway of sleep full of shadows that bulged out of the walls after me. They whispered, *No today, no tomorrow. The end of the day will find you dead. No today. No tomorrow.* I turned to run and struggled to break free. Soft hands soothed me until I heard familiar voices.

"Can that be, Xablanque?"

"Yes, cousin. Today is the first day of February."

"But that means two weeks have passed since your last reading of the days, and time is out of pace."

"Yes."

"If the lords can make the days pass so quickly, can they not make them pass February 29?"

"I do not know the answer to that."

"It frightens me," Huna said.

I felt her tremble and opened my eyes. "Did I hear right? It's February first?"

"Yes, True Jaguar, it is."

"Okay, then, the question is what are we going to—"

"The lords of Xibalba have prepared a place for you to rest," a messenger-guard said from behind us.

I turned to look at him and suddenly thought I knew why they all looked somehow familiar. "Where are you from?"

"Here, True Jaguar. We're all from here."

"You didn't come from someplace on the surface?"

"No. Only the guns and clothes come from the surface. We steal the guns from the Communists and the clothes from the Americans. The Italians sell us ammunition and give us the sunglasses. You like them?"

"Very nice," I said, "very nice. But why do they give you the sunglasses?"

The messenger laughed. "So they will not anger us. You must know of the Italians. They hate terrorism, so they try to love terrorists. We told them that if they didn't sell us the ammunition and give us the sunglasses, we would become terrorists in their country. They even offered to sell us French jet fighters, but we have no way of getting them here."

I stared at the grey reflection in his glasses and saw how much emptiness there was in Xibalba. "Who do you deal with, the Cosa Nostra?"

He spat. "Never. They are scum on a cesspool. We deal only with the Italian government. Now, up. I must take you to Razor House."

If what he had said hadn't been so absurd, I might have laughed. Instead it depressed me, because I was all the more sure that these messenger-guards were Arab terrorists—for all that they looked Mayan. "What happened to the twins in the old story when they went into Razor House?" I asked Xablanque as I climbed wearily to my feet. Every muscle that moved protested with pain.

"You are hurt," Huna said.

"The boys promised the knives in Razor House that they would taste of the flesh of all the animals on earth," Xablanque said.

I shook my head. "That doesn't leave us much to offer them, does it?"

Xablanque smiled, then turned to follow the messenger. "Perhaps, and perhaps not. We shall see what happens, True Jaguar. Be surprised by nothing."

Huna fell in step beside me and took my hand as the messenger led us down Yellow Road away from the direction of the circle of the lords. The native women in their bright clothing turned away from us as we passed. The men, some with AK's slung from their shoulders, followed us with their black eyes. Naked children ran squealing into dark alleys. The smell of boiling cabbage and the chords of Hispanic rock and roll drifted out of several doorways we passed, but we walked without talking—Huna for her own reasons, me because I was fighting the pain—until we came to a brown, stone building set well back from the road by itself. The glyphs above the door read, RAZOR HOUSE.

"This is where you may rest until the next game," the messenger said.

Xablanque led the way through the low doorway and Huna and I followed. As had happened at Dark House, a stone door fell behind us and locked us in. In Razor House, however, plenty of light came through the large windows. I looked around almost in disbelief.

Except for a path from the door to a raised wooden platform in the center of the room, and the ceiling above that platform, the floor of Razor House, the ceiling, and all the walls were covered with knives—pocket knives, camp knives, butcher knives, carpet knives, flint knives, paring knives, hunting knives, throwing knives, obsidian knives, fillet knives, survival knives, bone knives, whittling knives, butterfly knives, skinning knives, jade knives, boot knives, carving knives, razors, bayonets, kindjals, stilettos, daggers, tantos, switchblades, and jambiyas. They all gleamed sharply as they turned toward us. It was the most incredible collection I had ever seen.

"Now what?" I asked when I reached the platform. Deja vu wasn't a strong enough term to describe what I felt. For some reason I was sure I had seen this room before.

"We want your blood," a chorus of curiously deep voices said. The knives appeared to be talking.

"Xablanque?"

"I do not know."

On impulse I reached over my shoulder and pulled my Crain Predator machete from its sheath tied to my pack. Waving it over the knives, I said, "You're going to have to beat my knife before we give up any blood."

The knives moaned. At least it sounded like a moan. Then they rattled like pagan sticks.

"We offer you the blood—"

Several knives flew through the air.

217

Instinctively I swung the machete at them.

They clattered noisily to the floor. More knives moaned and rattled.

"Stop!" Xablanque commanded. "We offer you the blood of the lords of Xibalba to wet your edges and their flesh to test your strength. What is our blood in comparison to that?"

"We want both," a singular voice said.

The knives chanted, "Both! Both! Both!"

"Then come and get it," I screamed. I whirled the blade and knocked dozens of knives off the ceiling. All I could see were the knives and how weak they were against my machete, so I waded into them, using the two-and-one-half-inch-wide flat of my blade to sweep them out of my way. The knives were at my mercy.

Screams filled the room—Huna's screams.

I spun around in time to see her pinned to the wooden platform by daggers.

Chapter Fifty

I heard myself roar as I charged back to Huna, scattering knives into the corners as I went. The Crain sang with the ring of steel on steel. Each shock of contact sent a thrill up my arm and filled the room with a keening that hurt my ears.

Xablanque knelt over Huna, pulling daggers out as fast as he could and flinging them aside.

Her eyes were wide with terror.

Only when I threw myself down beside her did I realize that the daggers were pinning her clothes, not her. She was not hurt. At least she wasn't bleeding. Not yet. Instinct told me what to do. "Get down, Xablanque," I said.

He huddled down so that Huna's face was protected by his body.

I passed the machete blade over her body with the flat of it parallel to the floor. The daggers popped out of the floor and slammed against the Crain's blade. Each dagger shattered into dozens of pieces that fell to the floor.

The keening in the room subsided and a new sound took its place, a sound that rose and fell in pitch like the tremolo of an organ's bass notes. I could feel the vibrations in my bones. Dust filtered down from the ceiling. My lungs gasped for breath.

Xablanque helped Huna sit up. "What is it?" she shouted over the vibrato.

Somewhere deep inside I knew what it was, but I didn't understand what I knew and didn't have words to explain it. I shook my head and climbed slowly to my feet, holding the machete over my head. My hands trembled.

The ceiling fell down. The walls caved in.

With a jolt of panic I dropped into a defensive crouch before I realized that the ceiling and walls hadn't fallen, but the knives had fallen from them. Again I stood, holding the machete over my head.

The mob of blades on the floor swayed like water surrounding the platform. The bass notes rose, then fell, then stopped.

The room fell still except for the occasional click of blade against blade.

"We recognize the greatness," a grating baritone voice said in a faintly Arabic accent.

"I am True Jaguar," I said, pitching my voice as deeply as I could in the hope of impressing them. The words came to me as fast as I needed them, and only for the flicker of an instant did I wonder where they came from. "I speak for the Great Blade. Who speaks for the knives of Razor House?"

"Jambiya the Wicked," the baritone answered.

"Present yourself, Jambiya the Wicked." The tone in my voice amused me, but I dared not smile.

After a brief clatter, a jambiya with a typically curved foot-long blade leaned against the front of the platform, its point toward me, its edge away. "What would the Great Blade have us do, True Jaguar?"

"Guard us, Jambiya the Wicked," I said without hesitation. "Protect us against the lords of Xibalba, and in return the Great Blade promises that each of you will drink of the arrogant blood of the lords and taste of their pompous flesh."

"We would like to drink their blood and carve their flesh," Jambiya said. "When can we do that?"

"Soon," I said, uncertain all of a sudden of how I had wound up in the position of talking to a knife named Jambiya the Wicked. My arms trembled with fatigue, but I was afraid to lower the machete, since it was what the knives seemed to respect. "After we have left Razor House, whet your edges and stay prepared. When the time comes, we will call for you, and you will know it."

"What do you want of us until then?"

"Guard us, as I asked before. Keep the messengers of the lords away from us while we rest."

"May we taste their flesh and blood, also?"

"Yes, when the time comes, they are yours for the cutting."

"We will guard you, then," Jambiya said.

I lowered the machete as slowly as my tired arms would let me and lightly tapped Jambiya twice with the flat of the blade, once on each side of his. He dipped his point, then slipped back into the mob of knives surrounding him. A vibrating bass sound again filled Razor House, but I sensed that it was a sound of approval, so I raised the machete over my head again and turned in a full circle so that the rest of the knives could see it.

Only when I stopped and put the Crain back in its sheath did I think about how silly I must have looked. A blush of embarrassment crept up my face as I took my pack off and sat down beside Huna.

"Incredible," she said.

I could see awe in her eyes and face, and it made me very uncomfortable. The knives clattered quietly around us.

"The gods are with us still," Xablanque said.

"Don't ask me what made me do that," I said. "Don't even ask me how I knew what to do. I can't explain it, because I don't know. And don't look at me like that."

"How can I not? You just saved our lives from a pack of bloodthirsty knives, and made them our allies against the lords, and you want me to look at you as though everything is normal?"

"Tohil guided you," Xablanque said. "Cristo watched over us. We are blessed, True Jaguar."

The three of us automatically crossed ourselves.

"Some rest would be a blessing." I pulled my sleeping bag out of its stuff sack.

"You two sleep. You're the ones who played the game. I will stay awake and guard us."

"That's not necessary. The knives will protect us."

The knives clattered in assent.

"Besides, if you're going to insist on playing the next game with Xablanque, you need your rest, too."

"He is right, cousin," Xablanque said. "We must all rest while we can. I think we're safe here, now."

"All right." She leaned over and gave me a quick kiss, then unpacked her own sleeping bag. We zipped the two bags together, took off most of our clothes, and climbed in. I lay on my back. She lay on her side with her head on my shoulder and one arm on my chest. For a few minutes we talked softly about how good it felt to be close to each other.

Then ever so slowly the edge of sleep cut my mind off from my ears, and I couldn't make out her words, and when I tried to speak, my words divided into fragments, and my tongue twitched uselessly on the floor of my mouth, separate from me and everything else. My body felt heavy and light at the same time as I floated free of it, but I didn't understand why or how, yet I knew enough to be confused by the sight of the canyon of spears, with its swollen river raging below me, choked with splintered trees and fragments of boulders.

Huna stood on one side of the canyon. I stood on the other. The rope hung between us in a deep curve. She waved for me to join her, to cross the gap. I waved for her to come to me. She took hold of the rope and began working her way hand over hand across the canyon.

No! I tried to shout. Nothing escaped my mouth. There was no sound anywhere.

Huna's belly was swollen in pregnancy. Her arms were weak and pale. Her movements slowed in the fearsome silence. She hung like a great weight on the rope. She was tiring too quickly. She wasn't going to make it.

No! I tried to shout again. *Go back. Use your pack sling like before. Go back. Please go back.* My throat constricted. No words rang in the air.

Time slowed. Air thickened. Huna barely moved. Tears I couldn't stop ran down my face and fell into a gaping hole below my world where sharp lines divided light from darkness.

A brightly colored bird landed in the middle of the rope, a macaw with a sharp, curved beak like a serrated knife, like a lobster's claw, and the same burnt orange color as a lobster's claw. The macaw sawed on the rope with its beak as Huna dangled helplessly, as I watched frozen in place, as the bird cut the rope in half, as Huna fell, holding the rope like a catfish on a trotline, and the macaw flew away, and Huna fell and fell, and a silent voice screamed in my head, *Shirlito! Shirlito!*

I knew I was dreaming, fought to get out of the dream, and couldn't escape. I fell with Huna and Xablanque and together we fell. Fish on a line, we fell into that gaping hole beneath my world, where they fell into the darkness and I fell into the light, and I was blinded and couldn't see Huna and couldn't stop falling, and couldn't wake up until—

My body jerked. I awoke in a sweat.

"You all right?" Huna mumbled.

"Yes," I whispered. "It was only a dream."

Only a dream. It was only a dream. Wake up and go home while you still can. Just click your heels together three times and say, "There's no place like home. There's no place like home. There's no place—"

No.

I tried to open my eyes, and when I failed, I concentrated on the reality around me—the wooden platform under us, Huna's relaxed breathing beside me, Xablanque's rolling snores, the barely perceptible clatter of knives in the distance. We were there, resting, in Razor House, in Xibalba. The canyon of spears was only a dream, a nightmare, a swirling, splintering roar of a silent nightmare where no one could speak, where separate bodies fell and fell forever into the gaping hole under my world, into the light of blindness, the darkness of—

My body jerked. My eyes opened. Xablanque snored. Huna breathed. The knives clattered. Outside macaws squawked at one another. We were safe. For the moment we were safe.

I shut my eyes again and counted slowly backward from one hundred until I slid below the numbers into the soft waves of dreams where jigsaw puzzles lay in pieces, and nothing was whole, and off in the distance I saw a man cut in half by a terrible blade of light and he was screaming.

Chapter Fifty-one

I jerked awake as Huna grabbed me.

Xablanque's scream died away with a faint echo.

"What is it? A nightmare?"

"Yes," he gasped. "Yes. A nightmare from Razor House. A curse from the lords."

"Me, too. A couple of them got me, too."

"I had no dreams," Huna said, "but I feel a terrible sense of isolation here." She hugged my arm.

"Me, too." I shivered. "This is worse than Dark House. How many more of these torture houses do we have to go through, Xablanque?"

He shook his head in the dim light. "Who can answer that question? The lords? Our gods Hunahpu and Xablanque had to face Chattering House, Fire House, and Bat House before they won their victory over the lords."

"So you guess we have three more like this to go?"

"I cannot make any guess. We have as many houses as we have to face. That is all I—"

"If you can't guess on something like that, we're in big— oh, never mind. Suddenly I'm not much interested in guessing. Not much interested in sleeping, either, for that matter. But maybe you two should try to go back to sleep so that you're rested up for the next game. I'll keep—"

"Shhh." Huna squeezed my arm and cocked her head. "Listen. Listen to that."

After a moment of listening I said, "I don't hear anything."

"Exactly. It's dead silent around here. And look, the knives are gone."

I couldn't hear anything from outside, and as I looked around the room I couldn't see even one knife with us there in Razor House. "That's spooky," I said to break the pressing silence, "real spooky."

"What does this silence mean, Xablanque?"

"How should I know? Why do you two always think I have the answers? Just because I know a little more about—"

"Just because you're the one who led us here and you're the only one of us in touch with—"

"Stop it."

Xablanque stared at her for a second, then looked at me and grinned. "We cannot even get a good argument started anymore before she butts in."

"Yeah, but it's such a cute butt."

"It is not," she said.

"Of course it is."

"How foolish of her to think otherwise." Xablanque sputtered the last word out and we all laughed. We laughed hard and freely, and as I finally calmed down enough to think, I tried to remember the last time we had laughed like that— probably before we entered Xibalba. When the laughter came to its natural end, I felt as though a stifling blanket had been lifted off of us and we could breathe again.

"So where do you think the knives went?" Xablanque asked.

"They're probably outside standing guard," I said. "And listen. The birds are back."

From outside came the sounds of Xibalba, mostly the squawks of macaws and the chattering of monkeys.

"I'm going back to sleep."

Huna ran her fingers lightly up my thigh, then paused and tugged at me in a way that left no question about what was on her mind. "Me, too," she said.

"I think we should all try to get more rest," Xablanque said. "Pray that our laughter has chased the nightmares away."

Huna and I contented ourselves with touching and kissing until Xablanque started snoring. Then we made love slowly and gently, and afterward touched and kissed for a little while before she fell asleep.

Even though I was completely relaxed, I knew I wasn't going to fall asleep any time soon. Something nagged at the back of my brain, something I felt certain was important. What it was, I didn't know.

I felt as though I had missed some big clue, some major answer to a question I hadn't been able to formulate. It was as though by recognizing the answer, I might learn what the question was, and then have something useful . . . maybe.

Vague. That was the word that described my feelings,

vague—also indistinct, fuzzy, and nebulous. Being True Jaguar didn't confer any enhanced thinking abilities on me, that was for sure. In fact, being True Jaguar didn't confer much of anything as far as I could . . .

Being True Jaguar . . . there was part of the answer. But what part? What was the question that being True Jaguar was partial answer to?

Who are you?

Ohhh . . . I sighed with great resignation. If I hadn't known I was True Jaguar, I couldn't have confronted the knives, could I? Could Jesus O'Hara Martinez alone have swung the machete and defeated them? No. I didn't think so, and I couldn't have done it by only pretending to be True Jaguar.

I *was* True Jaguar. I knew that just as surely as I knew that I was also Martin O'Hara.

The second part of the answer locked into the first. I was both—True Jaguar and Martin O'Hara. For the first time in my life I was complete, whole. Leader and follower, aggressive and passive, emotional and rational, all were part of one big me that had never been balanced before.

My first impulse was to wake Huna up and share my discovery with her. That made me smile. My *discovery* was something she and Xablanque had been trying to tell me from the beginning. I had discovered what they already knew—or more to the point, I had accepted what they knew. With an embarrassed grin, I decided to wait till Huna awoke before sharing my *discovery* and acceptance of the obvious.

Yet as I lay there in Razor House I gradually realized that my acceptance was even larger than I had thought, because it opened me up to possibilities I would never have considered before. The future—my future, our future, Huna's and mine —grew suddenly wider and brighter as I caught my first glimpse of the new opportunities that awaited us.

Just as suddenly, that glimpse grew dark.

What good were all those opportunities without Huna? What good was this growth in me if I lost her and the babies? And what miserable chance did I have to save them here? Should I try to force her to leave Xibalba with me?

Only when I formed that question did I fully understand where my twisted thoughts had been leading me. If I accepted myself as True Jaguar, then I had to accept my role in this story Xablanque had rolled out for us. If I accepted myself as True Jaguar, I had to accept the responsibility for stopping *cometa Xibalba*. There lay the only hope for our future and the future of our children.

Forcing Huna to leave Xibalba with me would be surrendering us all to death. If I couldn't find a way to stop the comet, there wouldn't be a future for anyone. It was that simple.

I lay there thinking about the future for what seemed like a long time before a voice awakened me and I realized that I had fallen asleep. The light coming in the windows seemed a little brighter.

"Call off these knives," the voice shouted. "The lords of Xibalba await you for the second game of deathball."

"Huna," I said, shaking her gently, "I think it's time to get up. Xablanque? Are you awake?"

"Yes. What is it?"

"Time to go play ball, I think."

"Get these knives away from me!" the voice said with more than a little panic. "Leave me alone!"

"Jambiya the Wicked," I called.

"Here, True Jaguar, brother of Great Blade," the knife answered from outside.

"Let the messenger of the lords pass and open the door."

My request was followed by a loud clattering before the stone door rolled open for us.

"Thank you, Jambiya," I said. "Messenger? Can you hear me?"

"Of course I can hear you, infidel. Make these knives leave me alone."

"Listen to me, messenger. Go tell the lords that we'll be there in a little while."

"They want you to come now."

"Jambiya?"

"Yes, True Jaguar?"

"Send the messenger on his way."

The messenger yowled and kept yowling until his voice faded away in the distance.

Xablanque chuckled.

"I don't believe it," I said. "Look at him, Huna. He's laughing. Well, almost laughing."

"He thinks the messenger's pain is funny."

"Of course. I forgot," I said as I pulled on my shirt. "His sense of humor is attached to pain, isn't it?"

"You do well, True Jaguar."

"Thank you, thank you. All compliments duly accepted. You think we've got anything left to eat in our packs?"

After we dressed, we moved outside. What we wanted was two, hour-long, hot showers—one for Xablanque, and one for Huna and me. Instead Xablanque got the camp stove going and heated water for us to wash our faces and hands with, and made a pot of coffee. I mixed together a porridge with our trail food and some instant oatmeal I found in my pack, while Huna spread out the sleeping bags to air.

Twice the messenger returned to tell us that the lords insisted we come play ball immediately. Twice Jambiya sent him on his way by pricking the messenger's butt. The second time I told him that if the lords sent him one more time, I would send all the knives after *them*. He didn't return.

Only after we had carefully repacked our gear and given Jambiya the Wicked and the other knives instructions to wait for our call for help, did Huna, Xablanque, and I go off down Yellow Road to meet the lords for the second ballgame.

Chapter Fifty-two

As the three of us walked up to the great ballcourt, I saw the asembled lords in the bleachers waiting for us, and for the first time noticed a giant calabash tree thirty yards or so beyond the other end of the court. "Xablanque, isn't that the tree that one of the twins . . . ?"

"That is the calabash tree known as Head of One Hunahpu," he said. "Do you see his face in its fruit?"

"Yes," I said, surprising only myself, "I do." It was a face that looked all too familiar.

"Are you ready to play?" Five Death asked.

"One Hunahpu watches over us," Huna said.

I sneezed, then said, "I hope so."

"Yes," Xablanque answered, "we are ready to play."

"You and me," I said to Xablanque as he took off his pack.

"We have already decided, T.J. Xablanque and I will play

this game, and you and I will play the next. Let's not argue about it in front of the lords."

"But I . . . don't . . ." Again I sneezed. And again.

"Are you all right?"

"I thought I was. My throat tickles a little and my nose itches, but I don't think it's anything to worry about."

"The same rules apply," Five Death said. "The first team to put the ball through the hoop twenty times wins the game. Bloody Teeth and Bloody Claws will play for the lords of Xibalba. Who will play for the imposters?"

"Xablanque and Hunahpu Woman will play to defeat the Bloody Fools," Huna said, putting the pads and paddles on.

"Don't aggravate them."

"Are those your best?" Xablanque called. "Don't you have some real ball players to challenge us?"

Bloody Teeth and Bloody Claws were already down on the court passing the ball back and forth. They looked damned formidable to me—especially Bloody Claws who glared up at me with pure hatred in her black eyes.

"They don't," I said, answering him with as much bravado as I could put into my voice. "Just those two losers."

"Come down here and ask that," she called, waving a gloved hand tipped with metal spikes.

I remembered how close I had come to choking her to death and wondered if letting her live had been a mistake.

"Kill them now and save the sweat," one of the lords shouted. The other lords shouted in agreement and the messenger-guards laughed.

"Send True Jaguar down," Bloody Claws said. "I have something for him." With one hand she lifted her pads to reveal two skinny breasts also tipped with metal spikes.

The lords roared their approval.

"I've seen dogs with better tits," Huna said as she climbed down to the court, "or were they pigs?"

"Pigs," Xablanque answered, climbing down beside her.

The bleachers erupted with boos and obscenities.

My laughter turned into a series of hacking coughs. What in the world was wrong with me?

"I'll teach you about pigs," Bloody Claws said, firing the ball at Huna.

I jerked as Huna jumped to the floor of the court, and

the ball sailed harmlessly over her head. Bloody Claws charged after it, straight at Huna, metal claws fully extended. Xablanque jumped on Bloody Claws's back and the two of them crashed to the ground.

"Begin!" Five Death shouted.

Huna chased after the ball. Xablanque and Bloody Claws struggled with each other to get to their feet. Bloody Teeth ran up the court to help his partner.

"Foul!" I screamed. "Foul!" The words raked my throat with pain.

"Fair," the messenger-referee said.

I coughed, then coughed again, then couldn't stop coughing. Xablanque elbowed Bloody Teeth in the gut and shoved him into Bloody Claws just as Huna got control of the ball. She passed the ball to Xablanque on one bounce, and he charged down the court to a lay-up shot followed by a second hoop and a third.

Bloody Teeth arrived in time to block the fourth shot. With one of his paddles he whipped the ball down to Bloody Claws, who grabbed it and ran squarely into Huna. By the time Xablanque got back up the court to help Huna, the score was tied three-three.

My coughing eased, but my eyes watered and in the few seconds it took me to clear them, I heard one of the lords shout, "Five to three."

I wiped my eyes angrily and saw Huna was down on her hands and knees, heaving. Bloody Teeth was kneeling on Xablanque's back.

"Six to three," the lords shouted as Bloody Claws put the ball through the hoop again.

The messenger-referee leaned against the opposite wall, smiling, and sudden anger swept through me. I jerked my Beretta out of its holster and fired two quick rounds. The referee collapsed, clutching his chest and leaving a red smear on the wall behind him.

Everything stopped. Time hung still. For the longest moment I felt sure the universe had frozen in place and I would be captured by eternity with a smoking gun in my hand, the animal in me exposed forever.

Bloody Claws stood there holding the ball, glaring at me. The lords stopped shouting. The gun was a living thing in my hand, pointed straight across the court at Thirteen Death. Any second it would go off by itself.

"Three to three," I said. My hoarse voice seemed to echo in the stillness. Out of the corner of my eye I saw Huna and Xablanque get to their feet, and only then did I realize that ten or fifteen messenger-guards had their AK's trained on me. They might kill me, but I would kill Thirteen Death.

"Six to three in our favor," Five Death said.

Someone moved off to the side. A lord jumped. I dropped into a crouch, squeezing the trigger without thinking. The Beretta barked and kicked in my hand.

Blood exploded all over Thirteen Death as Soul Burner caught the bullet and hung in the air.

I squeezed off a second shot as Soul Burner's body crumpled out of the way, but Thirteen Death had ducked.

"Stop!" she screamed.

"Three-three," I screamed back past the ringing in my ears.

"Yes! Yes. Three to three." She crawled behind Pus Master and Jaundice Master.

Suddenly I realized that the messenger-guards weren't going to fire without her orders—or maybe not at all. They could easily have killed me, but they hadn't, and I didn't know why. Yet I dared not take my eyes off of Thirteen Death to see what the guards were doing. "And no more cheating!"

"Yes. I mean, no. No more cheating."

"And a new referee," I said, my sights steady on her head where she peeked from between Jaundice Master and Stab Master, an unfamiliar smile shaping my lips.

"Yes. Yes. A fair game with a new referee. Now stop this craziness."

"Tell your messenger-guards to put down their rifles. In fact, tell them to stack all the rifles together—and their ammunition."

She stared back at me without saying anything, so I squeezed the trigger and loosed a round barely over her head. The bullet exploded against the rock behind her. Jaundice Master and Stab Master flinched away from Thirteen Death.

"All right! All right. Do as True Jaguar says."

I heard what sounded like fear in Thirteen Death's voice, and something else, hatred, maybe. Glancing around, I real-

ized that Xablanque stood at the right end of the lords' bleacher
with an AK trained on the guards. Huna stood slightly off to
his right with another AK held to the back of Bloody Claws's
head.

Huna smiled. "Are you okay?"

"I'm fine. You?"

"We're okay."

Bloody Teeth lay face down and still in the ballcourt. The
messenger-guards began stacking their weapons as Thirteen
Death had commanded them to do, and I couldn't escape a
great sense of power that slipped into me. Defeating the lords
of Xibalba was going to be easier than Xablanque thought.
They understood power and force, and at the moment we had
the upper hand with both. All we had to do was retain that
power position and we could beat the lords, destroy the comet,
and be done with Xibalba forever.

"Why don't we just shoot the comet down?" I called to
Xablanque.

"We can't."

I sneezed. "We could try, couldn't we?"

He looked at me intently before he nodded. When the
last of the messenger-guards put his rifle and ammunition on
the stack, Xablanque rocked back on his heels and fired four
or five rounds from his AK almost straight up in the air at the
scissortail above us.

The lords laughed nervously. "You are all three fools,"
Thirteen Death said.

"Don't push your luck, bitch," I said, resettling my sights
on her.

She grinned. "So shoot me. Another will take my place
as I took the place of Seven Death. The lords of death will
always prevail in Xibalba."

"We'll see about that," I said. Some deep impulse made
me pull the trigger. Thirteen Death fell backward with a little
black hole over her left eye. Her body twitched only once.

Someone moaned. Five Death stood, threw his hands up,
and wailed to match the ringing in my ears. The other lords
wailed with him.

Chapter Fifty-three

The lords left the great ballcourt almost silently, their messenger-guards carrying the bodies of Soul Burner, Bloody Teeth, and Thirteen Death ahead of them. Huna, Xablanque, and I lugged all their rifles and ammunition to our side of the ballcourt.

We had barely finished doing that and were catching our breath when a familiar voice cried out, "Fools! Idiots! Now you've done it. Just wait and see. Wait and see. How do people survive on the surface if they're all as stupid as you?"

"And hello to you, too, Lefthanded Hummingbird," I said to the buzzing blur of color darting around us. "What are you trying to tell us?"

"Trouble's coming, now," he said, stopping to perch on Huna's outstretched left arm. "Real trouble. Thirteen Death is going to look like a mosquito compared to who's coming next."

"Spit it out," Xablanque said. "Who's coming?"

"I don't know her name. I just know she'll be worse. They're always worse. Kill one of them and a worse one will take his place. And if you kill a she-lord? No god can help you then. Not even me."

I coughed several times, making my sore throat and my still-ringing ears hurt even worse. "Well, that's nice to know, Hummingbird, but I think I'm more worried about this cold I'm catching than I am about Thirteen Death's understudy."

"Stupid. Overstudy is more accurate."

"What difference does it make? If my pistol will kill two of them, these AK's will take care of the rest of the lords—and any over-and-under replacements they drag on stage."

Hummingbird turned his head away. "If you will follow me, I will lead you out of here, now, Hunahpu Woman."

"Why? You said I would live, didn't you? I want to help them live, too."

"Fools!" Hummingbird screeched, launching himself into the air. "I have warned you. Don't say I haven't. But I can't do anything else." He climbed above us in a buzzing zigzag.

"I can't help you, you know. I've done all I can. You're on your own. On your own."

"Thanks," Xablanque called as Hummingbird's buzzing faded.

"Thanks for what?"

"He did warn us, True Jaguar."

"So?" I snuffled and felt angry and cynical, but I wasn't sure why.

"Don't we owe him thanks for warning us?"

"No, we don't. We thanked him for his help with identifying them and that's all he's done for us."

"Perhaps," Xablanque said. "But perhaps we should listen to him. He does live here, and he does—"

"All right. Who's worse than Thirteen Death?"

A frown creased Xablanque's forehead. "I don't know, higher death, perhaps. Eighteen Death? Twenty Death? I don't know."

"Twenty-one Death," Huna said quietly.

"What kind of name is that?" Xablanque asked.

"It is death after the end of life and before the beginning of life," she said, looking past me. Her eyes seemed to be focused in the distance.

I turned around, but saw nothing unusual. "What are you looking at?"

"The Tree of One Huñahpu." Her voice was distant.

"Why? What do you see?"

"The past. I've been here before."

"Of course you have," Xablanque said. "Your genius has been here before."

"Beyond that," she whispered.

As I turned to look at her, I saw a fully armed messenger-guard approaching. "Heads up. Here comes company."

"Salaam, mighty ones, and greetings from the lords of Xibalba."

"Where'd you learn your lines, in a bad movie?"

"The lords ask you to wait here for them," the messenger said, ignoring my comment. "The game will resume."

"Tied three-three," I said.

"Yes. That is the wish of the lords."

Huna smiled at me. "We will wait for them."

"But not all day," I added.

The messenger nodded and walked back the way he came.

"Now, Xablanque, if you would tell us what day it is on the surface, we will know how long . . . or will we?"

"No. Besides, I have a feeling that we are all right for the time being."

"But we must win this game," Huna said. "Why don't we practice while we're waiting for them."

They climbed back down to the court to practice, and I sat next to our munitions stack removing the bolts from the AK's. There were Pakistani, Indian, Chinese, Russian, and Albanian models of the AK in the stack, but the three I kept were all Chinese T-56 models that were in better working order and cleaner than the rest.

After putting all the bolts in my pack and blowing my nose, I emptied all the distinctively curved magazines and was surprised to find that none of them were more than half-full. Apparently the messengers liked to travel light. Using some patch material I found in one of the bandoliers, I cleaned the ammunition before reloading it into the magazines. All the while I kept an eye on the practice session and was pleased to see that Huna was guarding the goal while Xablanque was trying to shoot. At least Huna wouldn't have to run so much that way.

My throat had that aching kind of soreness back in the righthand corner. With water from my canteen, I washed down two aspirin, then rinsed off a pebble to suck on so my throat would stay moist. I was almost finished loading the last of the ammunition into the magazines when I heard the lords returning accompanied by fully armed messenger-guards and several young peasant girls in embroidered purple dresses beating on little drums tied to their waists.

"Here they come," I called hoarsely, "and it looks like Bloody Teeth is with them."

"Who is leading?" Huna asked as she and Xablanque climbed up out of the court.

"Some woman lord, a head taller than Five Death—a head taller than all of them, for that matter."

I handed Xablanque and Huna each a loaded rifle and the three of us stood there with our rifles at the ready, watching the jumbled procession arrive. The messengers were out of step and didn't seem quite sure of who was supposed to do what when they arrived at the bleachers. The lords struggled to get their feathered capes out of the way as they climbed up to their seats, and as usual, squabbled amongst themselves.

Only the new, tall lord displayed much dignity. She sat on the top row of the stone bleachers, and everyone except Five Death sat below her. "I am Twenty-one Death," she announced in a voice that sounded conversational when it reached us. "This is my companion, Five Death. The rest of you will introduce yourselves to your guests."

"They already know who we are."

"They're not guests, anyway."

"Invaders."

"Scum."

"Kill them. Stuff them full—"

"Silence." Her voice was calm and almost sweet, but the lords quieted. "Now, introduce yourselves to our guests."

"I am Mind Burner."

"Spirit Burner," the new male lord said.

"Stab Master."

"Trash Master."

"Skull Scepter."

"Bone Scepter."

"Jaundice Master."

"Pus Master."

"Bloody Claws."

"Bloody Teeth." He either wore a new headdress or a bandage under his old one, and his eyes burned with anger.

"Now, tell us who you are," Twenty-one Death said.

I elevated the barrel of my AK so that it pointed in her general direction, and only when I felt sure she was aware of it, I said, "I am True Jaguar, grandson of grandsons of Seven Jaguar who was son of Great True Jaguar. These are my—"

"Great True Jaguar had no children."

"Yes, he did," Xablanque said.

"Who are you?"

"Xablanque."

"That is impossible. Xablanque died when—"

"And I am Hunahpu Woman."

The lords gasped as though they had heard that for the

first time. Twenty-one Death's whole body twitched, but she quickly tried to cover it. Her forehead wrinkled. "You have come to play ball, I understand . . . for your lives."

"For *cometa Xibalba*."

"Only if you win."

"Of course."

"How foolish of us to think otherwise," Huna said softly.

I wouldn't let myself laugh, but a quick glance at Huna showed her grinning to her ears. "When we win, great Twenty-one Death," I said, "you will destroy *cometa Xibalba*."

"When you lose, we will take your lives."

Releasing the bolt on my AK sent a round into the chamber for everyone to hear. "Not unless you reconfirm the deal we made with Thirteen Death."

Twenty-one Death smiled. "The arrangement stands confirmed as you made it with my poor dead sister. Now let us play ball."

Chapter Fifty-four

"First, I have a riddle for you," Xablanque said. "What has two heads, two tails, two legs, and signals the defeat of the lords of Xibalba?"

Twenty-one Death laughed. "Foolish Xablanque, you think that you are the answer to your own riddle, but you are not. It has no answer here in Xibalba, because the lords will never be defeated."

"You will be today," Huna said. She laid her rifle down, gave me a quick kiss, then started climbing down to the court. "Xablanque and I will defeat your best."

Bloody Teeth and Bloody Claws climbed down to the other end, and an unarmed messenger climbed into the middle with the ball. He immediately threw it into the air.

"Begin!" Twenty-one Death shouted.

Bloody Claws reached the ball two steps before Xablanque reached her, but he grabbed the ball and lowered his shoulder into her at the same time.

Bloody Claws grunted loudly as she flailed her arms, trying to keep her balance.

Xablanque stumbled over her falling body and hit Bloody Teeth. Bloody Teeth fell, and Xablanque shot the ball through the hoop twice before either Bloody Teeth or Claws got back into the game.

"Go!" I screamed. "Get 'em, Xablanque."

Somehow Xablanque managed to make two more hoops before Bloody Claws knocked the ball away from him with her left paddle and charged down court. She made one hoop, but Huna blocked the next shot straight into Xablanque's hands. He ran up court and made one hoop before Bloody Teeth took a rebound.

"Eight to four!" I shouted. "Eight to four!"

Bloody Claws made two hoops before Huna blocked her, then Xablanque answered with three hoops of his own. I screamed encouragement for all I was worth.

Several times Bloody Teeth and Bloody Claws pulled the score to within a point. But even with the referee calling ten fouls on us and only one foul on the lords, when Xablanque bounced a perfect shot off the backstone to make the twentieth hoop, we were ahead by three, and the final score was twenty–seventeen. Huna was jumping up and down in our end of the court. Xablanque was smiling up at me.

I tried to scream for joy, but all I got out of my throat was a hoarse roar.

"They cheated," a lord shouted.

"The imposters cheated."

"Imposters always cheat."

"Kill them."

"They're the killers."

"What about our Bloody Wimps?"

"Shut up, Pus-for-Brains."

"Watch your mouth, Garbage-breath."

"*Silence!*"

"Shit pile."

The lords quieted, but they never shut up.

"Crap Head."

"Rotten Guts."

"It seems you were right," Twenty-one Death said all too politely above the grumbling lords. "You have won today. If I remember what Five Death told me, tomorrow we play basketball, three on three."

"That's right," I said, sucking on my pebble for all it was worth.

"Snot Master."

"We have a new room for you to stay in," Twenty-one Death said, ignoring the continued bickering of the other lords.

"Surprise, surprise," Huna said flatly.

"Pissy Claws couldn't fight her way out of bed."

"The messengers will show you."

"What about you, Boneless? What can you do?"

One of the lords chased several of the others off the bleachers.

By the time Huna and Xablanque finished changing out of their equipment, the lords and all but two of the messengers had left. We followed the messengers down a smelly, twisted alley from the ballcourt to a tall, narrow building that leaned against the face of a cliff and looked out across cultivated fields toward the jungle. In the distance I heard birds and monkeys.

A small set of glyphs beside the door of the building said, CHATTERING HOUSE. The three of us stood in front of the doorway and looked around for a moment, then Xablanque led us into the building.

"Throw out your guns," one of the messengers called.

"Come in and get them," I called, turning around and firing a short burst back outside.

A stone fell across the door, but the room wasn't totally dark. Dull grey light filtered down through the dust in the air from windows high above us.

Xablanque and Huna sat on the stone floor, holding their ears and laughing.

"What's so funny?" I asked as I put the rifle's safety on. I could hardly hear my own voice for the ringing in my ears. "What's so funny?" I shouted hoarsely. Pain shouted back from my throat.

"You, True Jaguar, you," Huna said. "If I didn't love you so much, I would laugh even harder."

After shaking my head and coughing several times, I said, "I don't understand."

"How can you understand?" Xablanque asked. "We have seen you changing, and what is funny . . . is, uh, I don't know. You tell him Hunahpu Woman."

She held out her hands. "Come here, T.J."

I coughed again as I crossed the small square room past her to the back wall where I leaned my rifle against the wall and shed my pack with a sneeze before I sat down beside her. She and Xablanque had played the ballgame against the lords, but I ached all over.

Huna put a hand to my cheek. "You feel feverish."

"Figures. I either have the flu, or a nasty cold, or I'm dying and these are my last hours on earth—or under earth, as the case may be." My body leaned against her of its own accord.

"You'll live, T.J."

"I hope so." I was serious. I wasn't planning on dying in Xibalba—especially not of the flu.

"What's in your first aid kit?"

"For a cold? Aspirin, aspirin with codeine, Rhinohistab, and penicillin, I think."

"You come prepared, don't you? If you brought all that, why haven't you taken some already?"

"I took some aspirin, but the rest of it is in the first aid kit for emergencies. I'm not going to take it unless it's an emergency." I sneezed and flinched. The muscles in my chest felt like something had twisted and jerked them at the same time. A weak growl of protest rumbled in the back of my throat.

She took my chin in her hand and made me look at her. "T.J., this is an emergency. You're sneezing. You're coughing. You're running a fever. You have to take the medicine. You've caught some kind of bug, and we don't have time for you to be sick down here. At the very least—"

"I'm not a kid. You don't have to lecture me."

"Then take it, all right?"

"Just the Rhinohistab."

She grabbed my pack and pulled it over to her. "And some more aspirin for your fever. Or the aspirin with codeine? Which?"

"Aspirin." I shivered. "Is it cold in here? Or is that just me and my cold?"

"It is cold," Xablanque said. "This is Chattering House, and it will probably get even colder."

"Oh, boy. Whoopee. We're in the coldest place in Xibalba and I'm coming down with pneumonia."

"We must put the three sleeping bags together," Huna said as she handed me six pills.

"What's this?"

"Two aspirin, two Rhinohistabs, and 500 milligrams of penicillin."

My first impulse was to say no to the penicillin, but considering the circumstances, maybe she was right. With some water from my canteen I washed them down. "So much for modern medicine," I said. "All those drugs in me and I still don't feel any better."

Xablanque had his sleeping bag rolled out flat on the floor. Huna opened hers and they zipped the two together. Then they opened mine and spread it on top. Even as I shivered watching them, I was damp with perspiration down the middle of my back. "God, I hate being sick."

"All right, in you go," Huna said.

"With or without my clothes?"

"With. In fact, get your down jacket on before you get in the bag."

"Won't we have to keep each other warm?"

"Yes, but that doesn't mean—"

"Then we need to get down to our underwear in—" A sneeze exploded in my nose. "Bless me," I said, pulling out my soiled bandana to blow my nose again. "Listen, we need to get down to our underwear in the bag and spread all our clothes between the two layers of bags to help hold the heat in."

"But . . ."

"That's the best way, believe me."

They did as I suggested and soon the three of us were snuggled down in the bag. I could feel their warmth beside me, but my back felt like we were laying on a block of ice.

"Welcome to Chattering House," I said with a shudder, "air-conditioning by the lords of Xibalba."

Neither of them laughed.

Chapter Fifty-five

I know I slept, but only in fits and starts. I constantly felt like I was just waking up shivering, cold sweat running down my spine feeding the frigid dampness under me. No matter how much I struggled to talk myself to sleep, it was all I could do to try to get warm.

Sometime in the middle of all the tossing and turning, Huna crawled out of the sleeping bag and got more pills, which she made me wash down with icy water from my canteen. I stayed awake for a long time after she climbed back in next to me, aware of how cold she had gotten and wondering how we were going to defeat the lords in basketball with me so sick.

Then I heard a quiet chirping sound close overhead, followed by my name spoken quietly as though a mynah bird or a parrot was talking. When I opened my eyes, I saw a small bird perched on the wall above us, a bird so colorless that I could see it only because it paced nervously up and down a crack in the wall, its small claws scratching the stone most irritably.

"So, True and Fat Jaguar, you're awake," it said. "Good. It's about time. Now, pay attention."

"Who are you?"

"Just pay attention, fat ball. The lords of Xibalba are in the latrine plotting against you at this very minute, and what I tell you could save your lives."

Xablanque snorted and shifted to his side.

"Who are you?" I asked again, my throat sore and aching.

"It is of no matter to you who I am. All you need to know is that I have come to help you."

"Go to hell," I said wearily, shutting my eyes.

"True Jaguar. True Jaguar." He called my name repeatedly and his voice rose and fell in my ears, but I did my best to ignore him and concentrated on my breathing, knowing I had to get some sleep.

"True Jaguar, listen to me. The lords have hired a real Italian basketball team to play you tomorrow, the Milano Lakers. Their center is six-foot-seven. They're going to kill you unless you do something about it."

I started counting backward from one hundred. Ninety-nine, ninety-eight, ninety-seven, trying to visualize each number in my head before continuing, ninety-six, ninety-five—

"And when the train arrives there are going to be a thousand Arab and Italian terrorists facing you and they'll have all kinds of guns and you won't, but if you don't win, Hunaphu Woman will die, and they'll string you up and hang you and bury your body in Boot Hill with no marker."

Ninety-six, ninety-five, ninety-four, ninety—

"Of course. How foolish of you to think otherwise. Hunahpu Woman will die and Xablanque will die and become catfish as their genius demands, but you will live in defeat and crawl on your belly out of Xibalba . . .

"Along the roller coaster ride, we will glide, side by side, and the world will know about the pit of the lords of Xibalba and beat their hired guns in the most important basketball . . . you and I, we will fly in your colorful balloon like Lefthanded Hummingbird except that he knows . . ."

Something told me I was dreaming, but I couldn't get out of the dream because the rent was still due and the landlord was standing on the porch, and I couldn't wake up because there was dinner to be cooked and babies to be fed and Shirlito to think about. . . . Oh, God, why wouldn't they leave me alone. Why wouldn't they—

"Listen carefully. That's what I've been trying to tell you, True Jaguar. That's why you have to pay close attention. I know how you can beat the system, and with only a thousand dollars down and payments of one-ninety-seven a month, excluding tax, title, license, and dealer prep charges."

Ninety-seven, ninety-six, ninety-five . . . until I opened one eye and saw a different bird sitting there on the perch hung with the icicles stuck in the crack in the wall, a bird that looked more and more every second like a snake with feathers, because my great-grandfather's great-grandfather knew its great-grandfather and all the old men and all the old gods and the laws were counted out to the people . . . ninety-seven, ninety-six, ninety-five, ninety-four, ninety-three, ninety-two, until I opened my eyes and saw perched above us, on the inner wall of Chattering House, the Great Plumed Serpent.

"Now you're paying attention. I like that in you, boy. There aren't many like you around these days, you know? Today's boys aren't taught any manners and they aren't taught to respect authority, and the ones that are, ones that have potential, run off to the cities to get jobs if they can, because the idea of seeing me in their dreams every night is like, real disturbing to them, you know?"

So I closed my eyes and counted backward, one hundred, ninety-nine, because I didn't want to know, didn't want to hear what the Great Plumed Serpent wanted from me, ninety-four, ninety-three, ninety-two, because I didn't dare let myself—

"Don't think you can get away now, kid. You've seen the illegal aliens sleeping in rabbit holes in the Texas valley—picking in the fields by day, hiding from Immigration at night—and you've seen the slums of Mexico City and you know that all the *campesinos* should be here with me and if they weren't so blinded by—"

"Shhh," I whispered.

Huna patted my arm. "You okay?"

I was surprised. "Sure. Go back to sleep. I'm okay."

"Mmmm."

But I wasn't okay and I knew I wasn't okay, because the Great Plumed Serpent had grown longer and fatter over our heads and it hung there twisted around a rafter that had been made from a whole tree.

"What do you want from me?" I asked.

Great Plumed Serpent smiled and showed two rows of small, sharp, white teeth curved back and serrated like shark's teeth—and folded into the roof of its mouth, fangs the length of a man's forearm. "I want no more than you can give," it said.

"Go away. Leave me alone. You're a dream, a bad dream, and I'm dying." I pulled the sleeping bag over my head.

"No. The others might die, Hunahpu Woman and Xablanque, but you will live. You don't have much time. You must live and crush the lords, soon. You don't have much time."

As I uncovered my head, I tried to understand what it was saying. "But Lefthanded Hummingbird said that I would die and Hunahpu Woman would live."

"He lied. He knows nothing. What can you expect from the god of bloody sacrifice? He is little more—"

I snuggled closer to her as though her warmth might protect us both. "But he said she'd live."

"Don't whine. She can't live. You have to live so that the lords can be—"

"Who are you calling a liar?" a new voice asked. It was Lefthanded Hummingbird.

"You, Huitzilopochtli," Great Plumed Serpent said.

"Well, eat a busload of Indios," Lefthanded Hummingbird said, "if that doesn't take the sacrifice, the old liar, blood-on-the-altar himself, calling me a liar. He's the one who's lying, True Jaguar, just like—"

"Shut up, punk."

"—just like he lied to convince the historians that he was somebody special in the ranks of the gods. You know who he really is? I mean, his real job? He's the gatekeeper. He's the one who—"

"I said, shut up." Great Plumed Serpent writhed above the rafter, darting its head in and out of the black corners, apparently searching for a Lefthanded Hummingbird that neither of us could see.

"Make me, feather-face."

Great Plumed Serpent's hiss woke me up with a start. I was shivering uncontrollably.

"Time for more aspirin," Huna said.

"Not much time. Can't be."

"Is. You need it now."

"I hate this," I said. "All mixed up. We have to hurry. Not much time."

She climbed halfway out from the sleeping bag, took hold of my pack, and dragged it to her. "I know."

"I was dreaming."

"Sounded more like nightmares than dreams."

The water from my canteen seemed even colder than before, I washed down the pills with as little of it as I could manage.

"How about some tea?"

"No."

"Yes," she said, pulling her shirt from between the layers of the sleeping bags. "It will warm you up and help you sleep."

Too tired to argue with her, I closed my eyes, saw Great

Plumed Serpent hissing at me, his glistening fangs lowered, and I opened my eyes again.

"It's ready," she said, handing me a cup as I propped myself on one elbow. "I'll wrap your jacket around your shoulders to help you stay warm."

She climbed back into the sleeping bag as I sipped the hot tea, but I knew I dared not go back to sleep. Yet eventually I set the half-full cup back down as the cold drove me into the sleeping bag where I pressed against Huna's side. Moments later when a voice called for us from outside, I pushed myself back up on one elbow and tried to take another sip of my tea. It was frozen in the cup.

Chapter Fifty-six

The messenger looked most displeased when Huna, Xablanque, and I straggled out of Chattering House dragging our gear with us. I felt like someone had beaten me up and left me for dead.

"So, you fingers-of-Satan survived this house, too," he said. "Well, in that case, the lords order you to come to the great ballcourt and play ball."

"After we have eaten," Xablanque said, throwing down his pack and taking out his sack of seeds and stones.

"Now," the messenger insisted.

"Shall we call Jambiya the Wicked and the rest of our friends from Razor House?" Huna asked. "You remember them, don't you?"

"I am only telling you what the lords have said."

"Then you can also give them our reply."

He hesitated.

"Get out of here, scum," a voice screamed from above.

The messenger turned and left on the run as Lefthanded Hummingbird buzzed past his head several times, then zigzagged to a landing on Huna's wrist.

"I dreamed about you," I said.

"That was no dream, stupid. Putrid Plumed Serpent was here, trying to trick you, but I wouldn't let him. I tricked him into thinking you were asleep."

I wiped the perspiration from my forehead. "It wasn't a dream?"

"No. . . . Aren't you going to thank me?"

"No." I snuffled to clear the drainage in the back of my throat and sat wearily beside my pack. Hummingbird moved from Huna's wrist to her shoulder as she started digging things out of her pack and seemed ready to poke her in the ear. Xablanque huddled over his stones, sorting, and counting to himself, totally absorbed in his divining process. I sat there in a dull fog, full of anger at my treacherous body and the lords of Xibalba and Lefthanded Hummingbird, wishing I could take Huna by the hand and walk out of here, knowing that we couldn't leave until our job was finished, trying to ignore the memory of Great Plumed Serpent's predictions about me living and Huna dying.

Xablanque moaned.

"What's the matter?" Huna asked.

"It is February 5," he said.

"The time here isn't even regular with itself, is it? How are we supposed to know when the comet will arrive?"

"I do not know."

"Damn." My curse was for the fluctuating time, the date, my cold, and everything else. I glanced overhead. The last hawk seemed to be closing on the scissortail—one last missile to destroy the comet.

"You had better do more than curse," Hummingbird said. "The lords will be full of other surprises this morning."

"Great Plumed Serpent said something about the lords hiring a basketball team, the, uh . . ."

"The Milano Lakers," Hummingbird said, "but don't worry. I headed them off."

"How?"

"I poked Gorbanifar the ferryman in the ear as they were coming across Blood River and they all fell off and drowned. Be careful, woman," Hummingbird said, jumping off Huna's wrist as she prepared to light the camp stove, and hopping over to stand in front of me.

"What ferryman? There was no ferryman—"

"Never mind. How are you going to play sick?"

"I'm not playing sick. I am sick." I tried to grin, but my face was too tired to move.

"Don't make jokes. You're not well enough to play."

"I don't get a choice. We told them the next game would be three-on-three basketball, and that's what it's going to be."

Huna put water on the camp stove to boil. "We'll do what we have to do."

Hummingbird made a sound more like a snort than anything else and suddenly flew away. I wouldn't miss him.

"I want a count of your emergency medical supplies," Huna said.

"Why?"

"Just count them."

I did as I was told. "Twenty-two penicillin, thirty Rhinohistabs, twenty aspirin with codeine, a hundred or more plain aspirin."

"Take three of the Rhinohistabs, and four each of the penicillin and the aspirin with codeine."

"I can't. That's too much."

"You have to if you're going to be any good to us in the basketball game."

"Aren't you afraid I'll be too doped up to play?"

"No. That much aspirin and codeine will kill most of your pain, but it shouldn't be enough to knock you on your cute butt."

"Well," I said, counting the various pills into my hand, "thank goodness for that, Doctor Hunahpu. Where'd you learn all this fancy medical technique?"

"DSA survival training. This tea will be ready in a minute."

DSA. Defense Security Agency. A dark shadow in the past. Where were they now? Where were we? Who were we? How in the holy names of Tohil and Cristos had we . . . ? Tohil and Cristos?

Huna handed me my canteen cup full of tea and I took little sips to wash the pills down one by one, trying to remember if the DSA was some figment of my dreams, or if it had once been real for me, as real as the lords and their grey Xibalba.

And the comet? Was it real? Would the earth really be destroyed if we didn't win? And how could we win if we didn't know when the comet would arrive? The questions rolled through my mind in an unending procession of illusion and reality.

Even as I sipped the tea and nibbled on the chocolate Huna gave me, I knew I could never again be totally sure of any reality.

Chapter Fifty-seven

We ate a quiet, undisturbed breakfast of trail food and oatmeal cooked in water. The cooking didn't do the raisins much good, and chewing them was hard work for me. All I really wanted to do was rest some more.

The messenger sat down the hill from us waiting in agitated patience. Only after a third cup of tea for each of us did we finally pack our gear, check and load our rifles and pistols, and leave the porch of Chattering House. To my surprise, I felt warm, somewhat refreshed, and less lightheaded than I would have expected with all that codeine in me.

When we arrived at the great ballcourt, Jambiya the Wicked and ten or twelve of his knife-brothers were waiting for us, and even cheered our arrival. Seemed that some of them had been following the games, and Jambiya decided they would make themselves visible to the lords, which was probably a very brave thing for him to do. Anyway, in exchange for the company of my Crain Predator, Jambiya and his brother knives offered to guard our gear while we played ball. We gladly agreed.

The lords then arrived and confronted us with a demand for a rule change. They wanted us to play basketball for four periods marked by the hourglass. Then following the fourth period they wanted a sudden victory period that wouldn't have a time limit, during which play would continue until one team was ahead by ten points. Xablanque and Huna were adamantly against the whole idea. I didn't care.

While they argued with Twenty-one Death and Five Death and all the other lords, I lazily practiced shooting baskets through the hoops at one end of the court. It didn't matter much to me what they decided. Nothing mattered much to me except the baskets. I found a comfortable rhythm of shooting, taking the rebound, and shooting again, all at a casual pace with soft shots and gentle rebounds.

"We're ready," Huna said suddenly from beside me. She took the ball from my hands without warning and stared at me. "How do you feel?"

I returned her stare and smiled, feeling for some reason as though my face was crooked. "I'm fine, beautiful. What do you mean, we're ready?"

"We're playing Bone Sceptor, Skull Sceptor, and Stab Master, five periods by the hourglass, whoever's leading at the end of the fifth period, wins. The game's going to start as soon as the lords get their team down here. Are you sure you're all right?"

"Sure. I'm okay."

She kissed my cheek. "I love you."

"I love you, too." The words came out of my mouth on a wave of positive pleasure, but the sight of the two Sceptors and Stab Master climbing down into the court knocked my good feelings away. Reluctantly I handed the ball to the referee, then stood there feeling very out of place.

The referee tossed the ball, Xablanque and Stab Master jumped for it, the game started, and I quickly found myself caught almost unwillingly in the middle of it.

My nose was clear and dry, my breath came hot and fast, and my throat burned. I knew my body was going to strike back when the game was over, but for the longest time it seemed to me like the game would never end.

The never-ending game. What a terrible idea. The torture of the damned. The curse of the innocent.

The game flowed back and forth through my senses like the sand through the big hourglass at the end of the court near the calabash tree. The game carried the world. Carried Bone Sceptor and Skull Sceptor and Stab Master up and down the court with Xablanque and Huna. Floated me through the pauses between periods. Pushed the two scores up side by side, point by point. Sailed my shots into the hoop. Carried me on a cushion of dull aches until suddenly the air filled with insane screaming and we stopped. The game stopped. The world stopped.

The lords screamed. "Foul!" "Foul!" "Cheaters!" "Kill 'em."

I fell to my hands and knees as my whole body tried to suck in air. This was the end, of everything, ever.

"Tie game," Huna gasped.

"No ties! No ties!"

"I knew this was stupid!"

"You're stupid."

"Shut your puking mouth."

"Play again."

"The game's over," Xablanque panted. "The game's over."

"Make them eat the basketball!"

"The game ends in a tie," Twenty-one Death announced.

"Tie, my ass!"

"Tie it round your teats."

"Send them home."

"That's stupid!"

"Send them to their graves."

"Send them to Bat House."

"Yes! Send them to Bat House! Send them to Bat House!"

The cry became a chant and the chant deafened us as we struggled out of the court.

"Bat House," Twenty-one Death shouted above the rest. The lords were suddenly quiet.

After gathering our packs, we allowed ourselves to be led away by one of the messengers.

BAT HOUSE, the glyphs on the grey stone building read.

Bat House, I thought. Couldn't we do anything here except play stupid ballgames and sleep in nasty houses? Was this why we had come to Xibalba? Was this why Tohil and Cristos sent us? Was this how we were going to save the world? It was all too confusing to me.

Jambiya and his knife-brothers came into Bat House with us. Xablanque built a big fire. Bats complained noisily above us, but stayed away from us and the fire. Huna forced the messenger at gunpoint to clean the guano off the floor and wash the floor down, but the place still stank until Jambiya pulled some aromatic logs onto the fire, and after a while the air smelled of sweet smoke. He and his brothers dragged in meat from somewhere and a big pot to cook it in. Then Huna made me take more pills, and I slept.

She kissed me awake and I ate. Eating took a long time because I was so stopped up I had to rest and breathe through my mouth between bites. The slow chewing and breathing gave me time to wonder exactly what the stew I was eating was made of, but after some consideration I decided I didn't feel good enough to want to know what was in the stew.

The Rhinohistabs were no longer keeping my nose clear, and every one of my joints ached. I made my pain known loudly to the world at large, in particular cursing Xibalba and all its inhabitants. At Huna's insistence I took more pills and slept again, dreaming of knives and basketballs and squeaking and beeping and fighting for breath, and when I woke up, I realized that the beeping was coming from Huna—from the watch in her hands, my watch.

"What are you doing?" The room still smelled of sweet smoke.

"Keeping the bats away."

"With what? My watch?"

"Yes. The bats don't like it at all. Maybe they think I'm an alien bat or something. Anyway, it works, and that's what matters. Now go back to sleep. Xablanque and I have everything under control."

I felt terribly lightheaded. "What time is it?"

She giggled. "According to this? Seven forty-eight P.M., August twenty-first."

"That's crazy. It doesn't make any sense."

"The watches stopped making sense a long time ago, remember?"

I barely remembered. That was way back in the past. I shut my eyes. When I opened them, I heard the beeping again. Or maybe I heard the beeping, then I opened my eyes. Or maybe my eyes beeped when they opened. "I hurt."

"You want more pills?" Xablanque asked softly.

I dug my bandana out of my pocket, found a small dry spot on it, and blew my nose clear. "No. I don't think so."

His hand rested against my neck for a few seconds. "You need more aspirin and codeine," he whispered. "You still have a fever."

"Whatever you say, boss. Is Huna asleep?"

"Yes. . . . True Jaguar, there's something you need to know, something we need to talk about."

"So talk."

He hesitated as he got the pills out for me. "It's about the creation story from the *Popol Vuh*, the story I was telling you as we came here."

"I remember." I did, sort of.

"You see, uh, when the boy-gods Hunahpu and Xablanque faced the lords of Xibalba, the boys let themselves be defeated and killed. Then they came back from the dead as holy catfish and tricked the lords into death."

I didn't like what he was saying. "Spit it out. What are you trying to tell me?"

"I'm trying to tell you that Hunahpu Woman and I may die here."

"And come back from the dead and trick the lords?"

"I don't know. I don't think so."

"What the hell do you mean, you don't think so? Besides, Hummingbird said Huna would live—she's carrying our babies—and the boys didn't have True Jaguar with them, did they?"

"No, but the Great Plumed Serpent said Hunahpu Woman would die." He held out his hand.

I took the pills and washed them down with tepid water from my canteen. The air smelled suddenly thick with bats and I could hear them squeaking and flapping around like pieces of leather slapping against each other. "Well, let's just believe Hummingbird and not worry about Great Plumed Serpent," I said. "We have no evidence that he's on our side, and Hummingbird, at least, is looking to help us so he can get revenge on the lords. Now I want to get some more sleep."

But I didn't get more sleep. I lay there mourning deaths that hadn't happened until a messenger called our names from outside of Bat House.

Chapter Fifty-eight

As soon as the three of us walked out of Bat House, the messenger ran away, wailing loudly, as though the world had come to an end.

"The lords will be furious," Jambiya the Wicked said.

"They ought to be used to it by now. We've survived all the other houses. Besides, this one was simple compared to the others."

"Bat House was where the god Hunahpu lost his head," Xablanque said.

"I'm glad I didn't remember that last night, cousin." She snuggled up to my arm. "Aren't you, T.J.?"

"Of course I am," I said through my stuffed nose. "Now, let's go beat the crap out of the lords so we can get out of here."

"First we will eat something," Huna said, "and you will take more of the medicine."

"And I will read the seeds and stones," Xablanque added.

So we ate, and I swallowed all the pills Huna handed to me, and Xablanque set about reading the stones, but before he finished I looked up and saw the third and final hawk fall from the sky, its wings broken, its tail clipped.

"Saints preserve us," I said, crossing myself. The final missile had failed. There was nothing to stop the comet but us.

Huna and Xablanque looked up in time to see the bird fall, and they, too, crossed themselves, but neither seemed surprised.

"Today on the surface of the earth, it is February 11. In eighteen days it will be the Day of True Jaguar and the comet will strike."

I whistled through my teeth and crossed myself again, seeing my hand moving involuntarily, realizing that I was renewing a childhood habit, hoping it did some good, praying wordlessly that Xablanque was wrong, that Cristos and Tohil could reach into the heart of Xibalba to help us.

"The timing's all screwed up," I said to Xablanque. "If we have to win two more games in order to make the lords destroy Lana's comet, do we have enough time? If there's no way to guess how many days we lose every time we sleep, shouldn't we—"

"I do not know, True Jaguar. I have no answers."

"Well, who does?" I sneezed. "Somebody'd better have some answers, because I—we—haven't gone through all this crap just to let Xibalba's screwed-up clock beat us, have we?"

"No, T.J., we haven't but we can't anticipate the future, either."

"What the hell's that supposed to mean?"

"Please, True Jaguar, do not be angry. What she is trying to tell you is something we discussed while you slept. Things here are not happening as they did in the *Popol Vuh*, so we cannot predict what will happen next."

"But what about—I mean . . . we can't just wait for things to happen to us. If we're here to go through some ceremonial battle for the life of the earth, we have to take charge of the battle." I looked from one to the other, and neither seemed about to disagree with me.

"All right, let's eat. Then we go to the ballcourt and announce that we're playing according to our rules from now on. Screw the lords. If they don't like it, we kill them. We played their game according to their rules, now they can play basketball according to ours."

An hour or so later, flanked on my left by Huna and Xablanque, each with an AK at the ready, and on my right by Jambiya the Wicked and his brothers, I stood across the ballcourt from Twenty-one Death and her retinue and repeated my demand.

"Never," she said.

I released the bolt on my AK, and a round slammed into the chamber. I raised the rifle and fired a round at the feet of the lords. "We play this game according to our rules," I said, "or I start killing you one by one until we get down to someone who agrees to be fair about this."

"Drop dead," Pus Master said.

With no great effort I shot him twice in the chest before he hit the stone bench, and I felt all the better for having done it.

Huna gasped, but I saw her raise her AK to her shoulder.

"Who wants to be next?" I asked. A quick flick of my eyes revealed the messengers standing nonchalantly at either end of the lords' bleachers.

"Hail Mary, full of grace, blessed be thy name . . ." I heard Xablanque whisper as his rifle came up, too.

"Kill them," Jaundice Master screamed in a voice that irritated my trigger finger.

I shot her through the head.

Her brains splattered over half a dozen of the others. Her body flew backward, then hit the stone steps with a heavy, wet thump. Lords scrambled over each other to get away from Twenty-one Death and Jaundice Master's body.

Several bloody macaw feathers from her headdress caught the breeze and danced brightly over her body for a second before drifting down beside her.

Quiet held the ballcourt. From the close-by jungle I heard the monkeys chattering nervously amongst themselves. Very deliberately I raised my sights until they rested on Twenty-one Death's forehead.

"Next?" I asked.

Her dark eyes stared back at me from either side of my front sight for the longest moment before she flinched. "Your rules," she shouted. "Stop this. We will play by your rules."

"Thank you," I shouted back, slowly lowering my rifle. Huna and Xablanque followed suit. "Thank you, Twenty-one Death. Your devotion to fair play and good sportsmanship is remarkable."

She didn't say anything as she took off her headdress and cape and started climbing down the bleachers. It took me a moment to realize that she was going to play basketball against us. Five Death followed her, and Trash Master followed him.

Huna walked over and kissed me on the cheek. "Time to play," she said. "You certainly got them ready for us."

"Their anger will be good for us," Xablanque said.

"Let's hope so."

"Look." Huna pointed to the sky.

Above us the scissortail was descending in a wide spiral of which we seemed to be the center. "Better give it all we've got," I said. "Doesn't look like the comet's going to give us much time."

We took off our gear, climbed down to the court, and after a few practice shots each, handed the ball to the messenger-referee. Without pausing he tossed it up toward the lords.

Five Death caught it, dribbled toward us, then bounce-passed the ball to Trash Master. He moved toward the center of the court as I took up my position under the basket and Xablanque went on the attack.

Trash Master passed to Twenty-one Death. She charged past Huna, ran into me, and made the first basket of the game. The lords in the bleachers broke into wild cheers.

We answered with three baskets in a row from Xablanque before Five Death managed to sink one and make the score six to four, our favor.

Huna stole the ball twice. Xablanque made two more baskets, and suddenly the score was ten–four.

The lords in the bleachers cried, "Foul! Foul!" and as if on cue, the referee charged us with a foul every time we got the ball until the game was tied ten–ten.

But Huna and I kept feeding the ball to Xablanque and he kept making baskets. After each one, Trash Master muttered something about the ghost of Cousy, and that made me smile. I don't think Xablanque understood it.

Slowly we began to pull ahead, by four points at the end of the first quarter, by seven at the end of the half, and by eleven at the end of the third quarter.

"We've got a good chance, now," I panted as we prepared to start the fourth quarter. I felt like hell, but I felt better than when we had started. "Let's keep our cool out there and we can make those three wish they'd never heard of us."

Someone should have warned the lords to keep their cool. The better we played, the sloppier they became, and it looked like we were going to run away with the game. They called a time-out with about a third of the sand left in the hourglass, which the timekeeper tipped on its side to stop the flow. She then started the flow of a small hourglass.

Several of the lords had come down to the court to confer with their team, and when the timekeeper announced the end of the time-out, I was surprised to see that Twenty-one Death had put her feathered cape back on.

"Foul," I cried, running up to the referee. "Technical foul. She can't wear that on the court during the game."

"Of course she can," the referee said.

"How foolish of you to think otherwise," Twenty-one Death added with a weary grin dividing her brown face.

"It's a foul," I repeated, "whether you agree to it or not. But just to show you that nothing's going to help you, I won't press it any further."

"Play ball," the referee shouted.

The tip-off went to Twenty-one Death, who dribbled down the court with it, cape billowing, loose feathers flying.

Huna tried to block her, but at the last second, Twenty-one Death spun around, backed into Huna, then turned and made her shot.

A low shadow crossed the court, and I glanced up to see the scissortail no more than a hundred feet above us.

Xablanque missed our next basket. Trash Master made one for the lords. Suddenly our lead was cut to seven points again.

I tossed the ball in to Xablanque. He passed to Huna who passed back to him on the way down court. Xablanque faked a pass to me, then drove toward the basket with a high dribble.

God's camera clicked and for an instant time stopped. I saw Twenty-one Death's hand back over her shoulder. I saw the long curved war club she held. I saw the terrible grin on her face.

"Xablanque!" I screamed.

Time started again. The ball flew toward the hoop. The club swung into Xablanque's head.

Huna screamed.

Xablanque's head flew from his shoulders. It sailed up, out of the court and landed beneath One Hunahpu's calabash tree.

Chapter Fifty-nine

Xablanque's headless body stood on its toes at the free-throw line. It leaned forward. Blood spurted out of his neck in pulsing arcs. His shooting arm stretched toward the basket. His knees were still bent, but he stood motionless in the grey stone light of the ballcourt as though balanced on the dark edge of eternity.

My head spun. The blood in my heart congealed into a frozen lump filling the center of my chest. My knees turned to trembling jelly as I stumbled to Xablanque's side. Tears blurred my vision and I angrily brushed them away.

Dear Jesus, I prayed, *take his soul*.

I heard the lords in the bleachers high on one side of the court whooping and laughing with joy, thickening the air with their disgusting breath. The odors of the rotting disease of their mouths and the vapors of Xablanque's blood and the stench of death clogged my nostrils.

High on the other side of the court, Jambiya the Wicked and his brothers growled in fury, yet made no move toward the lords, as though waiting for some allowance from me.

But I was caught in that tableau, paralyzed and frightened, wanting only escape from—I sneezed.

A sudden quenching darkness filled the court. Silence choked off every sound as almost immediately the darkness was replaced by a freezing light.

Twenty-one and Five Death fell away from Xablanque's rigid body and covered their eyes. Trash Master huddled in obvious fear at the end of the court.

The light descended, brilliant, blinding, cold, double-shafted, split by a finger of darkness. It chilled my sweaty skin and drove me away from Xablanque's body to the wall of the ballcourt and drove Huna into my arms.

Angry, confused shivers ran through us as we both tried to see where the light was coming from. It glared off the dull stone and the bright blood, too harshly for anyone to look at it.

Huna and I wept as we sank down the wall to our knees. Whether we cried in fear or sorrow, in fright or grief or shock, I did not know.

Then, without warning, the light dimmed to the intensity of a photographer's floodlight. As it dimmed even further, it landed in a shower of sparks and fire on Xablanque's shoulders where his head should have been. Down his back, almost to his heels, hung the split tail of a platinum bird. On his shoulders the bird's body settled itself in its wreath of sparks as though nesting on his blood-soaked neck.

Slowly this new Xablanque lowered his arms and turned to face us.

Each of the bird's cold, metallic feathers gleamed with a singular brilliance. It stared at us with its golden eyes. When it spoke, its beak never moved, but its words sounded in the center of my brain.

"I have come," it said. *"Why have I been called?"*

"To destroy the surface of the earth," a weak voice answered. "But you are too early. You're supposed to hit the earth on the Day of True Jaguar."

"*Why have I been called?*" the scissortail repeated, ignoring the voice.

No one answered it the second time.

"*I am cometa Xibalba, greatest of all comets. I have defeated your destroyer hawks. Who dares call me here, then refuses to answer my question?*"

"You are Death," I said with a voice not my own. "You are the greatest death of all, the death of the soul. Go back to the hell you came from."

"*I am home, but I am not what you say. Don't lie to yourself, mortal.*"

"Then have you come home to die? Is this to be the death of Death?"

"*No, I am not the death of Death. I am the death of Hope. With me dies mankind's hope for the future.*"

"You lie," a distant voice cried.

"You are nothing but a comet."

"A weak, cheap, dirty comet—and you're too early."

"Go. Wait till it is time. Then do your job and be gone."

"Get out of our ballcourt."

The bird laughed a deep, startling laugh, but even as it laughed, a haze fell over its shiny surface.

Suddenly Xablanque's body ran up the steps on our side of the ballcourt with the laughing bird clinging to his shoulders where his head should have been. Sparks, fire, and flashes of darkness trailed behind him.

Laughter and shouts of triumph startled my ears.

"Run, you stinking comet."

"That's right, get out of here. Go do your job!"

"And take that smelly corpse with you, *cometa Xibalba.*"

Huna and I scrambled up the steps just in time to see the inexplicable creature run into the jungle behind One Hunahpu's calabash tree. A scorched path marked his route.

The referee blew his whistle. "Play ball," he shouted.

I turned toward the noise.

Twenty-one Death jumped by herself, took the ball, ran to our end of the court and made an easy lay-up shot. The referee threw the ball to the other end of the court where Five

Death waited for it. Five Death took the pass, ran to our end, and made his own lay-up.

"Forty-eight, fifty-one," someone called.

Trash Master shot us the one-fingered salute.

I stared at them, too stunned to understand what they were doing.

"Time!" Huna shouted. "Time-out."

"Time-out, mortals," the referee said in a mocking echo. "T.J."

My eyes saw her mouth move, my ears heard her words, but I couldn't make sense of what she said.

"T.J., listen to me. We have to finish the game. It's our only chance. We have to beat the lords. Do you understand?"

I nodded because it seemed like that's what she wanted me to do, but only as she led me back down to the court did the meaning of her words sink into my brain. "We can't play." I sneezed. "Not now. Not after what . . . Xablanque . . ."

"We have to." Tears ran down her face. "We don't have a choice. Xablanque would demand it of us."

"I warned you," a voice cried from overhead.

That voice, that obnoxious voice released a force inside me that sharpened my brain and dulled my aches and pains. "Go to hell, Hummingbird," I said as I pulled free from her grip.

"This is hell, True Jaguar."

"No, it's not. It's only a bad imitation." I jumped down the last step and looked across the court at Twenty-one Death. My body ached and my nose itched, but I pushed those sensations aside. "The score's fifty-one, forty-four."

"Fifty-one, forty-eight," Twenty-one Death said with a smile that showed all her blunt, yellow teeth.

I roared as I charged across the court and threw myself on her. My hands clamped themselves around her thick, ropy neck as we fell to the stones. Her war club skittered down the court.

"No more cheating, you stinking bitch," I screamed, "or I'll choke you all to death one by one. And I'll let Hummingbird poke out your eyes, and puncture your ears."

She struggled under me and the lords screamed in the background, but my grip tightened and Hummingbird zoomed in close to her face.

"Now, True Jaguar? Can I poke her now?"

"Yes."

"No! No! Don't kill me." The words rasped their way out of Twenty-one Death's throat. Her eyes bulged to the edges of their sockets. Thick yellow tears oozed down her face.

Hummingbird poked at her left eye. She twisted her head. His beak stabbed into her eyebrow and dark blood oozed out.

"Enough," I said in a voice so calm and quiet it frightened me. "Both of you."

"You said . . ."

"I'm sure you'll get another chance, Hummingbird."

"What about us?" Jambiya called from above.

"You'll get your chance, too."

"Now?"

"Soon, I think." A glance to my left showed Huna holding Five Death on his knees with one of his arms twisted high up into the middle of his back.

"My throat," Twenty-one Death whispered hoarsely.

I eased the pressure on her throat, but I didn't release her and her black eyes still bulged. "You have to play fair from here on out," I said. "Promise me that."

"Yes, I promise."

"Because if you don't, I'm going to let Lefthanded Hummingbird poke you and Jambiya the Wicked and his brothers slash you, while I kill each and every one of you with my bare hands. Do you understand?"

"I understand."

"Then let's play ball." I pulled her to her feet by the neck as I stood up.

The referee looked uncertain. Hummingbird zoomed past the referee's head and nicked the end of his nose. "Play ball, True Jaguar said."

"Play ball," the referee said. The timekeeper tipped the hourglass up. The referee threw the ball into the air, but I was the only one who went for it. I sneezed, then passed the ball to Huna, and she dribbled down the court with Trash Master only making a half-hearted effort to slow her down. Five Death stood in the middle of the court comforting Twenty-one Death.

Huna shot and made the basket. The timekeeper shouted, "Game's over. Mortals win, fifty-three, forty-four."

"The lords file an official protest," Five Death said.

"What? Why?" I asked as I walked straight toward him, ready to choke him, too, if I had to.

"Because you only had two people on the court. The rules call for three against three."

"What? You mean you want to protest because we had fewer—"

"The protest is filed," he said. He turned and began to help Twenty-one Death out of the court.

Without warning I sneezed again, and a flood of resistance drained from my body.

Chapter Sixty

Huna and I sat silently leaning against each other beside the ballcourt long after the lords left. Occasionally I sneezed or blew my nose, but we didn't talk because there wasn't anything to say. Xablanque was dead, and his death seemed all the worse with his body driven into the jungle by the comet-bird than if his body had lain there in front of us. The sorrow I felt was like an empty pit inside me—a pit lined with anger. Yet I knew what Huna had said earlier was true. Xablanque, if he were there, would demand that we continue.

Hummingbird flitted around us for a while, but when neither she nor I responded to his badgering, he promised to be at the next ballgame. Then he flew away. Of the knives, only Jambiya remained with us.

"This is bad, True Jaguar," Jambiya said, breaking a long period of silence.

"All death is bad," I said, but my words sounded empty and trite.

"I mean this lack of confrontation," Jambiya said. "We should have killed them all when they were here. I could have summoned my brothers quickly and we could all have drunk their blood as you promised us."

Huna shivered. "Bring all your brothers to the next game."

"What are you talking about?"

"The next game will be the showdown. When we win, they must destroy the comet."

I blew my sore nose and wiped it with my overused bandana. "You seem awful sure of us winning."

"We have to win, T.J. That's why we came. And now Xablanque is the answer to his own riddle, two heads and two tails that mean the defeat of the lords. After the comet is destroyed, Jambiya and his brothers can slake their thirsts with the blood of the lords."

With a long sigh I shook my stuffy head. "Yeah, well, Xablanque lost one of his heads, didn't he? And we still have to beat the lords first. That's going to be the real trick, isn't it, with Xablanque dead and gone? How are we going to beat them if we're two against three? You have some way we can cheat them out of an overpowering victory?"

"Fairly. We have to win fairly."

"Right." What else was there to say?

Again it was Jambiya's voice that broke the silence. "Messenger coming," he said. "Armed."

Only then did I look around and realize that our rifles were missing. I dug frantically in the side pocket of my pack, pulled out my pistol, and checked to see that it was loaded. Then I held it ready to fire, just in case.

"You are good with your hands, *effendi*," the messenger said.

"What's that supposed to mean?"

"Nothing, honored sir, nothing. Come with me, please, and I will show you where you must sleep until the next game."

"Fire House, I think," Huna said as we climbed to our feet. "The boys spent a night in Fire House when they were down here, so I guess that's next on the list."

When we reached the low, roofless building, however, the glyph on the gatepost read JAGUAR HOUSE.

"Maybe this is a good sign," Huna said.

A jaguar roared from inside the house. Many pairs of glowing eyes stared out at us. Other jaguars roared in response.

"And maybe not," I said.

"I'll go first," Jambiya the Wicked said, and he plunged through the doorway ahead of us.

We paused, but heard nothing. "Me next," I said, holding the pistol in front of me as I went through the doorway.

The interior of Jaguar House was at least forty yards square and not much darker inside than outside. Prowling its edges were more jaguars than I could count, maybe a hundred or more, all of them staring at me as I surveyed the room.

"It's all right," Jambiya called. "I told them who you were."

"So?"

"They're obviously impressed," Huna said from behind me.

"Me, too," I said softly. "Now what?" The stone door closed behind us, and every one of the jaguars suddenly seemed twenty feet closer. "We're dead meat."

"No, we're not. Stop thinking like that."

"How else am I supposed"—I sneezed—"to think?"

"Who are you?" a voice asked from the opposite wall.

"Us?" I looked hard, but couldn't tell which of the animals had spoken. "I am True Jaguar and this is Hunahpu Woman. You've met our friend Jambiya."

"We know the wicked knife. His voice is powerful and his blade is sharp, but he is easy to avoid, and like his brothers, his bones are brittle and he would shatter easily on the stones if we should—"

"Hey," Jambiya said, "try me, fur face."

"Be still, knife. Tell us, you who claim to be True Jaguar, what are you and the pregnant woman doing in our house wearing the names of gods?"

"We were sent here by the lords to rest," Huna said.

A jaguar somewhat smaller than the rest stepped toward us. "You were sent to be eaten."

Jambiya whistled softly. "Touch them, and I'll slit your throat and gut you."

"Brave talk, brittle one, but foolish. We eat whoever comes to us." With gutteral rumblings, other jaguars padded into place beside the speaker.

I raised my pistol and aimed at the jaguar speaking. "We have come here to rest, Little Jaguar Heart. Leave us alone."

The rumblings turned to growls. "How do you know my name?"

"I am True Jaguar, grandson of grandsons of Seven Jaguar, son of Great True Jaguar," I said with that voice I had reluctantly come to recognize as my own. "I know you dream of killing the lords and sucking the marrow from their bones." I sneezed and flinched, feeling vulnerable to the snarling pride of jaguars around us.

"You, Little Jaguar Heart, know that only True Jaguar can set you free from this house where you are imprisoned. Now, either leave us alone, or face my wrath."

"Do you have enough bullets of wrath for all of us?"

"Perhaps not, but I have enough for you."

Jambiya whistled loudly. Knives clattered through all the high windows. Jaguars leapt snarling out of the way. "And we have blades for those who escape the bullets," Jambiya said.

"Stop it, all of you," Huna shouted. Suddenly, inexplicably, the knives and jaguars stilled their noises. "We have not come here to fight jaguars who should be pleased to meet their name bearer. We have come to defeat the lords of Xibalba."

"Be still, woman. We will eat you in time."

Huna stepped past me and in her hands was my Crain machete. "Come try to eat me now," she said.

Little Jaguar Heart leapt toward her. I dodged sideways into a crouch to get a clear shot at him.

Huna lopped off his head with one swipe of the machete. She caught the next jaguar in midair on the upsweep, cutting it in half. The third howled and lost its front legs. The fourth screamed and lost its hindquarters.

No fifth jaguar leapt at her. The sound of heavy breathing and the smell of fetid breath filled the room. I never had a chance to shoot—but I never needed to.

Huna stood ready, the machete wet with blood. All the jaguars in sight had knives hanging under their chins, edges pressed against the fur of their throats.

The pieces of jaguars scattered around Huna on the floor rolled slowly together and piece by piece reassembled themselves until all four jaguars stood before us, whole again. My mouth dropped open.

"You are good, Hunahpu Woman," Little Jaguar Heart said.

"Because we are on the side of Tohil and Cristos," she answered.

"Perhaps. Now, call off your knives. We will not harm you."

"We want more than that," I said without thinking. Jambiya and his brothers hung in place at the jaguar throats. "We want your allegiance against the lords."

"That is dangerous, man."

"Life is dangerous, jaguar."

"What can you offer us that we don't already have?"

"Freedom from the lords. Freedom from this house. Freedom to roam the jungle and live like real jaguars."

"We will think on it."

"You don't have time to think on it. Either give us your word and allegiance, or the knives will hack you all into so many pieces you will never pull yourselves back together."

For the longest time no one moved and no one spoke.

"Let's hack them up and be done with it," Jambiya finally said.

"It's up to them," I answered.

"I would choose freedom," a voice from behind Little Jaguar Heart said.

"Choose quickly," Huna said. "We must rest before the next game against the lords."

"Freedom," a new voice growled.

"Freedom," a chorus of others added.

"Allegiance to True Jaguar!"

"Allegiance to Hunahpu Woman!"

A general roar followed and I got the distinct feeling that these jaguars had been waiting for this opportunity for a long time, for so long, in fact, that it had taken Huna's action and our combined threats to make them see the possibilities. I lowered my pistol.

"The vote seems to be in your favor," Little Jaguar Heart said above the noise. "We pledge our allegiance to you two for a taste of lords' blood and freedom."

Deep in my gut I knew we were safe for the first time since we had entered Jaguar House. "Jambiya," I shouted, "call off your brothers."

When Huna lowered the machete and turned to me, I could see great washes of tears rolling down her face.

"It's all right," I said, taking her into my arms. "It's going to be all right."

"Xablanque," she whispered, and I knew that part of our lives would never be all right.

Chapter Sixty-one

We sat close beside each other leaning against the back wall of Jaguar House, but at Huna's insistence, neither of us slept. I wanted to sleep. God knows I wanted to sleep. Every joint in my body ached, as though I'd hiked a thousand miles. My brain had passed exhaustion into numbness. I needed to sleep. But we didn't know if we should risk the time change that every previous sleep period had brought with it. If we were going to stop the comet, our timing had to be correct, but there was no way to know what time it was anymore.

The jaguars asked a hundred questions until Huna gave up on trying to answer them one by one and simply told the story of what had happened to us since our arrival in Xibalba.

I listened and added details when I could, but it was hard for me to remember very clearly what had happened when we first arrived, almost as though the three people who walked out of that cave into Xibalba had been three different people than the two of us who sat in Jaguar House and our brother, the comet-zombie Xablanque, lost in the jungle beyond the great ballcourt.

With all the concentration I could muster, I tried to remember those three people—Reyes, Velasquez, and me—tried as hard as I could to remember especially who I had been and what I had thought at that moment we entered Xibalba. But the images were all too hazy, too distant, too unimportant. Whomever Jesus O'Hara Martinez had been when he arrived, he had since been buried somewhere deep inside me, far away from my life as True Jaguar, and I had no illusions that he would ever emerge again.

Yet I wondered about him. Could O'Hara have loved Shirlito Velasquez as much as True Jaguar loved Hunahpu Woman? Would O'Hara have grieved for the *brujo* Cacabe Reyes as I grieved for my companion Xablanque? Could O'Hara have killed without mercy or threatened the lords of Xibalba with his bare hands? Would O'Hara have willingly faced the jaguars?

The answers to those questions might have been interesting if I could have found them, but I knew they had no meaning. If ever we got back to the surface, if ever I had to be O'Hara again, never could I be the same naive O'Hara who wandered into Xibalba back in the dim past of my recollection. That much I knew for certain.

What I was totally uncertain about was who I really would be on the day we escaped from this disgusting underworld. Worse, I had no way of knowing. How could True Jaguar live in the high tech world on the surface? How could O'Hara suppress True Jaguar? Would he want to?

Did any of those questions make any sense? Who could I be, if not me? Who could I become, if not me? *Me* wasn't some creation carved from the stone of my ego, was it?

No. The world shifted and changed from moment to moment. So did I. When I changed my behavior, when I changed my actions, then the person who was me changed, also.

The old O'Hara was dead and gone. But if we got back to the surface, back to good old Weatherford, Texas, True Jaguar would be shifted and changed, too. Poof. Out of the hat, just like that, because neither O'Hara nor True Jaguar colored all the next shapes of the person I would be, could be, should be, wouldn't it be wonderful, the future as we came to know the sunny side of the street, the dark side of the force . . . open to the elements, open to the windmills of change—two quarters, dimes, and pennies, lots of pennies breeding in the dark—and I could be anyone better than you were . . . I could be anyone . . . O'Hara could be . . . T.J. . . . True Jaguar . . .

"T.J.? T.J.?"

"Hmm?" I looked around and saw jaguars curled up against each other and heard them snoring and muttering, but I had to see the piles of knives here and there around the floor before I fixed the place as Jaguar House and sorted Huna's voice from the voices in my head.

"Are you listening to me? You can't go to sleep."

"I wasn't sleeping."

"You were snoring."

"That was the jaguars."

"It was you. I can tell the difference between you and them."

"I don't care. I wasn't sleeping. I was thinking."

"Think without snoring, then. Or better yet, think aloud and we'll help each other stay awake."

"What time is it?"

"There! I knew you were asleep."

It took me a moment to figure out what she meant. "We don't know the time, do we?"

"No. When the messenger comes for us, I will read the seeds and stones like Xablanque did"—she paused with a sharp intake of air—"and we will know the day. But here, who knows the time? I doubt that even the lords of Xibalba know because it has no importance to them."

"How could it? It doesn't mean anything here."

"Exactly."

How would people live without accurate timekeeping, I wondered? Would a lack of clock time make the world a different place? Would we approach life differently if we only had sunrise and sunset to mark each day, or would we be like Alice and the Mad Hatter, late for a date about a quarter till nine when the moon comes over the mountain and that didn't—

"T.J.!" She elbowed me.

"Uh, I'm sorry. But my mind keeps drifting and my eyes won't stay open."

"You can't go to sleep. At least one of us was awake the whole time we were in Bat House and still we lost a week of surface time."

"Then what difference does it make now? If we're going to lose the time anyway, we might as well sleep. Huna, I'm bushed, beat, tired, exhausted. I'm full of penicillin and aspirin and antihistamine and codeine and phosgene, and I have to get some sleep. I have to."

"If you were full of phosgene, you'd be dead."

"So prove to me that I'm alive."

She turned and leaned against me. Her tongue darted into my ear. Her hand ran up the inside of my thigh. "You're alive," she whispered when she felt my reaction.

I trembled and shouldered her tongue away from my ear. "If we follow through in that direction, there's no way you'll keep me awake afterward."

She kissed my shoulder. "Well, we just won't go all the way."

I closed my eyes and leaned my head back against the wall. "Boys have a name for girls like you."

"What?"

"P.T."

"What's a P.T.?"

"It's a girl who gets you all worked up, then won't let you go all the way."

"Hmm."

"Why don't you read the seeds and stones now?"

"What do you mean?"

"Read them now," I said. "We haven't been here very long, and the last time Xablanque read them it was February 11, right?"

"And if the time's accelerating even when we're awake . . ."

"Then we can get some sleep."

"After we go all the way?"

"Yes. Of course."

"How foolish of you to think otherwise."

I tried to smile. "So what are you waiting for?"

She dug through Xablanque's pack until she found his leather sack of seeds and stones. In one of his small stoneware bowls she set fire to a piece of copal, then started counting out the seeds, then adding stones at intervals I couldn't make sense of. But every few minutes I rubbed the sleep out of my eyes and forced myself to concentrate on what she was doing.

Huna worked slower than Xablanque usually did, but I knew that speed wasn't the problem when she added a second piece of copal to the smoking bowl and started counting over again. Finally she finished the second time and started putting the seeds and stones back in the sack. "It is February thirteenth," she said without looking at me.

"Which means we're losing time even if we don't sleep?"

"Yes, I think so." Her voice trembled.

"What's the matter?"

"I am frightened, and I wish Xablanque were here."

"Me, too. Both."

She came to me, then, and curled up in my arms, and for the longest time we held each other without saying anything. I think I slept. I certainly drifted in and out of semiconscious limbo, and I suspect Huna did, too. However, we were both awake when the stone door rolled away and the messenger called us out of Jaguar House.

If I had been in a better humor and my nose hadn't hurt and my eyes hadn't burned and my body hadn't felt like warmed-over death, I would have laughed at the expression of disbelief on the messenger's face when we came straggling out behind a line of eighty or ninety knives. His expression turned to one of terror when the jaguars followed us out, and he left in a hurry.

One of the long knives took our canteens and brought them back in a few minutes full of clear cold water. Huna cooked some oatmeal and made me eat it along with a heaping handful of pills, then made me drink four cups of tea, and sent one of the knives for more water before the messenger returned.

As usual, we took our time packing up. Before we left, Huna read the stones. To our complete surprise the seeds and stones said it was February 8 on the surface. She double-checked it. "February 8," she said with a shake of her head. "Time's going backward."

"God help us," I muttered. "What does that mean?"

"I don't know."

"Any ideas on what we should do next?" I asked as we followed the messenger with our escort of knives and jaguars.

"Play the game and keep an eye on the time every chance we get. What else can we do?"

"What about the comet?"

"I have a strange feeling it will be back, T.J."

"Then when it comes, we'll have to try to destroy it no matter what's going on with the lords."

"Yes. . . . We never did make love," she said, taking my hand.

"After we've defeated the lords and destroyed the comet."

The corners of her mouth barely turned up, but there was a brightness in her eyes. "I'll hold you to that."

I squeezed her hand. "Of course you will."

Huna smiled ever so slightly. "Let's go beat the lords."

Chapter Sixty-two

"Two against two," I said as I took off my pack and laid it beside Huna's.

"You can't change now," Twenty-one Death answered from the lords' bleachers. Her voice trembled, and even from where we stood I could see her black eyes darting back and forth along the lines of knives and jaguars on our side of the court. "The agreement was three against three."

"But that was before we lost Xablanque."

"Sounds like a personal problem to me." She turned her back on us and joined the huddle of lords, probably to get away from the stares of the jaguars.

"Don't worry, T.J., we'll be all right. I have a feeling about all this."

I took the Crain machete out and laid it on top of the pack. "Me, too, only mine isn't a good feeling—but it's actions we have to trust, not feelings. You ready?"

She bent over slowly and touched her toes without bouncing. "Let me stretch a little more. You go down and practice if you want to."

I climbed down, but a step before I reached the court, the referee threw the ball at me. Not to me—at me. I caught it as I stumbled down the last step, then staggered halfway across the court before I caught my balance.

"Great move," one of the lords shouted weakly. "Do it again."

I ignored her and dribbled toward the closest hoop, but I knew it was going to be some great basketball game with us outnumbered three to two and me so tired I couldn't even walk straight. My first practice shot missed the hoop by an easy foot and bounced off the wall. So did the second. The third was an air ball. My fifth shot was the first one to go through and already my arms felt like lead.

"Fancy, fancy."

"Watch out, Twenty-one Death. He's practicing deception."

"Yeah, he wants you to think it went through the hoop even when it didn't."

I missed the sixth shot.

"When they lose, can we have him drawn and quartered? We haven't drawn and quartered anyone in a long time."

"Great idea!"

"All right!"

"He'll be the d-and-q dude."

They all laughed nervously.

My seventh shot went in, and so did the eighth, but the catcalls and jibes from the lords didn't stop because I was finally finding my touch.

Twenty-one Death and Five Death practiced at the other end of the court with Spirit Burner, then moments after Huna joined me, the referee shouted, "Let's play ball!"

"Give her a chance to practice," I said.

"Play ball."

"You want me to call Jambiya the Wicked down here to cut out your vocal chords?" I asked.

The referee looked up at our fan club. Jambiya rocked on his handle. Little Jaguar Heart snarled. "Practice time," the referee shouted.

"Play ball," Twenty-one Death called in a strained voice as she ran to the middle of the court.

I trotted over to join her. "We may not have to play. I may just call on our friends to come down here and help me kill you all."

She turned her back on our side of the court. "It's time to play ball."

I spun around and brought myself nose to nose with her. "I'll tell you when it's time to play, bitch, and that's when we'll start the game—when I tell you, not before. By the way, how's your throat today?"

Without blinking she turned and ran back to their end of the court.

I walked over to where Huna was practicing and talked to her as she shot baskets. "We'll have to concentrate on defense, you know, blocking their shots whenever possible. And one of us will always need to stay close to our basket."

"You're the one in the worst shape. You stay and be the guard."

273

"Okay, but you watch out for them at the other end. Shoot from as far away as you think you can make the shot, then get back down here as quickly as you can. Don't worry about rebounds at their end. We'll let them have those for free. The ones down here are the ones we can't afford to lose."

She shot four or five more baskets, then handed me the ball, and gave me a quick kiss. "I'm ready any time you are."

"Referee, let's play ball."

Huna and Spirit Burner faced off at center court. Spirit Burner got the ball on the jump and Huna ran to help me. Five Death took a bounce pass from Spirit Burner and scored the first two points.

I passed the ball in to Huna and she charged down the court, passing Twenty-one Death, then stopping suddenly and taking a shot from a long thirty feet. The ball hit the rim and bounced away.

Spirit Burner made the next basket for the lords. Huna made her next shot from a little closer in. Five Death scored twice more.

"Eight, two," the lords shouted from the bleachers.

"Kill those suckers."

Huna dribbled down court, but Twenty-One Death ran into her from behind and knocked the ball away.

"Foul!" I shouted.

The referee ignored me. Jaguars roared from above us. Knives clattered.

"Foul on the lords," the referee shouted.

"Cheaters!"

"No foul! No foul!"

The jaguars roared again. The referee handed the ball to Huna and she bounced it in bounds.

"Foul on the humans," the referee said. "Illegally putting the ball in play."

"How else are we supposed to put the ball in play?" I asked as I ran to confront him. "We're short a man."

"No, you're not," a voice boomed. Xablanque's body flew into the court in the clutches of the platinum, scissortailed comet-bird.

I cringed at the sight of the bird's talons sunk deep into Xablanque's blood-stained shoulder. My stomach turned over and I wanted to vomit. Xablanque's body was very obviously dead, but the comet-bird was animating it like an obscene puppet.

"Unfair!"

"Illegal player!"

"Technical foul!"

"SILENCE!" the bird roared.

Everything stilled in the echo of that voice. Then from the jungle came the nervous chattering of monkeys and the squawks of macaws. The comet-bird stared around with its golden eyes. "I will play with the humans," it announced.

"We don't want you," I said.

"You have no choice."

"We do!" Five Death swung a curved war club in a great arc as he shouted.

The comet-bird jerked Xablanque out of the way.

Five Death swung again and again.

"Stop!" Twenty-one Death shouted.

Five Death ignored her.

The comet-bird dodged this way and that, sometimes jerking Xablanque's body, sometimes being jerked by it.

I stumbled out of their way and pulled Huna to my side, fascinated and repelled at the same time.

Spirit Burner joined the attack, swinging his war club in wild circles as he charged the comet-bird from behind.

"No!" Twenty-one Death shouted. "Stop, fools!"

The comet-bird barely had time to turn before Spirit Burner's club connected in an explosion of sparks. The bird sailed off Xablanque's body into the corner of the court. Spirit Burner's club sailed after it. The comet-bird lay twitching and screaming in the corner. Its edges burned.

Xablanque's body collapsed and twitched in a silent parody of the bird.

Chapter Sixty-three

Instinct made me run for Five Death's club. As I snatched it off the stone floor almost without breaking stride, I saw the comet-bird struggling to its feet.

In an instant I saw that enemy I had come to face for what

it was. The comet-bird hadn't lied to us. Its shiny metallic feathers covered a terrible darkness that bled now through the club wound Five Death had given it, and I saw in its black blood the death of my hopes and dreams, the loss of everything I valued. With all my strength I swung from my heels at the rising comet-bird.

"Nooooo!" a lord screamed as the club went through its arc.

"Aaaaa!" I screamed as the club made contact.

A silent starburst filled the court.

The force of the blow threw me to the ground.

Jaguars roared. Owls screeched. Lords moaned in agony.

Somewhere I heard Huna calling me, but my open eyes were blind.

Thunder hit me. It shook the stone court, buffeting my body against the wall over and over. "Huna," I cried. "Huna."

A whirlwind sucked the air from my lungs and whipped my clothes against my body. Wind tore hair from my head and dug under my fingernails. Wind beat me almost senseless.

Then slowly, ever so slowly, the thunder rolled off into the distance and the wind subsided. I raised myself to my hands and knees, but I still couldn't see, and the buzzing in my ears was almost overpowering as though a giant saw were cutting its way through my head. I trembled in fear.

Hands touched me, gentle hands. A voice made noises behind the buzzing. Huna. It had to be Huna who helped me to my feet and led me slowly away. "I can't see," I said. My own voice echoed in my distant mind.

"I can't see," I said as loudly as I could, "and I can't hear. Is that you, Huna?"

"Zzzz," a voice said. She patted my hand. With her steadying me, and me feeling my way, we climbed the steps. After easing me to the grass, she laid me back, and a few moments later laid a cool damp cloth over my eyes. It felt so good, I cried.

Dreams followed the tears, vague visions of contentment and peace pierced by screaming shafts of blackness and the babble of angry voices rising toward hysteria.

When I woke up, the cloth was almost dry. I heard voices arguing in the distance, hysterical voices I recognized from my dreams and from before.

"T.J.? Are you awake? I think the lords are planning something."

As I pushed myself up on one elbow, the cloth fell off my face, and I opened my eyes. Everything looked fuzzy and too bright, like the bad television reception out in the country, but at least I could see. I squinted at Huna and tried to smile. "What happened? How long was I out?"

"Not very long—an hour, maybe. But the comet escaped."

"We failed?" Had I screwed up our one chance? I felt sick. "What about Xablanque?" My voice thickened. "At the least we have to bury him. We owe him . . ." With deliberate care I rolled over onto my hands and knees, then stood up and looked around.

Xablanque's body still lay crumpled in the court. Neither the lords, nor Jambiya and his brother knives, nor the jaguars were anywhere to be seen. But from behind the lords' bleachers I could hear the lords arguing with one another. "Where are the knives and jaguars?"

"I don't know." She stood up beside me, fatigue written into her face. "And right now I don't care. While you bring Xablanque's body up here, I'm going to pull everything out of our packs that we don't absolutely need so we can travel as light as possible to try to find the comet."

"For Xablanque's sake," I said.

"Yes."

I kissed her cheek. Climbing down into the ballcourt, my knees trembled to remind me just how weak my body was. Eight or ten long silver tail feathers lay scattered about the court, and some instinct made me collect them. After marveling a moment at their slick, fine texture, I stuck them in my belt. Climbing back up with Xablanque's dead weight over my shoulder took every ounce of strength and determination I had.

As I reached the top step, Huna screamed. I looked up and saw Twenty-one Death charging around the end of the court with a black war club in her hand.

I dumped Xablanque's body and scrambled weakly over to where Huna was digging frantically through our packs.

"The guns," she shouted. "Our pistols are gone!"

Twenty-one Death was only yards away.

With a fierce pull, I jerked my Crain machete out of its sheath. "Get behind me!"

When Twenty-one Death realized I was armed, she slowed and began to circle us, her club held shoulder high, her black eyes full of hatred.

"Haven't you had enough, bitch?" I asked, brandishing the machete.

"You're going to die. Both of you stinking mortals. You almost ruined everything." She stepped closer and swung her obsidian toothed club back and forth. "Your puny machete is no match for this."

"You think you're tough? You've never faced a blade like this one. Come on over here and find out how puny yours is. We'll see—"

An angry roar filled the air. Lords shouted. Knives clattered. I glanced across the ballcourt. The lords scrambled up their bleachers pursued by jaguars and knives.

Twenty-one Death swung at me.

"T.J.!"

I ducked and spun away. It was a mistake. There was too much space between me and Huna. She had a short camp knife in her hand, but it would be useless against Twenty-one Death's club. "Jambiya!" I shouted. "Help!"

With a fierce swing of her black club, Twenty-one Death broadened the gap between me and Huna. Suddenly I was very much aware that the steps leading down to the ballcourt were close behind me. A wrong move and—

"Die, bitch!" I screamed as I charged Twenty-one Death.

She stepped backward and swung her club.

I sidestepped her blow and swung my machete. Beyond her, Five Death charged Huna. "Look out!"

Time slowed. My machete cut halfway through Twenty-one Death at the waist, but came to a jarring halt when it hit her spine.

Her eyes bulged. Her mouth opened. The obsidian club tumbled from her hand. She stared at me in disbelief. Then her body fell sideways, jerking the machete out of my hand.

Huna shouted in anger.

I turned.

Five Death swung his club backhanded and missed her.

I scrambled to get the machete without taking my eyes off Five Death and Huna.

He faked a sidearmed swing that turned into an overhead and his club crushed Huna's skull.

Chapter Sixty-four

I knew Huna was dead before she hit the ground.

Dead.

Huna dead.

Just like that.

Blood covered the handle of my Crain machete, but it was not slippery. It fit my hand like vengeance fit the hand of God, and it set out to finish earning its Predator name.

Time slowed until the only thing that moved was me. I dove into a liquid somersault toward Five Death, with every nerve in me concentrating on what had to be done. As I rolled up and out of the somersault, I swung the Crain with such force that it chopped Five Death's left leg off above the knee. The blade cut halfway through his right leg before it slid free.

Sometime later—it seemed like days later—I stood over the crippled lord and plunged the Crain's double-edged point into the center of his chest. Then I fell away from him to kneel beside Huna's body.

Time returned, and I wept.

I wept for a long time.

The weeping and the time seemed part of the same thing inside me—the time held the tears and the tears pulled the time forward. Or backward, or up or down, or sideways. It didn't matter in that hell-hole. Nothing mattered.

The comet had escaped. The earth was finished. True Jaguar was finished. I was finished.

When I stopped crying, I sat there looking at Huna's body until I saw Shirlito Velasquez and I felt like O'Hara, and I wondered how I could leave her and Reyes down there. And how could I not? There was no way I could get their bodies out of Xibalba. All I could do was dig their graves and mark them well, and if the DSA wanted to come down and get them, that would be just fine—if there was a DSA on the surface, or a surface anymore.

Off in the distance I heard the snarls of jaguars and a faint sound that might have been the grating of knives on bone. A scream drifted on the wind to me, twisted and turned by the currents of air so that it sounded like Huna. I wiped my face, then forced myself to my feet and looked around for something to dig with. All I saw was my Crain machete standing in the chest of Five Death. It wasn't meant for digging, yet it would have to do.

At first I didn't want to touch it, but I forced myself to take a firm grip on the handle and pull. The machete didn't budge. Very reluctantly I put my left foot on Five Death's chest beside the blade and jerked the machete free.

"What are you going to do now?" a voice behind me asked.

"Cut your damn head off," I said as I spun around to confront Lefthanded Hummingbird who buzzed back and forth over Huna's body. "You lied, you miserable s.o.b., and I'd like to get—"

"I didn't lie."

I swung the machete at him even though I knew he was out of range. Tears blurred my already fuzzy vision. "You said Huna would live. Does she look like she's living to you?"

"I didn't lie."

"Just get the hell out of here," I said, brushing the tears roughly from my eyes. "I've got to dig a grave."

"He'll be angry if you do that."

Lowering myself to my knees, I asked, "Who?"

"Him in the tree. Xablanque—One Hunahpu."

"Who?"

"Xablanque. The head in the tree."

Instinctively I looked over at the calabash tree.

"Go ask him if you don't believe me."

"All right, I will." I don't know why I did it, don't know why I believed Hummingbird, but I walked around the ballcourt and up to the calabash tree.

"I'm glad you came," one of the calabashes said.

"What do you mean? Who are you?"

"Look at me closely. I am Xablanque. Can't you see that?"

Stepping closer I did see that— "Don't be ridiculous."

"Nothing in Xibalba is ridiculous."

"Of course."

"How foolish of you to think otherwise."

I stood in silence, eyes on the ground. The voice was definitely Xablanque's. "What do you want from me? You want me to bury you with your body?"

"Yes, no, well, not exactly. I want you to take your machete to the jungle immediately behind me and there you will find a croton tree. Cut it down and build a funeral pyre with its trunk and branches."

"You want to be cremated? I don't think I can do that."

"Please, True Jaguar, listen to me. Build a funeral pyre with the croton tree. Put my body and Hunahpu Woman's body side by side on the pyre—and my head, don't forget my head—then set the pyre on fire and make sure we burn down to ashes."

"Well, Xablanque, I can burn you, I think. But Huna? I don't think I could stand to burn her body like that. I think I'll just bury her."

"No! You have to cremate us both on a pyre made from a croton tree."

"Why?"

"I can't tell you why."

"Then I won't do it."

"You have to."

"I won't"

"Then you are condemning Hunahpu Woman to stay in this underworld forever."

"What do you mean?"

"Just that. If you don't cremate her, she'll never escape from this hell."

Chapter Sixty-five

Hummingbird led me to a croton tree, but after what seemed like hours of hacking on it with my Crain machete, I began to doubt if I would ever get it cut down. Between my fatigue, my stuffy nose and head, and the numbness that had settled around my soul, I couldn't find much energy to put behind my blows. Even though the machete was up to the task, I wasn't. I collapsed at the foot of the croton and wept.

Xablanque was dead. Huna was dead. And the comet had escaped. We had failed. On top of everything else, my fever was out of control again. That made me giggle sadly.

"We have come to help, True Jaguar," said the familiar baritone voice of Jambiya from close in front of me. "Most of the lords have been caught, stabbed, and killed, and the jaguars even now are feasting on their ancient stinking carcasses. The head of Xablanque told us about the cremation, so, we returned to help you."

"Thank you, Jambiya the Wicked," I said, wiping the tears from my eyes.

"We mean no offense to you and the Great Blade, but if you will move to get out of the way, we will do the work."

I forced myself up and away from the croton tree, and Jambiya and his brothers attacked it with a vengeance. They had hacked about two-thirds of the way through when something rubbed against my leg accompanied by a guttural purr, and I jumped sideways.

"Forgive me," Little Jaguar Heart said, "I did not mean to frighten you."

"It's all right," I said, stepping back and scratching him behind the ears. There were still a few dark traces of blood on his muzzle.

He purred and rubbed his arched back against my leg. "We feasted on the lords, now we've come to help haul the wood."

"Thank you."

"No, thank you, True Jaguar. It is you who set us free. We are sorry about what happened to Hunahpu Woman and Xablanque."

Tears rolled down my hot face again, but I tried to ignore them.

"Timberrrrr!"

The croton tree crashed down away from us and soon the knives were hacking off manageable pieces and the jaguars were hauling them away. I dragged the biggest piece I could out of the jungle, then began building a pyre midway between the calabash tree of One Hunahpu and Xablanque, and the ballcourt. I had to stop frequently to rest and drink water, and I dosed myself good with penicillin, Rhinohistabs, and aspirin, none of which seemed to help. Eventually, however, we had used all the wood from the croton tree, and I guessed that it would be enough to do the job.

That finished, I lay down and slept.

Dreams haunted me—nightmares. I fell endlessly and was pursued through thick mud where I had to urinate and couldn't while demons rubbed wet sandpaper on my face—and I woke up to the sight of Little Jaguar Heart licking me.

"We fear for you," he said. "You are very sick."

"I know. I fear for myself." But I didn't, not really, not for my physical self, not for the me who could be attacked by things so ordinary as colds and fevers.

No, I had this terrible feeling that my physical self would be all right and I would cremate Huna and Xablanque in order to save them from eternity in hell. Then I would leave and walk up to the surface where a different hell awaited me. And though I might not live very long in a world destroyed by a comet, without Huna, however long I lived would seem like eternity.

"It is time to light the pyre," Xablanque said. His voice was like a hook and line that jerked me into the present.

With great resignation I climbed out of the sleeping bag and stood up. There atop the pyre were the bodies of Hunahpu Woman and Xablanque—with his head in place, his missing neck hidden by a collar of leaves. He stared at me.

"Must I, Xablanque?"

"Yes. It is time."

Not knowing what else to do, I put on my dirty jeans and shirt, took the camp lighter from my pack, and walked over to the pyre. Knowing that hesitation might lead to failure, I squatted down and held the lighter's flame to the kindling-size croton branches. They caught fire with surprising ease, and I moved quickly around the pyre igniting all four sides.

The flames grew rapidly.

"You must make sure we are totally consumed," Xablanque shouted. "Then leave Xibalba the way we entered. If you escape with the comet's feathers, that is as good as destroying it."

Every instinct in me wanted to put out the fire, but I stood back. As the flames engulfed the whole stack of wood and the bodies of Xablanque and my beloved Huna—Huna carrying our babies now dead in her womb—I crossed myself and recited the Lord's Prayer aloud. I must have recited it several times, because I caught myself in the middle of it and realized I had said those same words but a few moments earlier. Nevertheless, I finished that recitation and started over, the rote of it holding me still, God giving me courage where I had none of my own.

When next I was conscious of myself, heat burned my face as I sat staring into the flames of the cremation pyre. I scooched away from the pyre until I reached a spot where the heat was more tolerable. The jaguars and the knives were all gone. In the heat waves above the pyre I saw Huna wearing a sky blue dress, smiling, walking toward me with a laughing child in each hand, and tears burst from my eyes. I lay down and cried.

Perhaps I slept. Perhaps not. It was difficult to know, but I didn't feel rested. The pyre, when I looked at it again, had settled into a middle level of burning, seeming to be neither growing nor dying down. My fingers felt cold, but when I put them to my face, it felt like I was as hot as the pyre, and I knew my fever still burned out of control. I forced myself to take more aspirin, then drink all the water that was left in my canteen before I crawled in my sleeping bag and slept for real.

Waking was easier the next time I opened my eyes, mainly because the macaws and owls and monkeys were flying in a great coordinated pattern in the sky above me, circling the comet rather like a rose window pattern from one of Europe's great cathedrals, and I marveled at the intricacy of it and the way it shifted like a slowly turned kaleidoscope until I remembered that monkeys couldn't fly, after which the monkeys sailed down from the formation and dozens of jaguars flew up to take their places.

The monkeys landed in a circle around me and complained bitterly that I had ruined their day by remembering that they couldn't fly, and begging me to forget that I remembered, so I did, and soon the monkeys joined the others in the sky, and the pattern they all flew grew even grander than it had been.

Chapter Sixty-six

Jambiya woke me by pricking my arm ever so lightly with his sharp point. There was a gentleness about it that brought tears to my eyes.

"True Jaguar, wake up. We need to know what we should do now."

I looked from him to where the funeral pyre had been and saw that there was nothing left but a low grey heap of ash-covered coals that reminded me of the remains of the big council fires we had at the Y camp when I was a boy. Even the feeling of something lost was similar. I tried to speak, but nothing came out. "Water," I croaked.

One of the large stainless steel survival knives dragged my canteen over.

"Thanks," I said after I drank, "and thanks for filling it for me. I don't know what you should do next, Jambiya." My voice was gravelly and congested. "You can do whatever you want, I guess."

"Even when the new lords come? Maybe we should leave with you, True Jaguar."

"New lords? What makes you think there will be new lords?"

"He's right. There are always new lords," Lefthanded Hummingbird said from his perch on Huna's pack. "But you, Jambiya, if you go to the surface, you will just be an ordinary knife. You won't be able to talk or move or maybe even think on your own. Better that you should stay here and be special than go there and be ordinary. True Jaguar, however, had better get out of here before the new lords arrive."

"You going to lead the way for me?" I asked with a sigh. I guessed it was time to think about leaving.

"No. There is no food for me on *ube Xibalba*. If I did know a way out where I wouldn't starve, I would have left here long ago. Skull Owl will guide you."

"Why should I trust Skull Owl? What's he ever done for me?"

"I don't know. But only the messenger owls can lead you out. They're the only ones who can see the true way."

"Well, then, go find Skull Owl and tell him I'll be ready to leave . . . soon. And speaking of messengers, what happened to those messenger-guards, anyway?"

"They weren't real," Hummingbird said.

I stared at him in disbelief. "What do you mean they weren't real? I killed one. He looked real to me when I shot him."

"He wasn't. None of them were. The lords created them out of your fears—out of your phobias—so they could keep you in line."

"You mean they found Arab terrorists in our minds, so they created illusions of Arab terrorists to guard us?" I shook my head. "Is that why the messenger-guards never shot at us?"

"Yes, and yes, again. Good for you, True Jaguar. Rather ingenious of the lords, don't you think?"

I nodded. "Yeah, I suppose so. I'm sure glad I didn't have a phobia about dinosaurs or something. That would have been scary as hell. But wait a minute. Their rifles were real. Explain that."

"Were they?"

"They felt real and functioned like they were real and they fired like they were real, and mine was real enough to kill a referee and shoot up the lords."

"Or did they just believe they were shot up?"

I looked down and saw the comet feathers stuck in my belt. Pulling one out, I held it up, surprised again by its cold brightness. "What about this?"

"That's real," Hummingbird said.

"You mean . . ." Fever burned in my head. "Never mind. I get the point." This was the wrong place and I was too exhausted to argue with Lefthanded Hummingbird, god of the Mehica, about what was real and what wasn't. I stuck the feather back with the others—remembering suddenly that Xablanque had said that if I escaped with the feathers that would be as good as destroying the comet. "Well, like I said, go find Skull Owl and tell him I'll be ready to leave, soon."

Hummingbird flew away. I sat and stared at the ashes, aware of how lightheaded I felt, aware that Huna and Xablanque really were gone, that there wouldn't be any babies for me and Shirlito to play with, no graves of "Velasquez" and "Reyes" for me to visit, no one who would understand what I had lost or how I had lost them—if there was anyone left above to understand anything.

A drop of rain hit me on the hand. Another hit my head, then another and another, big drops the size of quarters. Rain in Xibalba? What next?

The embers of the cremation pyre whispered, *Yes. Yes. Yes*, as the drops of rain hit them.

I found my poncho in the bottom of my pack, but by the time I got it on I was soaking wet. Through the heart of a strange stillness of air, the rain increased, hit harder, faster, heavier, straight down until I felt like I was standing under a waterfall.

The ground turned into a foot-deep lake. The ballcourt filled like a swimming pool. I slogged my way over toward the lords' bleachers, looking for some shelter, and as I reached the bleachers, the rain seemed to slacken considerably.

Turning to go back and gather up my gear, I thought the rain looked heavier over the pyre. I stared at it. More rain was falling directly on the ashes of the pyre than anywhere else. A turbulent pool of water surrounded the remains of the pyre, and a riverlike current ate at its edges and washed its ashes away as though Hurakan, the god of rain, were washing the grit of Huna's and Xablanque's bones away to some better place. Maybe Xablanque had known something like that would happen and that was why he had been so adamant with me about burning Huna's . . .

My teeth chattered, and my face burned as I leaned against the lords' bleachers, shivering and wet under my poncho, watching the rain wash the funeral ashes away, feeling the rain wash the tears from my face as well, tears for the woman I loved, for our children in her womb, and tears, too, for the man who had so bravely led us into the heart of Xibalba.

When the rain finally slackened and stopped, and the water drained away, there was little more than a clear patch of earth left to mark where the cremation pyre had been. Our equipment was soaked, but since I was going to leave most of it behind, I didn't care. All I needed was enough water and food to get me out of Xibalba—and enough aspirin, because this fever that raged through my body showed no signs of breaking, and I knew that if it got too high, it could kill me.

That thought was appealing, but as I sorted and packed, I tried not to think about how comforting it would be to just to close my eyes and go to sleep and never wake up. Something stronger, more basic inside me wanted to get out of there, out of Xibalba and all it stood for, and the fever would have to kill me before that need to escape would be defeated.

Skull Owl showed up just as I was ready to put my pack on. "You must go now, mortal," it said, hovering its skull-shaped, legless body in front of me. "And leave those tail feathers here."

"Screw you."

"The lords are not pleased."

"The lords are dead."

"The *new* lords are very much alive. The world requires an evil underworld, you know, and someone to rule it. There will always be lords of Xibalba."

"Then why don't they face me themselves? Tell them to come on down here and we'll play water polo for their lives," I said flipping my hand at the ballcourt brimming with water.

"One would be foolish to challenge the new lords."

"You know, Skull Owl, I'm almost tempted to hang around here and see what these new s.o.b.'s look like."

"I would not recommend it, mortal."

"And I wouldn't give a moldy mango in a hurricane for what you recommend. But don't worry, deathbird. You show me the way out and I'll leave, because I have nothing to stay around this disgusting place for, anymore."

"Leave the comet's tail feathers as the lords command."

"No."

He stared at me with his black unreadable eyes. "It is your life to waste as you please. Follow me, then."

Skull Owl flew ahead and I followed, forcing myself to put one foot in front of the other down a stone path between two buildings to Green Road, then up onto Green Road.

"Can you find your way back from here alone?"

"No."

"Mortals," he said with more than a little disgust. Again he flew ahead, hovered near the stone walls lining

288

the road until I caught up, then flew farther down the road. I saw no natives nor any sign of them. Maybe they, too, had been killed by the knives and jaguars.

Fever ate at the inside of my skull, building pressure, squeezing sweat out of every pore. Vision blurred. Skull Owl doubled and became two birds leading me, then four. Only my need to get out of there and my realization that I could walk through all the hallucinations that confronted me, kept me staggering along.

Chapter Sixty-seven

I saw Huna that first time we met, saw Huna, who was Velasquez, when she questioned me, saw how beautiful she was with her perfect Mayan face, especially beautiful when she bent over naked in the motel, and when I woke up to her in bed curled up against me . . . saw her in front of me on Green Road, motioning me into her arms, felt her wrapped around me, kissing my face, whispering like the fanning of wings in my face, hearing Skull Owl telling me I was walking too slowly . . . and walking faster into her arms because she waited for me there in the shimmering light . . .

"Best of all," she said, "because we have each other . . . that our children—"

"Our children? What about our children?"

"We will have many children who will—"

"Our children are dead! . . . Dead! Dead! . . . You killed them! You and Xablanque-Reyes and Tohil and Cristos. They'd be alive if it weren't for you. You killed our children, damn you to hell!"

Killed our children, hell . . .

Killed your children, well . . .

Kill your children well. Don't mind the smell, that they will die by.

And wash their bones away. No place to pray, no place you can go cry. . . .

For your days are done, no seeds and stones, to tell the time by. . . .

*Oh, don't ask your children why, you had to let them die,
'cause you know they hate you.*

The little guitar riff at the end of the song intrigued me,
because I always wanted to be able to play guitar and make
the strings talk like that.

Or the harmonica. I tried the harmonica, but never quite
figured out how I was supposed to hold my tongue and suck
and blow and move the thing back and forth all at once. In my
head, though, I played a sweet harmonica.

Except, that wasn't right, was it? For one clear moment
I knew I had to get control of myself.

I stopped. I wiped the tears from my face. I drank some
water and took some aspirin. I walked again.

My clothes steamed with the heat of Xibalba and the heat
of my fever. Unsure about where I was going or why, I kept
following a strange bird who looked familiar, following a disgusting bird. Sometimes he hovered in front of me, but when
I tried to talk to him, he flew away from me. All I knew was
that I had to follow him.

Why? Did anyone know the answer to that question? Why
was this bird so important? Where was he leading me? Why
did I feel compelled to . . .

For an instant I wasn't sure who I was. Then I knew. I
knew for certain. Huna was dead. Babies were dead. Xablanque was dead. Velasquez was dead. Reyes was dead. And
why? Why?

Because I was Death. I was Cruel Death, Unstoppable
Death, Invincible Death. I was the Great White Indian *Brujo*
of Death. Who else could I be? And that disgusting bird was
my familiar, my guide, my little devil incarnate, leading me
to . . . ? The bird was Owl Bird . . . no, Skull Bird . . . no,
Skull Owl. Skull Owl! That was it. Skull Owl was my devil
bird and he was leading me to Xibalba.

"We're off to see Xibalba, the underworld of the gods, a
wiz, a wiz, a wiz, a wiz, if ever a wiz there was. The—"

"True Jaguar!"

"If ever there was, the wizard was, the problem was because, because—because, because, because, because—"

"True Jaguar!"

I stopped and stared at Skull Owl. "What? Why are you

shouting at me? Don't you know that you are my slave and I am your master?"

"This is the crossroads," Skull Owl said. "There is the path that leads to the exit from Xibalba. So long as you follow the stone-lined path and get out before the comet finds you, you will be safe."

"What if I get lost? What then? Will I be lost forever in Xibalba? Huh? What about that? What can I do if—"

"Just follow the stone-lined path. I will check on your progress occasionally. If you get lost, I will guide you back to the path. However, if you stay on the path, you won't get lost, so I won't have to check on you, will I?"

"Of course you will. How foolish of you to think otherwise!" I shouted. Then I broke into convulsive laughter and finally had to sit in the middle of the crossroads where Red Road, White Road, Black Road, and Green Road all came together. There at the exact center of the crossroads, I laughed until the pain was too overwhelming, then I cried until I couldn't breathe, blew my nose and coughed up gobbets of black sputum, and then lay down and fell asleep.

Sweat running into my eyes woke me up. Every muscle I moved cried in protest, but I forced myself up into a sitting position with a clear understanding of what I had to do. First water and aspirin. Then on my feet against my body's painful resistance. Then stumble down off the crossroads and onto the rock-lined path. I had to get out of Xibalba.

With the feathers! I checked my belt. Still there.

The path dropped from the crossroads, then rose gradually up a hill. Step by small step, curse by loud curse, I climbed that hill, the pack on my back like the weight of a thousand worlds. A hundred steps short of the crest, I couldn't walk any farther. I shucked the pack, took out the medical kit, and fastened it to my belt beside my canteen opposite the side where my Crain Predator hung. If I had to fight my way out, if I was confronted by the comet, the machete was the only weapon I had left. I washed down some penicillin and aspirin with codeine, tied the sleeves of my down jacket around my waist, and forced myself up the hill, leaving the pack behind me.

Once over the top of the ridge, I stumbled down the trail almost at a run. My legs burned with pain. My knees threatened to collapse. But I knew I couldn't stop, knew I had to keep going no matter what I felt, no matter how great the pain. In the distance someone called for True Jaguar, but I kept going.

The path leveled out and disappeared into thick jungle. I slowed to a steady walk, counting a cadence I had learned in the army to keep me moving.

"You had a good home, but you left. You're right. Your mother was home when you left. You're right. Your father was home when you left. You're right. Your mother, your father, your sister, your comet, they all were home when you left. You're right. Sound off! One, two. *Sound off.* Three, four. *Cadence count!* One, two, three, four, one two . . . three four!"

But Huna was dead when you left. "You're right." *Xablanque was dead when you left.* "You're right." *Xablanque and Huna and all of the babies, they all were dead when you left.* "You're right!" *Sound off.* "One, two!" *Sound off.* I stumbled and fell.

When I climbed to my hands and knees and looked up, there in front of me at the end of the path I could see Pus River. Then I could smell it. Then I vomited up water and stringy mucus, heaving and straining to empty an already empty stomach.

Only after the spasms stopped did I dare struggle to my feet. I rinsed out my mouth with the last of my water, wondering where I would find more water and if I could escape Xibalba without it. Then taking very deliberate steps, I followed the path to Pus River's edge and there to my surprise, saw what remained of the bamboo bridge we had built across it.

Some of the bridge's sections had lost part of their bamboo, but the span was complete from one side of Pus River to the other. After only a moment's hesitation, I turned around and walked away from the river until I was thirty or forty yards from it. I turned, took a deep breath, screamed at the top of my lungs, and ran for the bridge.

The bamboo cracked under the impact of my first leaping step. Pus spurted up. I never broke stride. I ran like the bridge was made of concrete. I focused on the other bank of the river.

More bamboo cracked. More pus spurted high into the

air, releasing jets of putrid gas. My left foot slipped. I stumbled forward. Out of control. Falling.

My right leg was jarred. Then my left. They buckled underneath me. I stretched forward and hung in the air for an impossible time before sliding into the dust on the river bank.

Dust clogged my nose and mouth. I couldn't spit. My tongue was swollen. My lungs gasped for air. I choked and coughed and sneezed and crawled my way up the river bank.

Tears rolled down my cheeks into the corners of my mouth. A dry tongue lapped them in, and finally I spit out a wad of mud the size of a baby's fist.

I cried some more and sucked in the tears and air, and when I could finally breathe at a normal rate, I forced myself to my feet and started up the path again through a haze that blurred the jungle where macaws squawked and monkeys chattered.

The path rose up a new ridge, and I barely remembered the sequence of rivers and ridges when we had all hiked into Xibalba. Blood River should be next.

Step by step I dared not look up to see how much higher the ridge rose above me, because I knew that if it was more then ten steps, I would die before I made it. All I could promise myself was ten more steps from where I stood.

Just ten more steps. With every step I promised myself ten more. Each step became number one of ten. I knew my feet could take ten more steps.

The world shrank to the path and the movement of leaden legs one slow step at a time. From dusty steps to gravel steps to rocky steps to slippery wet steps to rocky . . .

As I turned around, I fell. There, a yard in front of my face, lay the wet step—a narrow slimy trickle of water across the path. I dragged myself forward on my belly and stuck my face in the slimy stream, greedily sucking up the warm, green water until my stomach bloated. Finally I rolled away from it and closed my eyes in relief.

Chapter Sixty-eight

Thirst woke me. Thick cotton pads covered my tongue. Warm glue filled my nose and ran thickly down the back of my throat. Hot, dry fire burned my itching skin. Yet I shivered until the last dark tentacles of dreams released my mind.

My unfocused eyes stared up at the grey sky, trying to make sense of the moment, trying to grasp and hold some reality, some truth I could cling to. The first thing I remembered was the water, the precious water, and I twisted my aching body over far enough to suck the slimy wetness into my mouth. After rinsing the layers of sticky cotton from my tongue, I forced myself to swallow all the water I could hold.

Then as I rolled onto my stiff back again, I remembered that Huna was dead. Or was it Velasquez? Or was it both of them?

Yes. Both of them. Huna and Xablanque. Velasquez and Reyes. Dead. Very dead.

Like Five Death and Thirteen Death and Twenty-one Death and Skull Sceptor and Bloody Claws. All of them, dead.

The babies, too. Dead.

But not the comet. Oh, no. It escaped. Goddamm comet.

I rolled to the water and drank some more. Besides the comet, only True Jaguar lived. Only O'Hara would walk out of Xibalba. That thought held me in a wordless question, but I couldn't hold the thought. It slipped away like the green water down my throat.

Fatigue coiled around my brain like a giant anaconda squeezing its prey, and all I wanted to do was give in to the pressure, to let the fatigue squeeze the consciousness from my brain and send me back to sleep—perhaps forever.

But from somewhere near the core of my being, from somewhere that was as much O'Hara as it was True Jaguar, anger rose up to fight the fatigue, and forced me to act. With more of the green water I washed down penicillin and aspirin with codeine tablets. That was the last of the penicillin, but for the first time since I had gotten sick, I wondered if what I had needed all along was quinine instead of penicillin. Was this some form of malaria I had? I laughed. What the hell difference did it make? I hadn't brought any quinine.

With a sigh I filled my canteen. Once I stood up and got my sore feet steady under me, I had to tighten my belt a notch. Almost immediately I jerked my jeans down and squatted beside the trail. Two bad signs, I thought when I pulled my jeans up again: diarrhea and weight loss. But there was nothing I could do about them, so there was no sense in worrying.

Releasing another deep sigh with a slow shake of my head, I started hiking up the path. Mobs of muscles pulled together to painfully protest every movement of my body. I hurt from the base of my skull to my toes.

Yet the pain really didn't matter. It had changed from something that I perceived to something that was a part of me, and despite the fact that I was still running a fever, I felt a little better, as though I had passed some critical marker on my journey. That better feeling disappeared long before I reached the top of the ridge.

The pain did matter, after all. Every twenty steps I had to stop and rest, to give the pain a moment to subside. Blood pounded in my temples and behind my ears with the steady drumbeats of a jungle headache. My thigh muscles burned. My calves ached. My feet itched with pain. But after each pause to rest, I forced myself forward again. When I reached the top of the ridge, I cried, because I knew going down the path would hurt almost as much as coming up had hurt.

While I stood there sipping the warm, slimy water from my canteen, I saw a oddly shaped bird wobbling through the sky off in the distance, perhaps the comet whose tail feathers were stuck in my belt. Or perhaps Skull Owl watching over me. But the bird never flew close enough for me to see it clearly before it sank below the tree line, and I decided I didn't care which bird it was. I didn't care if it was the Great Plumed Serpent himself. I was determined to make it out on my own.

Well, maybe not totally on my own. Almost instinctively I crossed myself and recited the Lord's Prayer as I followed the path down the other side of the ridge. Skull Owl might have been marking my progress, but Tohil and Cristos were watching over me. Without proof, I knew that both of them were real and that their presence strengthened me. Yet I also knew that they didn't care in the end what happened to me.

If they had truly cared about me, they wouldn't have let Huna die. Or they would have let me die in her place.

Odd thoughts for a painful march down the ridge, I decided, and tried to dismiss them, but they wouldn't go away. For the purest second I knew the fever was causing all the craziness, but that knowledge only seemed to spur it on. Thoughts of dying, death, self-sacrifice, and suicide walked down the trail with me and served no good other than to numb my pain a bit.

I saw the bird again, wobbling, flashing, and in a moment of clarity I understood that it was the comet, the scissorbird, my silver nemesis. Then it was gone again and I didn't care.

Only when mosquitos started biting my face, and I realized that I was nearing Blood River, did my thoughts return to the present. By some lucky accident, my Skeeter Stop was in the medical kit, and once I got it on, the little beasts contented themselves with buzzing my ears. Fifty steps later I came out of the jungle to the cleared bank of Blood River and saw a most peculiar sign that certainly hadn't been there when the three of us had come this way before.

Arching over the path on my side of the river, a gaudily painted, red, green, and purple sign read:

GHADDIFI'S FERRY SERVICE
negotiable terms

Almost immediately I saw the ropes that led from the sign on my side of the river to the sign just like it on the other side of the river. The ropes ran through woven grass hoops attached to the corner posts of a large bamboo raft tied to my side of the bank. The raft was ours, by the look of it.

Posted beside the path stood a large square piece of weathered plywood with notices painted on it in English, Arabic, French, and some other language. The English part read:

IF ALLAH BE PLEASED,
THERE WILL BE NO AMERICANS, JEWS, SOUTH
AFRICANS, ENGLISH,
AZTECS, CHRISTIANS, WEST GERMANS, MEXICANS,
INFIDELS, SUNNI DOGS,

TRUE JAGUAR

OR OTHER UNCLEAN PASSENGERS ALLOWED ON THIS FERRY.

"Welcome, *effendi*," a voice called from a grass hut I hadn't noticed up the river bank. "You wish to ride on my ferry?"

"Yes," I said to the figure who appeared from the doorway, "I would like to cross the river on your ferry."

A fat, dark-skinned man wearing only tattered khaki shorts and a red and white checkered cloth like an Italian tablecloth wrapped around his head waddled down the bank toward me. A wailing kind of music trailed out of the hut behind him. "I am Akeem Gorbanifar Abdallah Rafsanjani, at your service, *effendi*. What do you offer in payment?"

The smell of Blood River, that smell of gore and death was beginning to turn my stomach. I had to pause a minute to think. There wasn't much I had left to trade for anything. "Like, what would you accept?"

"Ah, *effendi*, that is a good question. Perhaps that handsome machete you are wearing would be sufficient," the fat man said, pulling an oily rag from his back pocket and wiping his face. "That is the famous Crain Predator Machete with which you killed Five Death and Twenty-one Death, is it not?" Even though his skin was dark, it had a translucent look. Flies and mosquitos buzzed around his head.

"Yes, but how do you know about that?"

"Several of the old lords fled this way before the jaguars and knives caught them. Jambiya the Wicked—Allah have mercy on his blade—told me the unbelievable story about the *effendi*'s Great Blade."

I shook my head, wishing I could think more clearly. "What else would you accept beside my machete?"

The fat man laughed. Little clouds of mosquitos rose like puffs of smoke from his skin. "My apologies, *effendi*, but you own nothing else worth anything to me."

"Then by the mercy of Allah, I ask you to take me across for free."

The fat man stopped laughing. "You are an infidel. I owe you no mercy of Allah." His fat nose wrinkled. "I should take your precious machete, cut your head off, and sell them both to the stinking lords."

297

"All right, it's your ferry. Whatever the price, let's go."

"Give it to me, now, *effendi*." He held out his hand.

"I will give it to you when we are safely across Blood River," I said, staring into his clear beady eyes. I felt like I could almost see through him.

Neither his eyes nor his hand wavered. "Now, *effendi*."

"When we are across. That's my only guarantee that I will arrive at my destination."

"And what is my guarantee, *effendi*?"

"You have none, Ferryman Rafsanjani. Either you take me across in exchange for my machete, or I take myself across and you get nothing. It's your choice." I wished he would hurry. The stench of Blood River had worked its way even into my clogged nose and all I wanted to do was get going before I threw up.

"You are rude, *effendi*, but I wish to own your machete, so I shall conduct this business according to your rules." He bowed with a sweeping gesture toward the raft. "After you."

"You first, please," I said, returning the gesture without taking my eyes off of him.

"Allah," he said with his hands raised and his head thrown back as he waddled ahead down the riverbank, "teach this infidel some manners, I beg you."

"I don't need manners, just a ride."

He led the way onto the raft, and as soon as he saw me step aboard, he pulled hard on one of the ropes. I almost fell off, but by dropping to one knee, I managed to stay aboard. For a long moment he stared at me unhappily, then started pulling us across Blood River.

I stayed on my knee, my hand on the machete's handle, my eyes on Ferryman Rafsanjani's back. It was curious, but he seemed to have a pattern of jungle tattooed on his back.

No. That was no tattoo. The jungle on the other side of the river was visible through his back.

The man was transparent.

Chapter Sixty-nine

Halfway across the swift currents of Blood River, Ferryman Rafsanjani started laughing—a deep maniacal laugh like one from a bad horror movie. When we reached the opposite bank, his fat body doubled over with laughter.

As quickly as I could, I stepped past him onto the shore, aware all of a sudden that I was drenched in perspiration. Not only was Rafsanjani transparent, so were the trees at the edge of the jungle.

"My machete," he said, holding out his hand.

I drew the Crain slowly and held it up, admiring its blade. Then with a quick swing and a growl of determination, I slashed through one of the grass ropes holding the ferry.

The ferryman choked in midlaugh as he straightened up and stumbled toward me, rage written all over his face.

I spun and hacked through the other rope.

Rafsanjani screamed as the raft slid away from shore. He scrambled across the ferry to grab the loose end of the rope before it slipped through the grass hoops. The bloody current ran too swiftly and pulled the raft from under the ropes which dropped into the river.

"You cheated me!" he shouted as the ferry floated free into the center of Blood River.

"No, I didn't," I shouted back. "You're not real. Hummingbird told me. None of you are real. You can't cheat a devil who isn't real!"

"Infidel!" he screamed. The raft twirled around a willow tree and disappeared downstream.

I looked up the path, then back across the river. The signs for the ferry were still there, but they seemed to have faded, and their lettering wavered in the heat. I suspected that by the time I got to the top of the next ridge, the signs would be gone completely—like Rafsanjani and his imaginary ferry.

How I walked to the top of the next ridge, I don't know. All I know is that when I got there, I sat down at the foot of a big slab of rock, looked back down the trail, and remembered no more than going through the jungle and starting the climb.

If Lefthanded Hummingbird had come along and told me I had flown the rest of the way, I couldn't have proved him a liar.

With a sigh I leaned back against the rock and closed my eyes.

With a painful start I sat up, opened my eyes, and listened.

A deep bass voice way in the distance called for me above the faint roar of Neck Canyon. *"True Jaguar. True Jaguar. Bring me my feathers."*

The comet-bird.

"Damn!" I cursed as I scrambled to my feet. I worked my way over the ridge top and started down the trail. How was I going to cross Neck Canyon and escape the comet? When I had left my pack behind, I had abandoned the only way I knew of crossing the canyon. How in Xibalba was I going to get across without the pack? How stupid could I be? And where was the damned comet-bird?

"Sick, not stupid," a familiar voice said.

I jumped sideways, lost my footing, fell, and slid head-first on my back twenty yards down the trail.

Lefthanded Hummingbird hovered above me. "Now, that was stupid, True Jaguar."

"Thanks," I said as I sat up. "What the hell are you doing here? Haven't you done enough damage to my psyche already?"

"I came to tell you something."

"So spit it out and leave me alone."

"I was right. Hunahpu Woman is alive."

An image of the cremation pyre filled my eyes. My hand rested on a fist-sized rock. I picked it up and heaved it at Lefthanded Hummingbird.

"It's true!" he said. "I swear it!"

I saw Huna's body wrapped in flames. I felt the heat of her death and the chill of my grief. My second rock almost hit Hummingbird.

He zigzagged away from me. "Stop it, you idiot. She's alive and waiting for you. But so is the comet."

I smelled the burning croton tree and the stench of seared flesh. My third rock hit Hummingbird, sent him tumbling through the air before he righted himself. After hovering a moment, he buzzed up the hill at me squawking obscenities.

"Get out of here you miserable, bloodsucking, Mehican bastard of a god!" I shouted back. "You damn fraud!"

He disappeared from sight and sound.

Only then did I wonder if there might be the slightest chance he was telling . . . the comet, maybe, but . . .

Sobs wracked my body and drove me to my knees. I saw Huna die. I burned her body. I watched her ashes wash away. But that hell-bound Hummingbird had to torture me with the memory of it. I shivered and held myself as I cried. Why? Why? What did he gain from such an awful lie?

How long I cried, I don't know. Eventually I found myself lying on the trail aware that my tears had stopped and my nose was overflowing. As I sat up and blew my nose, I knew there was no sense in me staying there, and as if to confirm that, when I got to my feet I heard that voice again, calling to me above the distant roar of the Canyon of Spears.

"True Jaguar. True Jaguar. Bring me my feathers."

Down the trail I walked, mind numb, body numb, only my ears alive, straining to follow the voice, suddenly eager to face the enemy who had drawn us into Xibalba—until I saw the rocks where we had anchored our ropes.

My body woke up. I ran to the rocks, looked at the grappling hook still firmly wedged between them, then stared sadly across the canyon. Both the rope and our grass line had broken free from the other side and now hung useless against the cliff on my side of the canyon.

The roar of water and broken trees and tumbling rocks filled my head as I stared down the cliff face until it finally occurred to me that I had to climb down into the canyon and try to find a way—

True Jaguar!

I looked up and saw the comet-bird wobbling down out of the grey sky, platinum feathers blazing, talons gleaming. Grabbing for the Crain and trying to duck at the same time, I fell backward as the comet swooped past me. One talon raked my arm, and blood welled out of the long gash.

The comet screamed.

Using all my strength, I pushed myself up on one knee and held the Crain out in front of me as I tried to prepare for the next attack. Only I couldn't see the bird.

He hit me from behind. Talons seared my back. I sprawled forward gasping in pain.

As quickly as I could, I rolled onto my burning back. Sweat ate at my eyes. But I could see the comet-bird diving again, wings folded, body wobbling.

At the last instant I swung the Crain up from the ground as hard as I could. The air exploded with light. I grunted with pain. The shock numbed my arm and knocked the Crain from my hand.

The comet squealed in terror. The air burned with sulpher.

I was almost blind as I scrambled around in the dirt trying to find the machete.

My hand touched the blade and quickly found the handle. As I rose to my knees, I could see shapes, but no details. "Go to hell, you damned bird!" I shouted back.

Its cries faded as its blurry image disappeared across the canyon. For a long time I sat back on my heels and panted. Finally I forced myself back to my feet and the canyon's edge. Staring down into Neck Canyon, I knew my only chance would be to climb down and try to find a way over the river.

I sat down and cut strips off the bottom of my jeans. With the strips wrapped around my hands, and the rope wrapped around me in a rapelling loop, I walked backward over the edge of the cliff. It had been too many years since my slight training in rapelling, and twenty feet down the cliff I knew I would never make it to the bottom.

Maniacal laughter drifted across the canyon.

The rope was too thin. It cut through the cloth into my hands and through my shirt and jeans.

Leaning almost perpendicular to the cliff, I stopped. The pain was unbearable.

My head spun. My vision blurred. I growled in anger and frustration, but my voice was lost to the roaring canyon.

Relax, True Jaguar," said an oddly familiar voice. *"Breathe deeply and take one step at a time. You only have to hold on for one more step."*

It was as though the voice was in the center of my head. I breathed deeply. I took another step down, surprised to feel a small ledge under my feet. That discovery let me relax a moment.

"Good. Now one more step."

One more step. Then one more step. Then one more step. My hands burned. My back ached. My head throbbed. I stopped. Breathed deeply. Then one more step. One more step.

The journey down became a series of repeated, painful, mind-numbing actions, as though I were performing a ritual of penance for letting Huna and Xablanque die. The voice talked to me softly in my head, encouraging me, steadying me. Demanding my obedience one sliding step at a time.

I couldn't place the voice, but I knew it. I had heard it before in a different key or different clef. Mother, father, teacher, boss, friend, god—whose voice it had been I didn't know. Nor did I care.

When I reached the base of the cliff, I collapsed on the scree of gravel, closed my eyes, and crossed myself, amazed and thankful that I had made it to the bottom. I meant to take some aspirin and codeine, but couldn't find the energy to do it. The gravel was so soft, so comfortable . . .

Chapter Seventy

When I awoke, I couldn't move. My whole body was stiff and cold, and I knew I had died.

A weak grin pushed at the corners of my mouth. Dead people didn't feel pain, and even my breathing hurt. My feet and ankles throbbed with pain that filled my boots. My shoulders felt like someone had twisted the muscles tight. No, I wasn't dead. I was all too alive in the midst of my pain at the bottom of the Canyon of Spears.

"I will get my feathers and you will die!"

When I heard the comet, I remembered what had happened and forced myself to sit up on the scree. Gravel slid down the inside of my shirt and under my belt.

"Now you must cross the river," a new voice said.

"How?"

"One step at a time."

I stared at the churning river. "What am I supposed to do, walk on water?"

"One step at a time." The new voice had a familiar tone of insistence.

"Sure. One step at a time." There was no rational reason to stand and start climbing over the gravel and rocks to the water's edge. Fever made me do it. I was going to die in the Canyon of Spears. Did it matter on which side of the river I died?

"Ah, we see you now, T.J. It is good to see you."

Was it Lefthanded Hummingbird? I looked up and around, trying to see the speaker. Only Huna ever called me T.J., but Huna was dead. "Where are you, you miserable bird?"

"We are here, in the river."

I looked down into the water. It churned with boulders rolling downstream and chunks of trees tumbling around them, but I saw nothing alive.

"Here."

The voice was Huna's. The beast that jumped up the current was a catfish four or five feet long.

A second giant catfish appeared beside the first. "Who are you?" I asked.

"We are Hunahpu Woman and Xablanque. We are Velasquez and Reyes. We have come to join you."

"They're dead. They're both dead. And I might as well be dead, too, because there's no way to get out of this canyon."

"We are alive. Look at us." They seemed to speak in unison.

"I see two overfed catfish, the color of my friends' ashes."

One of them swam closer, leaping over trees and boulders in the current, more like a dolphin than a catfish. I didn't even think that catfish could jump like that.

"Listen to me, T.J.," the catfish said in Huna's voice. "You have to believe. We will help you across here, then meet you at the top."

A bitter laugh stumbled out of my mouth as I sat down on the rock. "Leave me alone. You're not real. You're malaria running crazy in my head. You're fever and bad dreams. You're the Death twins come—"

"T.J.! Stop it."

I pulled my knees up to my chest and looked up and away from the beast. "You're the Death twins come to mock me."

"Jesus O'Hara Martinez, you had better listen to me."

TRUE JAGUAR

"Why? . . . You're not real. You'll disappear like the ferryman. Leave me alone!" I closed my eyes and rested my head on my knees, feeling the heat from my forehead through the damp jeans. Tears rolled silently down my nose.

"Martin, I love you," the catfish said. "You have to trust us. You have to believe. We can help you across the river. Xablanque says there are stone steps up the other cliff—steps you can climb to meet us at the top."

The damned catfish kept talking to me, first one, then the other, trying to make me believe they were the genius of Hunahpu Woman and Xablanque, except that they kept switching names and sometimes called each other Cacabe and Shirlito. Their voices were grief in my ears.

I was too tired and listless to move, but my fatigue and pain made it easier after a while to ignore what they were saying. Instead, I tried to concentrate on the sound of the water and the cracking of the trees, tried to lose myself in a roar that was bigger than all of us. Perhaps I slept, too, I don't know. But when I looked down at the river again, the catfish were still in front of me, still talking.

"What do you want from me?" I asked.

"We want you to believe in us. You have to believe in us or we cannot complete our transformation. Once you believe, you can cross the river on our backs."

I laughed so suddenly, I choked on my saliva. "Do what?"

"You can cross the river on our backs. We will carry you."

"Right. Just like dolphins?"

"Yes. But you have to believe first. You must, or we will die."

"Forget it. Go away. Leave me alone."

"Martin, we need you. Someone has to believe in us, truly believe, for the change to complete itself."

Something in her voice suddenly made me face what I had been trying so hard to avoid. I wouldn't have been talking to her unless—"I do believe in you—in a way."

"Do you believe we are Hunahpu Woman and Xablanque?"

I almost said no, but the word caught in the back of my throat and abruptly shifted to a sigh.

True Jaguar! True Jaguar! Bring me my feathers! the comet called from high above me.

I looked up, then looked at the fish. This was the final line for me to cross, and I knew it—the final line between who I was and who I would become. My hesitation lasted only a moment longer. "Yes, I do believe in you. I don't want to be crazy. I don't want this whole thing to be an hallucination, a bad dream, a nightmare. I want to believe you're real."

"Wanting to believe is the first step toward real faith," the Xablanque-fish said.

"Yes, I do believe." I said it and I meant it—or I wanted to mean it. I didn't know. It was hard to think. "You are Huna and he's Xablanque and I'm going to ride across the river on your backs."

The catfish squealed happily. "Come on, Xablanque, line up beside me."

The other fish swam up beside her.

"Now, kneel on our backs, T.J."

I did what she said. Clutching their dorsal fins I slid down onto their backs, one swollen knee on each fish. Cold water covered my feet and calves and soaked my jeans.

"Ready? Hold on," Huna-fish said.

"I'm as ready as I'm going to get."

As soon as they moved I knew I was going to fall off. Their bodies twisted and bucked like slick broncos. They lunged into the current and out from under me.

The frigid water knocked the breath from my lungs. A log banged against my side. I gasped and sputtered as I fought to keep my head above water. Cold pain stabbed through my skull.

Chapter Seventy-one

Something crashed into my leg. I crashed into a rock. My head bounced like a peach pit. I gulped for air and swallowed ice. Panic drove my arms and legs against the current.

A tree limb raked my head, driving me under water again. After I fought my way out from under it, I choked down as much water as air.

My body was lifted, then jerked down into the current.

I was pushed and pulled and yanked and tossed until I lost all my bearings. Things hit me. I hit things.

All the air disappeared from the world. A frozen hand squeezed my windpipe closed. I gave up. My body went limp, floating into the whirpool of death to join Huna and Xablanque and Reyes and Velasquez.

The end.

My knees scraped gravel. My hands grabbed basketball-sized rocks. My head broke the surface and I gasped in desperation.

Something shoved me repeatedly from behind until I crawled shivering and gasping from the river onto a tree-strewn gravel bank.

"Build a fire, Martin. You have to build a fire."

It was true, so I did it. Chattering and shaking as I worked, I cut some limbs from the driftwood with my Crain machete, then broke them over my numb knees into usable size. Cold wind cut through my wet clothes as I peeled dry strips of bark from one of the trees with the machete. Using the bark as starter, I got some kindling burning with my camp lighter. Then I added larger pieces of wood as fast as the fire would accept them until the flames leapt eight or ten feet into the air. Only then did I begin to warm up.

"We have to go now," Shirlito's voice called.

I stared at the water's edge and saw the two catfish side by side. "Damn you! I could have drowned."

"You did not drown, Senor O'Hara."

"But I could have."

"Yes, Martin, but you didn't."

The fire drove steam from my clothes, and the warmth encouraged me. "All right. I didn't drown. Now, how do I get out of here?"

"When you are dry, walk upstream until you come to a knife-shaped pinnacle of rock. Behind that you will find the steps up the cliff. We will meet you at the top."

"Okay, but what if . . ." I shivered.

They were gone, swimming upstream, leaping high into the current like strange trout or salmon, seeming to grow even as they got farther away, and to change shape until they looked like dolphins playing as they swam out of sight.

307

I turned away, suddenly conscious of the burning heat on my back. On impulse I stripped off my clothes and draped them across pieces of driftwood in front of the fire with the comet's tail feathers tied in a bunch behind them. The aspirin with codeine had turned into white mush in the bottom of its container, but I sucked out what I thought was two tablets worth and washed them down with several handfuls of river water. My canteen was gone along with my down jacket, lost in the struggle with the current.

Crazy laughter drifted down on me. *"You naked mortal. I will get my feathers and destroy you."*

"Come on," I shouted, Crain in hand. When the comet-bird didn't appear, I shook its threat off. That bizarre swim across the river had knocked my fever down for a little while and given me some lucid moments, but already I could feel the fever rising again and with it, lightheadedness. To my surprise, though, my back felt less raw, and when I felt along my arm where the comet had slashed me open, the wound was tender, but it had already healed shut. Or maybe the cold had closed it. I didn't know. My body didn't have much reserve left, so as soon as my clothes were dry, I put them on and started working my way upstream around and over the rocky riverbank.

After locating the knife-shaped pinnacle of rock, and climbing over the debris behind it, I found crude steps carved into a crevice in the face of the cliff, and began the grim climb. Every five or ten steps I had to stop and rest, but knowing I was crossing the last barrier on my way out of Xibalba helped me start up again after every rest.

"My feathers! I'm coming for my feathers!"

"Go to hell!" I shouted back. I couldn't see the comet, but it sounded closer. Only when I rested halfway up the canyon wall did the truth of what was happening hit me. I was being screamed at by a comet, while I climbed secret steps that a catfish told me about.

I shook my head and kept climbing, concentrating only on raising one aching foot above the other until I stumbled on the last step and sprawled into the grass at the top of the canyon wall, cherry bombs bursting in my head where an old Mayan god dressed in shiny metallic feathers was holding a two-fer sale of deathballs used by the lords of Xibalba to defeat the mortals from the surface who fled dead man's curve in terror after their loss and found their specialty department collapsed on the funeral pyre in the rain . . .

The air shuddered. Instinct made me move. I rolled over in time to see the comet wobbling down at me—wobbling damn fast. As I tried to get the Crain out of its sheath, I threw my feet up.

The comet hit my boots just as I kicked at it. The shock somersaulted me backward. Pain rammed its way up through my spine. As I struggled back to my knees, the comet hit me from behind. My chest bounced off the hard ground.

Fighting my way back to my knees once more, I saw the comet turn and tumble straight toward me. It screamed. I slashed out with the Crain. Sparks filled the air. A beast roared. My arm went numb and the Crain fell to the ground.

Something said that was the end, that the comet was too strong for me and my machete, but something else wouldn't let me quit. I picked up the Crain with my left hand and kept the comet in sight. It still wobbled, and a dark stain dulled its shiny feathers on one side. As I rose to my feet to meet the next attack, pain flashed in my eyes and my body wobbled, too.

The comet turned in a high arc and dropped toward me, its wings whistling. The very air shuddered again. It was time to win or lose—I knew that—and I had to believe I could win. True Jaguar would not be defeated by *cometa Xibalba*.

I raised the Crain and put my left foot back to steady myself. The ground shifted under my foot. A frightened glance showed me I was standing on the edge of the canyon.

The comet never slowed. I swung the Crain Predator with every ounce of strength I had, throwing my body behind it like a pitcher throwing a fastball. The stainless steel blade sang as it cut through the air. The ground gave way.

"True Jaguar!" Someone shouted my name.

The Crain struck home. The comet screamed, and so did I.

Pain swallowed me whole. The world exploded in a brilliant flash. Thunder roared. My eyes fell out. My ears fell off. My left arm disappeared. A claw raked my right arm. I fell headfirst, deaf and blind, to my death below in the Canyon of Spears.

Chapter Seventy-two

In my dream a gorgeous woman kissed the end of my nose ever so lightly—kissed me with little noisy pecking kisses that tickled. When I tried to brush her away, she giggled.

When I awoke and opened my eyes, a gorgeous woman was kissing the end of my nose. She had the face of a Mayan goddess, and I was too stunned to try to brush her away. Finally a small, sane voice from the corner of my mind told me what I needed to know and I loosed a long sigh with an odd sense of relief. I was hallucinating again. That was the only possible explanation. But even so, it hurt to look at her and see how much she looked like . . . like Velasquez.

The woman's smiling face pulled away from mine. "Hello, Martin. I told you we would meet you here."

With another long sigh I closed my eyes and felt my forehead. Fever. Still lots of fever. "What happened?" The roar of Neck Canyon surrounded us.

"You destroyed the comet, Martin."

"I did?"

"Yes. Then Cacabe grabbed you and kept you from falling into the canyon."

I raised my hand. She clasped it between hers and held it to her breast. She felt so real that I cried. Even the rough cotton blouse she wore felt real.

Looking directly into her dark beautiful eyes, I said, "Been hallucinating for days, maybe weeks, maybe since the DSA arrested me. Maybe I'm dead and this is hell and they're torturing me with dreams. Maybe there's—"

"Shhh. Don't talk now. Cacabe has made some tea for you to drink that will make you feel better. It's an old Indian cure for malaria."

"Help him sit up."

She put her arm under my shoulder and pulled me up. The delicate scent of her body stirred me in a hundred positive ways even as I moaned in pain at the movement of my sore muscles.

"I'm sorry you hurt so much," Velasquez said.

Suddenly Reyes appeared in front of me holding out a floridly engraved silver cup.

"Here, Senor O'Hara. Drink this. It should not be too hot for you."

Velasquez took the cup and held it to my lips. For a moment I wanted to fight the illusion, to make them both disappear the way the ferryman had disappeared, but then my cracked lips smiled. The ferryman was an illusion. Velasquez and Reyes were real. Understanding and accepting that didn't mean I could explain why I believed it—even to myself—yet most of my doubt had disappeared.

What could I do but drink? The tea tasted bitter and salty, but there was a hint of sweetness in it, too, and I was so thirsty I drank the whole cupful. I looked at the cup for a moment, unable to decipher the embellished script, but for some reason I knew the motto was in Queche. "More, please?"

Reyes grinned and took the cup. "Of course. Anything for the man who destroyed *cometa Xibalba*."

Bending slowly forward, I stretched some of the painful tightness out of my muscles and I noticed the scabbard from my Crain lay empty by my leg, and my bones remembered the force of the blow when the Crain struck the comet. The Crain was gone. There was no way it could have survived its clash with the comet, I was sure of that. But then, the comet hadn't survived its clash with the Crain, either. Finally I pulled myself into a cross-legged sitting position and studied Velasquez's beautiful face.

"You're pregnant," I said without thinking.

"Yes."

Reyes handed me a second cup of tea.

I sighed and drank a little. It tasted less bitter than before. "I'm not crazy, am I? This is real."

She leaned closer to me and put one hand on my knee. Her dark eyes softened. "You're not crazy, and I don't want you to go crazy. You're Jesus O'Hara Martinez, True Jaguar, my beloved Martin, father of the babies in my womb. That is reality. That is what you must accept."

"And all this?" I asked with a weak wave of my left hand.

"It is real, also," Reyes said. "What we have lived through was real. Your defeat of *cometa Xibalba* was real."

"All of it," Velasquez added. "It's all real."

I drank the rest of the tea without looking at either of them, then gave Reyes the empty Queche cup, and looked down at where my dirty, bruised hand rested on top of Velasquez's hand. "It would be awful to wake up from this and find out"—my eyes lifted and locked on hers—"and find out that this was a dream. I don't think I could take losing you again."

"You won't," she whispered. "You won't lose me. I won't let you. I love you too much."

Like a mud dike, something gave way inside me, and acceptance flooded the last dry fields of my doubt. Little tears ran from the corners of my eyes.

Velasquez pulled me into her arms and rocked me against her breast. "It's all right. It's going to be all right."

The tears that followed were tears of relief, and when I finally pulled free and looked at her, I could feel the idiot grin on my face. "So now what? Now we're all back together, what do we do?"

She bent over and kissed my forehead and my nose and my mouth. They were the most real kisses I ever tasted.

"First that," she said with a smile. "Then as soon as you feel strong enough, Cacabe says we need to leave."

"I'm ready, now. Just help me get on my feet and let me work the kinks out of my legs."

"Are you sure?"

I grinned, feeling suddenly happy. "Yeah, I'm sure." She helped me to my feet, and though my whole body was sore and cried in protest, it didn't hurt as much as I expected it to. "Where'd you get those clothes?" I asked, looking at the un-dyed, rough-spun cotton shirt and pants, and the reed sandals they were both wearing.

"Shooting Owl and Macaw Owl brought them to us at the source of the River of Neck Canyon," Reyes said.

"Who?"

"Shooting Owl and Macaw Owl. They are the first and third Keepers of the Military Mat. Skull Owl is the fourth keeper and One-Legged Owl is the second. They brought us the tea and cups, also. Let me tell you how we've changed."

"Never mind. This is the path out of here, isn't it? Let's get going."

"Don't you want to know how we changed?" Reyes asked.

"I already know. I got braver and stronger and more self-confident. Huna—Shirlito got more—"

"That is not what I mean."

"That's what I mean. . . . What am I going to call you?" I asked as she took my hand and walked beside me, easily matching my slow, stiff pace.

"Whatever you wish, Martin."

After a moment's consideration, I said, "I think Shirlito, but in some ways you'll always be Huna, too."

"And you'll always be T.J., but I shall call you Martin."

"Don't you really want to know how we changed?" Reyes asked again.

"Of course. How foolish of you to think otherwise. Shirlito accepted who she was and got—"

"The genius of Hunahpu and Xablanque did it, really," he said, ignoring me, "because they remembered changing the same way when they tricked the lords One and Seven Death, then came back as catfish who became men and fooled the lords with a magic trick."

"You're not paying attention, Senor Reyes. I don't care about that part."

"Yes, but it is truly an interesting story, Senor O'Hara, and if you would listen to it, I'm sure you would agree."

"Shirlito will tell me later," I said, "after I have rested and gotten over this sickness I have. Okay?"

"No."

"Yes," Shirlito said almost at the same time.

"No, you must listen," Reyes continued, "so that if you ever come face to face with the lords again, you will know what—"

"Never!" I spun around to face him. "Absolutely, positively, never. Got that? Never. Read my lips. Nev-er." I turned again, took Shirlito's hand with a jerk, and started up the trail.

"Why is he so stubborn, Shirlito?" Reyes asked.

"Because you helped him find his true self."

"No. It is because he has thought too long like a gringo. Too long his spirit has lived with the *norteamericanos*."

I stopped again and turned around more slowly. "Reyes, you can quit your carping right now. I have done what I had to do. I have come to Xibalba and destroyed the comet. I have grown and changed and accepted things I couldn't even imag-

313

ine before. So just stay off my case, will you? I'm tired. I'm sore. I probably have malaria and god knows what kind of intestinal critters, and the last thing I need is you griping at me. Okay?"

He nodded slowly. "I understand. Yes, okay."

"Good. Now can we get out of here?"

Chapter Seventy-three

The trail rose gradually as we walked side by side with Reyes ahead of us. At the entrance of the cave we paused and looked back over the jungle hills of Xibalba, then without speaking, we turned away from the underworld and walked into the cave. There the incline was steeper. The air was cool, too cool, and raised goose bumps on our arms.

"How are we going to cope with the cold when we get to the top?" I shouted to Reyes.

He stopped and his toothy smile looked green in the light of the phosphorescent *lampara Dios* on the cave's ceiling. "It will be summer when we reach the exit. Look at Shirlito."

We stopped and I looked at her. Her swollen belly had grown visibly since my awakening. "That's not possible."

"I can feel it changing, step by step," she said.

"This is no place to have a baby."

"Babies. That is why I am growing so big."

"Baby, babies. One or a dozen, this isn't the place."

"You know what I want?" she asked as we continued walking. "I want to see Torelli's face when we show up again."

"Why? What in the world for? You think we'll see him?"

"Oh, we will see him. The DSA will keep him on our case for the rest of his life just because he let us escape."

I shook my head. "Great. Here I am worried about you having the babies before we get out of here, and you're telling me that Torelli's going to be waiting for us. How in the hell are we going to get away from him this time?"

"The situation on the surface may have changed in our favor since we left." She rubbed her arms. "Brrooo!"

Every time I looked at her, her belly looked bigger. I put

my arm around her shoulders and pulled her close to me. "How much farther, Reyes?"

"I do not know, Senor O'Hara."

We walked for what seemed like hours, always up. "When are we going to get out of here?"

"Do not worry so, my love. Things will work out for us."

For her sake I tried to smile, but—

"Here!" Reyes shouted. He stood barely visible ahead of us.

When we reached the boulder with the steps cut in its face, he had already climbed down. I remembered those steps would take us to the floor below the sacred kiva. Then we would have to climb up two ladders to get out. Suddenly I was afraid. "What if Torelli really is waiting for us up there? The last thing we heard was gunfire."

Shirlito started down the steps into the darkness. "*Que sera*. We will cope with it, if and when it happens."

When I reached the bottom of the ladder I could barely see Shirlito, but on the other side of the low cavern I could see a dim, dusty shaft of light. "Almost there," I said, taking her hand to steady her across the rough floor.

"I am excited," she said as she climbed.

"Well, I'm scared."

"I guess we balance each other."

I smiled. "There's something to be said for that."

Reyes waited for us in the shaft of dusty light at the foot of the last ladder.

"Sun's probably shining out there," I said. "Damn it will be good to feel the sun again."

"I will go first and scout the area," Reyes said. "If there is no one around, I will come back for you."

"Does it matter? I'm ready to sit in the sunshine."

"Me, too," Shirlito added.

He climbed the rough ladder, up through the curtain of eagle feathers and beads. Shirlito went next. As soon as she cleared the eagle feathers and beads, I followed. Standing next to Shirlito on the top of the kiva, I knew something had changed. "Something's different about this kiva."

"Yes. Look out there."

My gaze followed her pointing arm out from under the

ledge where the pueblo—"This is a different pueblo altogether."

"Shhh."

The sound of a girl's laughter was followed by Reyes's voice. "Shirlito! Senor O'Hara! Come this way." He stood in the sunlight next to a wall at the end of the pueblo, where an adolescent Indian girl grinned at us from ear to ear as we climbed through the pueblo to join them. I kept shifting my eyes, expecting DSA agents to pop from out behind the rocks at any time, but none showed up.

"This is Melinda Straightfoot. She has been waiting for us."

"August is my month to wait here," she said proudly.

"Why? And how did you know we'd come out here?"

"You are She Blank Man and Hundakoo Shirt Woman and Mountain Lion Man, and the whole Ute nation waits for you. We have watchers at every holy kiva. I am honored that you chose mine to appear." She squatted down and started digging in her daypack.

"You honor us by waiting," Shirlito said.

"You said August? Is that right, Melinda?"

"Yes," she said, pulling out a hand-held citizens' band radio. "Today is the third day of August, and I will call the council house for someone to come pick us up."

I looked from her to Shirlito's belly full of babies and guessed that August wasn't unreasonable.

While Melinda spoke her own language into the radio, I helped Shirlito sit at the foot of the wall, then sat beside her. "It's almost a letdown getting here," I said, "no DSA, no lords with clubs, no CIA, no Skull Owls. Boring."

Shirlito put her head on my shoulders. "We could do with some boredom for a little while. . . . You feel very hot."

"Fever. Maybe Melinda has some aspirin."

"Yes, I do," Melinda said, handing the radio to Reyes. "You tell them that I am not playing games." Her voice shook.

Reyes turned, put the radio to his head, then turned away and began talking so softly I couldn't hear what he was saying.

"Adults are so stupid," Melinda said in disgust. "They give us jobs and lecture us about how important it is for us to be responsible, then when we do what they said to do, they act like we're kids playing games. All I have is Midol." Suddenly she looked from me to the bottle in her hand and blushed.

"That will do. That and water. Lots of water."

She handed me a large round canteen from her pack and I gladly washed two of the Midol down with grateful mouthfuls of tepid water that tasted like iron.

"They believe you now," Reyes said, handing her the radio.

"Yeah, except now they've broadcast in English and the feds will hear it and come after us. Adults!"

"No," Reyes said. "We spoke in Spanish."

"So? There's lots of Mexican feds. But maybe they didn't hear you. So where did the council house boss tell us to wait?"

"Here. They said they would honk for us."

"How far is it from here to the road?" I asked.

"Not too far. Quarter of a mile, maybe—and it's easy trail." She knelt suddenly by Shirlito's side. "Gosh, I got so excited I didn't even think about you being pregnant. When's your baby due?"

"Babies," Shirlito said with a big grin, "twins, and they're probably due late this month."

"While we're waiting, Melinda, why don't you tell us what's been going on this year."

"You mean since Lana's comet exploded?"

"Sure. Start there. When did that happen?"

"February twenty-eighth. I'll never forget it. The day before leap year's day. Us and the Russians had sent some missiles up to shoot the comet down, but none of them made it. Then this real weird thing happened, you know. You could see it from here. The comet wobbled for a week, then this strange silver cloud moved through the sky and when it reached the comet, it started to fly apart—the comet, I mean. Took it two days almost until it was busted into pieces so small we couldn't see them anymore. It was neat." Melinda took a deep breath. "And right after that, the blue corn sprouted, and the adults told us that meant you were alive."

I squeezed Shirlito's hand, silently thanking God that the destruction of the comet had been real. My eyes closed by themselves as I listened.

"Then there's been all this legal stuff about the trial about you and the feds on the reservation that the council's worried about, but I don't understand most of that because, well, you know how adults are about explaining things to kids my age. They think we're all retarded or something. But I can tell you that Henry Great Bear and some of the others are in court today to get a permanent disjunction, or something, against the feds, but nobody thinks it's going to happen because no white court is going to rule for Indians against those feds, you know, because it's like the CIA or something."

"Are any of those feds here now?" Shirlito asked.

"I don't think so—at least they're not supposed to be, because the council got a temporary disjunction against them back in May or June, but I don't think that will keep them away if they know you're here."

Shirlito asked another question that didn't quite make sense to me, but I was too tired to try to figure out what it was like to . . . sunshine on my shoulders through blue and orange sky—when Shirlito shook me. Our transportation had arrived. A dusty blue Suburban waited for us at the bottom of the trail with a man and a woman standing by it. They rushed up to help Shirlito the last hundred yards and left me to stumble down by myself, but I didn't mind.

As soon as we were all settled and the Suburban started down the road, I fell asleep again and didn't wake up until we came to a stop in front of Alan Lodge's house. It looked a lot bigger in the noontime summer sun than it had looked in the winter covered with snow—and more festive. Ears of blue corn hung from the exposed rafters across the front of the house along with corn husk dolls, eagle feathers, beads, and strips of red ribbon.

There were already people there expecting us, and as soon as they found out that I was sick, they hustled me off to bed, fed me broth and some kind of medicine, and let me sleep.

I woke up with a start, not knowing where I was, but in the moonlight I could see Huna beside—no, Shirlito, the pregnant Shirlito—beside me, and I felt better. Somehow I found my way down the hall to the bathroom. A woman I had never seen was standing outside the door when I came out and she made me drink a big glass of evil-tasting stuff and swallow some pills before she would let me go back to bed. I could still taste the medicine when I fell asleep.

Chapter Seventy-four

Morning sun on my face woke me up. Shirlito still slept, so I slipped out of bed, put on the heavy blanket robe and lined slippers I found by the bed, went to the bathroom, then to the kitchen where I found Henry Great Bear drinking coffee.

"Are you supposed to be out of bed?" he asked.

"I don't know. Do you have any more coffee?"

"Sure."

I took the cup he held out to me and sat at the table. "So how have you been, Henry?"

"Better than I've been in years, my friend. Fighting the feds can be fun for an old man."

I sipped the coffee. It was too hot. "Are we winning?"

"That we won't know for a couple of days. That was a hell of a thing you three did."

"Thanks, but Cacabe and Shirlito deserve most of the credit. Any idea what's going to happen with the DSA and all?"

He shook his head. "Only the court can answer that."

We talked for a while and he filled me in on what had been happening in the world for the past eight months, then I got dressed and discovered that the tribe wasn't going to wait for some white man's court decision before celebrating. The party had started the night before without me and people arrived all through the day.

Reyes became our official storyteller, and he seemed to thrive on the attention. Shirlito and I entertained smaller groups. Occasionally someone forced me to swallow pills, washing them down with glasses full of their evil brew, and occasionally I napped. By the time the party got cranked up in the barn after supper, with music even a pregnant woman could dance to, I felt better than I had in, well, who knew how long.

Somewhere in the middle of the evening Alan Lodge asked me and Shirlito to come to the house with him. Waiting for us there were two men and a woman all wearing business suits and grim faces. Henry introduced them as the tribal lawyers, Barbara Moon, Michael Wolf, and Leo Melenson.

"We have the ultimate respect for what you did," Barbara Moon said.

"Those of us who believe it," Wolf said with a glance at Melenson.

"And we hope the court will grant a permanent injunction against the DSA to keep them from coming onto the reservation except by invitation of the tribal government."

"Why isn't Reyes in here to hear this?" I asked.

Michael Wolf shook his head. "If any persons whom the United States government considers foreign nationals are present on the reservation, we do not want to know anything about such persons, and in fact, demand that we remain ignorant of that possible state of affairs."

"As I was saying," Ms. Moon continued, "we have no guarantee that the court will grant our request, so we are here to suggest that you give immediate consideration to your future."

Shirlito and I shared a look that answered a question I didn't need to ask. "We would like to stay here on the reservation until our babies are born."

"I'm sure that the tribal council would be more than pleased to have you stay here for as long as you wish," Alan Lodge said.

"All of us?" Shirlito asked.

"Yes," Henry Great Bear said, staring defiantly at the lawyers, "all of you."

"Good. What are our chances, Ms. Moon—with the injunction, I mean? Slim and none, or better than that?"

"Better, we hope, but we just won't know until tomorrow."

"There's a third possibility," Melenson said, speaking for the first time.

"I'm sorry, I guess I don't understand what the first two possibilities are."

"The circuit court could deny our request for a permanent injunction, or the court could agree to issue a permanent injunction, or the court could order some compromise."

A glance from Shirlito showed her concern. "Like what?"

"That would depend on the court, but we know that somehow today the DSA found out you were here and their attorney's filed a motion asking that, should a permanent injunction be issued, they be given the right to debrief you here on the reservation."

"You mean they could come here and question us?"

"Yes, with one or more of us present during the questioning."

"What are the chances of that?" Shirlito asked.

"Ms. Velasquez, it isn't our business to attempt to second-guess the court. However, it would be prudent of you to—"

"What Barbara means is, we're chicken—wouldn't give you a lizard's tail for your chances of escaping the DSA."

"Well, as an ex-agent for the DSA, I can say that—"

"Oh, be careful, Ms. Velasquez. The DSA does not consider you an ex-agent. That is part of the difficulty here. The DSA claims that the Ute Mountain Utes are harboring a renegade agent—to use their term—in addition to a foreign national, and a known national security risk."

"You bastards," I said. "All you lawyers are just alike—no matter whose side you're on. Why didn't you spell that out in the first place?"

"Because you should have known it," Wolf said. "She should have, if you didn't."

"He is right, Martin. I should have known. But so much has happened, so much that has nothing to do with the DSA, that I have not taken the time to gather my thoughts." She stood up. "We thank you for your efforts and will anxiously await the results tomorrow. Excuse us, please."

She left and headed for the bedroom and I followed, hearing the start of an argument as soon as we left the kitchen. By the sound of it, Henry Great Bear was not pleased with the lawyers.

"We cannot abandon Cacabe," Shirlito said as soon as I had closed the bedroom door.

"I know that. But those lawyers are right about one thing. We don't want to be visible until after the court hands down its decision tomorrow—especially since the DSA obviously has spies on the reservation."

"You know, if the DSA catches us, we could end up spending a long time separated," she said. "We have to hide. We have to go underground."

I put my hands on her shoulders, leaned over her belly, and kissed her. "I'm glad you've got a head for these things."

"Well, I certainly do not have the figure for it."

"I like your figure. Pregnant becomes you."

"Thank you. I will tell Cacabe the bad news."

"Good."

When we reached the kitchen, the lawyers were gone. Alan and Henry were washing dishes and arguing.

"Listen, you two," Shirlito said, "can you quit growling at each other long enough to help a pregnant woman?"

Only Henry laughed. "What do you want, pregnant woman?"

"Someone to take the three of us to a safe hiding place tomorrow—someplace only that person and you will know about."

"I will take you," Henry said, "and Alan will be the only one who knows where."

"Where?" Alan asked.

"Shut up and think. If I don't tell you where we're hiding, you can honestly tell anyone who asks that I didn't tell you. But you know me and I know you, and if we win the injunction, you come looking for us where *you* would have taken them, okay?"

Alan nodded, but still didn't smile. "I don't know anything."

"Good. We'll leave at daybreak. I'll wake you."

The moon was rising over the mountains when we rejoined the party, and close to setting before we finally broke away and returned to the house. None of us wanted to leave. The Utes were satisfying a deep hunger the three of us felt for the company of good, decent people.

It didn't take us long to go to sleep, and it wasn't long after that before Henry Great Bear shook me awake.

"I'm sorry, Martin," he said, "but you have to get up. The DSA is here."

Chapter Seventy-five

"Hello, Torelli," Shirlito said as she and Reyes and I walked into the living room. In addition to Torelli, there were five strangers in suits sitting there, plus Henry Great Bear, Alan

Lodge, and the lawyers Moon and Melenson. Torelli nodded slightly, but said nothing.

"Please have a seat," Moon said, motioning to three chairs that faced the rest.

I took heart from the fact that she seemed to be in charge rather than Torelli, but I was afraid she might be in charge only long enough to turn us over to him.

"The Tenth Circuit Court of Appeals has issued a permanent injunction forbidding the United States Defense Security Agency or any other entity of the federal government or the governments of the states of Colorado and Utah acting on behalf of the Defense Security Agency or on their own volition from entering the Ute Mountain Ute Indian Reservation unless specifically invited to so enter by the tribal government of the Ute Mountain Utes, except when in hot pursuit of a criminal suspect or—"

"Can you get to the meat of it?" I asked. "We don't need all the legalese. Are we going to be arrested or not?"

Moon looked annoyed with me, but she kept her voice level. "No, *but*, the terms for granting the injunction stipulate that the DSA shall have the right to question you, with a lawyer of your choice present, of course, over a period not to exceed seven days, nor seventy hours, nor more than five consecutive hours, nor more than ten hours in one twenty-four-hour period."

Shirlito squeezed my hand. "So, Torelli, you can question us, but we go free after that. All three of us?"

"All three of you," Moon said. "The court decided that since—by their own admissions—none of the governments which had attempted to destroy Lana's comet with rockets had succeeded, and since the DSA—by its own admission—could not disprove that your actions had succeeded in destroying the comet, that neither the DSA nor the federal government had grounds on which to arrest or detain you for questioning beyond the period agreed upon."

"Woo," I said with a big sigh of relief. "Am I glad to—"

"We still get to question you, O'Hara," Torelli said.

"So? We'll tell you exactly what happened."

A look of panic crossed his face. "Not now. Later. One at a time, using proper procedures."

"It's simple, Torelli. We went to the Mayan underworld,

called the land of Xibalba, and played basketball with the lords of pus and trash and death for the right to kill the comet. And we won. I killed the comet. That's it."

Torelli smiled, but it was not a nice smile. "You're such a damn smart mouth, it makes me sick. You think you can tell us some cock-and-bull story like that and have us accept it?"

"It is the truth, Torelli," Shirlito said.

"How do you expect us to believe that?"

"Like the lady says, it's the truth."

"That you went into some mythical underworld and played *basketball*, for God's sake, in order to destroy a comet? You expect us to believe that crap?"

"Of course," Reyes said, "how foolish of you to think otherwise."

The three of us looked at each other for a second, then broke up laughing, and I knew we would be all right. Compared to the comet and the lords of Xibalba, Torelli and the DSA were going to be pushovers.

*A potent dark magic stalks the
island kingdom of Ark,
drawing power from the people and the land.
Ages past, it fueled the War of the Wizards.
Now it rises again.*

CÐE SERVANCS OF ARK

By Jonathan Wylie

☐ **Volume One: THE FIRST NAMED** (26953-4 •
$3.95/$4.95 in Canada) The powerful wizardess
Amarino has usurped Ark's throne, killing the king
and sending his three sons into hiding. But an
ancient prophecy foretells a great conflict for the
throne against only one prince . . . in a battle that
only a true Servant of Ark could win.

☐ **Volume Two: THE CENTER OF THE CIRCLE**
(On sale in February 1988) • 27056-7 • $3.95/
$4.95 in Canada) A generation after the first
confrontation, Prince Luke faces his father's old
enemy in a new and terrible form.

And coming in July, the final chapter in THE
SERVANTS OF ARK trilogy: THE MAGE-BORN
CHILD. Don't miss it!

Buy **THE FIRST NAMED** and **THE CENTER OF
THE CIRCLE** on sale wherever Bantam Spectra Books
are sold, or use the handy coupon below for ordering: